Drugged is the exciting misadventure of Heather Blanchard, who accidentally crosses paths with a Detroit drug gang and has to run for her life. Patricia Hartman is a master of creating colorful characters through fast-paced dialogue you can't forget and poignant moments that touch your heart. And the white deer? You will not be able to put this book down.

—Jan Rader, Director, Mayor's Council of Public Health & Drug Control Policy, Retired Fire Chief, City of Huntington, WV, Featured on Netflix Documentary *Heroin(e)*

Patricia Hartman has done it again, giving us a fast-moving, fascinating suspense filled with intrigue, drug gangs, the FBI, DEA, and surprises. She fulfilled her promise from book one to answer what happened to Heather. She introduces us to Dexter—a menacing character you can't forget. Her characters won't let you go as you travel with Heather, battling the forces set out against her. Hartman brings it all together and yet leaves you panting for the next book.

—James W. Geiger, Former FBI agent and prosecuting attorney and author of *The Gospel According to Relativity: Constant Value in a Changing World* and *Christianity and the Outsider: A Lawyer Looks at Justice and Justification*

DRUGGED took me on a page-turning, heart-wrenching journey that defied probabilities while captivating my imagination! This fast-paced thriller brought me on a totally unpredictable adventure with deeply intense characters and surprising yet satisfying storylines. Author Patricia Hartman thrills again. Do not miss this one!

—Anne V. Alper, Attorney Former Assistant State Attorney, Broward County, Florida

DRUGGED

PATRICIA HARTMAN

Quote from Lewis, C. S. on page 5 (1962). *The Problem of Pain*. New York: Macmillan

ISBN: 978-1-955309-42-4

Cover photos: ForestPath, iStock/aniszewski; white deer, iStock/giannimarchetti

Author photo: Malcolm Yawn

Published by EA Books Publishing, a division of
Living Parables of Central Florida, Inc. a 501c3

EABooksPublishing.com

Pain insists upon being attended to. God whispers to us in our pleasures, speaks in our conscience, but shouts in our pain: it is His megaphone to rouse a deaf world.

– C.S. Lewis

Dedication

This book is dedicated to all the front-line workers battling the opioid crisis in America, including doctors who don't overprescribe; paramedics who answer the calls; law enforcement agencies who root out the illegal sources; judiciaries with drug courts focused on rehab; prosecutors who pursue big pharma pushers of opioids; journalists who shine lights on this issue; drug rehab facilities that truly rehab; and all those families who have lost loved ones from this epidemic.

* * * SPOILER ALERT * * *

Don't read this book before *Poisoned* (the first book in this series). *Drugged* will immediately give away Poison's plot. In fact, don't read this page. Just sayin'.

If you do read this first, you'll want to know the following:

Poisoned featured Julie Wheeler, a veterinarian living in the idyllic town of Hearthstone, West Virginia. She's married to Richard Wheeler, the county's chief prosecuting attorney. Gorgeous Nicole Marley (Richard's assistant) dropped off her poisoned German shepherd (Dog) at Julie's clinic, then disappeared crying hysterically. Then Richard disappeared. *Drugged* picks in the middle of *Poisoned* when Julie had just left to follow up on some information about Richard's whereabouts. *Poisoned* is Julie's story.

Drugged's main character is Julie's sister, Heather Blanchard, who was staying with Julie after her fiancé dumped her a month before. Heather leaves Julie's house in a drunken stupor, leaving the reader to wonder what happened to Heather. Now you'll find out.

There may be appearances or references to these characters from *Poisoned*:

- Max Enders – the FBI agent who was working undercover in Hearthstone
- Doc Robert Blanchard – Heather's dad, who's also a vet
- Catherine ("Cruella") Blanchard – Heather's awful stepmother

- Nicole Marley – Richard's assistant Prosecuting Attorney
- Sheriff Mack Mc Connell – Richard's long-time friend who was blackmailed into cooperating with Jerry Hayes
- Jerry Hayes – the corrupt assistant sheriff working for a Detroit crime organization
- Tom Cruz – a corrupt deputy who poisoned Dog but fell for Heather
- Smitty – Detroit's enforcer sent to clean up the Hearthstone mess
- Sarah – The Wheeler's housekeeper and Julie's childhood friend
- Jubilee – Julie's cherished horse, named after a song her mother had loved

Now, lower that lap bar. Heather's ride is about to begin.

Chapter 1

Tuesday, October 24
10:45 p.m.

FOURTEEN TEQUILA SHOTS HAD EARNED HEATHER BLANCHARD the Downtown Saloon's drinking championship title. But not one of those drinks had helped her forget her troubles. And now, the agave elixir whipped her brain like an F5 twister.

She fumbled an armload of shoes from the bottom of her sister's guestroom closet toward her half-filled suitcase. How was she ever going to escape Julie's house before Dad arrived from D.C.?

Her stomach lurched again. Her last bathroom bout had already dumped its contents. Shoes formed a trail as she raced for the toilet, dropped to her knees, and heaved nothing into the cold porcelain throne.

Dear Lord, help me. I promise I'll never drink again.

She rose and stood before the blue-streaked blonde staring back at her in the guest bath mirror. She pushed her tongue out of her cottonmouth. Yuck. She uncapped the blue mouthwash and tried to swish away the bile. While the cool mint could eliminate ninety-nine percent of germs, it couldn't wipe away even one percent of her messes.

Dog whimpered. The German shepherd sat erect outside the door beside the red oak banister near the top of the staircase, watching her, his black ears crowning his black and tan face.

"Don't you judge me too. You're my only friend."

He tilted his head. Had it only been twelve hours since she'd dubbed him "Dog" after his near-death poisoning? Maybe she should bring him. But he wasn't hers to take.

Take? Heather shook her fuzzy head back into gear. Dad'd be there any minute.

She raced back to the guestroom, picking up her breadcrumbs along the way. She dropped her footwear in the suitcase that contained all her worldly treasures, zipped it closed, and tugged it off the pillow-topped four-poster bed. Staggering from the guestroom, she slammed her shoulder against the door jamb that must have moved in the previous five minutes. Pain shot down her arm. "Ow!" She rubbed her shoulder and cursed the door.

Dog tipped his head in disapproval.

He couldn't possibly understand what it was like to be her.

Heather pushed her shoulders back and inhaled deeply. "I can do this." She nodded. "One step at a time." Ten steps to the banister.

The view from the top of the foyer's summit reminded Heather why the farmhand had had to carry her up here just an hour ago. Like a cat up a tree, there were no safe options down. And that hardwood floor below? Where was her rescuer?

Heather trembled as she waited for the headspin to stop. Just thirteen stairs. If she could just make it to the landing. *The landing.* Ha! Might be safer to sit and scoot down like a toddler.

Dog nudged her leg.

She patted his head. "Okay, we've got this."

With Dog at her side, Heather gripped the handrail and celebrated each step—her suitcase punctuating her progress. With only three steps to go, her legs buckled, launching her face forward to the unyielding floor below. An image of a rich boy in a pig's trough surfaced from deep in the crevices of her brain. Sunday school stories. All lies. Like the one about God loving her.

Dog licked her face.

"At least *you* love me."

She rolled over, scratched behind his ears, and then struggled to push herself up. Heather leaned against the wall and surveyed her sister's perfectly appointed house. Logs smoldered in the fireplace. Thick oriental rugs lined the hallway and decorated the living room. Julie had woven their mother's horse-themed paintings into every inch of her décor. She'd even mounted Mom's horse-harness mirror by the front door. Everything in its place.

And not one of Heather's masterpieces was to be found. Nothing to show for her life. She formed a lopsided "L" on her forehead with her thumb and finger. "Loser." No wonder everyone wanted to get rid of her—even Tom. Just when she'd hoped . . .

She shook her head. Why should he want her? Why should *anyone* want her?

Dog whimpered.

The looming grandfather clock bonged eleven. *Dad.* Heather righted her suitcase and grabbed the handle. She had to get to the garage. After surveying the distance to the closet, she drew a long breath and wobbled forward, thankful for the entry table to help her steady herself. An envelope scrawled with "dad," and a heart on it stopped her. She ran her fingers over it. Sealed. Was Julie tattling on her?

She ripped off the flap and unfolded the perfectly handwritten note.

> *Dear Dad,*
>
> *Sorry about leaving. I left to look for Richard. I know I told you he disappeared and was cheating with Nicole. I was wrong. She's an undercover FBI agent.*
>
> *Be careful who you talk to. Sheriff Mack can't be trusted. He was working with the mob—not by choice but blackmailed. No one in the sheriff's office can be trusted, especially* <u>*Deputy Tom Cruz*</u>*. He was dating Heather. Watch what you tell her . . .*

What? Didn't Julie trust her own sister? And Tom . . . the mob? Impossible. He was the only one who understood her. Nothing made sense.

Heather dropped the letter and crumbled to the floor, unable to read another word. Weren't sisters supposed to be best friends? First, Julie accused her of hiding Richard's affair. Wasn't it Julie who had told the world about her pregnancy, but not Heather? Talk about keeping secrets. Now Julie believed Heather was involved with the mob? How could she?

No more. Heather lifted her head, gathered her resolve, and stood. Dizziness tilted her world. She waited for it to pass.

Dog cocked his head and whined.

"I'm fine. I'll be fine."

Dog's ears perked.

"Even *you* don't believe me."

She opened the closet door to retrieve her faded-rose coat—Tom's favorite. Heather bit her lip. Tom. It couldn't be true. She shook her head and then pulled on the coat. Suitcase in tow, she weaved unsteadily through the kitchen and laundry room, Dog trailing.

She paused at the door. Those pleading eyes. How could she leave him? She stooped to explain but fell on her backside. Heather righted herself.

Dog's sad eyes met hers.

"I can't take you, boy. There's nothing I'd like more. I don't even know where I'm going. But believe me. You're better off without me."

Dog cocked his head.

She patted him, kissed his snout, and stood. Despite his whimpered protests, she closed the door on her only friend. Heather's heart sank as Dog scratched at the door. But it was time. Dad could show up any minute.

She popped the trunk of the red Prius her dad had given her for graduation. The painting Heather had created for Julie and Richard's tenth anniversary stared at her from within. She tossed the framed artwork to the garage floor where Richard's car should have been.

She shuddered. Had something terrible really happened to him? She pushed the thought away. He had to be okay—everything always worked out in the Wheeler's Shangri-La. Richard would show up, and then they would make up, have a baby, and live happily ever after. That's how it worked in Wheelerland.

Heather tossed her pathetic suitcase into the trunk and dropped into the driver's seat. She pressed the garage door button, backed out, and crunched into the stately oak tree that would shade the driveway next spring, but now cast an eerie shadow over her.

She looked in the rearview mirror and formed the L on her forehead, then jammed the gear shift into drive and raced off, hoping never to see that tree or any of them again.

Chapter 2

11:00 p.m.

DEXTER MILLER TANGOED HIS DIAMOND-STUDDED WIFE past the orchestra and around the marble-columned ballroom floor. He loved showing off her perfectly sculpted body, barely hidden beneath her evening gown. So provocative. Never a shortage of double takes when Mary Ellen mingled among Detroit's elite benefactors.

His secure phone vibrated. Mary Ellen frowned as he guided her off the dance floor.

"I've got to take this."

"You promised." She pouted her lush red lips.

"I'll be right back." He ran a finger down her cheek to her bare neck, then kissed her deeply. Her head tipped back as if asking for more as her body settled against his. After two decades, he still knew how to leave her breathless. Instead of taking the call, he should be racing her home. He forced himself to release her.

"That's not going to work," she called after him as he snuck out the French doors to the deserted rooftop patio. But he knew it would.

The frigid Detroit wind pierced his chest as he made his way between the patio tables to the hedged railing. He snugged in his earpiece and returned the call.

"Boss. Sorry to interrupt."

"This had better be important. I've spent all night warming Mary Ellen up. Her temperature just dropped twenty degrees. What—"

"Mr. Williams!" a voice with a tinge of Brooklyn called from behind.

Dexter turned as a short rental-tuxedoed man he didn't care to know approached. He quickly donned his politician smile. "Hold on, Christina." He spoke loudly, hoping to embarrass the man for the interruption.

"Sorry, sorry." The man held up his hand, stumbled back, and bumped into a table. But didn't leave. "Far be it from me to—"

"No, no. It's okay." He needed to get rid of this man. He put on his best Southern roots twang. "How can I help you?"

The man shoved his hand forward. "Great speech, Mr. Miller."

Despite the man's lack of pedigree, Dexter relinquished his hand and held on for a vigorous workout.

"Never thought I'd write a check that big for any cause. Whew. Philanthropist of the Year, my—" The Brooklynite tipped his head down. "Well, in a place like this, let's just say my rear."

He chuckled as Dexter reclaimed his hand and feigned amusement.

"More like Philanthropist of the Decade. Or Century. Am I right? Am I right?"

"Thank you, Mister . . ."

"Rizzo. Frank Rizzo."

"Well, thank you, Mr. Rizzo. No greater compliment than a large check to a worthy cause. But truly, it's only by God's grace that I'm able to do what I do." Dexter stretched his smile to its limits.

"Wow. That's humble." Rizzo shook his head and held up a finger. "You inspire me, Mr. Miller."

"What could I say that wouldn't make me sound proud?"

They both laughed.

Dexter pointed to the phone. "Do you mind, sir? I'm just checking in on our children. School night, you know. Is there anything else?"

"No, no. Of course. You need to check on the kiddos." Rizzo pointed toward the ballroom. "I'll just let myself out—or should I say, in." The man all but bowed before turning back toward the ballroom and returning to the gala.

17

"What was that about," Charlie asked through the earpiece.

"Probably looking for money. Never mind him. What is it?"

"West Virginia."

Dexter cursed, then checked around to be sure no one else was waiting in ambush. "Hearthstone again? I thought you took care of that."

"I did . . . well, I am. We'll be up and running by Friday." He paused. "Are you sure you want to go down there?"

Ribbon-cutting ceremonies were what left punks like Rizzo in awe of him. Dexter pictured himself holding the oversized scissors. As much as he had loved donning his construction hat to break ground, the opening was the pièce de resistance—especially since those West Virginia hicks would be helping him celebrate his drug rehab center on one side of town while his meth lab opened on the other. And that was just the start.

"Will the opening be a problem if everything's under control?"

No answer.

"Charlie?"

"Let's talk after everything's wrapped up."

"There'd better be no problems. This project's already gone over budget."

"I'm sure it'll be fine."

Dexter paced between the patio tables. Fine never meant fine. "Then what's the problem?"

"It's those brothers."

"We're getting paid tomorrow, right?"

"That's just it. They say they're going to be short."

"How short?"

"Half."

Dexter let out a string of expletives. He peered into the ballroom, reminding himself how fleeting respect could be. This was why he had rules about business conversations in public. He forced a mono-tone, ensuring each word was safe. "We can't have that now, can we?"

"No, sir."

"Are they stealing from me?"

"Bones says they're telling him they have to drop prices to move the product. The competition is undercutting us. And it's not just the brothers. We're getting the same reports from the whole state."

"Do you believe it?"

"Not my place, boss. But the eldest is driving a brand-new Porsche 911 Turbo."

"Last time I checked, I wasn't paying him enough for that."

"No, sir."

"I think we need new management."

"Yes, boss."

"And, Charlie?

"Yes, sir?"

"Get my money back first. Nobody steals my money."

"Yes, boss."

Dexter tapped the phone to disconnect the call. Deep breath in. Hold. Out. He reapplied his smile, adjusted his bow tie, and returned to his coy first lady just in time for a rhumba—the dance of love.

Chapter 3

11:50 p.m.

HEATHER PERSEVERED THROUGH THE TEQUILA FOG to get as far away from Hearthstone as possible. Driving drunk one mile on a straight road in a town where the streets rolled up at ten was a piece of cake, but the foothills were not so kind. She clenched the steering wheel like the lap bar on a roller coaster. Twists and turns churned her already queasy stomach. Her head swayed as she tried to navigate between the barely-discernible lines. At least there was no traffic.

She fumbled for the high beams to light up her dark world. An oncoming car flashed its lights and laid on its horn. "Get a life!" At least she was staying between the lines she could see. These yokels shouldn't be out this late anyway.

She opened the window to blast her fuzzy brain clear. Whoa. Blast was an understatement. When had it gotten so cold?

Where was she going to go, anyway? Chicago? Her dad was sure to look for her there . . . Who was she kidding? Nobody cared. Maybe she should stop at a hotel. Hotel? There weren't twelve hotels in the entire state of West Virginia.

How had it come to this? Homeless. Rejected. Unable to have children. It was all so unfair. Tears flowed, clouding her already blurred vision. She wiped them away with her sleeve. Oh no. Her mascara. She couldn't mess up Tom's favorite coat. She leaned over to grab her purse from the floor. When she looked back up, a white deer leaped from the forest and froze in the middle of the road, staring straight at her.

"Noooo!" Heather yelled as she yanked the steering wheel to avoid the buck. The car careened over the edge, then barreled down through trees and brush. Time slowed.

The Prius cleared the bushes just before it launched from the embankment into the river below.

The impact was deafening. The car jolted to a stop as it crashed into rocks, the airbag exploding in her face. Her ribs. She couldn't breathe.

The Prius shifted and turned. Metal scraped as the car dropped down the cascades, then settled. The river raced past her, just below the open window. The vehicle jerked from its position and inched further downstream. Freezing water poured in. Forcing the airbag down, Heather pushed herself into the raging torrents just as her car lurched and disappeared into the river below.

The freezing current dragged Heather's battered body over rocks and underwater. She struggled against numbness to reach the branches of a downed tree. As she pulled herself back to grab a larger log, something stabbed her ribs. She shrieked and let go. The gushing river propelled her into more rapids, where she tumbled into a wave pool, rolled over a boulder, and was tossed against a log. Debris pounded her as she turned her body to hold on. Her weak arms dragged her numb torso to the muddy bank and into a bed of pine needles.

Safe at last, she curled into a fetal position and tugged her coat's wet hood over her head. She was too cold to even shiver. She closed her eyes. First aid training echoed in her mind. *Shock. Organ shut down. Lie down. Elevate legs. Keep still. Loosen clothing. Cover with blanket.*

But there was no blanket and no one to care.

Was this it? Was this all there was when you died? No pain? Just cold? No troubles? Only peace. How easy it would be to fall asleep—to slip away. Her problems drifted away.

Chapter 4

Wednesday, October 25
1:00 a.m.

THE TRAIN WHISTLE RIPPED HEATHER FROM THE DEATH she should have died. Metal screeched as wheels ground along the tracks across the river. A heavy engine and coal cars rumbled along, coaxing her into some forgotten crevices of her mind.

The L . . . Chicago . . . the art studio . . .

She smiled as she floated among the art critics fawning over her masterpieces. *Elegant dresses . . . tuxedos . . . sipping wine . . . string quartet.*

"Where's Keith?" a friend asked. The studio gala morphed into a dark, sterile corridor. She ran from room to room. *The bedroom . . . her bed . . . a naked model . . . the look on her husband's face.* "No, no, no."

Darkness . . . laying on a table . . . feet in stirrups . . . a vacuum . . . "it's all over" . . . pain . . . my baby. "Somebody help me."

A dog whimpered. *Dog?* She opened her eyes, tequila still imprisoning her brain. *Darkness . . . a river . . . a train lumbering along on the opposite bank . . . pain . . . freezing . . . the white deer . . . the river . . . her car.*

The dog whined again. Mustering enough energy to tip her head back, Heather located the source. A tan-and-black-faced beagle shepherd immediately began bathing her face in love. "Jasper?" She blinked. Was she dreaming?

It couldn't be Jasper. He'd be long dead by now. Her stepmother had made her give Jasper up when she was six because it was *sooo* important to move to the city. "It's for your best," she had said, but Heather knew better. Cruella was trying to erase all evidence of her real mother.

"Okay, okay," she said, pushing the golden-eyed puppy back and herself up on her elbow. Agony gripped every inch of her body as she relived the river's churning wash cycle that had not spared her from even one rock. How was she even alive?

The dog tipped its head, wagged its tail, and barked. Heather reached toward the youngster, then realized the dog lacked the anatomy that a Jasper would have. Her tail beat the air as she came forward.

"Did you come to save me?"

The dog jumped back and barked as if inviting her.

"Are you lost too?"

A forest surrounded her. How long had she been there? Heather now wished for the gift she had rejected. *Oh, Dad, my generation doesn't wear watches. We have cell phones.* Now, where was her cell phone? She looked toward the rushing waters.

At least she was alive. Ha! The alcohol must have kept her blood from freezing. But she was freezing nonetheless. She had to get to the road. Otherwise, no one would ever find her body. No evidence of her existence. How poetic.

The dog barked and came to her side as if he could help her up.

Icy clothes clung to Heather's body as she fought her pain to erect herself. Her teeth chattered relentlessly, despite clenching them with all her might. She fingered the honestly-earned rips in her jeans.

As she scanned the surrounding trees for a path, the white buck bounded out into the clearing and stood. Staring. Mocking her. Her ribs screamed as she bent over, grabbed a handful of rocks, and launched them at her enemy. "This is all your fault!"

The deer scampered up the embankment into the trees. The dog barked, then followed the way her destroyer had gone. The dog stopped, came back for her, and whined. Was that the way to the road? The only sound was the rushing river.

Barking, the dog waited.

Heather took a few steps, but her toes gushed in the water buckets her boots had become. She hobbled to a fallen log, emptied the water, and wrung out her socks. If she was going to walk any distance, she'd have to put them back on to avoid blisters. It was like putting on a wet bathing suit right out of a freezer.

Boots on, she wiped her forehead with her mucky sleeve. Blood. No mirror to find its source.

The dog tipped her head as Heather struggled her socks and boots on. She backed a bit and barked.

Heather stood. Her mind said stay, but her boots followed the dog up to the two-lane road the deer had forced her off. Which way had she come? Did it matter? She had to start walking. What was that expression about the longest journey? A step. Just a step. The dog barked and went right. Even a dog could do a better job of navigating her life than she had.

———

1:35 a.m.

THE MOON HAD SET BEYOND THE TREE LINE, making the yellow blind curve sign almost imperceptible. How many miles would they have to walk? Had it been a mile?

Shaking, Heather crossed her arms over her chest, hoping to generate heat or at least keep what little body warmth she had to herself. Unlike her carefree companion, Heather jerked her head toward every howl, hoot, and crackle of brush. Could this mix-breed take on a black bear or wolf? Do you stand tall to scare them off, or do you turn and run?

Like she could do that anyway. She could barely walk between the piercing chest pain and the numbing cold, much less chase off a bear. She hugged herself tighter.

Rounding the curve yielded more of the same nothingness. Heather dropped to her knees and broke down. She longed for the four-poster bed of her betrayer's house. Maybe she should crawl back to her sister. Or even her dad, even if Cruella was part of the package. *If* she survived.

The dog licked her tears away. Heather rubbed the dog's neck. "Save yourself. I'm done."

The dog tugged at her sleeve, but despair would not release her.

"Go. There's no use. I can't make it."

The dog tilted her head and whined. That stupid dog was going to die here with her.

In the distance, headlights crested the road and flooded her soul. The beagle shepherd nudged her and barked. Heather hobbled to her feet and waved her arms wildly with her last ounce of energy. "Help!"

The silver Porsche dropped a gear, slowed as it approached, but then gunned the engine as it passed.

Hope drained from her body as she crumpled to the pavement—her life force drained. Nothing left. At least somebody would find her body there. The dog lay next to her as if even she had given up. Heather didn't have the energy to comfort the dog. She closed her eyes.

A throaty engine revved.

Heather lifted her head as the Porsche returned. The dog did circles in a celebration dance. The car stopped fifteen feet away. The bright headlights illuminated the roadside stage she found herself on, but they made it impossible to see her audience. She scrambled to her feet as a man emerged from behind the car door.

"Yo! You okay?"

The dog barked a warning. Dogs were better judges of character than she had ever been. What did the dog know?

The silhouette revealed a height north of six feet. She'd never stand a chance against him but wouldn't last without him. Her liquor-soaked mind wouldn't let her solve the dilemma.

The man cursed and disappeared behind the door.

"My car!"

The man reappeared. "What?"

"A deer . . . I drove into the river." Heather began to cry.

The man moved toward her, but the dog barked him back in front of the headlights.

"You wanna call off Fido?"

Heather patted her leg. "Come on, girl."

The dog came to her side and sat.

The man didn't move. "Your car is *where*?"

Heather looked back at the woods and held up a weary arm, pointing toward the car's graveyard. "I crashed into the river. I don't know what to do. I lost my cell, my purse, my money . . . everything."

The man muttered, then batted the air. "Listen, I ain't no AAA. You wanna call someone? Here." He held out a phone.

Heather shook her head and broke down, blubbering. "There's nobody."

"You in some kinda trouble, ain't you?"

"No. At least not from the law." What could she say? He'd never understand. "I'm sorry, I'm freezing. Can you just give me a ride?"

"A ride?" The man jerked his chest forward. "Do I look like an Uber? I just got this ride."

Heather dropped her head into her hands and bawled. "Go on. Why should you care?" She waved a hand down the road. "Leave me here to die."

The man cursed again. "All right. All right. Man!" He muttered something about his momma. "I'll give you a ride to Huntington. That's it."

"I was headed to Chicago."

"I ain't going to Chicago."

"Huntington's fine." Heather moved toward the car and smacked her thigh. "Come on, girl." The dog let out a low growl.

The man stepped back. "Whoa. I didn't say nothing 'bout no dog. Forget that."

"But she saved my life. It's either both of us, or you can leave me here to die."

The man swatted the air down. "Forget it." He swung around and got in his car. He revved his engine, gunning it a few hundred feet, then squealed to a stop. The reverse lights lit the road for his return.

The passenger window lowered to reveal his profile—a strong, jutted chin. Pierced ear. Shaved head. "You getting in or what?"

Heather yanked the door open as the man tilted the passenger seat forward. The dog jumped into the just-her-size back seat. Despite Heather's dream of riding in a Porsche, she only cared about getting warm at this moment.

"He better not have fleas."

"She," Heather said, carefully lowering herself into the seat. Every bone in her body hurt.

"What?"

"She. The dog is a she." Heather grimaced as she tried to find a comfortable position. A shiver jerked her body. "Can you turn on the heat?"

He pushed her seat warmer button and raised the temperature. "Anything else, lady?"

"Yeah. Thank you."

Without looking at her, he shook his head, then grumbled, "I'm gonna be sorry I did this." He reached for the gearshift, exposing a tattoo on his forearm—a fleur-de-lis around the letters MCM.

Heather had seen gang tats in Chicago. The gang members she'd come across hadn't driven Porsches. And they definitely wouldn't have picked her up. She reassured herself it didn't mean anything and pushed her seat back. Luxury enveloped her aching body and soul. The dog was settled in and sound asleep.

"My name is Heather. What's yours?"

"None of your business." He made a three-point turn on the narrow road with even narrower shoulders to get back on track.

"You're right, but it'd still be nice to know."

He hesitated, shifting in his seat. "Tyrone."

"Tyrone. That's Irish, isn't it?"

"What?"

"Tyrone is an Irish name."

"Yeah, right. Goes with my red hair."

"I'm serious. I helped a friend pick out a baby name once. I think it means you're from a particular place in Ireland. Or . . . it could mean your Greek. It means lord."

He gunned the engine and banked the curves. Were it not for her injuries, she would have loved every minute. Even so, she started to nod off.

"Heather," Tyrone said as if he was testing her name, not getting her attention.

She opened her eyes.

"Chinese, isn't it?" Tyrone cracked his first smile.

"Very funny. Scottish actually. My mom named me for my light hair. She was an artist."

"Was? She dead?"

"Yeah. She died when I was four." Her mind flashed to her mom's artwork in Julie's office and house. Safe and warm places. What had she been thinking—or not thinking? But her brain processor had closed shop and would not let her in. She shut her eyes.

"I gotta make a call."

She peeked her eyes open. "Um, huh."

"Call Johnny." Tyrone switched to a Bluetooth device he'd stuck in his ear.

"What's wrong with you? You in bed already? . . . I think Melissa got you hooked . . . Nah, man, you made your bed. You're the one that wanted to get away from home . . . Tell her I heard that, and I'm 'bout to come there right now and straighten her out . . . Listen though, we got some trouble . . . I'll tell you when I get there. Oh, and I got a surprise for you . . . Nah, if I tell you, then it won't be a surprise."

Surprise? Was she it? Was he a trafficker? Images of being bound and forced into an unthinkable life flooded her mind. She needed out. But if she got out here, she'd die for sure. She had to go along—at least for now. She closed her eyes.

———

2:15 a.m.

A CAR DOOR SLAMMED. Heather jerked from her sleep.

Streetlights cast gloomy shadows through barren limbs onto a cracking street lined with old brick houses. It was still dark outside. The car was parked, and Tyrone was gone. A dog whimpered from the back seat. Her neck protested her attempts to straighten.

Tyrone appeared outside her window, his breath visible in the cold. "Don't move. I'll be back."

Like she had a choice.

Tyrone walked up the front sidewalk to the house they were in front of. He mounted the four cement steps to the porch and knocked on a tired green door, then bounced up and down like a boxer before a fight as he waited.

Where were they? Was this Huntington? Brick porches and roofs sagged. Chain-link fences encased grassless yards littered with stained mattresses and rusting children's bikes. Every third house lacked any evidence of life. And of the occupied, only darkened windows. Was this where he was dropping her off?

Shivers overtook Heather as the car cooled. The dog jumped into Tyrone's seat and wagged her tail as she licked Heather's face.

"You'd better not be there when Tyrone comes back."

The puppy sat up like she owned the car.

A light came on in the neighbor's house's side window to the left. The curtains moved back and then dropped. The light went off.

Tyrone pounded the door. The porch light came on, exposing tubular metal chairs to Tyrone's right. The door cracked open, closed, then opened wide. Tyrone disappeared inside. Was this his girlfriend's house . . . or worse? He *was* crossing West Virginia in the middle of the night in a Porsche.

29

What was Heather waiting for? She was in a city. She pulled the handle and stepped outside the car. The dog followed. A door slammed at the house on the other side of the nosy neighbor, and a shaggy man stumbled down the porch steps. He stopped when he got to the sidewalk, turned back toward the house, and shook his fist. "I don't need you anyway, woman! You ain't nothing!"

The dog barked. Heather steered the dog back into the car, jumped in, and pulled the door closed. The man turned toward her and stared. He swayed in the moonlight.

Heather's heart thumped against her chest. The dog barked suddenly, startling her and setting her nerves further on edge. She stroked the dog. "Shh."

The light came back on in the nosy neighbor's window. The curtain moved.

The dog's barking intensified as the man staggered toward her and stopped at the front fender. His clothes were as wrinkled and dirty as his face. Heather shrank into the seat's leather. The deranged man banged the car with his fist and laughed as he stared at her. The dog jumped into Heather's lap, lunging at the dash.

Tyrone shot out from the front door of the house.

"Hey, what you doing to my ride?" He leaped from the porch, dropped a leather bag, and launched himself at the man. The man tried to break away, but Tyrone quickly caught up and punched him, knocking him out cold.

Heather had never seen such brute force. Even the dog was quiet. Tyrone reached down, grabbed the man by his jacket, and dragged him back to where he'd come from. His body hung like a corpse from Tyrone's grip, yet Tyrone seemed to carry his weight without effort. Who was this guy?

Tyrone dropped the man on the sidewalk in front of the house, slapped the air, and yelled something she couldn't make out. He returned to pick up his bag, then deposited it in the Porsche's trunk.

He yanked the passenger door open and motioned as he said, "Get out."

"Here? I don't even know where we are."

"I done got you here. Now get out before somebody sees you . . . *and me.*"

The curtain was still pulled back at the nosy neighbor's house. Heather's side rebelled as she swiveled and rose. The dog followed.

Tyrone pointed to the house.

Heather looked at the green door but couldn't move. He slammed her door shut.

"Go on, lady."

Heather took a step toward the house. Next door, a shadow stood back from the curtains. A witness? She willed her feet forward.

The green door opened. A man who could have been Tyrone's twin waited.

Behind her, a car door slammed. She jumped as the Porsche's engine revved. She turned in time to see Tyrone speed off down the street, bank a hard left, and disappear.

"What you waiting for?" the deep voice asked.

Heather turned back to the man. He held the door open.

"Come on." He cursed his fuel bill.

She looked left. Despite witnessing Tyrone pummel the man, the shadow still watched, but no police came. Would the shadow report seeing her when she disappeared? Her teeth chattered. She hugged herself tighter. The man two doors down was still lying in a lump on his sidewalk. What was she doing? One phone call to her dad would end this.

"I ain't got all night. You coming or what?" The man stepped onto the porch, and the light fully revealed his face.

She stared in disbelief. She'd spent a semester in college studying countenance and painted a piece she called "Good Mother." This guy was virtually the same as her model. It was surreal. And unmistakable. This was the face of a man who'd had a good mother.

31

A sweetness—an imprint on the child's soul—a phenomenon that intrigued the artist in her.

"What you looking at? You comin' or what?"

Peace overcame her. He was no tough guy. Heather started forward, but the dog growled her protest.

"Naw, naw, naw. Tyrone didn't say nothing 'bout no dog."

She stopped. "Like I told Tyrone. I don't go without the dog."

He stared at her. "You serious?"

Heather stood firm.

A towheaded little girl with Shirley Temple curls came through the open door and wrapped her unicorn jammies around the man's jeans. She looked up at him. "Uncle Johnny, who's that lady?"

"She's Uncle Tyrone's friend. She's gonna spend the night with us." Johnny pulled the little girl back. "Get back inside."

"Aww, look at the doggie." The little girl raced down the porch stairs before he could stop her. She giggled as the dog licked her face.

"Olivia! Get back here now."

"But, Uncle Johnny."

"Now."

Olivia straightened and returned to the porch. "What about the homeless lady and the dog?"

Homeless? She *was* in tatters—and she technically had no home. She needed a warm shower, clean clothes, money, and a place to sleep. She *was* a homeless lady.

Johnny regarded Heather as Olivia pleaded. "Please, please, please?"

He swept his hand toward the door. "Okay, the dog can come."

"Yay!" The little girl patted her leg. "Come on, puppy."

The dog's tail wagged as she followed Olivia up and into the house. Heather did likewise, watching Johnny's face for some sign of welcome. She stopped and held out her hand. "My name is Heather."

He tipped his chin up. "Yeah."

"Thank you for letting us stay. We'll be out of your hair tomorrow."

"Hmmm . . ." He shut the door behind her. "We'll see."

The house's tired exterior masked the treasure hidden within. Whoever had decorated this living room understood color, contrast, and function. The furniture choices were rustic yet elegant—each piece unique but working together. None overstated.

Petting the dog, Olivia squatted on the thick area rug that seemed to have been tailor-woven to mirror the palate of colors. The original paintings captured West Virginia landscapes and native wildlife. Heather had never seen this artist's work, but she hungered for more. How had this décor ended up in a neighborhood like this?

Heather turned back for her host's cue. Johnny pointed to a carved, tulip-shaped oak chair by the front window next to a soft burgundy Riviera sofa. "Wait there."

The chair was fantastic. It appeared to have been made from one tree trunk. It must have taken a month to chisel each of a dozen petals that invited you to snuggle in. She stroked the smooth finish of the oak masterpiece before removing her coat and settling in. The chair's comfort matched its beauty. Heather ran her finger along the magnificent grooves that formed this flower.

Johnny headed past the dining area on the right to the large kitchen entryway that exposed most of the kitchen to the living room. "Melissa's coming down. She'll know what to do with you." He stopped at the entryway and turned back. "Olivia."

Olivia looked up.

"Don't guess it'll do any good to tell you to get back to bed."

Olivia giggled. "Isn't the puppy *sooo* cute? Can I stay up just a little longer? *Pleeease?*"

Johnny shook his head as he turned on the kitchen light. "I'll let your momma deal with you." He retrieved a beer from the refrigerator, then leaned back against the kitchen entryway wall to the right looking toward the stairway. He shook his head and took a swig.

Heather's stomach lurched at the sight of the brown bottle reminding her of the torture she had thrust on it just a few hours before. How was she even functioning . . . or alive, for that matter?

A toilet flushed overhead.

"Johnny?" a voice called from above.

Johnny looked up, then at Heather, shook his head, but didn't say a word.

"Johnny!" Fuzzy purple slippers with purple pajama legs peeked out from the top of the staircase. A blonde stopped halfway down, glared at Heather, then back at Johnny.

Olivia hopped up and ran to the staircase, the dog following. "Mommy, mommy, look at the puppy." She waved her mother down. "Come here. Isn't she soooo cute?"

Melissa focused on Heather for a moment, then on the dog. "Johnny, you deaf?"

Johnny wagged his head. "I heard you."

"Then come up here . . . *now.*"

Johnny pushed off the door jam and started up the stairway to scorn. "I don't need this stuff."

"But, Mommy. Come and see the puppy."

"In a minute, baby." Melissa looked at Heather with a pinched face. "Pardon us . . ."

"Heather."

"What?"

"My name is Heather."

"Pardon us, *Heather.*" Melissa disappeared. Johnny followed.

Olivia came to Heather with her big brown eyes wide. "Where did you come from?"

Should she say? Little kids aren't known for keeping secrets. *Less said* . . . "Not too far away."

Olivia rubbed the fur of Heather's coat draped over the arm of the chair. "Are you homeless?"

Heather couldn't hold back her giggle. "I am today."

"Mommy said we're supposed to be nice to homeless people." Olivia pointed to the cuff. "Is that blood?"

"Yes, I got a boo-boo on my head."

Olivia's eyes scanned Heather's head. She reached out and gently touched a sore spot on her forehead. "Does that hurt?"

Strained voices drifted down the stairs, drawing both of their attention.

Olivia looked at Heather. "Uh oh. Mommy is mad at Uncle Johnny."

Heather should have run when she had the chance. But she needed a shower and some sleep. She rose and walked to the bottom of the stairs. "Melissa?"

Melissa came into sight and looked down, head tilted.

"I don't want to cause any trouble." She pointed to the front door. "I'll just be on my way." Heather grabbed her coat from the chair and tugged it over her shoulders, trying to avoid touching her bruises. She called for the dog.

Olivia raced to the bottom of the stairs. "No, Mommy, don't let her go. You told me we have to be nice to homeless people. You said we have to help them."

"Hold on," Melissa called out as she descended the stairs.

Heather stopped and turned back.

Melissa dropped from the last step. Her face was taut.

"No, really. We'll be okay. You don't have to worry about us."

Olivia wrapped herself around her mother's legs. "Mommy, you said we have to help them."

Melissa crossed her arms and cocked her head. "So?"

"So, what?"

"What's your story? What kind of trouble are you in?"

"No—it's nothing like that. Not that my story's a good one." It was so stupid that she never wanted to tell anyone. Hitchhiking in the middle of the night? What could she possibly say to make what had happened sound . . . normal . . . or even reasonable? But it was what it was.

"I got drunk and crashed my car in a river. I lost everything. I would have died if Tyrone hadn't shown up when he did."

35

Melissa didn't respond or react in any way for a long moment. She just eyed Heather.

"Listen, we'll just leave."

Melissa dropped her arms. "No. Olivia's right. With that story, you have to be telling the truth. No sane person would admit to that. Stay the night. We'll figure all this out tomorrow."

"I'm really sorry. I promise I'll get out of your hair in the morning. I need to sleep off this day. I'm happy to sleep on the couch." As soon as she said it, she knew Melissa wouldn't want her filthy clothes on her lovely sofa.

"You don't need to do that. You can bunk with Olivia since you're her new best friend."

Olivia jumped up and down. "Yay! A sleepover! I never get to have a sleepover."

Melissa eyed Heather. "You look like you're probably my size."

"Ha." Johnny laughed from his post midway up the stairs. "She could be your twin."

Melissa gave Johnny the evil eye.

Johnny put his hands in the air. "I'm going back to bed." He turned and disappeared.

Melissa looked back to Heather. "You take a shower. I'll bring you some fresh clothes." She pointed upstairs. "First door on the left."

"Thank you. Thank you. I promise I'll repay you when I get settled."

"No need." Melissa looked at the dog. "What are you doing with him?"

"It's a her. Do you happen to have anything she can eat? She's probably hungry."

"I'll feed her, Mommy."

"Bedtime, Olivia."

"But, Mommy."

"Now."

Olivia hung her head and petted the dog one last time before saying goodnight and pouting her way up the stairs. Heather called the dog over.

Melissa went into the kitchen. "Does she have a name?" She opened a cabinet door and retrieved a couple of bowls.

Heather walked to the kitchen entryway, then looked back at the dog.

"Not yet. That dog saved my life tonight." Heather chortled. "Sounds like an Elton John song."

Melissa began filling one of the bowls with water from the sink. She nodded and smiled. Heather wanted to paint that smile. Chiseled face full of history. She'd have to ask later.

Melissa filled the second bowl with canned tuna, then put both dishes on the floor for the dog, who raced over and began lapping water loudly at Melissa's feet.

Melissa leaned back against the counter. "Would *you* like something to drink?"

"Just some water, please."

"Nothing stronger?" Melissa asked with a nod.

"No, that's what got me in this trouble to begin with." The liquor fog was finally lifting—no more of that foolishness.

Melissa opened another cabinet, grabbed a glass, then held it under the refrigerator's water dispenser. She offered it to Heather.

"Thank you." Heather drank it down, hoping it would relieve her cottonmouth. It helped, but only sleep would cure her of her self-inflicted damage.

Melissa tilted her head. "Where were you going when you crashed?"

"Who knows? Chicago . . . maybe."

"Sounds like there's a story there."

"Not one for tonight. I'll head upstairs for that shower if you don't mind. Thanks for all you are doing. I don't think I'd be as gracious as you."

Melissa smiled. "Gracious? Hm." She looked at Heather for a moment, her eyes narrowing. "You don't seem like the type."

"What type?"

"The type that Tyrone brings around."

"Does he bring women around a lot?"

"Let's just say you seem like you've lived a better life than the people I usually see." Melissa was almost staring at her. "I don't know what it is, but there's something familiar about you. I can't put my finger on it, and I don't know why I'm saying this, but you're welcome to stay a few days. Might be nice having you around—for Olivia." Then she chuckled. "But don't tell Johnny I said that." She winked.

For the first time since the crash, Heather relaxed. Melissa's comments confirmed what Heather was sensing—an unexplainable connection. Too much to process after this day. She pointed upstairs. "First door on the left?"

"Yep. Leave the door unlocked, and I'll put some clothes on the counter. Olivia's room is just next to it. She'll probably be in the top bunk."

"You're really okay with me bunking with her."

Melissa nodded and grinned. "She's taken a liking to you. Or maybe it's the dog."

The dog's whine reminded Heather that she would need to be walked. Was she even house-trained? "Does your backyard happen to be enclosed?"

"Yeah, why?"

Heather pointed to the dog. "It will save me from taking her for a walk. I don't even have a leash or collar."

"No worries. I'll let her out while you shower. I had a dog not that long ago." Melissa's smile disappeared.

"Sad story?"

"Let's just say evil is alive and well." Melissa leaned down to pet the dog. "So, no name yet, huh?"

"Why don't we let Olivia name her? I bet she'd love that."

"I'm sure she would." Melissa stood. "Yes. I think we're going to get along just fine." She smiled. "Now go on. The sooner I get you settled, the sooner I can get some sleep. And give me that coat. We can take it to the cleaners tomorrow."

"Thanks." Heather handed over the blood-stained coat encapsulating the day's troubles and headed up.

Heather gasped as she opened the door to the eloquently decorated bathroom. Exquisite Wedgewood-like tile work and retrofitted antiques—wow. Heather was looking forward to finding out more about the hostess who had tried to hide behind the hardened mask.

The shower controls required a master's degree in engineering to operate. Various shower heads surrounded her as she stepped into the mini spa. Just turning on the regular shower was a coup. The warm water engulfed her and drained away the last of the alcohol's hold.

When she pulled back the curtains, pink pajamas and fluffy slippers awaited her on the vanity. Wearing someone else's panties unsettled her, but what choice did she have? They looked new enough—and clean. If she were Melissa, she'd toss them once they were returned.

A note sat on top of the clothes.

> *Feel free to sleep in. I'll take care of the dog and try to keep Olivia out of your hair. I threw your clothes in the washer. We'll go shopping tomorrow to get you some new ones—the holes in your jeans are beyond stylish rips. Must be weird putting on my undies. Sorry. They're clean.*

She chuckled. Melissa got her.

Heather snuggled into the jammies. The cut on her head had reopened a bit. The cabinet drawers yielded bandages and ointment. A sticky note on a toothbrush read, "At least this is new." Heather smiled as she applied bubble gum toothpaste—the same brand her mom had bought when she was little.

After blow-drying her hair, Heather was finally clean, warm, and dry. Except for the bandage and bruises, she looked human again. A Little Mermaid nightlight illuminated the bathroom when she flipped the switch off. Another nightlight guided her around the corner to Olivia's room. Heather's heart melted as she gazed upon Olivia curled up on the lower bunk with the dog. The dog raised her head, then lowered it again. Olivia didn't stir.

Heather climbed up to the top bunk. She shifted to find the least painful position and then covered herself with the safety of the Little Mermaid bedspread.

Tomorrow's unknowns began to torment her until Melissa came to the door, smiled, and mouthed goodnight. She reciprocated, and Melissa disappeared. She closed her eyes on a day that had somehow taken a miraculous turn for the better.

Chapter 5

10:00 a.m.

THE FLOOR-TO-CEILING GLASS WALLS OF HIS OFFICE afforded Dexter and his hundred-and-fifty pound Great Dane, Rockefeller, a kingdom view of the sales force working the new-car buyers below. Twenty years to reach this pinnacle, as evidenced by his new state-of-the-art dealership. America's largest showroom boasted models of every color and option imaginable. Big-screen projectors offered action and adventure on plexiglass walls. Even at ten a.m., his salesforce was busy writing orders while his brother Matty whipped lattes and cappuccinos at the full-service coffee bar. Complimentary, of course.

Dexter patted Rockefeller's head. "This is success, my friend. This is success." Rockefeller tipped his black-on-tan face up and sat a little taller.

This year, Detroit had done its part with bold new designs and colors that captured its buyers' imaginations. His regular customers had already gotten ahead of the Joneses by pre-ordering the updated models when they were first announced. Because he knew the right palms to grease, he still had plenty of inventory, making him the most powerful dealer in the Upper Midwest.

As she walked across the sales floor toward the coffee bar, his assistant Nancy modeled her perfectly fit, royal-blue suit. A man in a tan trench coat wearing a funny little brown cap sat on a stool drinking a coffee and chatting it up with Matty. Was that the man from the previous night? Mr. Brooklyn? What was his name? Something Italian . . . Rizzo . . . Frank Rizzo.

What was he doing there? And why was he talking to Matty? His stomach tensed.

Nancy said something to Matty, then joined the conversation. She pointed up to Dexter. Rizzo turned and tipped his hat toward him. He reluctantly waved back. Rizzo shook Matty's hand, then followed Nancy across the floor. What was she doing? She knew better than to let anyone up without approval.

He shut his office door and took a seat on his throne. Rockefeller took his position next to Dexter. Why was he letting this gnat get under his skin?

Nancy buzzed him. "Mr. Miller? I have a Mr. Rizzo here to see you."

"What does he want?"

"He said he forgot to leave his donation check last night at the gala, and he'd like to thank you again for the work you're doing for the charity."

Keeping up images was a waste of time, but he was well-versed in the importance of word-of-mouth. One positive encounter might be shared with one person if you were lucky, but a negative one would be blasted all over social media and relayed to everyone they knew. Understanding these business rules is what made him number one.

He looked at Rockefeller, who was always ready for company. Deep breath in. Hold. Out. "Please show Mr. Rizzo in."

Applying his money-maker smile, Dexter stood just as Nancy opened the door for Rizzo. He charged Dexter with the same zeal as the night before.

"Mr. Miller. Wow. What an honor it is to see you again." He eyed Rockefeller. "Your dog. Wow. He's a beauty—and big."

Dexter didn't comment or offer his hand but kept the desk between them. He pointed to the black leather bucket-seat chairs in front of him. "Please, have a seat."

"Thank you." Rizzo sat.

Rockefeller moved around and sat next to Rizzo—something Dexter had trained him to do. Rockefeller's sad eyes were face-to-face with Rizzo's. Dexter loved to watch his guests squirm. The gentle giant would never hurt anyone, but his guests still didn't like it.

Rizzo kept looking at the dog, then back at Dexter. "Is Fido here safe?"

"Harmless as a flea, they say."

Rizzo leaned away. "I don't want to take up your time. I'm sure you need to get back to work." He looked around. "Wow." Rizzo popped up and walked to the glass wall. Rockefeller didn't move. "Look at that view. You can see everything from here." He turned back to Dexter. "And they can see you. No privacy here, huh?"

Dexter couldn't help himself. He hadn't yet tired of this new toy. "Zaza, please dim the showroom walls."

Dimming the showroom walls, a sexy electronic voice said as the glass turned a creamy opaque.

Rizzo's mouth hung open. "Wow. Wow. I guess you can afford that when you're number one in sales. That's what Matty said. You must be very proud." Rizzo chose the chair farther from the dog. Rockefeller moved to his side. Rizzo leaned away.

"Yes. It's been a lot of work, but I feel the Lord blessed my work because I always give back."

"That's what I say too. Well, I wrote a check last night, but when I got home and told the missus about your new rehab center in that poor state of West Virginia, she said we needed to double our donation. Compared to what you're used to, it's small—heck, you probably make more in one week than I'll make my whole life—but what can I say? I was inspired." Beaming, Rizzo handed over the check.

Dexter took the check, glancing down as he did. One hundred dollars. A glass of wine costs more.

"That's very generous. Let me make sure this gets right over to them." He pressed the intercom button on his desk phone. "Nancy?"

After a long moment, she appeared at the door.

"Sorry, Mr. Miller. Charlie's on line six. He says it's important. Would you like to pick it up?"

The secure line.

"Yes, I'll take it." Forcing a smile, he held up Rizzo's donation. "Can you get this check over to the charity?"

"Yes, sir." Nancy retrieved it, then left.

"Pardon me while I take this call."

Rizzo held up his hands. "No worries."

Dexter picked up. "Good morning, Charlie. I have someone with me. Nancy said it was important."

"Boss? We got a problem."

Dexter maintained his smile. "We?"

"That vet—the prosecutor's wife. She got an attorney, and they got a judge to substitute for the magistrate . . . you know."

"I think we need to have a meeting to discuss this. I need to say good-bye to my guest. I'll call you back." Dexter hung up and stood. He smiled down at Rizzo. "Factory problems. I need to deal with this. I truly thank you for coming by with the generous gift. I hope you'll pardon me."

Rizzo stood. "No, no. It's no problem. And hey—nice thing you're doing for your brother."

"What's that?"

"Matty. He told me what a great brother you are and how you've cared for him his whole life. Seems like a nice enough fella—well, you know, for . . ." Rizzo wagged his head. "You know."

He knew all too well that people had trouble dealing with his brother's "cognitive challenges," as they called it these days. "Yes. I know. All I did was give him a job, and he's very good at it. Now if you don't mind . . ." He pressed the intercom button again. "Nancy? Would you show Mr. Rizzo out?"

Rockefeller returned to Dexter's side as Rizzo headed for the doorway. He turned back at the door and tipped his hat. "See you around." Nancy closed the door after him.

Not if Dexter could help it. He sat, patted Rockefeller's head, and called Charlie on his secured cell.

"Have you lost your mind calling—"

The door opened, and Rizzo poked his head back in. Rockefeller stood.

"Oh, sorry. You're on the phone. Never mind."

Nancy appeared at the door flustered. "Sorry, Mr. Miller, I tried to stop him."

"My mistake." Rizzo began backing out.

Dexter forced a smile. "It's okay, Nancy. What is it, Mr. Rizzo?"

Rizzo stepped back inside, eyed Rockefeller, and stayed by the door holding his hat like a man that needed a favor.

Nancy pulled the door closed.

"Well, it's just . . . I have a nephew who needs a good deal on a new car. Well, not a new car, you know. A good used car. And I was wondering if you could help a fella out."

Finally, Rizzo had admitted why he'd come. Dexter pressed the intercom.

"Nancy? Would you introduce Mr. Rizzo to Chris and ask him to help Mr. Rizzo with a generous discount?" He looked back up at Rizzo and raised his cell phone. "If that's all, Mr. Rizzo . . . my call."

"Oh, yeah. Sorry."

Nancy escorted him out, closing the door behind them. Rockefeller sat.

Shaking his head, Dexter returned to his call. "Sorry, Charlie. That strange little man from last night was here. But never mind him. I thought you took care of this problem."

"There was a delay, and before our girl could finish the job, they pulled the vet out to go to a bail hearing."

Dexter stood and paced as he unloaded an expletive bomb. Rockefeller's ears raised. "Where does this leave us?"

"It's still an open-and-shut guilty—especially with her husband and the old sheriff gone. Hayes says the evidence to put her away is solid. We should still be able to finish up what we started, and everything will be back on schedule."

"It'd better be."

"Oh, one other thing. We can't find Cruz."

"Who?" Dexter shook his head.

"Deputy Cruz. Hayes's nephew. He was getting chummy with the vet's sister. He might have lost his stomach for this work . . . or he might have turned."

"Find him."

"You still planning on going to Hearthstone Friday?"

Dexter cursed as he pounded his glass-top desk. "You think I'm going to let some punk nephew or hick vet stop me from opening that rehab?"

"No, sir."

"Do I have anything else to worry about?"

"No, sir."

"Good. Do you have the award ready for the eleven o'clock sales meeting? That new manager is blowing the roof off our sales quotas."

"But, sir, with all that's going on—"

"What's my rule about *buts*, Charlie?"

"Got it, sir."

Chapter 6

10:20 a.m.

"HEATHER?"

Heather peeked her eyes open. Olivia stood on the bunk bed ladder with her hand laid gently on Heather's leg. Her eyes were wide as if she were awakening an alien.

"Mo-o-o-m-m-y-y-y, she's a-wa-a-a-ake!"

The dog joined Olivia in her announcement.

Heather sat up and rubbed her throbbing temples. Her bruises forced her to remember her poor choices.

Melissa came into the room carrying Heather's cleaned and folded clothes. "Olivia. Did you wake Heather up?" She set the clothes on a small white table next to a toy tea service, then pulled Olivia off the ladder.

"But, Mommy . . ."

Melissa shook her head and looked at Heather. "I'm sorry. I did my best to keep her out of here." She leaned down and gave her daughter a soft pat on her behind. "Now go downstairs, young lady. Let Heather wake up in peace."

"No—no, it's fine," Heather said.

"See, Mommy. She wants me to stay." Olivia bounced with excitement.

"You heard me—get downstairs."

Olivia pouted her lip and hung her head. "Come on, puppy." The dog followed her out the door in lockstep.

Sunlight streamed through the white sheers above the tea table. Heather held up her hand to block the excruciating headache the bright light exacerbated. "What day is it? I feel like I've been sleeping forever."

"I guess that means you slept well."

"I don't remember the last time I slept so soundly."

"Yeah. I kinda figured." Melissa winked. "It's Wednesday. Not all that late." She checked her cell phone. "Just ten thirty. How're you feeling?"

"Like someone who crashed a car into a boulder in the middle of a freezing river after drinking half a county dry."

"That bad?" Melissa scrunched her face.

"Considering how bad it could have been, I'm just glad I didn't kill anybody. I've never been that drunk."

Melissa nodded. "Yeah." She pointed to the clothes. "Well. Here are your clothes, along with a pair of my jeans . . . in case you agree with me that yours have too many holes."

"Thank you. I guess they're pretty torn up."

"You like pancakes?"

"I'm a pancake junkie."

Melissa smiled and started to leave.

"Hey, Melissa?"

She turned back, resting her hand against the door frame. "Yeah?"

"Thanks. You'll never know what your kindness means to me."

"It's no big deal."

"No, it really is. You don't even know me." A tear slipped from her eye.

"Stop. I haven't been all that nice. Remember, I was ready to throw your butt out last night." She grinned. "Come on down to the kitchen when you're ready." She left the room, shutting the door behind her.

Compared to the beautifully appointed living room, Olivia's room was bland. It had all the right toys for a girl—an elegant dollhouse,

Little Mermaid bedspreads, the tea table in the corner with its too-small-for-adults chairs, and a dressing table. But the room lacked a theme. The white walls cried out for Neverland or a castle in a far-away place. Maybe she could repay them with a mural.

Heather carefully eased her hangover down the ladder. She donned her shredded jeans. Melissa was right about the holes. She switched to Melissa's and gave herself a once-over in the full-length mirror on the back of the door. A perfect fit. She should toss her holey ones, but that would look like she expected Melissa to give these clothes to her. And that part about going shopping? Why would Melissa want to do that? Heather was a complete stranger—and based on how Heather had landed on her door-step—a total loser.

But the idea of shopping together stirred her heart in a way she had not felt for a long time. Or maybe never. She couldn't explain it, but her soul needed this friendship. Maybe she was just being emo-tional. She needed to make sure she didn't overstay her welcome. She would thank Melissa and be on her way, with a promise to repay her for the clothes.

She opened the door and followed the scent of bacon and coffee downstairs. When she emerged from the stairway, Olivia and the dog hopped up from the living room floor and ran to her.

"Come watch my favorite movie with me." She pulled Heather to the sofa.

Heather complied, giggling as Olivia snuggled in next to her. "Really? *Aladdin* was my favorite too. I always wanted to be Princess Jasmine."

"Me too!"

"Hey, if *Aladdin*'s your favorite movie, why do you have *Little Mermaid* pajamas and bedspreads?"

Olivia pulled back. "That *used* to be my favorite a looong time ago." Her head bobbed, emphasizing her words.

"*Ooooh.*" She suppressed a laugh.

Melissa emerged from the kitchen, grinned at them, then slipped her phone from her jeans and snapped a photo. "I see Princess Jasmine has kidnapped you."

"It's okay. It's *our* favorite movie." Heather grinned, pointing back and forth between herself and Olivia.

"Well, why don't you come and have breakfast before Aladdin starts all that wishing."

"But, Mommy, Heather loves *Aladdin*."

"Don't worry. She can come back and watch it from the beginning after breakfast."

Olivia's face lit up. "Really?"

"If she wants to." Melissa returned to the kitchen.

Heather touched Olivia's nose. "You know it."

Olivia smiled and settled back for the movie as if Heather had never been there.

Heather found Melissa at the counter, pouring coffee into two mugs. "You're a natural with kids. Have any of your own?"

There was that question. Her stomach tightened, but not from the hangover. "No . . . I can't."

Melissa stopped pouring and looked back at her. "I'm sorry. Sounds like I hit a nerve."

"Let's just say 'safe abortion' is a myth." Heather touched her permanently-barren belly. "I almost died."

Melissa winced. She turned around fully and leaned against the countertop. "Oh, my God. What happened?"

Where should she start? Did she even want to? Remembering the abortion clinic's lies—lies she'd allowed herself to believe—only further reminded her of how she got there. "Maybe when I'm feeling better?"

"Absolutely."

"Great. Inhale." She brought her hands into prayer position, closed her eyes, and took two yoga breaths. Exhaling, she opened her eyes and dropped her hands.

"Better?"

"Almost." She pointed her nose to the aroma. "Ah, there it is—the scent that carried me downstairs like riding Aladdin's carpet."

Melissa chuckled. "Have a seat." She pointed to one of four chairs around the small round oak table in the breakfast nook. Only one place was set. Of course, the family would have eaten at a normal time. "How do you take your coffee?"

"Milk and sugar, if it's not too much trouble."

"Got it."

An oak hutch filled with delightful rooster accouterments flanked the table to the left of a bay window. These nick-nacks captured Heather's attention. They weren't tacky but rather the kind that bespoke authentic farm life. And the painting on the wall on the right—a farm, just like the one she grew up on until Cruella took it away.

The painting drew her to step closer. It was almost identical to the one in her sister's office, except this one revealed the golden palette of fall. She examined the details. Brush strokes like her mother's. And the colors . . . all the radiance of a bright fall day in Virginia capturing light the way her mother had.

She checked the bottom of the painting for a signature. There wasn't one—one of her mother's trademarks. *How can I take credit for the glory the Lord had created?*

Heather shivered at the memory. How she missed her mother.

"Heather?"

She forced her attention back from her childhood to Melissa, who was carrying the two mugs of coffee to the table.

"I'm sorry. This painting . . ." She looked back at it. "I would swear this is the farm I grew up on. I was five or six when we moved away." She shook her head. "It's almost identical to a painting my mother did. But that's impossible. Isn't it?"

"What?" Melissa stood beside her and looked at the painting as if she'd never seen it before.

She turned to Melissa. "Do you mind if I ask where you got it?"

"Well, that's a story." Melissa fiddled with the diamond ring on her finger, then sat in the chair next to Heather's spot across from the painting.

Heather took her seat, looking from Melissa to the farm.

Melissa pulled her coffee cup from across the table and wrapped her hands around the mug. "I got it from a grandmother I didn't know I had. After she died, a lawyer called and said I'd inherited her estate."

"You didn't know her?"

Melissa pursed her lips and shook her head.

"I'm sorry. That's personal. I shouldn't have asked."

"No, no. It's just that . . . Well, it just happened. I haven't even processed it yet." Melissa searched Heather's eyes. "When he called, I discovered my entire childhood was a lie."

"What do you mean?"

Melissa examined Heather for a long moment, then took a deep breath. "I have no idea why I'm telling you this. For some strange reason, I feel like I can trust you. Except for Johnny, I never trust anyone. Even with him . . . let's say there're things he doesn't know. But there're times like this when he doesn't get me."

"I'm all ears." Heather almost reached for Melissa's hand, but the tough Melissa she had met the night before might withdraw. She was already stretching her boundaries.

"Let me get your breakfast first."

Melissa busied herself as Heather took a slow sip of coffee and pondered the painting. Melissa returned and set a plate of blueberry pancakes and bacon in the middle of the table, then retrieved a serving fork, butter, and pancake syrup.

"Jasmine and I have already eaten, so help yourself." She gestured toward her culinary gift, then sat and returned to her seat.

Heather forked a couple of pancakes onto her plate and covered them with syrup. "These look great." Her hungover stomach decided against the bacon, even though its smell was what had enticed her. "I haven't had blueberry pancakes in years. My favorite." Heather cut a forkful and savored the bite. The flavor of love. Yes, this was just what she needed. "All right. I'm all ears."

Melissa looked at her fingers laced around her coffee mug. "Here goes." She took a deep breath. "About a month ago, my grandmother's attorney called. He told me she had passed and left me her entire estate. Other than my brother, I didn't even know I had a family."

"I can't even imagine."

Melissa paused as if she was reliving something or searching for words. "I grew up in the foster system. They told us our parents were dead. When I asked the attorney why my grandparents didn't take us, he said I should come to his office in D.C. to get my questions answered."

"D.C.? That's funny. Our farm was outside D.C."

Melissa scrunched her face and looked up at the painting.

"So, you went to see him?"

"Yeah. The next day. Wait here." She jumped up and left the kitchen. She returned with a manila folder and sat, placing it in front of her. Tears formed in her eyes—something Heather hadn't expected.

"It's okay if you can't."

"It's just . . ."

"What?"

Melissa opened the folder to an article from a New Hampshire newspaper. She pushed the folder so Heather could read and pointed to the headline: couple sentenced to fifteen years for child neglect.

Heather put her fork down and picked up the article. "What's this?"

"It's about me . . . and my brother. I was too young to remember it. I wasn't even two." Melissa bit her knuckle. "How could anyone do that?" She looked past Heather toward the living room, where Olivia's childlike voice echoed the joyous melody of "Friend Like Me" pouring from the video.

She looked back at Heather. "We were, like, Olivia's age. I'll never understand."

Heather scanned the article.

Children naked . . . four-year-old boy tied to a bed with a dog collar . . . urine soaked through mattress . . . covered with feces . . . two-year-old girl shivering in a crib . . . parents' areas clean . . . treated dog better . . .

Heather covered her mouth as she read, unable to process the scene's horror. Why was it always the women who could have babies who did this stuff while women like Heather were doomed to no children? But Heather had had an abortion, so who was she to talk? She kept reading. "They only got fifteen years? That's not right. Did they at least castrate him and rip out her womb?"

Melissa shook her head.

"Are they out of prison?"

"They did get out, but my dad died of a heroin overdose, and my mother died of cancer."

"That's weird. My mom died of cancer too. I thought I had it bad when my father married my wicked stepmother." At least Heather had her dad and sister. She should call them, apologize for being a jerk, and beg them to let her come back.

"So, where was your grandmother while all this was going on?"

"That's the saddest part. She didn't know we existed until somebody called her after we went into foster care. My mother had run off with some guy, had a baby, and sold that baby—"

"You're kidding."

"You can't make this stuff up. After that, she hooked up with another guy, got married, and had us. We were put into foster care when we were taken from our home.

My grandparents had no idea. As soon as they found out, they tried to adopt us. They jumped through all kinds of hoops to get us from New Hampshire. After several months, they did, but then my brother started acting out. He hit me with a baseball bat. He became dangerous at school. They think he killed some of the farm animals. He was getting out of control."

"Did the attorney tell you all this?"

"No. My grandmother left a letter and photos. And some other articles and reports."

"So, what happened?"

"My brother had what they call attachment disorder. When kids aren't loved by the time they turn four, they can become like sociopaths—no ability to bond and no conscience." Melissa's voice had become almost a growl. "The guardian ad litem said he should have gone into a therapeutic home right away." She held onto her mug with both hands. "I know it wasn't my brother's fault, but when my grandparents reported his behavior to New Hampshire, the social workers took me too instead of just picking up my brother. This was over the objections of psychologists and the guardian, who told the court I was bonding and in a good place. The social workers didn't care. They said they don't like to break siblings up."

Melissa's body tensed. Her knuckles had become white around her mug. "Because of my brother, I missed out on being adopted by two loving grandparents. Instead, we went from home to home. He eventually ended up a criminal. I was abused and moved around for years. The reports showed how the social workers lied about everything. They ignored all the professionals. My grandparents fought so hard for me." She broke down crying, covering her face with her hands. "I could have been loved."

Olivia and the dog came to Melissa's side. The dog nosed Melissa's elbow and whimpered. Olivia's eyes were wide.

"What's wrong, Mommy?"

Melissa quickly wiped her eyes, then turned to hug her daughter. "Oh, Mommy's sorry, sweetie. I'm just sad that my grandmother died. Remember when we went to get your pretty things—your dollhouse and table?"

Olivia nodded.

"Now go on back to the living room. Heather will be in to watch *Aladdin* with you in a few minutes."

"Promise?"

"Yes—just a few more minutes," Heather said.

Olivia kissed her mom's cheek and left.

Melissa pointed up. "Did you see that dollhouse in Olivia's room?"

"Yeah. It's magnificent."

"My grandfather made that for me." Melissa smiled sadly. "The attorney said they spent thousands of dollars trying to get us, then keep us, then get us back. But New Hampshire cut them off. The letter from my grandmother said my grandfather died of a broken heart."

"Do you remember anything?"

"I have some vague recollections. Some came back when I looked at the photos. It all runs together after a while. You go from home to home with all your worldly goods in a pillowcase."

Melissa twirled the diamond ring on her finger. "This was my grandmother's. And I got that cool hand-carved chair, Olivia's dresser, and the paintings. And then there's that Bible." She pointed to the buffet.

Heather scanned the shelves to find the well-worn Bible sitting amongst a host of cookbooks. Heather wanted to retrieve it, but she hated Bibles.

"There isn't a blank margin in the whole thing. And I have a faint memory of her telling me about Jesus." Melissa shook her head. "How could she have believed in a God that would let this happen to two little children?"

"Don't ask me. I've always tried to figure out why God let my mother suffer and die. If anyone was a saint, it was Mom."

"I'm sorry. How old were you when she died?"

"Four."

Melissa's face contorted. "Four? I was four when they ripped us from my grandparents."

They both looked toward Olivia. Melissa said, "I need to make sure four is her best year ever." She rose, took both coffee mugs from the table, then went back to the coffeemaker for refills.

Heather pushed around a piece of pancake on her plate. "Why didn't your grandparents stay in touch?"

"The state made it impossible. They searched for me but didn't find me." She grinned. "Of course, I made it more difficult. I live a little under the radar." She returned to the table with the coffee. "My grandmother insisted her attorney hire a private investigator to continue to look for me, even after she died. The attorney said it gave her peace knowing that someday she would be able to help me and let me know that I was loved."

"No other family?"

"My mom had a sister, but they didn't have a good relationship either. My grandmother's letter didn't explain what happened, but there was a fight, and they never spoke again. She warned me never to let that happen to my kids."

"What happened to your aunt?"

"She died. Cancer." Like Heather's mom. It couldn't be. Heather's mind began tracing her ancestry as Melissa continued.

"My grandmother considered including her other daughter's family in the will, but apparently, they were well-off financially. She figured after having gone through foster care, I'd likely need the stuff more."

"And your brother?"

"He's serving a life sentence for murder."

"Wow." How could she ever complain about her family again?

The dog barked.

Heather jumped in her seat.

They both laughed, then rose from the table together. Heather headed toward the living room to quiet the dog. Melissa followed.

Olivia ran to the front window. "Uncle Johnny's home." Olivia squealed. "He's home. He's home!"

The dog stood with her nose nearly touching the front door, barking with increasing intensity. "Quiet," Heather said as she called the dog to her.

The dog obeyed and sat without another sound, looking up at her as if awaiting a treat.

"Wow—well-trained." She hadn't expected that. If only she had a doggy snack.

Melissa pulled the door open. Johnny stood on the porch with a grocery bag in each hand.

"Uncle Johnny!" Olivia screeched and launched herself on his leg, demanding to be picked up.

"Let me put these down." Olivia released him as he juggled the groceries toward the kitchen.

Olivia looked up at him. "Did you get anything for me?"

"We'll see."

Melissa winked at her daughter, then walked over and kissed Johnny. He handed her a grocery bag. "They didn't have the ice cream you wanted, but I think you'll like this."

"Ice cream? Can we have some, Mommy?"

"That's not breakfast food."

"But I already had breakfast."

Melissa put her hands on her hips and gave Olivia "the look." Olivia dropped her head and returned to the movie, calling the dog as she passed. "Come on, puppy."

The dog obeyed.

Melissa peeked into one of the bags. "Pistachio with chocolate chips. Almost as good. Thanks." She rewarded him with a kiss.

Johnny put the second grocery bag on the kitchen table, then turned to Heather. "Did you get some good sleep?"

"I did. Thanks for taking me in."

"You sore? I crashed my ride a couple years back. Airbag went off." He pressed a palm to his chest and grimaced. "Hurt for weeks."

"It only hurts when I breathe." Heather grinned, drawing a smile out of him. Was this the same tough guy from last night?

He tipped his head toward Heather's plate. "Looks like you got some of Melissa's famous pancakes. She must like you, else you'da got cereal."

"Well, either way, I'm forever indebted."

Johnny emptied the contents of a plastic bag onto the table—dog shampoo, two dog bowls with little hearts, a pink collar, and a retractable leash.

Heather smiled. "Wow. You're the best. You know she's not my dog, though, right?"

"Yeah, well, that dog needs a bath either way."

Heather grabbed the collar. "I've got an idea. This will be great." Johnny and Melissa followed Heather as far as the kitchen entry-way. Heather went to the sofa, where Olivia was engrossed in the movie. "Look what your Uncle Johnny got." Heather held the collar out. "How about you name her, and then you can put the official collar on her."

Olivia jumped up, took the collar, and squealed. "Really?"

Heather nodded.

Olivia stepped back and looked around the room and then at the movie. "I'm gonna name her Abu—just like Aladdin's monkey."

Everyone chuckled.

"Abu it is." Heather sat on the sofa. "Here, you put it on while I hold her." She held the dog's back gently. "Now say, 'I hereby dub you, Abu.'"

Olivia repeated the prescribed words and snapped the collar in place.

Abu's tail wagged as she accepted the honor.

Olivia gave Abu a big hug, then hugged Heather and Johnny. "Thanks, Uncle Johnny."

Melissa opened her arms. "What about me?"

Olivia rushed to and hugged her mother until *Aladdin's* magic carpet ride drew her away.

Heather's mind exploded with images of a mural for Olivia's room. "Olivia."

Olivia turned her head slightly from the TV but kept the corner of her eye on the carpet ride.

"How would you like it if I painted your bedroom wall with Aladdin and Jasmine riding on the magic carpet?"

Olivia jumped up and clapped her hands, now entirely focused on Heather. "Really?"

"If your mom says it's okay."

"Mommy?" Olivia ran to her mother, who was putting groceries away with Johnny.

"Yes, sweetie?" Melissa asked.

"Heather says she can paint me a magic carpet ride on my wall. Can she? Please, please, please?"

Heather joined them in the kitchen. "Of course, it will take a couple of days. I don't want to overstay my welcome."

"Mommy?" Olivia's eyes were as round as an owl's.

Melissa laughed. "Of course. We can pick up supplies when we go shopping."

"Yay!" Olivia danced, then pulled Heather to sit with her on the sofa. Abu snuggled next to Heather's feet.

"Well, I can see why you got the dog shampoo." Heather stood. "Where can I bathe her?"

"In the tub upstairs," Melissa said. "Just—"

"No, no." Johnny stepped forward and leaned over to pat Abu's back. "Olivia and I will wash Abu while you and Heather go shopping for some clothes." He straightened, then stuck a hand in his pocket. He pulled out a thick, folded stack of bills and handed it to Melissa.

Face taught, Melissa looked at his hand, then his face. "We need to talk." She grabbed his arm, and they disappeared out of sight into the kitchen.

Melissa's reaction raised her hair like a cat being threatened. Where did that kind of cash come from? Because of Heather's desperation and their kindness, she hadn't allowed herself to consider their circumstances. But Melissa's reaction demanded her honest assessment of the last dozen hours.

Heather's mind retraced her encounters. Picked up by a gang-tattooed man driving a Porsche in the middle of the night . . . taken in by a couple who didn't know her . . . described by the brother as a gift. Then there was Melissa's comment about not being the usual type of girl Tyrone brought. And what were both of them doing there on a weekday when the rest of the world was out working for a living? This was not good. It was lousy thinking that got her here, and she didn't want *not* thinking to make things worse—if that was possible. She needed to leave.

Melissa reappeared wearing a soft smile. "Heather, you all done with your breakfast?"

"Yes—but you've been hospitable enough. I don't want to outstay my welcome. I should probably call my family and get back home."

"Dressed in what?" Melissa asked. "Listen. Johnny just cashed his paycheck, and he's feeling generous. Let's go before he changes his mind."

A paycheck from what? She dared not ask in front of him.

"I want to go, Mommy."

Johnny scooped Olivia up. "But you named the dog. And you know what that means?"

Olivia shook her head.

"You get to give her her first bath."

"Really?"

"You know it," Melissa said.

"Okay, but will you get me something too?"

"We *are* getting you something. Art supplies so Heather can paint your wall."

"Yay!" Olivia ran and hugged Heather's legs. "Thank you, Aunt Heather."

Aunt. Heather's heart melted.

Melissa turned to Heather and set her hands on her hips. "Ready?"

Heather froze. She couldn't get her mind off the cash or Melissa's reaction, but looking down at Olivia, she realized she couldn't break her promise. What could possibly happen if she stayed a couple of days? Maybe she could get it done in one. And Melissa's story? And that painting? Was it possible that they were related?

"Earth to Heather." Melissa waved her hand in front of Heather's face.

Heather forced a smile. "Okay, if you're sure I'm not imposing."

Heather stooped and looked into Olivia's eyes. "Thanks for taking care of Abu for me while we're gone." She hugged Olivia, then stood and headed for the door with Melissa.

"Oh, my coat," Heather said, turning back.

"I took it to the cleaners this morning," Johnny said. "It'll be ready in a couple of days."

Melissa opened the coat closet next to the door revealing a variety of outerwear, from lightweight jackets to full winter coats. "Here. Take your pick."

Heather thanked her, then pulled a pink down vest from its hanger. She slid it over her shoulders. Melissa grabbed a navy down jacket, then closed the closet door. "We'll be at the Huntington Mall. Will you put Olivia down for a nap after lunch?"

"I'm too old for naps, Mommy."

"Not until you're twenty." Melissa opened the front door for Heather, then stepped out after her.

During the short drive, Melissa babbled on about everything, from the mall's offerings to Heather's fashion preferences. Heather's focus was on how to get out of this mess. Was Melissa really this excited to go shopping, or was she trying to distract Heather from the cash?

Melissa pulled into a parking space but didn't turn off the engine. She rested both hands on the top of the wheel, took a deep breath, and turned to Heather.

"You know, I thought we were becoming friends back at the house, but you haven't said two words since we got in the car. What's going on?"

Heather's stomach knotted. On the one hand, she was right about their connection. And their business was none of hers, but she couldn't shake the feeling she should run. She turned in her seat to look Melissa square in the eyes. She needed to gauge her reaction.

"It's the money."

Melissa's hands dropped from the steering wheel. "I told you, Johnny cashed his paycheck."

"Does that really work for you?"

"What do you mean?"

"Either being lied to or lying to yourself. But judging by your reaction, I think you're trying to convince yourself everything's okay. Nobody cashes checks anymore. And nobody lives in that neighborhood if they have that kind of pocket change. And nobody drives a Porsche and then wakes people up in the middle of the night so they can take in a stray woman and dog." Heather paused. "You can tell me it's none of my business, but I need to know what I'm getting myself into."

Melissa lowered her head to the steering wheel. After a long moment, she raised it and turned in her seat to face Heather fully.

"Let's just say I don't *actually* know where the money comes from. I just know I'm not involved."

Heather's heart pounded. "Does pretending you don't know make it okay?"

Melissa's face reddened. "Yes, in fact, it does. And I'm not going to sit here and defend myself—I have my reasons." Melissa's voice rose as she continued. "I don't think you're in any position to judge me. Maybe you'd understand if you hadn't had that abortion and had your own kids."

Heather's breath caught. Melissa's weaponized words crushed her heart. Had Melissa just said that? Heather should have known better than to trust someone she had just met, especially in her weakened emotional state. Maybe her hangover made her drop her defenses.

Hot tears built in the corners of her eyes. "I should never have shared my pain with a stranger, but I thought you were different. You're like everybody else—sitting in judgment on my life."

"Yeah? Talk about judging, Ms. Black Pot. Like how you're questioning my choices? Let me tell you about Johnny. He's the only person who has ever truly loved me. He loves my daughter. He rescued me, and as far as I can tell, he rescued you too. And if that's not good enough for you, you're free to leave." She glared at Heather.

Heather sat stunned. She closed the mouth she hadn't realized was hanging open and replayed Melissa's words, the words of a woman doing her best. What kind of friend was she? She hadn't even asked Melissa what was going on or why she had made her choices. Instead, she had jumped to conclusions and judged.

Melissa was right. Who was Heather to question anybody? Her life had been a series of bad decisions. She took a breath. "I'm sorry. You're right. I had no right to judge you. I'm the mess that showed up on your doorstep."

Melissa's face softened. "You know, you should question the money. Then when I explain, you have a right to choose what you do with that information. I've made my choice, and I won't judge you if you leave. If I were you, I'd probably run. But I'm hoping you'll at least go into this mall with me, let me get you some clothes, and be my friend."

How Heather needed a friend like Melissa, someone she could relate to. She stared out the windshield, not seeing the mall in front of her. The past month replayed itself in her mind . . . all the reasons she had run first from New Mexico and then from her sister's. Was she ready to go back now? She could call her dad. He'd come in a heartbeat. But all the problems she needed to process would still be waiting for her, and Julie never could relate. Like Melissa, she wasn't in the mood for judgment. And forget going to Dad's. Cruella would never let her live any of this down.

Heather still needed to get perspective on her life . . . like Melissa had said about her need to process the lies her life had been. Maybe they were kindred spirits trying to figure out the cards they had been dealt.

Heather opened the car door. "What do you say we go shopping?"

Chapter 7

2:15 p.m.

"MISTER MILLER. MR. BOONE."

Their tuxedo-clad host swept his hand toward the back of the mahogany-crafted restaurant as the scent of sizzling steaks confirmed Dexter's choice of lunch establishments.

"We have your table ready. Right this way."

"Thank you, Maurice," he and Charlie said in unison.

Maurice led the two men to Dexter's private booth tucked into the back corner, surrounded by empty tables. He knew better than to seat anyone within earshot.

Dexter claimed his usual spot—back to the wall. Charlie stood away, surveying the table set for three. Dexter had intentionally not told him that Donny would join them for their normally-private lunch meeting. Charlie needed reminding that, despite his right-hand man status, he was not the only one granted an audience with Dexter Miller.

If only Dexter had an intellectually-challenging friend who loved the sport of testing human behavior. He'd bet a Bugatti that Charlie would question *Maurice* about the extra setting but not dare ask Dexter who'd be joining them.

Dexter eyed his subject with great anticipation. He waited, savoring each moment. *Three . . . two . . . one . . .*

Charlie looked at Dexter, then pointed to the table. "Maurice, there will only be two of us—"

Maurice reached to remove the extra setting, but Dexter lifted his hand from the table to stop him.

"It's okay, Maurice. Another guest will be joining us."

Charlie shot him a look. Dexter suppressed his smile as the worm twisted on the hook, then sat.

"Let me know if you need anything else." Maurice tipped his head and backed away as their waiter arrived with a tray.

"Good afternoon, Mr. Miller. Mr. Boone." The waiter delivered three plates of deviled eggs with caviar. "When the chef heard you were coming, he prepared your favorite—New Zealand elk with ground cardamom."

Dexter smiled, his pallet already savoring the treat. "That's why we're here, Frederick. The hors d'oeuvres are magnificent, as usual. You truly know how to take care of us."

"Thank you, sir." Frederick bowed and left.

The wine steward brought a bottle of New Zealand red, showed it to Dexter, and then poured a sample. Dexter nodded his approval.

"Anything else?" the steward asked as he poured three glasses.

"No, no. Everything's perfect," Charlie said.

The steward kept his eyes on Dexter. "Mr. Miller, are *you* good?"

Charlie tapped the linen tablecloth with his middle finger. Even the service staff reminded Charlie of his place.

Nodding, Dexter released the steward to his other patrons, then waited a long moment to allow Charlie to sulk before raising his glass for his next zing.

Before Dexter had promoted him, Charlie had been the most successful sales manager in the dealership's history. What a contrast to his recent inept performance. And now Donny was blowing away all of Charlie's sales records. Of course, Donny only managed one business—a legitimate one that didn't require getting his hands dirty. But dirty hands were well rewarded and enjoyed more power. And for that, Charlie would have to pay his dues, just like Dexter had.

"To Donny and October sales. I didn't think we were going to hit our goal. And a week ahead of time."

Charlie complied with a weak smile. "To meeting goals."

A moment later, Maurice approached with Charlie's possible replacement.

"Here's the man of the hour." Dexter rose and shook Donny's hand. He pointed to the empty place setting. "Join us. We were toasting your early victory. Doesn't that make fourteen straight months?"

Donny nodded, feigning humility.

"Congratulations."

"Thank you." Donny beamed as they both sat while Charlie pasted on a smile. They toasted Donny's accomplishments again.

Charlie's phone rang. Dexter gave him a death stare. He knew the rules. But Charlie held the phone for Dexter to see. *Hawthorne.*

Dexter grabbed the phone, pressed talk, and said, "Hold on." He looked at Donny. "Give us a minute."

Donny's face dropped. He looked over his shoulder and pointed across the room to the bar. "I'll just get a drink."

Dexter nodded.

Once Donny had walked away, he held the phone to his ear. "Why the hell are *you* calling? You know better."

"Mr. Miller?"

"Oh great. Sure. Just say my name out loud." He squeezed his fingertips across his forehead. Idiots surrounded him. "This had better be important."

"I'll make it quick. Our office just got the heads-up. The FBI, DEA, and U.S. Marshals raided Hearthstone's sheriff's office and the lab. That prosecutor is alive, and that informant you thought you had—Jake—is FBI. There was a hearing. They exposed Hayes . . . everything."

The call ended.

Had Hawthorne hung up? Nobody hung up on Dexter Miller. He held the phone away from his ear and stared at Charlie, then threw the phone against the booth's wall, breaking an unlit oil lantern. Fellow diners across the restaurant turned.

Charlie sat wide-eyed as Maurice rushed over. "Is everything okay, Mr. Miller?"

Dexter had just broken his no-public-displays rule. But he was not about to break the one for no apologies. "We're fine. The phone must have grazed the lamp when I returned it to Charlie."

"Well, we shouldn't have placed the lantern in such a precarious position, sir. I'll speak to the staff about their error." He snapped his fingers, and a host of servers sped over, cleared the table, then replaced everything within a minute under Maurice's supervision. "I believe your lunch is ready, sir. Would you like it now?"

"Give us a few minutes. Thank you." Dexter forced a smile.

Maurice bowed slightly and left.

Donny pointed from himself to the table as if asking permission to return. Dexter held up a hand. Donny raised his glass and turned back to the barmaid.

Dexter didn't know where to begin. How hard could it have been to set things up? Two years of work. Whoosh—all gone. He put himself back together.

"Why on earth is *this person* calling to tell you about a sweep of the whole West Virginia operation?" Dexter pounded the table, rousing the neighboring diners to turn again. He lowered his voice. "It's not *his* department. He's not supposed to call. And how on God's earth did you not know about this?"

"A sweep?"

Was that all he heard? "Oh, wait. I didn't even tell you the good parts." Dexter suppressed his building anger, forcing a low monotone. "Our Hearthstone informant was an undercover FBI agent."

Charlie slumped in his seat.

"The prosecutor isn't dead. Oh no—he's very much alive. I can hear him on the stand now, can't you?" Dexter glared.

"Smitty." Charlie sat up as if he had redeemed himself.

Dexter sat back, astonished that he even had the nerve to speak. "What?"

"Smitty's there. He can handle this."

Dexter processed everything he knew about Smitty. The thug had handled problems before, but nothing this big. Dexter squinted his eyes.

"He'd better. Let's just say I'm not happy about any of this." Dexter rose, planted his knuckles on the table, and leaned into Charlie's face. "This mess had better be cleaned up before I fly there Friday. Do you understand?"

"Yes, sir."

He made his way to the front door, excusing himself as he passed by Donny at the bar.

Outside, his driver jumped out of the Rolls-Royce Phantom and opened the door for him to slip inside the acoustically-insulated perfection of the Privacy Suite back seat. Debussy's *Arabesque No. 1* played, inviting him to breathe and purge the day's ills. Rockefeller greeted him with a sloppy kiss. How did this driver always know precisely what he needed? This man may well have been his longest-serving employee.

The driver lowered the cabin window. "The office, sir?"

"No, no." He was in no mood to deal with mundane customer problems. With his luck, that Rizzo fellow would show up wanting something else or complaining about his nephew's deal.

And he couldn't go home. Mary Ellen would ask questions he couldn't answer. He needed time to regroup. "How about the lake house?"

The driver nodded. "Excellent choice, sir. I'll let the staff know you're coming."

The privacy window raised as Rockefeller lay on the floor and Dexter snugged into his melodious rest. Could anything else go wrong today?

Chapter 8

2:20 p.m.

A RAINBOW OF CHOICES SPANNED THE LUGGAGE STORE'S floor-to-ceiling walls, displaying every possible suitcase size, shape, and material—either an artist's dream for palette variety or a nightmare for having to pick just one. Heather breathed in the sea of color. From across the store, a perfect earthy green beckoned her. She passed between the displays to its eye-level cubbyhole and wrestled the largest hardshell bag to the ground.

Turning to Melissa, Heather grinned as she modeled her new traveling companion." What do you think?" She pushed up the sleeve of her borrowed jacket. "It even matches my tattoos."

"I love it."

The tag revealed the color—Lotus Temple. She flipped it and scrunched her face at the price. "Are you sure about this?"

Melissa held up the five bags of clothing they had purchased along the mall corridors. "How else are we going to get all these clothes out of here?"

A sales clerk approached. "Find what you need?"

"I think so." Heather pointed to an empty display table at the center of the otherwise unoccupied store. "Could we use that display to pack the bag with the clothes we bought?"

Melissa smiled and presented the bags.

"No problem. I'll snip the price tag so you can pay and then pack away."

"Here, I'll go pay while you start packing." Melissa followed the clerk to the register while Heather lifted the suitcase to the table and began unfolding and refolding her new wardrobe.

Melissa had turned out to be a smart shopper, anticipating Heather's every need. Bras, panties, cosmetics, toiletries, shoes. At least a week's wardrobe. Every time Heather had protested getting another item, Melissa insisted she treat herself.

Their earlier falling out had given Heather something she had not had before with her friends or family—a weird kind of freedom. As ridiculous as it seemed for a relationship less than a day old, Heather knew they would be friends regardless of their circumstances. Whether Heather stayed or went, Melissa still wanted to be friends and work through life together. Somehow, Heather felt emotionally at home. She just needed to figure out how to stay safe. And maybe she needed to help Melissa consider the wisdom of her situation.

Melissa returned and helped Heather finish up. Heather handed her the bag containing the Aladdin book she had picked up to help her with the mural. The book was filled with vibrant illustrations Olivia was sure to love. They still needed to pick up the art supplies.

Heather closed the suitcase, dropped it to the floor, and pulled the handle up.

"I'm starved. Let's find a restaurant here and have a drink."

Heather's stomach lurched. "I don't know about the drink part, but lunch sounds great."

"How about Ruby Tuesday? They have an amazing salad bar." Melissa pointed to the right.

"I'm in."

With Heather's treasures in tow, they made their way out and turned right into the hustle and bustle of the mall's interior corridor. Several stores down, a voice called from behind them.

"Oh, ma'am!"

The girls turned as the luggage sales clerk raced toward them, holding out a wallet.

"Ms. Thomason, you left this." She blushed as she handed it over. "Sorry, I had to look inside to find your name on your driver's license."

Thomason? Heather froze as her mind tried to piece together the revelations.

Melissa took the wallet, thanked the sales clerk, and then turned back to Heather. "Thank goodness, she caught up with us. I'd hate to have to wash dishes to pay for our lunch."

She stared at Melissa, still trying to process. "Thomason? Your name is Thomason?"

Melissa nodded, scrunching her face. "What? Did you have a bad experience with a Thomason or something?"

"Thomason was my mother's maiden name. Rosalind Thomason."

Neither girl budged. Heather examined her what—her cousin? Her blond hair. Height. Thin build. What was it Johnny had said? *Twins.* The artwork. The story. Their inexplicably quick connection.

Melissa's face twisted. "You don't think . . ."

"Cousins?"

Melissa's phone chirped. She slipped it from her back pocket. Whatever was on the screen blanched her face. She looked up. "We've got to get back to the car." She yanked the battery out, shoved both pieces into her purse, and dug out a flip phone. Richard called them burner phones. Said they couldn't be traced. Said drug dealers kept boxes of them around . . . *drug dealers.*

"What's going on?"

"I'll explain later." Melissa tugged at Heather's arm.

"No." Heather jerked back. "Not until you tell me what's going on."

"I'll explain in the car. I'll tell you everything. Please." She nudged Heather's elbow again, but Heather stepped back.

"Not until I get answers."

Melissa squinted her eyes and then waved Heather off. "Never mind."

She rushed off towards the exit but stopped, shrugged, and returned. She reached into her purse and handed Heather a wad of cash. Her eyes softened. "Sorry we didn't have more time together. I hope you reconcile with your family. Maybe someday. . . " She shook her head, turned, and hurried toward the exit doors.

Heather stood mystified. It was never a good idea to rush where angels feared to go, but what if Melissa was her cousin? How could she leave her family—one she hadn't had the chance to know? Without another thought, she grabbed the suitcase handle and ran to catch up with Melissa at the doors.

Squaring off with Heather, Melissa spoke slowly as if to ensure that Heather caught every word. "You are going to have to make a decision right now. I just got a 9-1-1 text from Johnny. It's our code for trouble. We've had plans to escape if Johnny ever needed to get away fast."

So much for Melissa not knowing what Johnny was into. Drugs? Trafficking? Nothing good. But she needed to give her a chance to explain—as much for herself as for Melissa.

"I'm coming—at least for the moment."

The two exited into the bright sunlight of the parking lot. Heather followed Melissa, heart pounding with every step. At the car, Heather lifted the suitcase into the back, pushed it against Olivia's car seat, and then jumped in. Melissa had started the engine and was reading something on the second phone. After a moment, she turned to Heather.

"This is the deal. We'll meet Johnny at the north end of the parking lot. He's going to take me to pick up a car so I can get away with Olivia. Then he'll take you to a bus station. Or you can stay here. You don't need to be a part of this, but I have to go now."

It was all too fast. As if by instinct—or perhaps, curiosity— Heather consented.

Melissa reached under the seat and took out a manila envelope. She removed a license plate with two magnetic strips running along the edges and a small metal tag. She placed the tag over the VIN on the dash.

"What's that for?"

"We don't want them to be able to trace us—at least for a few days."

"Them" sounded ominous, but Heather didn't ask.

"Grab your bag," Melissa said as she climbed out.

Heather got out and complied. "We're leaving the car?"

"Yep."

Melissa snapped on the license plate. "Let's go."

Melissa led Heather to the same mall entrance they'd just left. They wove their way through the mall's center and out the north entrance to a two-tone brown camper waiting alongside the curb with Johnny and Olivia in the front.

Johnny pulled forward. Olivia's eyes lit up as she jumped up and disappeared around her chair. Melissa pulled the RV's side door open to the living area, where Olivia bounced for joy. Abu barked and danced with her.

"Mommy, Mommy. We're going on a road trip."

"I know. Are you excited?" The tension in Melissa's voice was thinly veiled as she stepped inside.

"Yes. I can't wait. Uncle Johnny says we're going to see Mickey Mouse. He said we might even see the Little Mermaid."

"Yes, sweetie, but not today." Melissa stepped in and sat on the end of one of the bench seats at the dining table on the opposite side of the camper and hugged her girl. Heather followed, tugging her suitcase in after her. She set it behind the captain's chair where Olivia had been sitting.

This was a first for Heather. She had not realized how comfortable a camper could be. Captain chairs for the driver and passenger to her right. A full kitchen to her left, with the bedroom and bath bringing up the rear. Large picture windows on both sides. Maybe if she got one of these, she wouldn't have to be a burden on anyone.

"Take a seat." Johnny swiveled forward from watching the reunion. "Time to go. It's not far, so don't worry about getting settled." As soon as Heather shut the door, Johnny eased off from the curb and began navigating them through the parking lot. Heather sat across the dining table from Melissa. Abu jumped into the passenger seat, anticipating a new adventure. Dogs always loved going for rides, but this had to beat all for a dog.

"When can we see the Little Mermaid, Mommy?"

"Well, honey, I'm not sure. But soon." She pointed to the front. "Why don't you go sit with Uncle Johnny? I need to talk to Heather for a minute."

"Okay, Mommy." She returned to the front seat. Johnny stopped the RV, shooed Abu down, then buckled Olivia in before getting into traffic.

"Here's some money for the bus and the trip." Melissa handed her some money.

Heather started to object, but Melissa held up her hand. "Don't argue with me. There's no time. Do you know where you're going?"

"Hearthstone. Not that I have a choice. I need to replace my lost driver's license." She half-laughed. "I just got my West Virginia license last week. I'd only been back with my sister and her husband . . ." Heather's mind flashed back to Richard's empty stall in their garage. Was he still missing?

"What is it?"

"When I left, my sister Julie had just found out she was pregnant, and my brother-in-law was missing. What if something bad happened to him?" Heather had been so focused on her own problems . . . *Problems?* Heather's breath caught. At worst, she had hurt feelings. What a brat. While her sister was dealing with her missing husband? What if that letter was true? She left Julie to face all this after finding out she was pregnant with a child she didn't ever think she could have? She hated the person in her soul's mirror.

"Oh my goodness. I've been so awful. I need to call Julie."

"I agree, but we only have a few minutes to discuss some things. Johnny will give you a phone when he drops you off. First, you know, you're not going to be able to bring Abu with you on the bus. We're happy to take her. It's up to you."

Heather hadn't considered the dog. Melissa would certainly take good care of her. But Abu had saved her life. Then again, Olivia probably needed her more.

"You're right. You keep her—if it's not too much trouble. Besides, how could I take her from Olivia?"

"Ha. That might be impossible."

Heather called Abu and hugged her, allowing Abu to kiss her face. Heather's heart hurt, and while it was true that she'd see Dog soon, she would miss this rambunctious puppy.

Melissa tipped her chin and smiled, then called, "Hey, Olivia, come here for a minute."

Olivia unbuckled and returned to where the girls were sitting. "Yes, Mommy?"

"Heather has something to ask you."

Heather took Olivia's hands and looked into her eyes. "Would you please take care of Abu for me?"

Her eyes sprang to life. "You mean it?"

"Yes, if it's not too much trouble. You'll have to give her baths, walk and feed her. Can you do that?"

"Oh, yes." Olivia danced in place. "I'll take real good care of her."

"Can I come and visit her?"

Olivia's face drooped. "You aren't coming with us?"

"No, sweetie. I need to get back to my family."

Her lips pouted. "I wanted you to go with us to see Little Mermaid."

"Not this time." Heather pursed her lips to let Olivia know that she felt her pain.

Johnny parked the RV in front of a white building surrounded by used cars with painted prices on the windshields. It appeared to be an old gas station with "Buy Here, Pay Here" painted on the office window. Above it was a LENNY'S USED CAR LOT sign. Johnny swiveled around, donned a pair of gloves, then retrieved two duffle bags from a cabinet above their heads, one all-black and another black with pink polka dots. He set the girly one on the table, then returned the black one to the cabinet.

Melissa rose.

"Remember, east on I-64 to our meeting place. Stop when you get to a rest area and call me. Okay?"

Melissa looked into his eyes. "Are we gonna be okay?"

Johnny took her hands. "Yeah. We got this all planned. Nothing can go wrong. Bulletproof." They kissed for a long moment. Johnny pulled back. "Now go on." He looked at Abu, then back to Melissa. "You want the dog in the camper with me?"

Olivia grabbed Johnny's arm. "No. Abu's my dog now."

Johnny raised both hands in defeat. "Your call."

"Okay, Abu can come with us." Melissa collected two bowls from the cabinet. "We'll need a water bowl and food dish." Melissa hooked up Abu's leash, grabbed the polka-dot bag, and stepped from the camper. "Give Uncle Johnny a hug and kiss."

Johnny scooped her up and hugged her. "Goodbye. See you soon." He held her for the longest moment.

"Come on, pumpkin." Keeping her head down, Melissa waved her out.

Olivia turned and jumped on each step like she was launching into a new adventure.

Just then, a rotund older man came out of the office with a large manilla envelope. "Melissa." He shook Melissa's hand, patted Olivia's head, and then looked up at Johnny. "I've got everything right here."

"You take good care of my girls."

"Don't worry. It's all under control. You need to get going. The camper might draw the wrong kinda attention."

"We'll be fine," Melissa said. "Please, be careful."

Turning away from Heather, Johnny closed the door, wiped his face, and returned to the driver's seat. "You coming up here?"

She joined him in the front. They waved to Melissa and Olivia, leaving them in the parking lot with Lenny.

"I've got to get out of town before I drop you at a bus station. There's one about an hour from here."

"Sounds good."

Johnny continued east on the busy four-lane road that narrowed to two through lanes with a center turning lane between. Businesses became fewer the farther they traveled. Neither spoke until Heather finally broke the silence.

"Do you really believe everything's going to be okay?"

He glanced at her. "It has to be."

That was not an answer. "Am I in danger?"

Johnny looked straight ahead. "It's better you don't know. We got a plan, and we're on schedule. Don't worry; you'll be out soon."

They turned off the busy highway and onto a curvy, narrow two-lane road that alternated between woods and residential areas. Heather flashed back to the twists and turns of the night before. Not quite as many here, but just as troubling. She closed her eyes for several minutes to escape the feelings, but she couldn't shake the memory. She turned to Johnny.

"Do you mind if I put on the radio?"

"Quiet." Johnny's face was tight as his eyes darted from the driver-side mirror to the road. He sped up.

"What is it?"

"Nothing! Just be quiet."

Johnny swerved to the left, then jerked back. "Get in the back and get low!"

Heather crawled back and sat on the floor. Johnny jerked the camper left, banging into something and causing a loud thud. The camper lurched as he pulled it back to the road.

A car's engine revved outside. Heather rose enough to peer out the picture window. A black vehicle beside them slammed into the side of the camper, knocking Heather back down. She crawled to a corner in front of the kitchen sink and the bathroom, then turned forward, using her arms to keep from falling over.

Johnny pulled left, banged the car, then regained control. Suddenly, Johnny's head jerked right and then flopped forward as a shot rang out. Blood splattered across the passenger area. The RV veered right, bumped, then rumbled over rough terrain as greenery and branches scraped the windshield and side of the camper until it crashed into a tree. Heather and her suitcase flew forward, slamming into the back of the passenger seat as the contents of the cabinets poured down around her. The large black duffle bag landed next to her on the floor.

"Get the money!" Someone yelled from a distance.

Johnny was dead. Was Heather next? She needed to get out of sight.

She tossed the black bag under the table, crawled into the space with it, then pulled her suitcase to her to block anyone from finding her. A door handle jiggled, but she couldn't tell which one.

"I can't, man. The door's jammed." He pounded on the door.

"Try the other ones," the more distant voice said.

Heather unzipped the black duffle bag. Inside were bundles of money—more money than she could count. A gun rested on top.

Outside, branches scraped the RV. Heather held her breath.

Another handle rattled.

"It's locked. Get the crowbar."

She had to move fast. She crawled out quickly, threw back the top of her suitcase, and dumped the clothes she loved so much. Using a blouse, she picked up the gun and set it on the laminate floor. She had no idea how to use it, but she might need to figure it out. She dumped the money into the suitcase, latched it shut, then crammed her clothes in the black bag and laid it in plain sight, right in front of the door. She scooted back under the table, picked up the gun, and wedged the suitcase in front of her to block any intruder's view.

"Here. Take the crowbar," one of the voices said. A second later, the front window shattered. "Aw, man, I ain't crawling through all that blood."

"Go around."

Outside, a branch cracked. The camper jerked forward a few feet and settled at a forty-five-degree angle. Heather braced her body between the benches and held the suitcase's handle before it could slide away. She peeked around the suitcase. The black duffle bag had fallen against the door. The smell of propane filled the cabin.

"Watch out, man. This thing's gonna crush us."

"We gonna be dead if we don't get that money. Get over there."

The sound of metal on metal came from the door.

A siren sounded in the distance.

"It won't open, man. This thing's gonna roll."

The gas tickled Heather's throat, begging her to expel the fumes from her lungs, but she couldn't let them hear her coughing. *Please, God—if you are really there—get me out of this. I promise to follow you all the days of my life.*

The siren grew louder as the door finally gave way. She peeked around the suitcase. The duffle bag lay in the pine needles below the door.

"Grab the money. Come on, man. Let's go!"

An arm tattooed with the same MCM as Tyrone's reached for the bag. "I got it."

The man looked up. Their eyes met. They both froze. The sirens' wail drew closer.

"Come on, man." The second man yelled. "They almost here."

The tattooed man disappeared. Two car doors slammed shut. Tires squealed. They were gone.

Heather released the fumes from her lungs in a spasm of coughs. The RV was going to blow. She let the suitcase and the gun fall out the door to the ground, then slid down after them, falling into the pine needle bed. She left the gun, grabbed the suitcase, pushed herself to her feet, and ran toward the woods. As she did, a white buck appeared from the treeline and stopped. He stared into her soul.

Heather froze.

The loud explosion was the last thing she heard.

Chapter 9

4:30 p.m.

DEXTER HATED TO ADMIT THAT HIS WIFE HAD BEEN RIGHT, but the indoor pool complex at the lake house was one of his best investments ever. At his wife's insistence and inspired by the Omni Grove Park Inn spa, three irregularly-shaped stonework walls transformed his four pools into a hidden grotto. The two-story ceiling-to-floor glass wall showcased passing sailboats on Lake St. Clair. Low sky-view ceilings supported by stone pillars contemplated clouds drifting by, enhancing the peace of floating in the mineral pool. Was there a more serene spot on the planet? If only this Grosse Pointe house offered more security, they could live here year-round. Still, more and more the lake house was becoming Dexter's private escape from it all.

He finished his workout in the lap pool before slipping into the mineral pool to float while underwater instrumental music streamed through his consciousness. After several songs, he moved to the mineral-water cascade to beat the stress from his shoulders.

"Mr. Miller?"

Dexter opened his eyes. His housekeeper and Rockefeller stood at the pool's edge, holding his Charlie-only cell phone toward him. "It's been ringing. I wouldn't have bothered you, but it hasn't stopped."

What now?

Nodding, Dexter climbed out of the cave, dried with the towel his housekeeper offered, and walked with Rockefeller to the plate-glass wall overlooking the lake he was not seeing. Taking a deep breath, he tapped to allow whatever bad news Charlie was bearing.

"Boss?"

"Hearthstone again?"

"No, boss. Smitty has that handled. It's the Johnson brothers. We took care of the two here. And their mom."

"But?"

"Well, we got their money, even though it was short."

Charlie would not have called incessantly for this. It was worse than trying to get the truth from his teenage twins. *"But?"*

"We took care of the other one too. But when the guys got to him, the camper he was driving ran off the road. The police showed up before we could get the money. Then the RV exploded."

"So, you're telling me my money is gone. What did I tell you?"

"Nobody takes your money, sir."

"And now?"

"Well, at least they can't steal from you again. And when the others hear, they'll think twice before they try it."

Dexter wasn't paying him to find bright linings. There was more. "What else?"

There was a pause. "Johnny had a girlfriend. She might have had the money. Hawthorne said a girl with a suitcase full of money was found near the RV. She was taken to the hospital. The FBI and DEA are all over this."

"How much did they get?

"Half a million."

Dexter cursed everyone but his mother. "Tell Hawthorne I want my money back."

"How's he going to do that?"

Dexter raised his arm and leaned into the glass wall. *Breathe in. Hold. Out.* "Is that my problem?"

"No, sir. I'll tell him."

"Is that all?"

"Well, Hawthorne said they don't think the girl was Johnny's girlfriend, but they're not sure."

"When you say 'girlfriend,' what exactly does that mean? Was she his whore or something more than that?"

"More than that."

"So, she knows stuff and might have more of my money?" He pounded the glass wall with his fist. "Who'd you send there?"

"Bones sent two of his Mongrels."

Dexter rubbed his chin. While he never understood why anyone would choose "mongrels" for their name, they were a gang like no other. Bloodhounds who would die hunting their prey.. "That's good. No loose ends, right?"

"They're on it."

"That wasn't my question."

"Right, boss."

He tapped the phone off and looked into Rockefeller's sad eyes. "Maybe I should put you in charge."

Chapter 10

Friday, October 27
9:50 a.m.

A HOST OF REPORTERS AND TWO TV CREWS AWAITED Dexter's limousine as it pulled in front of his newly-constructed Hearthstone Drug Rehab Center located at the edge of the downtown. The irony that this town—and this state—celebrated his keep-them-hooked business model was delicious.

He had wanted to locate this two-story brick facility next to the sheriff's office, but *his* sheriff had convinced him otherwise—the same sheriff who now sat in jail. Hayes had been right, though. He needed a half-acre for the fifty-bed facility he had dreamed up, one rivaling those of the rich and famous. Plus, being on the edge of town would not draw as much attention when they were getting midnight deliveries from semi-tractor-trailers. But then again, it's not like these hicks would be awake after nine. The Downtown Saloon was the only place open late—all the more reason for his location.

The trip had been grueling, with Mary Ellen plying him with questions about the sheriff's office bust two days before and who could do those things to this sweet community. Dexter had patted her leg. "We built this rehab just in time. Those guys were ready to open a meth lab—if you can believe that." She had kissed him and reminded him how great he was for doing this. Good thing she didn't know how much money he had lost on that lab, not to mention the two years of work down the drain and the costs to exterminate the associated problems.

Mary Ellen fidgeted with Dexter's tie to make him perfect. He leaned forward and kissed her.

"You know I married you only because I needed someone to make me look good."

She grinned. "You stole my line." She patted his tie into place. "Ready?"

"In so many ways." Dexter kissed her again and got out when the driver opened his door. Dexter held his hand to his beautiful wife, and she raised herself to reign over this magnificent achievement. Her charm could melt the heart of his most dangerous foes. An impenetrable shield for the press and his greatest admirer. She was the total package.

With camera shutters clicking around them, the press stuck microphones in their faces and called out their simple questions. He and his bride made their way up the sidewalk to stairs that cascaded from the columned veranda extending the length of the building. Dexter held Mary Ellen's arm as they mounted the stairs to the red ribbon draped between two stanchions. The governor's new drug czar stood next to the mayor with oversized scissors and an even bigger grin.

If they only knew.

Dexter held out his hand. "Mr. Secretary. Mayor." He bowed in obligatory deference and took his place next to them. Mary Ellen joined as they posed for the news stations to shoot their canned shots. She always made the photos worth his trip.

The secretary took out his index cards from his inside coat pocket, stepped to the microphone, and began his address. As he droned on, Dexter scanned the crowd. *Rizzo*—standing at the back of the crowd next to one of the ancient oak trees that flanked the front sidewalk. When their eyes met, Rizzo gave that stupid four-finger wave and tipped that ridiculous hat. Rizzo in Hearthstone? No way this was an accident.

"Dexter?" the secretary said, making him suddenly aware that the sight of that man in this town had caused him to zone out. Dexter never lost control.

"Sorry . . ."

Had he just apologized too? A sign of weakness. He forced "the smile."

"Yes, yes. I was admiring this wonderful crowd gathered here in this beautiful city."

He delivered the rest of his speech, hitting every planned high point and ensuring the town that this institution would clean up this county and raise the city's economy.

". . . And if you want to thank anyone, thank my wife. This was all her dream." He took a half step back and raised his arm in an honor pose. Mary Ellen held up a hand and blushed at the applause.

"And now, Mayor, would you join me in cutting the ribbon to a new day in Hearthstone?" Dexter motioned for the mayor to join him, which he did.

The men snipped, and the applause erupted. Dexter again searched the crowd for Rizzo, but he was gone.

Chapter 11

_10:30 a.m._

MAX ENDERS SCANNED THE WHEELER BARN'S LOFT bedroom to ensure he had packed everything. The simplicity of the one-room accommodations had served him well during his undercover farm-hand stint. And what could be better than hanging out on a farm—although he could have done without mucking the horse's stall. But the housekeepers' cooking made it all worthwhile. He was going to miss Sarah's smile and fried chicken most of all.

"Well, goodbye, Jake," he said to the Red Sox ball cap on the top of the dresser. It was always weird closing down an alias. It was like the death of an old friend. Once again, his alias was a hero, and Max was a nobody until his next assignment. His mandated time off for his gunshot recuperation meant it would be a while.

Nothing compared to the incredible high FBI undercover agents experience when they rounded up the bad guys. Yet nothing drained him more than being submerged in a pit of vipers for months. He looked at his sling—always a badge of honor before, but now . . . Was the injury worth it?

Maybe he was getting old, but there was a growing uneasiness in his soul. Perhaps it was working with Richard Wheeler. That guy had risked everything, including a great life with an amazing woman, to help the FBI take down the corrupt sheriff's office. No one could have anticipated him almost losing Julie and their unborn child because of it. Even field agents didn't risk their families. Prosecuting attorneys weren't supposed to catch the perpetrators—just make sure they got a new address and an orange suit. But in the end, Richard was about to drive off into happily-ever-after with his bride Julie and a baby on the way.

But where was Max—FBI man-of-the-hour—heading? To an empty apartment, arm in a sling. No wife. Not even a dog. Just loneliness and echoes of his ex-wife's parting words: *I'm done trying to compete with your job. Have a nice life, Superman.*

He carefully seated the cowboy hat on his head as he checked his image in the mirror. Cowboy was not an act. It was in his DNA. He had missed the hat while he played Jake, but too many would have recognized his signature look.

Tethered to her stall, Jubilee eyed Jake as he descended the stairs into the main barn area. She tossed back her elegant chestnut head and whinnied her disapproval. He dropped his bag and picked a brush from the rack above the workbench. "It's okay, girl. Your momma will be back to riding you soon enough."

Jubilee's eyes widened, and she jerked her head up.

"Okay—okay—I'll come to visit you too."

Her eyes relaxed as she accepted his strokes.

"It's time." He returned the brush to the rack. "Goodbye, old girl."

She bobbed her head up and down.

He nuzzled her neck for a long moment, then picked up his bag and stepped out into the perfect sun-filled autumn morning—blue skies and sixties with full sun. He paused to breathe it all in, then headed to his blue soon-to-be antique Ford F-150 pickup. He tossed his jump bag onto the back seat and retrieved the special-order package that had arrived just in time. Nothing could ever repay this couple for what they'd done, but he hoped that the gift would at least bring two smiles.

Max hopped in, tossed the package on the passenger seat, then rolled down the window to let in the day. He drove down the dirt road, past a car holding two U.S. marshals sent to protect the Wheelers. Richard was in the brick driveway looking between a row of five suitcases and the open trunk of Julie's surprise gift—the sunshine yellow Mustang convertible that Julie had always wanted.

Dog ran up to his truck as he pulled in front of the first of three garage doors. Dog barely waited for him to open his door before demanding his attention. Max placed his cowboy hat on his seat, then stooped to accept Dog's wet greeting and give him a one-armed hug. "I'm going to miss you too."

Max walked over and patted Richard's shoulder. "I hope you're not trying to get all those in that trunk."

Richard shook his head and grinned. "She says she needs it all. Who am I to argue?"

"Hold on." Max returned to the truck, pulled the treasures out of the package, and brought them to Richard, holding them behind his back. "I got you something for the road." He held up two yellow ball caps emblazoned with a Mustang.

"Wow. "Richard's face lit up. "Those are perfect." Richard reached for the caps.

Max smacked his hand back. "Uh uh. I get to see Julie's face."

Anticipating a joyous sendoff, Max followed Richard and Dog up the front porch and into the entry hallway, only to find a tense Julie standing at the bottom of the staircase. She glared at the older blonde standing next to Julie's dad across from her. It had to be the infamous "Cruella." Max had heard story upon story of Catherine, the evil stepmother who had terrorized the girls after their mother had died. She wore a politician's smile and a tailored outfit better suited for the country club than a farm.

And what was going on with Julie's sweet dad? The Doc Blanchard that Max knew was the life of the party. The man who stood before him had been transformed into a beaten-down old man. Max hadn't heard what had been said, but Cruella patted his hand like a mother making excuses for her child.

Richard glanced at Max, shook his head with the I-told-you-so look, then smiled and said, "Look who I found trying to slip away."

Julie stepped forward and carefully hugged Max around his sling. "Going somewhere?"

"Yes, ma'am. Right after I deliver your Mustang hats, color coordinated with your new ride." He pulled the caps from behind his back.

Julie's face lit up as she took one of the caps and pulled it on. She turned toward the wall and checked it in the mirror by the front door. "It's perfect."

Max retrieved a yellow bandana from his pocket with "Dog" emblazoned on it. He handed it to Julie. "And this."

"Where did you ever find this?" Julie bent to tie the bandana around Dog's neck. "Now we're stylin'."

Richard handed his phone to Doc Blanchard, "Can you get this picture?"

Doc Blanchard's demeanor brightened as he stepped forward to get the shot.

Richard and Julie stooped on either side of Dog. "Come on in here, Max," Richard said, waving him to kneel behind Dog.

"Say 'stinky feet,'" Julie's dad took the picture, then handed the phone back to Richard.

Bobbing her head and tapping Doc Blanchard's arm, Catherine said, "Well, now that you've all had your fun, aren't you going to introduce us?"

Max had never seen a woman who could so thoroughly express disdain through a perfect Southern smile. He had been warned, though.

Julie's face pinched, and she stepped forward. Richard reined her in, then held his hand out toward Max. "Max, I'd like you to meet Catherine Blanchard, Julie's stepmother. Catherine, this is Max Enders, the FBI agent we told you about."

Max put on his best Southern. "Nice to meet you, ma'am."

Catherine nodded.

He looked at Richard. "Well, my job is done here. The marshals are here to escort you to Chincoteague. Hopefully, you'll be able to relax while you enjoy your second honeymoon. I'm headed off for a few weeks of R and R myself, and then I'm sure they'll assign me to my next post."

Sarah emerged from the kitchen. "Is that Jake—I mean Max—I hear?"

"Yes, ma'am."

"You wait right there. Don't even think about leaving before I get back." Sarah held out her hands like she was telling a dog to stay. "Great hats, by the way." She pointed to Richard and Julie, then disappeared into her magical kingdom.

Doc Blanchard shook Max's good hand. "I don't know what would have happened if you hadn't been on the job. Thank you for protecting my little girl."

"Yes, thank you," Catherine said. "She is so precious to us."

Max ignored Catherine. "My pleasure, sir. Now I leave her in your hands."

Doc Blanchard's face twisted as he glanced up the staircase. "Son, I know this isn't your job, and it's not FBI business, but can you check around for Heather? That girl is a magnet for trouble, and I feel like she's in trouble or something."

"Oh, he's exaggerating," Catherine swept her hand through the air.

Julie's face reddened. "For God's sake, Catherine. Quit interrupting and let Dad talk."

Catherine's face reddened. "Well, I'm just saying . . ."

"Just stop saying." She turned to her father. "Go on, Dad."

Go, Julie! Even Max wished he could smack the woman. "Go on, Doc Blanchard. What is it?"

"I can't explain it. Yesterday, this feeling of dread came over me when I was taking a nap. No . . . it was more like a nightmare. Heather was running. There was an explosion. Then I woke up sweating." He shook his head. "I just don't get dreams like that." His face squeezed. "Well . . ."

Max had just carried Heather up the stairs a few nights before. Had something terrible happened to her? His mind flashed back to the nights he had worried about his sister when she was out partying. But Heather wasn't an addict. At worst, she was a spoiled-rotten drunk.

"What is it, Dad?"

"I haven't had that vivid a dream since your momma got sick. I had a dream then too. It was like I knew she had cancer before the doctors did. Because of that dream, we got the right doctors who helped her have more quality time with you girls. Your momma claimed it was the Holy Spirit's work."

Julie reached for her dad's arm. "Holy Spirit or not, why didn't you tell me? I've been having dreams about her as well. Not as definite as an explosion, but where Heather is calling for help, and I can't get to her." Julie's face pinched. "They were so real."

"Well, we all know that Heather's a nightmare," Catherine said.

Wow. Nicknaming her Cruella was no exaggeration.

Richard took Julie in his arms. "Babe, why didn't you tell me?"

"I didn't want to worry you . . . or anybody. Everyone's already walking on eggshells around me."

"Can you look into it for us?" Doc Blanchard asked.

Max knew the pain Doc Blanchard felt. How many times had his mother begged him to find her baby girl? Besides, he didn't have anything else to do while benched.

"I can't officially do anything, but after all your family has sacrificed, the least I can do is check around. I'll let you know if there's any word on her."

Doc Blanchard grabbed Max's hand and shook it hard as if Max were his new best friend.

Richard took his turn next. "This means a lot to us all." He glanced back at Catherine as if daring her to speak, then turned back to Max. "Thanks, man."

Max nodded. "Thank you for all you've done. I'll look into it. Meanwhile, I hope you'll be able to relax and enjoy yourselves—even with the detail watching you. And I'll do my best to find Heather."

"I feel better already." Julie hugged Max. "Now, go find her."

Sarah emerged from the kitchen with a wrapped container. "Just you wait a minute."

"Is this what I think it is?" Max sniffed out the pastry and fruit scents.

"Yes sir, your favorite—and my specialty—cherry cobbler."

Sarah's dishes and hugs had always taken him back to his aunt's great cooking and comforting arms. "You have no idea how much this means to me. If that husband of yours ever loses his mind and gives you up, I'll marry you in a minute. You are one special woman."

"That's the second offer I've had today."

Everyone except Catherine chuckled.

"Now go on and get out of here before I decide to run off with you." Max tipped his head to the family. "Thank you all again for allowing me to share in the richness of this family. You are very special people." He held up his prize, grinned, and turned toward the door.

"Let me get the door for you." Richard grabbed the dish from him, and the two walked together to the truck. Max opened the driver's door, donned his cowboy hat, and climbed in. Richard set the dish in the back seat, then shut the door and shook Max's hand through the open window. "Thanks again, man."

Max tipped his chin. "Thank *you*." He started the engine, then pulled away, lifting his sling in salute. The momentary fullness of Max's heart trickled out as he drove down the driveway, leaving behind farm life and great West Virginia small-town folk. But it was time. He just didn't know for what.

As Max found his way to the interstate, Doc Blanchard's words about the explosion niggled him. He hadn't wanted to alarm them, but there had been some chatter about a vehicle explosion that week. He had been too busy with the takedown to pay attention to the reports.

It was time to call Alex. If anyone could find something or someone, it was her.

He pressed the steering wheel button and directed the hands-free system to place the call.

"Well, hello, handsome. Did you miss me?" Her smile reached through the phone, tugging his lips up.

"You know I did."

"Aren't you on leave . . . like, didn't you get shot or something?"

"They can't take me down that easy."

"One of these days . . ."

"I know. I know. Listen, I need a favor. You know Richard Wheeler—the guy we worked with in Hearthstone?"

"Yeah."

"Well, his looney sister-in-law took off drunk a couple of nights ago, and they're worried about her. We can't officially get involved, but I've got a bad feeling about this. I think we need to do a little digging."

"Does *we* mean me?"

Max smiled. "Who else is the master of all things known or knowable?" He could hear the grin on the other end.

"Flattery. Have you resorted to that?"

"Whatever it takes."

"Name?"

"Heather Blanchard."

The computer keys clicked.

"She's from Virginia, went to college in Chicago, lived in New Mexico, and recently moved to West Virginia with the Wheelers."

"Got her. Clean as a whistle. Not even a smudge on the glass."

"What's the deal with the explosion near Huntington? Her dad said his dreams involved an explosion. What do you have on that?"

"His *dreams*? Are you actually chasing dreams?"

"I've been chasing you, haven't I?"

She giggled. "Oooh, lookie there. A camper exploded near Huntington after being run off the road. The driver was burned beyond recognition, but the DEA thinks it was one of the Johnson brothers from Detroit. Um . . . Johnny Johnson. Wow—two of his brothers and their mom were killed in Detroit on the same day. Execution-style. Somebody didn't like their family. They've been on the DEA/FBI watch list for a while."

"Anything about a girl?"

"Yeah—a blonde was found near the camper. They think it was Johnson's girlfriend, Melissa Thomason. She was pretty torn up. She had no identification with her, but she had a suitcase filled with half a million dollars. They believe it's Johnson's money. She's in a coma, so they haven't been able to talk to her yet. But it doesn't look like it's the Blanchard girl."

"Yeah. Heather's a total flake and a drunk. Her boyfriend was a crooked deputy in Hearthstone who ended up helping us save Doc Wheeler. It doesn't add up. Can you ping her phone?"

"Not that you have a warrant, but what's the number?"

He gave it to her.

"Nothing. Like it's off."

His stomach jumped. "Listen, would you let me know if you hear anything that might be related? They say she runs away when she gets in a mood, so it's probably nothing."

"I'll keep my ear to the ground."

"You're a doll. I owe you lunch."

"Yeah, if I ever collected on all your promised meals, I wouldn't have to pack lunch for a year."

"Later, Alex." He punched the end button just as a Tudor's Biscuit World billboard came into view. It was his last chance to grab one of West Virginia's famous staples. He banked right at the exit. He parked next to a limousine—not a regular site in West Virginia or a fast-food restaurant. The darkened windows would not reveal the passengers to Richard as he walked by. He got in the line behind a black-suited man in a cap who could only have been the limo driver. The man turned to him.

Max tipped his hat. "You with that fancy car?"

"Indeed, I am," the man said with a baritone voice.

Max grinned broadly. "We don't see many limos in these here parts. And biscuits?"

He smiled back. "He heard about these biscuits, and we had to come."

"Must be important or rich to travel in that style."

"Yes, sir. He's both."

"Can you give me a hint of who he is?"

"Mr. Miller wouldn't mind. He just cut the ribbon on Hearthstone's new drug treatment center."

"You don't say." Max had seen enough rehabs dealing with his sister. "I watched that place go up. Didn't realize it was ready to open. Mr. Miller, you say. I don't think I know a Mr. Miller. He from around these parts?"

"Next," the restaurant clerk said.

"Excuse me." He stepped up and placed his order, waited for his quickly-packed bag, then walked outside to the limo.

Whoever Mr. Miller was, it was good that someone was stepping in to help clean up the havoc the gangs were wreaking on this drug-infested part of the state. Hopefully, he enjoyed his biscuits.

Chapter 12

Sunday, October 29
_1:00 p.m._

BEEP... BEEP . . . BEEP . . .

Excruciating pain—a vice crushing her temples. She peeked her eyes open. Shards of light pierced through her body and into her soul. She squeezed her eyes closed, but the agony remained. Tears dripped from the corners of her eyes. Maybe it would go away if she lay still or went back to sleep. Was she dying? If it stopped this torture . . .

Beep... Beep . . . Beep . . .

Canned laughter—a TV sitcom. *Can't someone stop the noise?* Each beep shot electrical pulses to her temples and forced tears to spill from her eyes. *Please?*

Beep... Beep . . . Beep . . .

Daring the pain, she squinted against the light pouring in through the picture windows on her left, topped with white pulldown shades not pulled down enough. An awful golden-tan textured curtain was partially drawn beside her bed . . . her hospital bed? What was she doing in a hospital? How had she gotten there? Her brain wouldn't work. The fog. She couldn't remember.

Above her, an IV bag hung from a twisted metal rack. Her eyes followed the plastic tubing to a bandage and needle in her forearm—her tattooed forearm. Had someone tattooed her while she was asleep? How long had she been there? Her temples throbbed.

She reached to comfort them . . . gauze . . . covering her whole head. What had happened to her? Why wasn't someone there explaining what was going on?

Beyond the golden-brown curtain that feigned happiness with its interspersed sunburst designs, the foot of the bed to her right was void of humanity. The wooden door to her drab, beige sterile room was propped open, muffled voices drifted in, and things on wheels rolled by, but no one came.

A brown guest chair sat guestless. Where was her family? *Who* was her family? Her heart thumped faster. She couldn't remember. Who was *she*?

She tried to sit up, but invisible knives stabbed her chest on the right side, shoving her back to the tilted-up bed and her two pillows. Maybe she shouldn't move. What if something was broken?

Testing for paralysis, she wiggled her toes. They worked. All was not lost.

Staring at the ceiling, she scanned her body like a mental MRI. Every inch screamed as if she'd been run through a clothes dryer. With one hand, she lifted the sheets and, with the other, pulled her hospital gown up to review her naked body. No casts. Bandages and bruises speckled her skin, but nothing indicated a severe injury or surgery. A plastic tube carrying a liquid she didn't want to consider flowed from between her upper thighs. She touched her abdomen like doctors do to find where it hurt. Every inch was sore, but nothing cried out as badly as that right rib cage. Had she been beaten and robbed . . . or raped? How would she know? She couldn't remember. She couldn't remember anything.

Her breathing grew fast and deep, but each rise of her chest speared her right side. What if a rib was broken and it was going to pierce her lungs? She needed to know . . . something . . . anything.

She opened her mouth to speak, but the sandpaper lining her throat prevented even an utterance. She strained again, but only a faint "help" escaped her mouth. Avoiding moving her right rib, she fumbled for the call button and pushed.

A red-headed nurse decorated in Halloween scrubs entered moments later and smiled down at her.

"Good afternoon, sleeping beauty. You're finally awake. My name is Nancy. I'm your nurse for the next few hours. On a scale from one to ten, how's your pain?"

Pointing to her neck, she could only manage a single word. "Hurt."

The nurse nodded and reached for the pink pitcher on the tray table. She poured water into a white plastic cup and tipped the straw toward her. She drank it down.

"I'm not surprised. You're pretty beat up. Do you remember coming in?"

Beat up? She blinked to jumpstart her memory. Nothing. "No."

"You didn't have an ID. Can you tell me your name so we can contact your family?"

The guest chair mocked her. She closed her eyes—nothing but fuzz. She shook her head as tears spilled down her cheeks. "I don't know."

"It's okay." Nancy patted her arm. "What do you remember?"

"Nothing. I don't remember anything." What if she never remembered? She began to cry, intensifying her headache. "It hurts." She pointed to the TV. "It hurts. Turn it off."

Nancy picked up the call button and turned it off. "You have a concussion. Pain and fogginess are common when you come out of a coma."

"A *coma?*"

"Yes, sweetie." Nancy reached for her gauze-covered head and fiddled with several spots. "You've been out for a few days."

"Days?" She blinked as her heart raced. "What happened?"

"All we know is that you were in an accident."

Why couldn't she remember anything? "Who am I?"

Nancy pursed her lips as she shook her head. "We don't know. We were hoping you could tell us."

100

"Nobody came for me?"

"Not yet, sweetie." Nancy's face pinched. "But then again, I don't think they released any information about you to the press."

Had nobody missed her for days? Wasn't this the digital age? How could they not know who she was? Maybe she'd been traveling out of her area. But where was home?

"Where am I?"

"You are in the St. Mary's Hospital in Huntington, West Virginia."

"West Virginia? Why would I be in West Virginia?"

"I don't know. Do you know where you should be?"

She had no idea. She was trapped in a body that didn't belong to anyone or anyplace. Heaving sobs magnified her agony. "It hurts, oh God, it hurts."

"Where?"

"Everywhere. I can't take it. Make it stop."

A dark-haired man with a midlife paunch, donning a white coat with a stethoscope draping his neck, entered her room.

"I see you're awake." He smiled, interacted with the computer screen by her bed, then approached the side of her bed opposite Nancy. "I'm Doctor Singh. Tell me, what's going on?"

"I don't know," she said between sobs.

Nancy patted her hand. "She doesn't remember the accident or who she is."

"Well, based on your brain scans, you have some swelling that could cause amnesia. Time usually rectifies it."

"Usually?" Her parched throat forced a cough, slashing her right side as if by dagger. She grabbed her side. "My ribs. I feel like they're broken. I'm afraid to breathe—like it will puncture my lung."

"Indeed. You do have a broken rib. Don't worry about it puncturing your lungs. Your rib is intact. It's only cracked. It's normal to fear a puncture, but it won't happen. I'm going to prescribe Percocet for the pain. It will help you relax so you're not afraid to breathe. Do you understand?"

She nodded. "What about my memory?"

"There are rare cases when a patient's memory doesn't return. But you're young and healthy. We expect a full recovery." He smiled as if that would encourage her, then looked at Nancy. "Would you grab a mirror?"

Nancy nodded and left.

"Other than your concussion and your broken rib, we did not find any other areas of concern. But, after a trauma such as you experienced, we need to monitor you in case there's any internal bleeding or something that didn't show up in a scan. Understand?"

She nodded.

"I'm going to apply some light pressure around your abdomen. Let me know how much it hurts on a scale of one to ten."

She winced as he prodded each spot on her abdomen and named numbers closer to ten than five. When he touched her right chest area, she recoiled in pain.

"Stop! Twenty!"

Doctor Singh held his hands up as Nancy returned with the mirror.

"Sorry. As I said, we only have the two areas of concern at the moment." He held his hand out to Nancy to accept the mirror and gave it to Heather.

She immediately held it up and examined the mummy's head staring back at her. She didn't recognize this woman. What was she supposed to look like? How could she not know? The swollen, cut, and bruised face screamed of a woman beaten by an out-of-control husband. Was she married? But it couldn't be abuse. Nancy had said it was an accident.

"What happened to me?"

Dr. Singh looked at Nancy, then back to her—almost as if asking permission. "From what we understand, you were in a camper that exploded after running off the road and hitting a tree. I saw pictures of the scene on the news. It's a miracle you survived."

She shook her head. "A camper? That doesn't sound right."

"You don't remember?"

Her head continued shaking its denial. "Remember? I don't know who I am or getting blown up." Her breathing quickened. She focused on the blank TV screen to imagine the news report, then on the vacant guest chair below it. "Wait—you said it was on the news? Shouldn't someone have seen me and called about me?"

"No, the news didn't show you. They only reported that there was an unidentified woman. I only know it was you because I saw the report and was here when you came in."

"Why didn't they show me in the report if you were trying to identify me."

Dr. Singh looked at Nancy again. What was he not saying? Why was he checking his words? He returned his gaze to her.

"Well, maybe that's a better question for the authorities. There are a couple of detectives here who want to interview you. They might be able to answer that question. Are you up to talking to them?"

"Detectives? Did I do something wrong?"

"They didn't say."

"But I don't remember anything."

"Well, maybe speaking with them will help you remember." He patted her hand. "Don't overdo it. I'll order the pain meds. Okay?"

She nodded.

Dr. Singh typed something into the computer, then turned to Nancy. "Would you show the detectives in and stay with her while they're here? I don't want her getting excited."

"Yes, sir."

He left.

Nancy gave her another swig of water. "I'll go get them."

Almost immediately, a black-suited man who could have doubled as a bouncer filled her room with his presence. He took an imposing stand between her and the window. Except for the light reflecting off his shaven bald head, his form was a dark silhouette that was too close for her comfort. Her heart raced. They didn't send a guy who looked like this for some camper accident. What was going on?

Another shorter suited man followed, who used a comb-over to conceal his baldness. Positioning himself at the end of her bed, he had a kind face with a couple of years hanging around his jawline. Was he studying her?

Nancy was last to come in, retrieving the rolling card from the left side and bringing it to her right, where Nancy played guardian.

"Good morning." The bouncer's deep voice boomed but with unexpected gentleness. Was he using a soothing voice to lull her into saying the wrong thing? What if she was a criminal? She couldn't fall for it. *The less said . . .*

The bouncer retrieved his ID from his inside jacket pocket and held it up for her. "I'm FBI Special Agent Eric Braun, and this is Dr. Dan Tolley."

Tolley tipped his chin up and smiled weakly.

"Doctor?"

"Not that kind of doctor. I'm a psychiatrist."

"Psychiatrist? What, am I crazy or something?"

Tolley chuckled. "No, ma'am. Nothing like that. You've been through a lot. The nurse told us that you have amnesia. I'm just here to help if I can." His face was soft, like a friend's. But psychiatrists couldn't be trusted. They never answered questions. They diverted.

"Are you a profiler?"

He chuckled. "Why would the FBI send a profiler?"

See? Already diverting.

She looked him squarely in the eyes. "You tell me, Dr. Tolley— why *would* the FBI send a profiler?"

Tolley grinned. "Very astute. You're clearly an intelligent woman."

"I wouldn't know."

She pointed to the water. Nancy gave her a sip as Braun cleared his throat and looked back at Tolley. Oh, no. Drinking water was a sign of nervousness. Of course, she *was*. She should never have agreed to talk to them when she didn't know who she was, much less what had happened to her—especially anything the FBI would be interested in.

"Okay then," Braun said. "Since we don't know your name, would "Ms. Doe" be okay?"

"As in Jane?" She winced as her head pounded with each heartbeat. "Sorry. My head." She rubbed her temples. "Call me whatever you want."

"I'm sorry to put you through this, but you might be able to help us solve a crime."

Or help you put me in jail. "Do I need an attorney?"

"Not that I'm aware of," Braun said, looking at Dr. Tolley and then back at her.

That was not an answer. She should end this before she did need an attorney. "My head is really hurting, and I don't remember anything, so this is wasting everyone's time."

"Maybe if we ask you some questions, you may remember something." Braun pulled a pad and pen out of his coat pocket. "What's the last thing you remember?"

"Nothing."

"Let's see if we can help you out with that. You were found on a highway just south of Barboursville. Do you know why you were there?"

"I don't even know where Barboursville is."

"You were found near a camper. Do you know whose camper that was?"

"No. I don't think I've ever been in a camper."

Tolley stepped forward. "Why do you say that?"

Again, with the psych questions—but it was one she wished she could answer. "I don't know. It doesn't feel like me."

Braun made a note. "What do you remember about the accident?"

"Accident? I thought it was an explosion."

"Explosion?" He straightened, lowering his hands. "I didn't say there was an explosion."

"Doctor Singh—or maybe Nancy told me."

Braun frowned at Nancy, who shrugged.

"She asked."

Braun raised his pad and pen again. "So, no memory of the accident or the explosion?"

"None." She moaned as she shifted to find a more comfortable position.

"Do you remember who was driving the camper?"

"Is that a trick question?" Her breathing quickened. "How would I remember who was driving a camper if I don't remember a camper?"

"I'm not trying to trick you. The goal is to help you remember. There was a male driver who was burned beyond recognition. Do you have any idea who that would be?"

"Someone died?"

Braun's face dropped. "Yes." He eyed her for a moment.

Is that why no one had come for her? Was it her husband? Did they think she had something to do with it? "Was anyone else killed?"

"No." Braun shook his head and returned to his pad. "Have you ever heard of the Mermaid Company?"

"No. Is it a tuna company?"

"We were hoping you knew."

She shook her head. The FBI did corruption and money laundering, didn't they? Was the mermaid company some shell thing?

"No. Did I work there?"

"It's registered in New Hampshire. Have you ever been to New Hampshire?"

"I don't think so. But then again, I don't know why I'm in West Virginia."

Braun made a note on his pad, then flipped the page. "We found a suitcase at the scene. It has your fingerprints on it. Is it yours?"

"Fingerprints?" She examined her fingers. "If you have my fingerprints, why don't you know who I am?

"They're not in our database."

"Why not?"

"Apparently, you haven't gotten a professional license, been arrested, or applied for a passport."

So, she wasn't a criminal, or at least she had never been caught if she had been. No passport? She couldn't be a drug smuggler.

"So, back to my question, is the suitcase yours?"

"I have no idea."

"The suitcase had a sizable amount of money in it. Do you have any idea where the money came from?"

That sounded like drug dealing or money laundering, for sure. Her heart beat harder. "A suitcase of money? That's ridiculous. No. Did you find my purse or cell phone?"

"Why do you ask?" Tolley said.

"Doesn't every girl have them?"

Tolley nodded.

"No passport? You say I had a lot of money but was traveling in a camper? Does that make sense to you? You'd think I'd have been on my way to Paris if I were rich." This was too much. An explosion? A suitcase full of money? She needed some time to think. But she needed to know what they knew too. And something told her there was more that they weren't telling her. She pressed her fingers against both temples.

"Listen, I feel like I've been run over by a truck, and you guys are grilling me with all these questions I can't answer. Can't you tell me what's going on? Why are you here?"

Braun smiled. "I get to ask the questions."

She closed her eyes and inhaled deeply. She hated that answer.

"Do you know how much money was in the suitcase?"

She tilted her head toward Braun and narrowed her eyes at him. "No, Special Agent Braun, I don't. How much money was there?"

Tolley let a half-laugh escape, then returned to stoic silence.

Braun tapped his pen on the pad. "Let's just say more than a thousand dollars."

She shook her head. "I just don't feel like I would have that much money in cash."

Tolley leaned forward. "Why is that?"

"I don't know. Carrying that kind of money is asking for trouble. Like a money launderer or a drug dealer."

Tolley's brow lifted. "What do you know about money laundering or drugs?"

Oh great. Of all things, why had she said that? But what if she was a criminal? The longer this interview went on, the more it seemed plausible. Maybe she should be thankful she couldn't remember. She couldn't say anything wrong. And she was finding out what they were after for when her memory did return. She needed to persevere.

"Nothing. As far as I know, I've *never* bought drugs, and I wouldn't know how to launder money except to throw it in a washing machine."

Braun made a note. "Do you have any idea where you were born or where you grew up?"

"No." She wished she knew.

"We found a gun at the scene. Is it yours?"

"No. I don't like guns."

"Why not?" Tolley asked.

"Because they kill people. What do you think?" It was the first time she thought she knew something about herself but didn't know why.

Braun frowned and touched his jacket where his gun probably rested at this very moment. He shifted his stance.

"Two men were seen fleeing the scene in a stolen car. Do you have any idea what they were doing there?"

"*Really?*" Her voice rose with her frustration. "Do you believe I would remember two men in a car if I can't remember an exploding camper?" She leaned forward slightly, but her rib yanked her back against her pillow.

She motioned Nancy for water. She took a long sip from the straw, eyeing her torturers and stretching every moment until the cup was empty. She asked for more and slowly finished that cup, this time noting Tolley studying her with his lips curved slightly to the right.

"Do you know who the president is?"

"No. Who is it?"

Braun shook his head.

She threw her head back against the bed and stared at the ceiling. She had learned enough to make her head spin and maybe enough to figure out what they were after. She looked back to Braun.

"This is stupid." She turned to Nancy. "Please make them leave. My head is killing me."

Braun pulled a card from his pocket and handed it to her. "We'll come back in a couple of days and see how you are progressing . . . if that's okay with you."

"We'll see."

Braun pointed to the card. "Call if you remember anything."

"Only if you promise to call me if you find out who I am."

"Deal." Braun closed his pad and tucked it back into his jacket. "You know, we're not the enemy. Especially if you have nothing to hide."

"I don't know if I have anything to hide. I don't know who I am, where I came from, or what I've done"—she looked at the agents as her chest tightened—"but I feel like I'm a good person." She looked up and blinked away the forming tears.

Tolley patted her foot. "Me, too."

Braun glanced at Tolley, and then the two headed toward the door.

"Wait. Agent Braun?"

He stopped and turned back to her. "Yes."

"Did you check the missing persons' reports?"

"Yes, ma'am."

"Does that mean nobody's missing me?"

Braun smiled sadly. "I don't know, ma'am." He gave a single nod. The two men left the room, leaving behind a Jane Doe with more questions than when they'd come.

Chapter 13

2:30 p.m.

SUNDAY DINNER—THE DELICIOUS JUXTAPOSITION of his mother's sweet Italian heritage next to his father's German no-nonsense manner. And Momma's Sunday gravy. Dexter's favorite, right after her ossobuco. It made his family's weekly flights to Chicago worth every minute.

He just wished his mother would let him bring Rockefeller, but the first time Dexter brought him, his mother banished him to the backyard and said never again. She'd raised enough kids and animals. His father said the dog's size must have been compensating for something.

Dexter sat on a barstool at the kitchen's island counter, picking off chunks of Momma's homemade Italian bread from a basket and dipping them into a dish of Momma's famous tomato sauce. Matty, the youngest of the three brothers, had sat beside him and followed suit. Dexter smiled as he remembered their bread-dipping days in Alabama when the three boys bunked together in one room. Such simple days. That was until his father became one of the premier neurosurgeons in the world and made them move to Chicago.

Mary Ellen ladled the browned braciole into the sauce that had already been simmering for hours. Cloud-diffused light from the kitchen window fell over her curves. Such a tiny waist, cinched tightly by the ribbon of one of Momma's aprons.

His mother smiled as she reminded Mary Ellen to be gentle with the pockets of love. Mary Ellen had always delighted his mother. And no wonder. His wife had an incredible ability to emanate light into any environment she inhabited—even when that environment included his gruff old dad. How had he gotten so lucky with his bride?

His father entered the kitchen, stood next to Matty, grabbed a piece of bread, and dunked.

Momma wagged a finger at them. "Don't you boys spoil your appetites."

"What mere mortal can resist your sauce, Momma?" Dexter said.

His mother leaned back against the Wedgewood-blue hand-painted Italian tile counter where Mary Ellen was working. Grinning, she said, "Mary Ellen told me you opened a drug rehab center. What a great thing you're doing. Isn't it Mike?"

His father nodded and dipped another chunk. "In West Virginia? Right?" He stuffed the bread in his mouth. With his mouth still full, he said, "You couldn't do something in Detroit or Chicago?"

Momma's eyes met Dexter's. Nothing was ever good enough for Dad. No surprise he hadn't come to the ribbon cutting, despite Dexter offering his private jet to get him there.

Mary Ellen set the ladle down and went to Dexter's side. "Well, *I'm* proud of him. The governor even sent his new appointee to the grand opening." She put her arm around him and kissed his cheek.

"That's my boy," Momma said, beaming. "Which reminds me . . ." She checked her watch. "Where's Michael?"

"Oh, I forgot to tell you. He called. He's still in surgery. He's not going to make it to dinner."

Momma's face dropped as she turned her back and wiped her cheek with her apron.

Dexter couldn't remember the last time Mike or his family had made it for Sunday dinner. He knew how much it meant to Momma. This was her second go-round playing second fiddle to a career—first his dad and now Mike. Dexter was all the more thankful that Matty and Dexter's family could be there for her.

His dad walked across the room to grab a bruschetta from the appetizer tray on the kitchen table.

"It's the price of doing the greatest work—saving lives." He turned to Dexter. "Something even your rehab center probably can't do. You know, those addicts go right back to it once they leave. Of course, you probably already knew that. Is that what enticed you to pursue this business—the revolving wheel of return customers? What's your angle on this venture?"

Momma looked back into Dexter's eyes. She knew the pain his father's comments brought, as only a mother could. It didn't matter how successful Dexter was, he would always be his dad's failure. Dexter hated to admit that his dad had figured out one aspect of his business model, but what he failed to acknowledge was his entrepreneurial genius.

His mother opened the drawer and began counting out silverware. "I suppose Kelley and the girls won't be here either?" Momma asked, keeping her head down.

"No. Kelley said they would wait for Michael and have dinner together."

"Matty?" Holding out the silverware, Momma turned to him and smiled sweetly. "Would you help me set the table? For seven, as usual. And would you confiscate your niece and nephew's phones and let them know we're sitting down to dinner?"

Matty accepted the silverware, retrieved the plates, and set off for the dining room. Grabbing the appetizer tray and a bottle of wine, Dexter followed. Dexter put out the dishes, and Matty did the silverware. Maybe it was time to get the twins to do this. They were teenagers, after all. Momma had her sons doing this when they could walk.

Dexter's private phone vibrated. He pulled it out of his pocket. Matty eyed him from across the dining room table. "Your trouble phone?"

"Why would you say that?"

"Because you always get grouchy after you talk on that phone."

"That's just because it's business. You know business is serious."

"If you say so." He smiled as usual. Happy was his only mode unless someone was making fun of him.

"I'm going to step outside for a minute. Don't forget to call the twins."

Dexter rushed onto the front porch and into the frigid Chicago cold that only the lake effect could stir up. His teeth chattered the moment a wind gusted through his sweater and froze his lungs. He should have grabbed his coat. He tapped the phone's screen to answer.

"It's Sunday dinner. This had better be good."

"The girl woke up. She has amnesia. Our guy got a picture of her. It's Heather Blanchard—the Hearthstone vet's sister. The FBI has already questioned her."

"How on God's green earth was the doc's sister involved with the Johnson brothers? And why didn't you know that?"

"There wasn't anything to know. She wasn't involved with them. I can't explain it. She only came to Hearthstone a month before the accident and was totally involved with Cruz for the whole month. We knew her every move. She came from New Mexico, where she had been for over a year. There's just no connection. She had to be hitchhiking or some other crazy thing. She left her sister's house the night of the doc's arrest and got blown up like twelve hours later. I'm telling you, there's no connection."

Dexter bounced in place to stay warm.

"So, she shouldn't have had our money or know about it?"

"I don't see how."

It was too cold to argue that it didn't answer Dexter's question.

"And you don't know where the Johnson girlfriend is?"

"No, boss."

"Do you believe you're the right man for this job, or is it too big for you?"

"No, boss. It's all under control. Bones has two guys working on leads to find Johnny's girl. They're getting close. Two guys are watching the hospital, and one is working on staff, just in case. And Hawthorne will report when something happens."

"Something'd better go our way soon."

Dexter tapped the phone off and stared at it. Matty was right. This was the trouble phone.

Chapter 14

Monday, October 30
7:30 a.m.

HOW COULD ANYONE SURVIVE, MUCH LESS RECOVER from anything in a hospital? Just when she'd get comfortable enough to fall asleep, boom—some villainous nurse would wake, poke and prod her, leaving her to another hour of sleeplessness. "Necessary with head trauma," or so they said. Wasn't sleep necessary for healing?

"Good morning." The new shift nurse beamed almost as brightly as the sun's first rays rising over the window sill.

Heather was tempted to growl but forced a grin. "Morning."

Miss Sunshine erased the night nurse's name from the marker board that still proclaimed last week's weather forecast. As if Heather couldn't read, the nurse announced her name as she wrote Charlene next to the other staff members that Heather doubted even still worked there. Still smiling, she moved to Heather's side to fuss with the monitors and the IV bag.

"On a scale of one to ten, what's your pain level?"

Why did Heather even wait for the question? She should say, "Good morning—ten—bring more drugs." Not that she liked how the drugs made her feel, but her pain level was off the charts.

"Eleven."

Charlene scrunched her nose. "No improvement?"

Was there? Heather imagined a pain scanner moving the length of her body. "My big toe isn't hurting."

Charlene chuckled. "There—something good."

"Hmm."

Dr. Singh strode in, reviewed her patient data on the computer screen, and took his position opposite Charlene. "Good morning."

"Eleven—bring more drugs."

Dr. Singh's face twisted. "What?"

"My pain level—it's everyone's favorite question."

"Okay. Okay." He grinned. "So where does it hurt?"

"Everywhere." She eyed Charlene and winked. "Except for my big toe."

Charlene chuckled and left.

"Good." Dr. Singh started his prodding.

Between pokes and groans, she asked, "Did you get the results of my brain scan?"

"Yes. All positive. The swelling is down. We'll still need to monitor it. Have you remembered anything?"

Heather's heart hurt. "No. Nothing. Of course, with all the drugs, my brain is fuzzy."

Dr. Singh furrowed his eyebrows. "Are we giving you too much?"

"No. It's just that it doesn't kill the pain—it makes me not care. Bothers my stomach too."

He patted her hand. "Give it another day. You'll begin to adjust."

"Another day? How long am I gonna be here?"

"At least until the swelling's gone. We would normally send someone with memory loss to a rehab center, but because you're technically indigent and without insurance—"

Indigent? Was she? She didn't remember ever not being cared for—but then again, she didn't remember anything. "How much does rehab cost?"

"I'm not sure, but it's in the thousands per day."

Braun had said there was more than a thousand dollars in that suitcase—not even enough for a day. "Where will I go?"

"Social services will send someone by. They'll help you get temporary housing. Hopefully, your memory will return before then. Let's concentrate on getting you better." He nodded. "Okay?"

"Do I have a choice?

After Dr. Singh left, Charlene returned with more meds as an orderly delivered a black tray with gray plastic dishes, including an entrée cover that made her breakfast look more like a fat flying saucer. Who designed this stuff? The food was already questionable. The orderly rolled her tray over her lap and left.

Charlene held out a cup and a pill. Heather swallowed and returned the cup.

"Can I get you anything else?"

"A mirror—one I can keep here."

"There's a mirror in the bathroom, sweetie."

"I know, but I just figured if I looked at it long enough, I might figure out who the stranger is looking back at me.

"I'll get you one." Charlene patted her hand like every other nurse—an action that must have been in the training manual—and left.

Heather examined her tattooed arms. No wrinkles. Some bruises. At least there wasn't a name inscribed because she wouldn't know whose name it was.

Charlene returned with a mirror. "There you go, sweetie. Hope it helps."

Heather held the mirror up and stared at her now unbandaged head. Blonde with blue streaks running through. She needed to wash that hair. Too old for college, but still young. Childbearing age. What if she had kids? What if they were in trouble? Her heart beat faster. Would they be put up for adoption before she remembered who she was?

A female orderly with bangs covering her eyes peeked into her room. Except for her dark hair, the girl could have been her sister.

Heather groaned. "Another test?"

The orderly walked to her bed, pulled the curtain around them, and looked intensely into her eyes. "Heather?"

"Heather?" She sifted the name Heather through her brain. "I'm sorry, I think you have the wrong patient."

The young woman put a finger to her lips. "Shh. It's me, Melissa. I cut and dyed my hair dark. Don't you recognize me?"

"Recognize you? You're kidding, right?"

Melissa cocked her head. "What are you talking about?"

"Amnesia." Heather examined Melissa's eyes. "I don't know my own name, and I don't know Heather or you."

Melissa's face twisted. *"Amnesia?* You don't remember me?" She rolled the food table to the side, sat on the bed next to her, and paused as if waiting would help Heather remember. Melissa's eyes widened. "Don't you remember coming to our house? The accident? Abu? Anything?"

She shook her head, hoping to shake some memory loose. Melissa seemed sincere—concerned even. "How do I know you?"

"I'm your cousin. Don't you remember your mom's painting? Anything?"

Heather shook her head. Melissa's eyes pleaded.

"I wish I could. You said my name is Heather. What's my last name?"

"I don't know. I know it sounds crazy, but you never told me. We just met last week. My boyfriend's brother picked you up after you crashed your car in a river. He brought you to our house because you were mad at your family and didn't want to call them. We figured out we were cousins. Then everything blew up . . . literally." Melissa's face pinched.

"You do know how strange that sounds."

Melissa nodded. "I can tell you about it later, but right now, I need to get you out of here before they figure out who we are."

"Who *we* are? What does that mean?"

"What happened to you was no accident. Some very bad men are after us."

"Why would anyone be after me?"

"You know the saying, 'wrong time, wrong place.'"

She stared at Melissa, straining to remember anything. "If I didn't do anything, why am I in danger?"

"Because a Detroit drug dealer thinks you have his money."

The suitcase.

"My boyfriend is—" Melissa's face dropped— "was one of their dealers. These guys thought Johnny was skimming money. He wasn't, but that doesn't matter to them. They killed Johnny and his family, including Johnny's mother."

"And this Johnny . . . are you saying I was with him in that camper? Is that who died in the explosion?"

Melissa nodded as she wiped tears from her eyes.

"So, you're not a drug dealer?"

"No, I'm a waitress. At a diner. It's where I met Johnny." Melissa choked up. Through tears, she said, "He cared a lot about me—more than anyone ever has. I have a daughter. Not his, but . . . he wanted to take care of us." She brushed back the tears and took a deep breath.

"Is that why the FBI came to question me?

"*The FBI?*" Melissa stood and paced. "Maybe it's good they're here." She ran her fingers through her hair. "I saw a car outside with two thugs that looked like they might be part of the MCMs. If the FBI is around, they can't come after you."

"But I don't have their money. Why would they come after me?"

"You think they're going to ask? You don't know these guys. They executed Johnny's whole family in one day. And they don't leave witnesses." Melissa sat back down and put her hand on Heather's.

"The FBI agent told me there was over a thousand dollars in a suitcase."

"A thousand? Are you kidding me?" She grunted. "It was closer to half a million."

"Oh my God!" She tried to catch her breath. "Oh my God!" The weight of the money began to sink in. "No wonder the FBI came to see me. Are you sure I wasn't involved—like the FBI can't tie anything back to me?"

Melissa shook her head. "There's nothing. Like I said, you just happened to be there."

"But if I'm innocent, won't the FBI protect me?"

"I don't know. If you don't know anything, what good will you be to them? It's called 'witness protection,' and you're not a witness. Do you think you can trust them?"

She didn't trust Braun. But that didn't mean she could trust this woman either.

"Why did you come for me? Is it for the money the FBI has?"

"You're kidding, right? You're never going to get that back."

"Then why?"

Melissa stared at her for a long moment as if she was asking herself the same question. "Call me crazy, but I've never had a family—at least not the kind that cares about one another. And with Johnny gone, I don't have anyone else. Plus, I feel like I got you into this."

Heather shook her head, hoping to release some tidbit—something she could trust. Nothing came.

"Listen, I got set up in another state, but I came back for you. I don't need money. Johnny gave me more than enough for both of us—at least for a couple of years—until this all blows over."

"A couple of years?" Heather tried to imagine life on the run. "Do I have other family?"

"You have an older sister in Hearthstone—Julie Wheeler. She's a vet. Your dad's a vet, too—in D.C. But if you contact them now, you might bring all this trouble on them."

"And if I come with you?"

"Like I said, I've got a safe place. My daughter's there with some church folks. That's where I was when I heard about the crash. You can go with us, or I can help you settle elsewhere."

Indigent. Wasn't that what the doctor had called her? How could she get by without money? But drug money? Could she really do that?

And what if the FBI found her? Wouldn't that make her look guilty? How smart was it to claim innocence and get back involved with the same people who got her into this in the first place?

"I don't know."

"Listen, Heather. I know what you're thinking. Isn't it only right that this money is used to protect you?" Melissa stood and pulled a phone from her back pocket.

"Look, I brought you a smartphone." She handed it to Heather. "Use it to look up what I've told you, but do not try to contact anyone who knows you, or the feds will be able to trace it.

"I'm leaving tomorrow, with or without you. Call me by noon tomorrow if you want to go. My number is programmed under 'Grandma.' She paused, looking Heather over. "If you don't call me by tomorrow, I promise you'll never hear from me again."

Melissa pulled the curtain back. "Please don't speak my name to anyone. I grew up an orphan. I don't want my daughter to be one."

Their eyes locked for a moment—the heart of a mother. The sacrifice Melissa had made had no equal.

"Mel—I mean, Nurse. Do you know if I have children?"

"You don't. In fact, you can't." Her lips turned down. "I'm sorry. I have to go."

Melissa pulled the curtain back to its original position and exited, leaving Heather at the proverbial fork in the road.

———

10:00 a.m.

HOW COULD SHE HAVE BEEN SO CARELESS? Fifteen percent power left. Would it be enough to call Melissa? She powered it down and tucked her connection to her family history away.

Everything Melissa had said was true. The Huntington newspaper reported the accident and the drug investigations. Other news reported her sister and brother-in-law were heroes, having helped take down a corrupt sheriff's office. An FBI agent was part of them. Braun couldn't be trusted.

She had hoped that her family's photos would jog her memory. Nothing. And worse, Julie had been jailed for murder and almost killed by an inmate. What if Julie had died?

She desperately wanted to call her family—to find out who she was—but Melissa was right. With all the trouble they'd had in Hearthstone, contacting them could only bring more danger.

Only one day. One day to make the choice that might decide whether she lived or died. Dead before she even knew who she was.

Heather reclined her bed and rearranged the pillows, but she couldn't get comfortable. Her head pounded. She pushed the magic button. Maybe more meds would help. She waited several minutes, but no one came. She pressed the buzzer again, but instead of a nurse, Braun appeared—along with Dr. Tolley. They took their usual spots—Braun in front of the window and Tolley at the end of the bed.

Braun smiled. "Good morning, Ms. Doe."

She flinched at the name. Was she a Blanchard like her father? Did it matter? She studied Braun. The only thing that mattered now was that she didn't let him know she knew who she was.

Charlene entered and looked the men over. Raising an eyebrow, she said, "Can I help you?" She took a sentinel stand by Heather.

"Yes. We'd like to ask Ms. Doe a few more questions."

Charlene turned to Heather. "Your call."

Declining would make her look like she had something to hide. She could do this. She pushed the tilter button to raise her bed and sat up. "My head and ribs are killing me, and I don't remember anything, so let's keep this short."

Charlene patted Heather's hand. "If you're okay, I'll just go."

"Could you get my meds?"

"Of course. Be right back."

122

Braun took a step closer. "Ms. Doe, have you remembered anything since we were here last?"

"I just told you—no." Her heart raced as she measured her response. It wasn't a lie. She had learned things but hadn't *remembered* anything.

"Did you find out who I am?"

Braun shook his head. "Remember the rules. We ask the questions."

"Who wrote these rules?"

Charlene returned and handed Heather a small cup of pills and water. She tossed them in the back of her mouth, took in a mouthful of water, and swallowed. She crushed the paper pill cup into a ball, then grimaced at a pain shooting through her head.

"Do you want the agents to leave?"

She did, but . . . "No, give me a minute" She inhaled. The pain abated. "Let's cut to the chase. Why are you here? Did I do something wrong?"

Tolley straightened. "Do you *think* you did something wrong?"

Not again.

"No—actually, I don't. I feel like I'm a decent person—unless that can change with amnesia or brain damage." She looked at Braun. "You know, you said Dr. Tolley was here to help me remember, but all he does is mock me."

Braun tipped his chin to Tolley.

"I'll stay quiet."

"I saw the news." Heather's voice rose. "You think the driver was a drug dealer, right? I wouldn't know how to do a drug deal if my life depended on it."

"Calm down. I told you we're not the enemy."

"*You* calm down. You come in here and pester me instead of letting me get rest. My head is killing me, but do you care? No. You keep coming back." Her head throbbed. She squeezed her temples as if she could push the pain away.

"I think you need to leave." Charlene stepped toward the door as if directing the men out.

"Ms. Doe, we're trying to help," Tolley said.

Heather scowled at him. "I don't know how. Can you give me my memories back?"

"Actually, discussing events might help you connect to your buried memories. The brain is very tricky. The information is in there."

"Oh, so you think I'm crazy? Is that why you're here?" She began to cry.

"That's it." Charlene crossed her arms. "Time to go."

Tolley stepped forward. "It's normal to feel frustrated. I apologize for upsetting you. Brain swelling pinches off connections to your memory. Hopefully, the connectors open back up when the swelling goes down, or the brain will form new connections." He patted the end of the bed and nodded. "Frankly, I'd be worried if you weren't frustrated."

Tolley's kind eyes caught her off guard. Did he care? All three of them stared at Heather for a long moment.

Braun started to leave but turned. "Two more questions?"

"If I say yes, will you leave me alone?"

He pulled photos from his jacket pocket but didn't reveal them. "So that you understand how important this is, last week, two of the Johnson brothers and their mother were murdered on the streets of Detroit."

That's what Melissa had said.

He handed her a photo of three people lying in pools of blood on a city sidewalk. She tried to process the horror of the scene but couldn't. She looked away and handed it back.

"Do you recognize anyone in the photo?"

"Oh my God, no." She looked up at him. "Why are you showing me this?"

"The Johnson brothers were part of the gang. They had another brother in Huntington. Johnny."

Braun showed her another picture—a man—or at least body parts that could have been a man. She turned her head away from the grotesque scene.

"Do you recognize him?"

"Should I?"

"We believe he was driving the camper before it exploded. The Mongrels put out the hit. They believed the brothers were skimming their money. Half a million." He paused and stared at her. "Exactly what you had in your possession when you were found."

"*Half a million?*" She glared at Braun. He had finally admitted it. "I may not be good at math, but that's about—let's see—$499,000 more than you mentioned, *Special* Agent Braun."

"We know the camper was run off the road by a stolen vehicle. The descriptions of the two men driving matched those of two gang members. If Johnny Johnson was driving the camper, then it only makes sense that the money was his. Or theirs."

Just like Melissa had said. Johnny's photo flashed in her mind. At least Melissa hadn't seen it.

"So, you believe the money I had belongs to this gang in Detroit?"

Braun nodded. "One more thing. Johnny lived with a young lady named Melissa Thomason. She and her daughter disappeared around the time of the explosion." He handed her a picture of Melissa with long blond hair holding a little girl. If this was how she looked before, even with her memory intact, she might not have recognized the dark-haired woman who had come to see her earlier. She looked so different in the photo. *Happy.*

"What about them?"

"Do you recognize them?"

Heather glared. "Do I really need to answer that?" She scanned the picture again. "Is she involved?"

"I can't comment on that, but if the gang thinks she has their money, then she and her daughter are in danger. You can help them by cooperating."

"Listen, Agent Braun, I may not be the brightest candle in the room, but let's review. You clearly know a lot about this gang and their money, the Johnson brothers, his girlfriend, and her daughter, but I am not hearing what you know about me." She handed the picture back, trying to look nonchalant. "That's what I need to know."

Braun hung his head. "We don't know anything about you."

"Well, neither do I, but it sounds like it's the gang's money, and I had nothing to do with this gang. Do you have anything—anything at all—that ties me to the money or drug dealing?"

"I don't think you understand. Even if you weren't involved, the Mongrels would kill you when they find out you were with him—if they don't already know."

The photo of the dead brothers and their mother flashed through her mind. If everything Braun said was true, that could just as easily have been her, and there was little she could do to protect herself. She had nothing and knew no one. Where could she run?

Maybe the FBI could protect her, but what if that wasn't their goal? Perhaps they were only trying to link her to this gang. Still, they might be her only option if she wanted to stay alive.

"I don't know what to believe. And I have no reason to trust you. You lied to me about the money."

Braun's eyebrow raised. "I guess you'll have to."

Unlike Braun, Melissa had been truthful and forthcoming. Melissa gave her a phone to verify her life independently, but Braun wanted to keep her in the dark. "No, I don't . . . I can't."

"You're making a mistake."

"Am I under arrest?"

"It's more likely you'll be a key witness when you get your memory back."

"Won't that put me in danger?"

"We'll protect you."

"But I'm not a witness now, am I?"

Braun looked at Tolley.

"And what's gonna happen if I don't remember anything before I'm released?"

Braun didn't answer.

"That's what I thought."

Braun shook his head and raised his voice. "Didn't you hear anything I said? No matter where you go, the Mongrels will find you."

"That's hard to believe when even the FBI can't figure out who I am." She looked between the two of them. "Now, gentlemen, I need to get some rest."

Braun took a half step toward her, but Charlene raised a hand like a crossing guard. "You heard Ms. Doe. Out."

They started for the door. Braun said, "This is a mistake, Ms. Doe."

"But it's mine to make."

Braun appeared as if he would speak again, but instead, he and Tolley shared a look, then turned and left without another word.

Heather inhaled a long breath. Charlene patted her hand.

"Do you need anything else?"

"No, thank you."

Charlene turned to leave but paused and turned back to her. Her face puckered. "Do you wanna know what I think?"

Heather nodded.

"I'm afraid for you."

She shrugged slowly. "What can I do?"

"I don't know. I'm glad I'm not in your place. I'll pray for you. But please. Be careful."

She left.

Her heart pounded as she retrieved the cell from under the covers. She slipped out of bed and pulled the curtain back far enough to watch for anyone coming. Sitting back on the edge of the bed, she restarted the phone and prayed there was enough battery. She pushed the button for "Grandma."

Melissa answered after one ring.

"Heather?"

The name still surprised her. "Yes."

"What's going on?"

"I'm in."

There was a pause.

"Why did you decide to come?"

"Research. Plus, the FBI agents confirmed everything you said. They know everything—except who I am. They even know about you."

Melissa uttered a few expletives.

"They didn't seem to want you. Honestly, they seemed concerned for you."

"Bull. They want to question me. But I don't know anything. Johnny kept me out of it."

"They showed me pictures of his mother and brothers. It was awful. They said Johnny was run off the road by two guys who matched the description of the gang members." She didn't dare mention Johnny's picture.

"What did you tell them?"

"I told them I didn't trust them and sent them packing. How much of their money do you have?"

"The other half. Well, and another half mill that Johnny stashed in safe places."

"Wow." Heather tried to picture that much money. "So, what's the plan?

"Tomorrow is Halloween. I'm going to dress like an orderly again. We'll change into Halloween costumes and walk out."

"What time are you coming? That FBI guy will be poking around."

"Tell them the doctor said you won't be out before Thursday. What time is the shift change?"

"Three."

"My goal is two-thirty, but don't freak out if it's later."

"What about my meds?"

"What are they giving you?"

"Percocets."

"Oxycodone?"

"No . . . I mean, I don't think so."

"Oh yes, it is. You'd better get off those. Most of Johnny's customers started with that stuff."

"I can't quit now. I'm in too much pain."

"I'll find some for you, but this is not my thing. I can't take the chance of getting caught buying drugs. You gotta promise to get off that stuff. Soon."

"Of course. I don't like the way they make me feel anyway."

"I'm serious, Heather. I'm not going to have a druggie around my daughter."

Her—a druggie? That would be the day.

"Anything else?"

"Nope. Just be ready. And get rid of that phone. Dunk it in a sink of water, then take the back off, crush it, and leave it on the top shelf of your closet. No one ever cleans there."

"But how will I get hold of you?"

The phone went dead.

Chapter 15

Tuesday, October 31
7:00 a.m.

THE FROSTY AIR STUNG MAX'S LUNGS as he finished his three-mile predawn walk with the six steps up to the landing of his Arlington colonial brick apartment building. The sling made his usual runs impossible and even frustrated his walks. Just as he reached for the keypad by the door, the brunette from 3B emerged wearing a curve-hugging electric-blue suit—every body part in place. He held the door open, unable to move his feet as her Chanel No.5 intoxicated his senses.

"Early run, Enders?"

"Wish I *could* run," was all he could muster as he worked to keep his heart rate down.

She ran her red-manicured fingers up and down the front edge of his sling as she pursed her glossy red lips. "Word has it you're supposed to be on R & R."

This woman knew everything. The FBI should hire her to do intel.

She smirked. "What are you running from, anyway?"

He should be running from this maneater, but he couldn't help himself. "Let me buy you dinner, and maybe we can figure it out together."

"Fat chance, buddy. But nice try. You know my standards—the next guy I hook up with will be my ticket to retirement. Although I will say that those government pensions are pretty tempting."

"Sorry, doll, my ex already staked her claim on half of that."

She shrugged as she tipped her head. "Oh well, a girl can dream, can't she?" She spun around and swung her perfectly-shaped posterior down the sidewalk all the way around to the driver's side of her red BMW, leaving him gawking. Opening the driver's door, she looked back and winked before disappearing into her carriage.

Max shook it off and turned back to the door he had let close. He punched the code, entered, and climbed the staircase to his empty Ikea-furnished apartment. He yanked his sling off even though the doctor had said to keep it on. He was determined not to need it.

He scanned the beige living area, then the white kitchen. He had already washed, scrubbed, vacuumed, and dusted every inch. Three more weeks of this? At least he'd get a reprieve when he returned to West Virginia to testify at the Hearthstone preliminary hearing the following week. For now, he took a shower and got dressed for nothing.

Max made an oversized bacon and cheese omelet—no match for the ones Sarah had made for him at the Wheelers. He was spoiled forever. Even worse, she wasn't there to clean his dishes. But what else did he have to do?

As he dried his white Corelle plate, his cell phone buzzed from the corner of the kitchen counter. Alex's face lit up the screen. He tapped the speaker button.

"Hey, doll, what's the word?"

"Two words. Trick or treat." She giggled.

Halloween. How could he have forgotten? It was his ex's favorite holiday. Her witch costume made all the more sense. "Well, which is it?"

"Treat, for sure. Remember that blonde near Huntington?"

"Yeah."

"It's not the dealer's girlfriend. And guess what?"

"You know I don't like guessing games."

"Sorry. It's the Blanchard girl. She has amnesia, so even she doesn't know who she is, and the agency hasn't figured it out yet. I didn't want to tell them until I spoke to you, but it's her, all right."

"Amnesia? Really? Can you send me her photo?"

His phone dinged.

"Already texted."

"Who's the agent in charge?"

His phone dinged again.

"Eric Braun. FBI. It's a joint DEA/FBI case. I texted you Braun's information and emailed you the case file. Heather's in St. Mary's Hospital, Room 452. You'll get there by one o'clock if you leave now—since I see you're at home and not on a beach in Aruba where I'd be if I had three weeks off."

"Spying on me again?" Max put her on speaker and moved to the bedroom to start packing. "It's a good thing I wasn't away. You're a doll, Alex. Hey—don't forward this intel. At least until I get there and speak to Braun."

"Are you kidding? What intel?"

"I owe you—"

"I know, I know. Another lunch. I'll add it to the IOU list."

"Actually, I think this one warrants a five-star dinner."

"Ooh—a promotion."

Max clicked off and checked the texted photo. It was Heather, all right. Blue streaks and all. If only he could call her family. But he knew better.

He topped off his jump bag with power bars and water, then printed out the case information. Who needed Aruba anyway . . . well, unless the trip involved Ms. 3B.

He snugged on his cowboy hat, ready for Mission Blanchard.

———

10:00 A.M.

HEATHER SKETCHED CHARLENE'S PORTRAIT with the art supplies her sweet nurse had gifted her in an orange pumpkin bucket earlier that morning. While unusual Halloween treats, the black witch had proffered that drawing might help her remember. It hadn't, but something about holding the graphite sticks felt right.

Braun knocked on Heather's open door, sporting a humble deportment and holding another small plastic pumpkin. "Trick or treat."

Her stomach tightened. Even with his warm smile, a homeowner opening their door to the bouncer would hand over the entire candy bowl.

Tolley was not with him. Maybe he wasn't on official business? Still . . . She waved him in, determined not to let her guard down. "Back again?"

He didn't take his usual Men-in-Black stand. Instead, he came to the door-side of the bed and set the pumpkin beside her. "A peace offering."

"Thank you." Heather laid her pad and black chalk on her table and then examined the contents—chocolate kisses and candy corn—her favorites. Or were they? "These are great, but not morning food, you know."

Braun chuckled. "Feeling any better today?"

"I guess so. I still don't remember anything. My ribs only hurt when I breathe, but my headache's not crippling anymore.

"I had broken ribs once. Hurt for months."

"Months? The doctor must have forgotten to mention that part." She was glad she'd be laying low wherever she was going.

"Has the doctor told you when you can leave?"

"He said maybe Thursday."

"Have you changed your mind about letting us protect you?" His eyes were soft with concern. Her heart beat faster as she considered telling him everything. Maybe he *could* protect her. Or maybe he was corrupt like that Hearthstone agent. He *was* here by himself.

The hospital's bedside phone rang. They both stared at the phone that Heather had not heard ring before. Who would call on a landline? Nobody knew who or where she was there except Melissa.

"Aren't you going to answer it?"

"It has to be a wrong number. I don't know anyone."

Braun looked from the phone to her. "What if it's someone who's recognized you?"

Playing cool, she picked up. "Hello?"

"Is the coast clear?"

"I'm sorry, you must have the wrong number." She hung up.

Braun's eyebrow raised. "Who was that?"

She glanced at the nurse's board. "Someone looking for Charlene."

"That's funny." Braun's gaze followed to where Heather's had been. "Isn't that your nurse's name?"

"Oh, yeah. I thought I had heard that name before. Maybe they thought she was here."

Braun examined her face. Could he tell she was lying?

She averted her eyes and reached for her temples. "Ow. I'm sorry. I need to call the nurse. Is there anything else?" She pressed the button.

Witch Charlene arrived, straw broom in hand. "You called, my pretty?"

"Cute." Braun chuckled. "You must be Charlene."

"Why yes, I am."

"Oh, someone just called looking for you."

Charlene's eyebrows squeezed together. "That's strange. They page me on my cell phone."

Braun turned to Heather.

She looked past him before he could make eye contact. "Can I get some meds? My head and ribs are killing me."

"Certainly, my pretty, I'll be right back." She cackled as she left the room.

"Thank you, *Charlene*," Braun called after her while his stare splayed her like a frog pinned to a dissection board.

"Well—if there's nothing else, I need my rest."

"Listen, I don't know what game you're playing or who that was on the phone, but your life is in danger. You don't know who you're toying with here. Please—" he paused, his eyes pleading—"let us help you."

"Help? Ha. You can't even figure out who I am. How can you protect me?" she said louder than she'd meant. "Out!"

Braun cursed. "You're impossible." He spun around and left.

"No—I'm in an impossible situation!" she screamed after him at her pain's peril.

Heather pounded the bed as Charlene returned and came to her bedside.

"Are you okay?"

"No—I'm not okay! How can I be? Make sure that man does not come back to my room!"

Charlene frowned and pulled back.

But Heather wasn't sorry—she couldn't take it anymore.

Chapter 16

12:00 noon

CHARLESTON: THIRTY MILES. Max finished his protein bar and checked his Google Maps app. Sixty-two minutes to Huntington. Time to call Braun. He pulled over and dialed.

"Braun." The all-business deep voice answered.

"Special Agent Eric Braun?"

"Yes, who's this?"

"Special Agent Max Enders." He switched to Bluetooth and pulled back onto the highway.

"Wait a minute. *The* Max Enders of Hearthstone fame?"

So much for undercover anonymity. "That's me. But how—?"

"You're a West Virginia rock star among the agents. When you've been battling this stuff as long as we have, it's nice to see a piece of the iceberg chipped away. What can I do for you?"

"Listen, I'm not on official business."

"I hope not. Didn't you get shot?"

"Flesh wound." His shoulder ached as he said it. "I've got a favor to ask and maybe some information on your Jane Doe at the hospital."

"What kind of information?" His voice tensed. "Do you know who she is?"

"I believe so."

"So?"

"First, the favor."

"You know it doesn't work like that. You can't withhold—"

"It's not like that, but I need you to understand the situation first."

"I'm listening."

"You have to promise not to do anything until I get there. In an hour—"

"What do you mean an hour? You're on your way here?"

"Yes."

"How long have you known?"

"Let's just say I found out today."

Braun cursed. "You know that's withholding."

"If I thought it would have made a difference, I would have called, but I believe—"

"I'll be the judge of that."

"Promise me you'll at least hear me out before you do anything."

"Okay, okay."

"I think that the blonde is Heather Blanchard. She's Richard Wheeler's sister-in-law. Does that name ring a bell?"

"Yeah. He's the PA who was helping you in Hearthstone."

"That's right. I don't see any way she could have been involved with the Johnson boy."

"Why do you say that?"

"Heather was staying with the Wheelers until the night Julie Wheeler was arrested. Pay attention to the timing here. Last Tuesday night—the night before the explosion—she got mad at her sister, got drunk, and took off around midnight." Max paused to give Braun a chance to process the timing.

"*When* did you say Heather left?"

"Midnight last Tuesday."

"Why do you think it's the Blanchard girl?"

"Last Friday, the family asked me to look into her disappearance— unofficially, of course. After they risked their lives for the Bureau, it was the right thing to do. I did some checking. This morning, I received a picture of your Jane Doe. It's Heather—blue-streaked hair and all."

"If the explosion happened about three on Wednesday afternoon, that's only fifteen hours after she left the Wheeler house. She had to have known them."

"Trust me—Heather was not involved with them. She's flaky and can tie on a mean drunk. But otherwise, she's about as innocent as they come. She'd been at the Wheelers for three weeks. Before that, New Mexico for a year. She's never been into drugs. She didn't have time to get involved with Johnson. I know. I had eyes on her until that night. There's nothing connecting them."

"Do you know how crazy this sounds?"

"If you knew Heather . . . well, let's just say trouble finds her. I'd bet she was hitchhiking."

Braun didn't speak for a minute. "Okay, let's say she's not involved. Why do you think you need to come?"

"The family asked. We owe the family at least this much. I know we can't call them, but perhaps if I meet with her, it will jog her memory. Is she a suspect?"

"Not really, but she is in danger. The gang believes she has their money, and we've seen a couple of their guys around the hospital."

"What? Why didn't you arrest them?"

"And destroy a two-year vetting of four agents? This gang has massive ties to drugs, guns, trafficking—you name it. We finally got a police chief willing to take them down, and they're about to pull the trigger. We can't mess this up for anybody. You know that."

Yeah, he knew that better than anyone. They almost lost Julie on their holy mission.

Braun continued, "She's supposed to be released in a couple of days. But I will tell you, she's been acting quirky. We're more than a little concerned she might try to run. The only thing we have going for us is she has no one or nothing to run to without the money—if she's telling the truth about her amnesia." He paused. "She's refusing witness protection. She saw the news about that corrupt FBI agent and the sheriff's office. She's sure I'm on the dark side."

"All the more reason for you to wait until I get there. Maybe if I talk to her, I can convince her I know her family. I might have better luck gaining her trust."

"You say you're an hour out?"

"I should be there by one."

"Okay, I'll meet you in the hospital lobby. Tall, bald, good-looking bodybuilder in a classic FBI suit. And based on the Halloween costumes around here, we'll stand out."

"White shirt, thin tie. Got it. I'll be the one in the cowboy hat and sling."

Chapter 17

_12:15 p.m._

HEATHER PUSHED HER PEAS INTO THE BROWN GRAVY, unable to take a third bite of the meatloaf that smelled better than it tasted. She tossed her fork onto the tray and pushed the table away. What if she and Melissa got caught? Her heart raced. What if Melissa didn't come?

The phone rang, jolting her from her fears and sending a stabbing pain through her ribs. She answered. "Hello?"

"Anyone around?" Melissa asked.

"No. Are you coming?"

The phone clicked off. Heather stared at the receiver and then hung up.

Daring the pain, she slid out of bed to peek down the soft, mint-green hallway full of ghosts, vampires, and even Buzz Lightyear. Braun was leaning against the window of the oak-framed nurse's station, back turned toward her, speaking with Witch Charlene. *Traitor.*

She leaned farther toward the elevators, careful to stay hidden behind a food cart. This was trouble. If Melissa came now, she'd be face-to-face with Braun. There was nothing she could do to avert this. She had to trust Melissa had enough sense to realize who he was and postpone. But how long would she wait?

She returned to her bed as pounding in her heart traveled to her temples. Closing her eyes offered no relief. She watched the clock. Five . . . ten . . . fifteen minutes passed.

A red-bearded man in a Frankenstein costume knocked on the door and entered. Unless Melissa had undergone some major surgery, it was clearly not her.

"Ms. Doe?"

"Yes?"

"Time for another brain scan." He checked her wristband and began preparing the bed for transport.

This couldn't be happening. These tests took a couple of hours. What if Melissa showed up while she was gone?

"I'm sure it's a mistake. Can you check?"

He laughed. "It's no mistake. Besides, don't you want to know if your head is getting better?"

"The doctor already said my swelling had gone down."

"Well, I guess he wants to be sure." Frankenstein raised the sidebars, unlocked the wheels, and rolled her into the haunted hallway. Braun was still there.

When they got to Braun, she raised her hand. "Stop for a minute." Frankenstein obeyed.

"Special Agent Braun, why are you still here?"

"Just keeping an eye out for my favorite patient. And—" he smiled as he held up her sketch of Witch Charlene "—admiring your artwork. This is good. Really good."

"Umm, Hmm." She examined his smiling face. "I could've sworn I told Charlene you're not welcome here. This is harassment. Am I under arrest?"

"No, ma'am."

"Then you need to leave. I can't rest with you stalking me." Heather looked at the turncoat nurse. "Can he be here if it hurts my recovery?"

"No."

"Then please ask him to leave."

Charlene retrieved her sketch. "You heard the lady. Please leave and call before returning—or I'll have to cast a spell on you." She pointed her fingers at him and wiggled them.

Braun shook his head. "Yes, ma'am." He looked at Heather for a long moment as if wanting to say more, but instead headed for the visitor elevators.

"We're good to go." Frankenstein guided her down a hallway past Braun to the staff elevators. They boarded and began their descent.

Where on earth was Melissa? Had she given up?

Dear Lord, If you're real, help me.

The elevator doors opened on the third floor. Melissa stood in the hallway dressed in green scrubs. Her face blanched. She looked between Heather and Frankenstein, then smiled.

"Oh good, you saved me a trip." Melissa grabbed the bar that ran along the foot of the bed. "They sent me to intercept you. They changed Ms. Doe's orders. I'll take her from here."

"Really?"

"Really." Melissa pulled Heather's bed out of the elevator, leaving Frankenstein behind. "Oh, and they told me you need to go to personnel. Said you had some paperwork to fill out—new tax laws, you know.

"I just did my forms," he said as the elevator doors closed, leaving the two alone in the foyer. Melissa rolled Heather's bed to the main hallway past groups of costumed staff. They made two right turns to a smaller, unoccupied hallway and stopped next to a supply room.

"Get off."

Heather's ribs jabbed her as she slid off the bed. Melissa motioned for her to enter the shelving-unit-lined supply room full of paper goods and medical supplies.

"Stay here." Melissa closed the door.

Where was she going? Heather cracked the door and poked out her head as Melissa rolled the bed back down the hallway and around the corner. She returned a moment later.

"Get back inside."

"Sorry." Heather backed up as Melissa shooed her in and then followed.

Melissa's face twisted as she yelled a whispered, "What if someone had seen you?"

"You're right." With all Melissa was doing for her, she needed to pay attention. Between the pain and the drugs, focusing was not easy.

Melissa grabbed a box from a shelf and removed a small bag from inside. She emptied its contents—wipes, gauze, bandages, ointment, and scissors. "Let me see your IV."

"What?"

"Just do it."

Heather held out her right arm as Melissa opened a sanitizer package and swabbed around the IV. She placed a piece of gauze over the IV, then pulled it out. "Hold this," she said, tipping her chin to the gauze.

Heather replaced Melissa's fingers. "Looks like you know what you're doing."

"Not really—just had a few of these. You wouldn't want me to put one in." Melissa grinned as she peeled a bandage and put it over the gauze pad. "That should do it." She cut off Heather's medical bracelet, pulled a large black department store bag from the top shelf, and retrieved two clown costumes.

"Wow, you thought of everything."

"I hope so." Melissa separated the one-piece jumpsuits.

Heather painfully bent over, pulled her costume to her waist, then removed her gown, leaving her bare-chested. "Bra?"

"Sorry. Guess I didn't think of everything." She waved it off. "With the frilly neckpiece, nobody will notice."

"A bra would probably hurt too much anyway." She pulled up the top and turned for Melissa to button it closed.

When they'd finished changing, Melissa stuffed their clothes in the bag.

"Did you come to my floor?"

"Yep. I saw a bald bouncer in a suit hanging out at the nurses' station. FBI?"

She nodded. "Special Agent Braun."

"Wouldn't want to cross him. After I saw him, I came back here and waited. I had just decided to try again when you guys showed up."

"I can't believe how you got me away from the orderly. Even I was convinced you worked here."

Melissa's eyes widened. "I was so sure our plan was busted." She added the trash and medical supplies to the shopping bag.

"What about masks? With my face?" Heather grimaced.

"Don't worry." Melissa pulled a makeup kit and a mirror out. "Better than masks, and with you being an artist, figured it'd be your thing."

Heather's heart warmed when she saw the cosmetic brushes, sponges, and face paint. She covered Melissa's face with white paint. With the black, she drew outlines of diamonds around Melissa's eyes and a clown frown. She filled the shapes in with blue and red, then dabbed on highlights. Melissa put on her red nose. It was perfect. Heather handed her the mirror.

Melissa turned it this way and that. "Wow. If all else fails, you can always join the circus."

Heather frowned.

"Sorry."

"It's okay. Probably would have been funny another time."

Opting for a happy smile, Heather painted her face, thankful that her bruises covered easily.

Once her face was perfect, they put on curly red wigs and floppy shoes. Melissa held up the mirror so they could look together. They looked like twins—one happy, one sad. In another life, she would have snapped a selfie. But this was not a day she'd want to remember.

Melissa added the paint supplies to the trash bag and shoved it on the top shelf. "Ready?"

All the commotion was stirring Heather's stomach, but she couldn't fall apart now or complain to Melissa. She prayed she didn't throw up. It would kill her ribs.

"Listen. We're clowns. We need to act like clowns." She hooked a horn to Heather's costume. "If anyone talks to you, blow this horn. Remember, clowns don't talk."

Heather didn't know if she was good at improv, but they were going to find out.

Melissa cracked the door and peeked out, then opened it wide. "It's clear. Let's go."

"Music to my ears."

On their way to the elevators, they passed a group of aliens huddled around a nurses' station. Melissa honked. The aliens laughed and pointed.

That was easy.

As they passed Smurfette, Heather tried her own horn. Smurfette's long yellow wig spread around her as she did a quick twirl and moved past them. This was really working.

She took a deep breath in the elevator foyer as Melissa pressed the button. She reached for the horn's bulb as the numbers over the doors decreased. The metal walls opened to six doctors, who chuckled at the horn's sound as they exited.

"Trick or treat!" one said as they passed.

Heather honked her horn again as she stepped in, causing another round of laughs. One of the men threw a thumbs-up over his shoulder. "Great costumes."

Heather flopped her shoes and honked again. Was she really doing this? Was she an extrovert? If only she knew.

The doors closed. Her stomach rose into her throat as they descended. Just a little bit farther.

The doors opened to the sunny first-floor hallway. Oak-framed windows surrounded a waiting area. A handful of un-costumed visitors sat on blue sofas and chairs. Heather followed Melissa to the right toward the reception desk between the windowed waiting room and the tiled entryway. A steady stream of ghouls, pirates, and

Dr. Seuss characters filed in and out of the front doors. A pumpkin and a queen operated phones and greeted visitors.

Another carpeted blue-furnished seating area filled out the other side of the reception. *Oh, no.* Braun and Tolley stood chatting on the carpet to the right of the doors. Heather's breath caught. Braun looked their way, then looked a little harder. Melissa honked her horn twice, garnering laughs from some elves as the pair wobbled toward the front door.

Someone called out, "Trick or treat," from behind them.

Heather honked her horn but didn't look back until she got through the doors. The agents hadn't moved but were looking in their direction. Just as she turned back forward, she bumped hard into a man wearing a sling, knocking him and his cowboy hat to the ground.

"Hey, watch it!" The cowboy raised his sling.

Stunned, Heather looked him in the eyes. Something about him—

Melissa grabbed her arm and pulled her toward a car across the drive, the driver waiting. Melissa opened the rear door. "Get in!" She shoved Heather inside, then climbed in behind her and shut the door. "Quick. Up the hill around the building. Go!"

The driver began to pull out but was stopped when a passenger boarded the car in front of them in the drive.

Heather looked over her shoulder. Tolley and Braun came out while the cowboy got himself up. Tolley picked up the cowboy's hat while Braun talked to him. Were they together? The man pointed at their car.

"Hurry! I think that cowboy recognized me."

The driver looked in the mirror. "You in some kinda trouble?"

Melissa handed him a hundred-dollar bill. "Now go!"

The cowboy started toward them. He called out to her. "Heather!"

"Go! Go! Go!" Melissa quickly slapped the back of the passenger's seat, punctuating her words.

The driver jumped the curb to the road that ran up the hill, a trail of crushed landscaping behind them. Melissa leaned between the seats and instructed the driver through a series of right turns to the backside of the hospital and down the hill on the other side. Instead of leaving the campus, they turned into a parking garage close to the hospital entrance.

"What are we doing?" Heather's heartbeat drummed in her ears. "We need to get away from here."

"I know what I'm doing." Melissa tapped the driver's shoulder and pointed. "Let us off at the elevator." She handed him another bill. "Here's a hundred to drive to the Huntington Mall. Will you do that?"

"For that kind of money? Sure."

They spilled out of the car and ran clumsily in their clown shoes to the elevator. They jumped inside before the doors were fully open. A strong urine smell overwhelmed Heather as Melissa repeatedly punched the fourth-floor button. The doors finally closed.

"What are you thinking? They're gonna find us."

Melissa shook her head. "First, they have to get to their car and put out a BOLO for the car we left in. They'll follow the driver until they figure out we're not in the car. They'll never look for us close by. By the time they double back, we'll be long gone. And with our new looks, they won't recognize us or our car even if they see us."

"They know our costumes."

"I'm not talking about that. You would never have recognized me from that picture, would you?"

"No, but what about me?"

"You'll see.

The doors opened to blinding sunshine, piercing Heather's eyes and sending shards of agony through her head. Melissa tugged her arm to hurry her to the far side of the garage's rooftop to a dull tan Grand Marquis with a peeling black vinyl top. The doors creaked as Heather climbed into the musty clunker with a torn roof lining and stained seats. Did this woman truly have half a million stashed away?

No time to turn back now.

Melissa jumped into the back and dumped a shopping bag onto the seat beside her. "Take off your wig and shoes and hand them to me. Then put these on," she said as she handed up a maroon sweatshirt and jeans.

Heather couldn't get the scratchy disguise off fast enough as Melissa tossed some sneakers forward. Melissa had no idea of the pain she was asking her to endure. She reminded herself that Melissa was helping her.

Melissa passed up some makeup remover wipes. "Let me know if you need more, then get the wig and clips out of the glove box and put it on."

Ten paint-covered wipes later, Heather pulled out the short red wig, pinned her hair up, tugged it on, and checked it in the visor's mirror. Ha. She liked it.

"Good look on you. We'll cut and dye your hair later."

Cut? Dye? Was that in character for whoever she was?

Melissa stuffed the old one in the bag, hopped out, threw the bag over the side, then slipped into the driver's seat.

"What'd you do that for? What if somebody saw that?"

Melissa cranked the car. "There's a dumpster down there. And God knows, even cops don't like to dumpster dive." She backed out and headed for the eight turns to freedom.

1:10 p.m.

MAX CURSED AND BEAT THE AIR IN DEFEAT as the clown's car hopped the curb and headed up the hill. He turned to Braun. "It was Heather. I'm sure of it."

Braun looked at Tolley. "Call in the BOLO . . . Silver Ford Taurus driven by a dark-haired, white male in his thirties . . . a happy and sad clown in the back. Tag number 2PS 123." He shook his head and looked at Max. "If *you* got that call, would *you* believe that BOLO wasn't a prank?"

Max mirrored Braun's dismay.

Braun pointed to the parking lot at the top of the hill where the Taurus had turned. "You're with me."

Max strained to keep up, but stopped just shy of the lot to catch his breath. Adjusting his sling, he scoped out the girls' escape route between the hospital and a brick building topped with HVAC equipment. Residences lay beyond.

A dark SUV pulled up beside him as its window opened. Braun motioned him in. "Come on, lightweight."

"Yeah, you try running in boots with a sling." Max opened the door and slid in. "They could be anywhere."

"You know,"—Braun pointed ahead—"I think this road dead ends in a worker's parking lot."

Braun hooked around in front of the HVAC building but found an exit to the residential road. Sitting at the stop sign, he banged the steering wheel and cursed. "The girls could have gone either way with dozens of possible routes through neighboring streets." He shook his head. "Why do I feel like we're the clowns? I hate Halloween."

"Heather's too much of a flake to have planned this. Got any idea who her accomplice might be?"

"Assuming Heather actually has amnesia, only one person makes sense." Braun turned to him. "It had to be Johnny's girlfriend."

"I don't get that. Why would she help Heather? Unless she thinks Heather has that money. But if they had talked, wouldn't Heather have told her she didn't have it?"

"Who knows? Maybe Heather was using her to get out. You want in on this detail—officially?"

"You bet."

"I'll arrange it. You can stay at my place. I have an apartment above my garage."

Max nodded.

Braun called in their status and requested his assignment to the case.

So much for Max questioning whether the job was worth it. He pictured Doc Blanchard's pleading eyes. It would be worth every minute if he could bring her back to her family.

After clicking off, Braun pointed back toward the hospital. "Let's get back up there, check her room and talk to the staff. Then we can get your car—"

"Truck.

"Why am I not surprised, cowboy? We can drop it by my place on the way to the office."

Braun waited for a tan Grand Marquis coming up the hill to pass, then turned left to make a three-point turn on the narrow red-brick road and head back to the parking lot.

1:25 p.m.

HEATHER'S STOMACH KNOTTED at the sight of the black SUV waiting for them to pass as Melissa drove up the red brick road. The cowboy. "Oh, my God—"

"Be cool. They're not looking for an old car with normal people. They're looking for a silver Taurus with two clowns."

As they passed the SUV, Melissa said, "Don't turn to look. Eyes forward."

"Are they following us?"

Melissa didn't answer, her eyes fixed on the rearview mirror.

"Well?"

With a deep breath, Melissa said, "They turned back into the parking lot. I told you."

"Doesn't sound like you were that sure. Where're we going."

"Not far. We're switching cars in case they have surveillance cameras in the garage. They'll assume we're far away by now. They'll never look here."

The Grand Marquis' suspension squeaked as the tires bounced over the uneven brick roads behind the hospital. "There." Melissa pointed and pulled behind a blue hybrid Prius parked by the curb lined with primarily lived-in houses.

The blood drained from Heather's face as a haunting feeling engulfed her at the sight of the car.

Melissa examined Heather's face. "Are you okay?"

"The car."

Melissa looked at the Prius and then back at Heather. "What about it?"

Shaking her head slowly, she said, "I don't know."

"We don't have time for this." Melissa shoved her door open. "Let's go."

Heather eased herself into that unmistakable new car smell, glad to be done with the stench of the old wreck, but still uneasy about this car. Her heart stopped as Melissa drove down the brick roads past the hospital, but beat again when they returned to real streets and finally the interstate.

"Where're we going?"

Melissa pointed straight ahead. "East."

"I can see that, but where?"

"I'll tell you in a couple of hours—just in case. I don't want you to have to lie."

That was good with Heather. She had lied enough. But still . . .

"What *can* you tell me?"

"We're going to a city large enough to avoid Nosy Nellies and still find the supplies we might need, but still remote enough to stay off the radar."

Unless Melissa changed direction, Virginia and the Atlantic Ocean were the only places east of them. "How long before we get there?"

"It'll be dark when we arrive."

The idea of Virginia was comforting . . . but why? It was an impression—nothing specific. How much longer would she have to live in the darkness of her own mind?

She located the seat lever and pulled on it to release the seat back. Her rib cage rebelled. "I'm so sick of this pain." She returned the back to its original position. "Did you get my meds?"

"Yes, but are you sure you want them?"

"You have no idea. Every time I move, it feels like my broken rib is gonna puncture my lungs. The doctor said it won't, but that's how it feels. If only I could relax."

Melissa retrieved a bottle from the console. "Do you know how addictive these are?" She shook the bottle. "I've lost too many friends to overdoses."

"I'm not going to OD. And I'm not going to get addicted. Just until the pain goes away." She took the bottle. "Got a drink?"

"No—sorry."

Heather swallowed one dry, then tried to find a comfortable seat angle, but it hurt no matter what she did. Before long, the pill started to take effect. That was better.

Chapter 18

_4:00 p.m._

HOW DID THAT POEM GO? _'Twas the afternoon before Trunk-or-Treat, and all through the dealership_ . . . Dexter grinned as he and Rockefeller surveyed his decorated empire below. Trunks full of candy, ready for the evening barrage. Preschoolers had pillaged his treasures before lunch. He would never have believed that it only took a bucket of candy to bring in over ten thousand potential buyers every year. What chumps.

Matty particularly loved dressing up. Spider-Man this year. And every year, Matty begged Dexter to dress up. Like hell. Especially after Mary Ellen made him put on that ridiculous Dracula outfit for the Halloween Ball at the club last Saturday. Eventually, Matty gave up and returned to making sure he had plenty of pumpkin spice for the lattes.

Maybe, he should reconsider. Dexter could threaten to sink in his fangs better than Luke Evans, Thomas Kretschmann, Gerard Butler, and even Bela Lugosi ever did. He waved his arm as if he had on a black cape. "I vant to suck your blood."

Rockefeller raised his head from the dog couch Dexter had custom-built for him as Nancy called from her office on the other side of the open door. "What?"

"Nevermind."

Dexter checked his watch. Maybe he could get to the lake house for a few hours before he had to return for the car giveaway at eight. He pulled out the secure cell, popped in his earbud, and dialed Charlie.

"Yes, boss?"

"I'm heading to the lake house. Anything I need to deal with before I go?"

"No, boss. The girl's still in the hospital. Still can't remember anything. Sure you don't want us to take care of her while she's there?"

"No, no. Too obvious. Needs to be an accident."

"Hold on, boss. One of my managers is calling."

Dexter paced in front of the glass wall as the seconds ticked by. He hung up. He didn't wait for anyone—his time was too valuable.

Managers' calls usually meant trouble. Charlie's men still hadn't located his money, Cruz, the Wheelers, or the old sheriff. They still hadn't eliminated the failed Hearthstone management, whose preliminary hearing was coming up the following Wednesday. Smitty's efforts were a joke, and not one Hearthstone loose end had been tied up.

The past week had brought too many phone calls from Charlie. Thankfully, Dexter had wisely heeded his MBA training to have layers of management. No way to connect any one thing to him personally. Well, maybe that's not exactly how they'd framed it in college. Perhaps he needed to write a how-to textbook to successfully operate his kind of organization.

Actually, his operation took pages from the Al Qaeda playbook by operating in cells—or pods, as Dexter preferred to refer to them. No pod knew what the other was doing. He really should write that book. Maybe he'd call it, *The Successful Disorganization.*

His phone rang. He let it ring three times to make Charlie squirm. "What is it?"

"The girl's gone. Our guys think she left in a clown costume, along with another clown. They also saw that undercover FBI agent from Hearthstone, Max Enders. He met up with the Huntington agents just before they chased the clowns. Word has it the girl was Wheeler's sister. Bones thinks the other one could be Johnny's girlfriend."

Dexter cursed. Were his pods touching? "How could that be?"

"We don't know, boss."

"Did Bones check with Hawthorne?"

"He tried, but Hawthorne didn't pick up."

That was not the right answer. "Is Hawthorne still on our team?"

"Yeah, boss. You know how it is. Sometimes he can't answer. It would blow his cover."

"What are you doing about all this?"

"The boys think they know where the girlfriend got her car. It's a guy who helps people disappear. They're confident they'll find her."

"They'd better."

———

4:15 p.m.

AN FBI RESIDENT AGENCY DOESN'T EVEN RISE to the level of a field office, so Max's expectations weren't likely to be dashed when they stepped off the worn elevator to Braun's floor. Introductions were made to the various suits they passed down the hallway to the agents' bullpen. Room dividers separated the eight desks stocked with mismatched desk accessories.

"This way," Braun said as they approached a glass-front office. The balding heavy-set man inside stood as Braun entered with Max just behind.

Braun pointed his hand to each as he made introductions. "Resident Agent in Charge Garth Hancock, this is Special Agent Max Enders."

Max removed his hat, set it on the desk, and held out his left hand for the awkward handshake.

"I kinda figured." Hancock pointed to Max's sling. "Dead giveaway."

He motioned for them to take the seats across from him, then took his own. "Great job in Hearthstone. We're glad to have your help on this one. I know you have a special interest in finding the Blanchard girl. We think whatever ties she's established may help

155

us nail the Mongrels. Sorry to say it, but she's likely the type of bait that will draw them out."

His stomach tightened at the thought they would use her like they had Julie.

The chief tapped the desk, eyeing Max. "You sure you're up to this? I had to pull some strings to get you back to work with that injury— you know how the service is about gunshots. Hell, you haven't even done your psych eval yet."

"It's the cowboy hat, isn't it?"

Hancock half-laughed. "Is it true what they say? Are you truly as proficient left-handed as right?"

Max grinned. "Yes, sir. It started as a stupid bet at the academy. Sure has come in handy, though."

"Well, good. I'm glad to hear it. Maybe we should make that part of our mandatory training." He laughed, then grew serious.

"I don't know what Braun has told you, but we have a joint task force working with the DEA to bring down the Detroit/West Virginia drug connection. Braun will brief you on the history and where we're at, but your focus will be locating the Blanchard and Thomason girls."

"Did you say Thomason?"

Hancock nodded. "What of it?"

Max sifted the name through his mind but couldn't place it. "I know that name. It'll probably come to me in the middle of the night."

"Always my best thinkin' time." The chief rose again. "Braun will show you a desk you can use and show you the ropes."

Max stood and returned his hat to his head. "Thank you for letting me in on this."

"Okay, then. Good hunting. Let me know if there's anything you need."

Max hoped he meant it. "Thank you, sir."

Braun led him out of the office to an empty desk in the bullpen. "You can use this desk if we're ever in the office—which I don't plan to be. For now, let's head over to the war room." They took two turns to a conference room with four whiteboards along one side of the table. Strings connected information cards and photos—some with Xs through them, including the Johnson brothers.

Braun picked up one of the phones in the center of the table and pushed a button. "Could you bring Agent Enders the file I asked you to put together? . . . Yes, in the war room."

"This is massive."

"Yeah, we have six agencies working together." Braun shook his head. "What really stinks is that there's already a new gang moving into Huntington. There are deep family connections here with Detroit." Pointing, Braun said, "Bones here is the head of the Mongrels. Can you imagine calling your gang Mongrels?

Max shrugged. "Nobody said they were bright."

"They wear MCM tattoos on their arms." Braun pointed to a photo. "With profits down, he's on the rampage. Somewhere up the food chain is a paranoid egotist who's convinced his people are skimming. He's killing them off to prove it." Braun pointed to the Detroit board with the largest number of X'd pictures. "Eight that we know of in the last week. Pretty soon, we won't have anyone left to arrest."

An attractive older woman delivered a thick manila file to Braun and left. He began sifting through the pages. "Most of the Mongrels are in Detroit, but with the number of thugs Bones has been sending, you need to be familiar with them all."

"Who were the guys seen at the camper?"

"We're not sure, but we think it's these two." Braun pointed out two men on the Detroit board. "They have two jobs—erasing problems and picking up money. They're the guys we saw at the hospital. I hope they didn't recognize Heather when she escaped."

"With that one-way street, we would have seen them."

"Maybe. But these guys have people everywhere."

"What did the Uber driver say when they brought him in?"

"He said he dropped them off in the parking garage across from the outpatient center. They were on the campus the whole time."

"Clever." Max contemplated the amount of planning that had been done. "These girls aren't going to be easy to find. We have to assume they have new identities and are long gone. The question is, how long gone are they?"

"For their sake, let's hope they're outside the Mongrel's reach."

"How far is that?"

"Good question. When you think you have it figured out, they pop up somewhere else."

Max picked up a photo of Melissa holding her daughter. He looked at Braun and pointed to the girl. "Maybe not so long gone after all."

Chapter 19

5:10 p.m.

"Heather. wake up."

How long had she been out? Where were they? Her neck rebelled when she righted her pounding head. Unlike Huntington's dull rolling foothills, they were now snaking through majestic mountains crowned in green pines amidst bare trees splashed with the remains of autumn. What was left of daylight peeked through the roadside forest like a strobe light.

Regardless of how she had turned, she hadn't been able to find a pain-free seat position. She never thought she'd long for a hospital bed. Her ribs threatened to pierce her lungs as she raised her seat back. "Dear Lord. Are we there yet?"

"You sound like my daughter. We have another couple of hours. But I gotta go."

"Me too. And my mouth . . . I need a drink." Heather turned her neck side to side to work out the stiffness. "Speaking of your daughter, where is she?"

She frowned. "I'll explain when we stop."

As they rounded a mountain, a green road sign came into view announcing Covington, 1 mile. Melissa tapped off the cruise control

"I thought we went east. Why are we in Kentucky?"

Melissa chuckled as she took the exit. "This is Covington, Virginia. We crossed the state line a few miles back."

No wonder Melissa was more relaxed. She pulled into a gas station and backed in on the far side next to red-doored restrooms—outside anyone's view. Red front doors on houses meant welcome. What did these mean?

Melissa pushed her door open. "Can you go in and get the key while I change our tags?"

"Change our tags?"

"Yeah. Virginia tags. No one will be looking for these."

Was there anything Melissa hadn't thought of—besides bringing drinks? And a bra.

A bell announced Heather's entrance into the ancient convenience store, crowded only with 1950s shelving units, Budweiser lights, and Marlboro ads. Weighing in at three hundred-something pounds, the black-lipped thirty-something clerk slid a magazine under the counter and glared at Heather like someone who had been caught with pornography. She flipped her straight black hair back over her shoulder, exposing her spiked dog collar. Did she need to be leashed?

The cash register displayed a sign in bold letters, restroom key for customers only.

Dare she ask? But she couldn't wait. It had been hours.

Before she could ask, the bulldog leaned forward, raised her pierced eyebrow, and said in a low growl, "It's for customers."

"I get that. I'll be a customer after I go. I won't want a drink until then—if you know what I mean."

The clerk eyed Heather, then handed over an eighteen-inch plastic rod holding a single key.

"Wow." Heather brandished the rod like a sword and smiled. "The key for relief and the rod for protection."

The clerk just stared.

She backed toward the door. "I'll just go now." The bell jingled, reassuring Heather she was out of the danger zone.

160

Outside, Melissa was finishing up at the back of the car. She tipped her chin toward the red doors. "Go ahead. Still have to do the front plates."

Sure she would find bugs and filth, Heather slowly pressed the red door open. Despite the worn condition, the white-tiled floor was clean, the paper products were stocked, and soap filled the dispenser. The scent of pine cleaner tickled her nose. She gripped the sink to brace for the sneezing agony she couldn't stop. If her rib wasn't cracked before, it was now. The meds must have worn off while she slept.

When she was done, she returned to Melissa, who was pacing next to the car. Heather handed her the weapon. "Hey, could I have some money before you go in? I need a drink."

"Oh, sorry, sorry." Melissa opened the trunk and pulled out a blue-jean-blue leather hobo bag with long tassels on either side. "Here you are."

"Great taste."

"It's your taste. You picked one like it when we went shopping last week—only it was in chartreuse. Thought this might not stand out as much."

"I picked this out?" Heather turned it back and forth. "Wow. I do love the tassels. I guess my tastes haven't changed, even if I don't remember what they are."

While Melissa bolted to the red door, she called back, "There's cash in the wallet."

Inside the purse, Heather found a cell phone and a matching wallet containing a Virginia driver's license with her as a redhead and the name Cynthia Lohman. Really?

Heather checked to be sure no one was watching, then counted the money. Several hundred dollars in various denominations—certainly enough to get a drink. She tried to be thankful for not being indigent, but was this better? A fugitive on the run?

Melissa came out. "Now we can talk."

Heather held up the driver's license. "Cynthia Lohman?"

"Or Cindy. I hope you like the name."

"Aren't Cindys blondes?"

"Ha. Not Cindy Lohman. It's better than Jane Doe, though, right?"

"I guess. Where did you get this picture of me with red hair?

"Remember when you and Olivia were watching *Aladdin* at my house?"

Heather shook her head. "Me? Remember?"

"Sorry. Anyway, I snapped a picture of you with my daughter at the house. A little photo magic"—Melissa waved the key rod— "and, voila! Cynthia Lohman."

"Oh, dear God. We have to get that key back to Spike before she comes after us."

Melissa scrunched her face. "What?"

"You'll see. Come on.

"No. You get your drink. Then I'll go in. I don't want to be seen together just in case someone asks about *two* girls."

"Good thinking. Be right back." Heather turned back to the store.

"Hey, Cindy . . . Cindy . . . Jane Doe!"

Heather stopped at the door and looked back. "I get it. It shouldn't take me long to get used to. I'm still not used to Heather. What's your name?

"Kelsey. Kelsey Gilbert."

"And your daughter's name?"

"Jasmine."

"Like in the movie *Aladdin*?"

"What makes you think Olivia isn't going to tell people our real names?"

"I told her these were our *Virginia* names. Of course, she's excited to be Jasmine."

"Okay, Kelsey."

Heather opened the door.

The bulldog turned at the sound of the bell and stared.

"Thanks for the key." She laid the key on the countertop. Hoping to elicit some goodwill, Heather smiled and waited.

The cashier scowled instead.

"I'm just going to do my customer thing now." She hoped Bulldog's lease was short.

The sole drink station offered six soda flavors, ice, and water. She hadn't had anything fizzy at the hospital. She eyed the beer cooler to her right. Melissa—or Kelsey may not have appreciated that. Maybe later.

She got drinks for both of them, checked out, and headed back to the car.

Melissa met her at the corner of the building.

"I got you a drink."

"Thanks. Would you set it in the car? I need some food. I'll be right back."

"Don't rattle her cage."

Melissa shook her head.

"Don't say I didn't warn you."

Heather returned to the waiting Prius, carefully lowered herself into the seat, uncapped the pill bottle, and eyed the contents—maybe two dozen tablets. Not even enough for a week, much less the months of pain Braun had warned her about. Her chest tightened. What was she going to do? What *could* she do? She downed one and chased it with her drink, then clutched her lifeline to her chest.

Several minutes later, Melissa returned with protein bars and a coffee. Heather tucked the pill bottle into her new purse.

"You weren't kidding about rattling her cage. Oh my God. She should come with a BEWARE OF DOG sign." Melissa replaced the soda with the coffee and handed Heather a protein bar. "I realized I needed that for the rest of the drive."

"Wow, that coffee smells good." Heather took a bite of her treat. She hadn't realized she was hungry.

"I figured you'd want to sleep, so I didn't get you one." Melissa started the car and returned to the interstate.

"You were going to tell me about your daughter—Jasmine."

"She's with a babysitter at the cabin I rented in Charlottesville.

"Charlottesville?"

"Well, Crozet, actually. It's just west of Charlottesville. The cabin's remoteness gives us less chance of being found."

"But you've been gone for days. How'd you find a babysitter you could trust for that long?"

"Believe me. I almost didn't leave. But the cabin's owners are the sweetest folks you've ever met—a retired pastor and his wife. He recommended this woman he's known for years."

"That's it? Did you at least know the pastor before?"

"No. And don't look at me like I'm a bad mother. I had my friend run a background check on the babysitter. She's as clean as a whistle—retired elementary teacher. And when I met her, both my daughter and I loved her. She knew the cabin property like the back of her hand, and there were all kinds of woodsy things they made plans to do there. It's like a sleep-away camp."

"Who'd you get to run the background check if you don't know anyone with your new alias?"

"It's the same guy who did the IDs, so he already knows me and my alias."

"And how did you know him?"

Melissa's face blanched. "It was someone Johnny knew and introduced me to."

Heather's stomach knotted. "You mean he has drug dealer ties? What were you thinking?"

"It's not like that. Johnny said nobody in the business knew this guy. He was safe." Water pooled in her eyes as she fingered the emerald ring on her left hand. She took a deep breath and wiped away the tears.

Not knowing how to comfort Melissa, Heather remained quiet for a while as the road signs began to feature Charlottesville.

"I feel like I've been here before. I know I love Thomas Jefferson's architecture, but I don't know if it's from studying it or being there."

"Not surprising. You're an artist, after all. We'll have to visit the University's Rotunda and Jefferson's home Monticello one day while we're here. It'll help keep Olivia busy."

"Isn't she in school?"

"Not yet. She just turned four."

Four. Heather shivered. An impression, but still no solid memory. "I saw her picture. She's adorable."

Melissa's face tensed. *"What?* Where?"

"The FBI agent showed it to me."

Her face froze. As her body wilted, she pulled to the side of the road. Sobs engulfed her. "Oh my God," she cried between breaths. "Oh my God. What have I done?" She buried her face in her hands. "All I wanted to do was give her a better life, and now she's a four-year-old fugitive."

Heather had been so consumed with her own misery, she hadn't considered what Melissa was going through—uprooting her entire life, leaving her daughter with strangers, and losing her lover. It was enough to put anyone over the edge.

She laid a gentle hand on Melissa's shoulder. "You did what you had to do. You did your best."

"That's not good enough. Look where it got me." She turned her reddened face to Heather. "Look where it got *you.*"

"Crying about it now isn't going to change anything." Wait. Had she just said that? What a pat statement. But Melissa's breathing began to slow, and she sat up straight.

Heather found a tissue in her purse and handed it to her. "Right now, we need to get you back to your daughter. And, based on the fact that I've had some pain meds—and I have broken ribs—somehow, I think you're the better candidate for driver." Heather smiled, hoping to evoke the same from Melissa.

It worked. Melissa's lips turned up slightly. "You're right. I need to get home to my girl."

She handed Melissa her coffee. "Now, drink up, and let's get there. I can't wait to meet her . . . again."

Melissa took a sip and pulled the car back onto the road toward their new lives. Whatever that was. Heather closed her eyes and tried to remember anything from her life before. Nothing. The drugs kicked in, and she was finally at peace.

———

7:20 p.m.

A SIREN'S SCREAM YANKED HEATHER from her sleep. She gulped a deep breath, immediately regretting her need to breathe.

"What the heck?" Her heart pounded. They'd been caught.

Melissa pulled to the shoulder of the two-lane paved road as a paramedic truck sped by, its emergency lights flashing eerie red silhouettes of bare trees against the darkness.

"Oh my God. I thought we were busted."

Melissa eyed her. "I bet. You were sound asleep."

The moonless night concealed the countryside that must have stretched beyond the white fences. Melissa pulled back onto the black pavement.

"Where are we?"

"Almost there. A couple of minutes away."

Tilting her seat forward brought a wave of agony that demanded another dose. Heather pulled out the precious bottle and downed a pill with the warm flat soda. Yuck.

Looking between the bottle and Heather, Melissa said, "Aren't you supposed to wait six hours between doses?"

"How would I know?"

"It's one pill, four times daily." Melissa bobbed her head as she lectured like a bossy big sister. "Twenty-four divided by four equals six hours. You just took one two hours ago."

"I don't care what they say! I'm in pain."

Melissa couldn't possibly understand what it felt like to fear breathing.

"Okay, okay." Melissa slowed and turned left up a short hill by a white-fenced pasture, then right onto a road at a wooden sign that read: MOUNTAIN HAVEN RESORT. Gravel road, pine trees, and dirt. Some kind of resort.

Nestled in a patch of woods on the right, an isolated pine cabin bearing a hand-painted whiteboard announcing this was the office. Melissa wasn't kidding—remote. Would their place be any better?

A tall, gray-haired man in a red plaid shirt and jeans emerged from the lighted doorway and waved them down.

"It's the owner, Doug. We'd better stop so I can introduce you."

"Really?"

"Sorry. I didn't think we'd see him this late." Melissa parked in the drive.

"Shouldn't you pull into the parking space?"

"Nah, this time of year, we're the only ones here. Come on. He's harmless." Melissa got out.

Heather pushed her door open and stood, but the frigid air and a wave of dizziness seized her. She gripped the door while she regained her balance, then quickly eased herself back down. This was crazy.

"Well, good evening." Doug met Melissa at the front of the car and hugged her like a parent that found a lost child. He was almost a head taller than her.

"Good to be back. Can't wait to see my girl."

"I bet. She might be a tad spoiled now—and full of candy and all. She made out like a bandit in that cute Jasmine costume." He chuckled as he turned with one arm still around Melissa and guided her toward Heather.

She forced herself back to her feet, closed the door, and smiled against her discomfort.

"You must be Cindy. Come on and give me a hug." He opened his arms and stepped toward her.

She blocked his advance. "Sorry, broken ribs."

Doug held out his hand. "Well then, this'll have to do until I can give you a proper hug." He shook her hand heartily, which didn't feel much better than the hug would have. "It's so good to finally meet you. Sorry 'bout your accident. My wife and I have been praying for you. And amnesia? I don't mind tellin' you, I don't think I ever met anyone with amnesia—or if I did, I forgot." He paused for a beat. "Get it? I forgot?"

Melissa laughed. Heather did not.

"I hope you'll understand it's not funny to me . . . not just yet anyway."

His smile fell away. "I'm sorry. If my wife were here, she'd scold me right now. Remember anything yet?"

"No."

His forehead creased. "Nothing at all?"

"No. In fact,"—Heather pointed at Melissa—"I'm not even sure I really know this woman or my real name."

Melissa's face froze until Doug chuckled, then she followed suit.

"I can't wait to hear all about it. How 'bout you gals come round for supper tomorrow night?"

Melissa pointed down the road in the direction they were headed. "Don't you think you ought to check with your wife before you go inviting us for dinner?"

"Heck, I do this all the time. After forty-some years, she's so used to it that she just makes extra food every night. We take the leftovers to the homeless folks, so it's all good."

Heather had been determined not to like him, but his smile and unassuming ways disarmed her. She reached deep inside her being, grabbed hold of some Southern roots she didn't know she had, and said, "You are the *sweeeeetest* thang, but every inch of my body is screaming. Kelsey, or whatever your name is,"—she winked at

Doug, who grinned back at her— "I need to get to bed. I'm flat-out exhausted."

"Oh goodness," Doug said. "That's my fault. I shouldn't have kept you." He opened Heather's door. "You gals go on now, but promise me you'll come on by tomorrow, you hear?"

Heather groaned as she lowered herself into the seat.

Doug grimaced. "Or whenever you're feelin' better—the missus is dying to meet you." Doug closed the door behind her and then went around to get Melissa's.

A true gentleman.

"Speaking of the missus, where is she?" Melissa asked.

"I 'spect she's still down feeding the homeless. They have a lot more people to take care of during the winter. Doing their best to keep them off the streets. One man froze to death last year over in Nelson County." He shook his head. "She'll be along any time now."

"Tell her I asked about her, okay?"

"Sure 'nuff. You and your sister get some rest, ya hear?" Doug closed Melissa's door.

He waved as they drove down the gravel road into the woods.

"Sister?" Heather stared at Melissa. "Do you think that might have been important for me to know?"

"Sorry—I thought it made more sense. I did leave my daughter with a stranger after all."

"Anything else I need to know?"

"Listen, I'm doing the best I can."

"I hope you can keep up with your story."

At an unmarked fork, Melissa turned left down a hill to cross over a berm that held a large lake back on the right. Light from the rising moon reflected off the placid tree-lined water that stretched to the mountain beyond. Heather wanted to paint the serenity of an imagined deer dipping its head for an evening drink.

On the other side, they moved up a hill past an unlighted A-frame with no vehicles in the drive. As they circled to the left, their headlights flashed across a sign: CABIN 7, APPLE BLOSSOM. Between the darkness, cold, and pain, it was hard to imagine anything as heart-warming as apple blossoms.

Melissa turned left up the drive to a log-encased parking area beside a weathered pine cabin lit only by their headlights. A wooden charcoal grill, picnic table, and galvanized trash can hinted at summer charms. Glints of light escaped the edges of the curtained windows evidencing life inside. A faded light blue Camry awaited their arrival.

"We made it. Home sweet home."

There was nothing homey about it, but at least she'd have a bed without nurses waking her at all hours.

The girls pushed open their doors. Melissa pointed toward the front right fender. "Watch out for the tree stump. I've tripped over it a couple of times."

Heather grabbed her hobo bag, got out, and located the stump with her phone's flashlight as Melissa opened the trunk, retrieved a jacket, and handed it to Heather. It wasn't worth the pain to put it on now since they'd be inside in a minute.

Melissa fetched a duffle bag from the trunk and then slammed it shut. Melissa's boots stomped their arrival as she mounted the two steps to the wooden porch. The porch light popped on.

"Mommy, Mommy! You're home." A blond version of *Little Orphan Annie* dressed in *Little Mermaid* pajamas flew out of a screen door to wrap herself around her mother's legs. Olivia was even more precious than the photo Braun had shown her.

Stooping, Melissa hugged the girl like a soldier returning to his girlfriend after a year-long tour of duty. "I missed you so much."

"I missed you more." Olivia squeezed Melissa tighter.

A fit brunette woman exuding an aura of power emerged from the front door pulling a suitcase with a purse draped on her arm. She uprighted her luggage by the door and turned to gaze at the reunion, her face aglow.

"She's been counting the minutes for your arrival."

This was the retired school teacher? No way was she old enough.

Olivia looked up at Heather with a scrunched face. "Heather? Your hair is red." She flew to Heather and wrapped herself around her legs as the sitter's eyebrows knitted together, and Melissa stood.

"Sorry, baby. I can't bend over. My ribs are broken." Heather rubbed Olivia's back, waiting to see how deep Melissa would dig this hole.

Drawing her hand to her chin, the sitter squinted her eyes as she stared at Melissa. "I know my memory is not what it used to be, but I'm sure you said your sister's name was Cindy."

Melissa scowled. "Well, actually, it's *Aunt* Cindy. Olivia, I raised you better than that. Now you apologize to Aunt Cindy."

"But Mommy—"

"No 'but Mommies.' You know Heather was a pretend name."

Olivia tipped her head down and, without looking up, said, "Sorry, Aunt Cindy."

Melissa winked at the sitter. "You've been with her long enough by now to know all about that imagination of hers. I hope she didn't wear you out playing pretend while I was away."

How lame. The sitter looked between them. Teachers were innate truth detectors. No way she was buying that.

"Hmm. Must be something she just does with you two.".

Heather's heart raced as an awkward silence settled between the three women for a long moment.

Melissa finally slapped her thigh and said, "Good grief. I forgot to introduce you. Cindy, this is Mary Ann."

"Well, it's good to meet you, *Cindy*. I'd hug you, but— Mary Ann pointed to Heather's side.

"Thanks. It's good to meet you too."

"So how *are* you feelin', dear? Your sister said you got pretty banged up in that accident."

"It only hurts when I breathe." Heather grimaced.

"Well, I don't guess you'd want to stop doing that." Mary Ann chuckled. "Well, dearies, you two get in and out of the cold. I'm sure you want to get settled so you can get some rest. I'll be getting on my way." She hugged Melissa and then Olivia before grabbing her suitcase handle. She turned to Melissa. "Take good care of our girls."

"Thank you for being there for us. I can't tell you what a comfort it was to have found you. I know Jasmine sure loves you."

"Thanks. She's easy to love." Mary Ann looked adoringly at Olivia.

"How much do I owe you?"

"It was only a couple of days. I feel guilty charging you. I had so much fun with her. Is three hundred okay?"

"I'm sure it must be more like five." Melissa handed her some cash.

"That's too much, sweetie. I know you girls can't work while your sister's on the mend."

Melissa's hand rejected Mary Ann's attempt to return some of the bills. "Not when you find the perfect person to watch your precious daughter."

"I do my best. Please call if you need me again."

"Don't worry. You're on my speed dial."

"Oh—I nearly forgot." Mary Ann retrieved a key from her purse. "Here you go. May God bless you all." She headed to her car.

Melissa opened the front door and guided Olivia inside.

Teeth chattering, Heather watched as Mary Ann pulled away, lighting the surrounding dark forest. Leaves rustled nearby. A white buck stepped into the porch light from behind a pine tree. Its beauty enraptured her. The elegant creature returned her gaze. Heather couldn't move. Something about the animal drew her. What was it?

Melissa called from inside. "Cindy. Come in before we let all the heat out . . . Cindy!"

The deer startled and disappeared as quickly as it had come.

Melissa came out.

"Did you see that?"

"See what?"

"The white deer."

Melissa looked around. "A white deer? How many of those pills have you taken, anyway?" She reached for Heather's hand. "Come on."

"No, seriously," Heather said as Melissa pulled her inside. "There was a white deer."

Melissa shut the door behind Heather. "Welcome home."

She swept her hand around the crowded L-shaped living area and kitchen as if she were proud of this pine-paneled, pine-floored living quarters centered around a pine table with three pine chairs.

Heather's heart sank as she scanned the room from the kitchen on her left to the green sheet-covered futon on her right. Not even the curtains matched. How long would they be here?

"You don't like it?" Melissa asked.

Heather hadn't realized her mouth was open. "I'm sure it'll be fine. I'm just tired." There had to be something good to say. A plastic pumpkin bucket smiled from atop the table. She looked at Olivia. "Is that pumpkin for me?"

Olivia ran to the table and held it up. "It's mine. Miss Mary Ann took me trick-or-treating. I got to be Jasmine. See all the candy I got?"

Heather dropped her hobo bag on the futon as Melissa peeked into the pumpkin. "Wow, honey."

"Can I have some, Mommy?"

Melissa examined her wide-eyed beggar. "Well, maybe one, but then it's off to bed."

Olivia swirled her hand inside the bucket, retrieved a miniature candy bar, unwrapped it, and stuffed it in her mouth. Melissa retrieved the wrapper and the pumpkin and returned the pumpkin to the table.

"Okay, now off to bed."

"But you just got home."

"I know, but Aunt Cindy and I are tired, and we need to talk. Go pick out some books to read. I'll be in in a few minutes."

"I want to talk to Aunt Cindy too." Olivia put on a delicious pout.

"Sweetie. Mommy has had a long day, and you know what that means?"

Olivia pushed out her lower lip. "That you're grumpy."

Melissa chuckled. "You're right about that. So, please mind Mommy. Okay?"

"O-kaaay," Olivia tucked her chin and drug herself toward a hallway beyond the stove, then turned back at the entrance. "Can I sleep with Heather—I mean, Aunt Cindy?"

"No, baby, not until she's feeling better."

"I won't bother her. I promise."

"No, ma'am. She needs her rest. Now go on—get to bed. I'll be right in."

"O-kaaay." Olivia looked at Heather. "Guess what, Aunt Cindy?"

"What?"

"Mommy said tomorrow we can go pick up Abu." She clapped her hands and jumped.

Heather looked to Melissa for a hint. "Abu?"

"That's the dog that saved your life. You gave her to Olivia."

"Abu, you say? I can't wait to see her."

"Off to bed, little missy," Melissa said sternly.

"Good night, Aunt Cindy." She disappeared around the corner behind the stove on the right.

"I love the blond curls. She's absolutely adorable. You didn't dye her hair. Aren't you worried someone will recognize her?"

"Hair dye is dangerous for kids under eight, so I don't want to risk it." Melissa gestured to one of the chairs at the table as if inviting her to girl talk.

Heather shook her head. "I hope you don't mind. I'm exhausted. Could I just get a glass of water and get to bed?"

"I get that. I know how tired I am. I'm sure it's worse for you. We can catch you up tomorrow."

Melissa moved to the decorator's nightmare disguised as a kitchen. Five different wood grains, three cabinet finishes, and two appliance colors in one-chef space. She pulled a glass from an open shelving unit hanging over a coffee pot that looked forward to the morning.

"Handing her the glass, Melissa said, "I'll show you your room."

Heather took a sip but didn't drink it all—in case she needed another pill.

The cabin shrank as they moved toward the bedrooms, and Melissa gave a tour of the obvious—bathroom on the left with a closet outside. The hallway was no more than a privacy space between two bedroom doors. Melissa opened the door on the left and motioned Heather past. "Here you go."

More oak paneling swallowed Heather as she strode to the middle of the bed's room—just wide enough for the queen bed. You'd have to turn sideways to get in, and there was certainly no room for a nightstand. The blue-and-white fake-quilt bedspread with matching pillow shams had been washed a few too many times. Two sconces on the far wall bracketed a space holding two nails begging for paintings. Lopsided miniblinds. Two doorless closets loomed to the left of the bed, one with a shelf in the middle stocked with some toiletries—her nightstand?

"Are there just two bedrooms?"

" Yep. It's all we need."

"You shouldn't have to share a room. I can sleep on the futon."

"Ha! Olivia's been sleeping with me since Johnny . . ." Melissa paused and took a breath. "Since we left Huntington. Besides, with your injuries . . ."

Melissa walked to a hanging wardrobe inside another doorless closet behind Heather on the wall between the bedrooms. "This should get you started." She pointed to the dresser next to it. "You'll find some pajamas, undies—*including* bras—in there. We'll go shopping when you're better."

Heather set her glass on the dresser and fingered the sleeve of a multi-fabric knit pullover blouse in the closet. "Good taste."

"I just got the same kind of stuff that you picked out when we went shopping."

Melissa returned to the doorway. "I put a toothbrush and toothpaste on the shelf so we wouldn't get them mixed up in the bathroom—unless you like bubblegum toothpaste." She tipped her head with a grin. "I also got you some basic cosmetics." Melissa looked around the room. "Need anything else?"

"How could I?" Melissa had done so much. The fullness of Heather's heart seeped from her eyes. "Thank you."

Melissa waved her off and grabbed the doorknob. "Stop it." Not looking her in the eye, Melissa said, "Now, get better. I don't do nursemaid too good."

Heather yanked the red wig off. How did anyone wear those itchy rugs regularly? She tossed it on the bed. The second drawer yielded injury-comforting flannel jammies covered in happily skating penguins. She carefully snugged them on.

With toothpaste and toothbrush in hand, she headed to the bathroom, pausing at Melissa's room to eavesdrop.

"And the white knight rode up to the castle wall . . ." She smiled. Cinderella? How could she remember a story character's name but not her own?

She shook her head and continued to the glorified closet stuffed with bathroom fixtures. Minions must have installed the hip-high sink with a single shelf holding bubble gum toothpaste, a mermaid toothbrush, and an *Aladdin* cup.

Her ribs screamed when she leaned over to rinse. How long since her last pill? She'd better take another to keep the pain from waking her during the night.

She finished brushing, then retrieved her pill bottle from her bag on the futon.

"Can I get you something?"

Heather jumped, not realizing Melissa had come out behind her. She shoved the bottle back into her bag. "No. Forgot my bag."

Avoiding eye contact, she held the bag up as proof. "Good night, again." Heather slid off to her room, her deceit clinging to her. But she didn't care. The pill would make it go away.

She moved the glass from the dresser to the closet shelf. She dumped the bag's contents on the bed, then picked up and opened the bottle. Several pills spilled into her palm. How many were there?

She spread the entire contents out onto the bed and counted. Twenty-six. Was that it? Every six hours? More like every four hours. That was six a day. That was—her heart pounded—four days of meds. She swept all but one back into the bottle and stared at it. She'd just had one before they got there. Should she save it? She did need the rest. A few naps in an uncomfortable seat had done nothing for her recovery.

She threw the pill to the back of her mouth and chased away her troubles with the water.

Chapter 20

Wednesday, November 1
8:00 a.m.

MAX SAT ON THE SOFA of Braun's second-story garage apartment, reviewing the files while finishing his second cup of coffee. The place couldn't have been more perfect. Great bed, comfy sofa, sufficient kitchen, and good lighting for late-night reading.

A knock sounded at the door. Max checked his watch as he rose. Eight o'clock. Right on time. He pulled the window curtain back. Braun in all his FBI glory, from the trench coat to the tie. Max pulled the door open to a rush of cold air. "Come on in."

Braun entered and looked around.

"What's up with the suit? Do I need to dress up here?"

"No, man. You're good." Braun said as they fist-punched. "I was groomed for this—makes me feel official. You, on the other hand?"

They laughed.

"Don't I know it. I've been undercover so long—moths may have turned my suits to Swiss cheese. Either way, I doubt they fit anymore." Max pulled at his belt. "Since R and R, even my jeans are fitting a bit too tight."

Braun walked to the coffee table and looked down at the papers from the dossier strewn across the surface. "Did you sleep at all?"

Max laughed. "Caught red-handed. What can I say?"

"Learn anything?"

"Yeah, but what wasn't there was the most important." Max pointed to the sofa for Braun to sit, then took a seat on the ottoman across the table. Max surveyed the photos he had laid out, then picked up a picture of Melissa. "There was almost no information about her—other than a few photos and a tragic foster home upbringing. But unlike her brother, she never got into trouble. It doesn't make sense. Why would she be with Johnny? No connections to his business."

"You're right about that. Before she met Johnny, she worked as a waitress and was living at the mission. One of the waitresses said they met at the diner. Said he came every day after that. Before she knew it, he'd bought her the house." Braun picked up the picture of her house. "Modest enough, but he paid cash for it . . . of course. Even put it in her name. Doesn't appear he expected anything in return. Melissa told her friend she'd go straight back to the mission if he tried to move in, but he stayed away. Kept going to see her at the diner, though. After a few months, she invited him to live with her."

Braun shook his head. "You know, Melissa's ex died of a heroin overdose. Maybe he felt responsible. Customer of one of his dealers. Next thing you know, she's raising a baby alone. Whatever it was, seems like he treated her different from the start." He dropped the photo on top of the others and leaned back into the sofa.

"The DEA was watching both of them and the house. They weren't dealing out of there. They never do. They recruit single moms desperate for money in neighborhoods to distribute for them. The only gang member that ever came to their house was Johnny's brother Tyrone. Nothing tied Melissa to their business."

"Nobody else ever came?" Max reached down and picked up a picture of a man leaving the house. "What about this guy?"

Braun took the picture and stared for a moment. "Oh, him? His name is Lenny Feldman. He owns a used car lot in Barboursville. A few days after this, Melissa had a new used car. We couldn't find any connections to the Mongrels—legitimate or otherwise. Lenny didn't take anything in or out—at least that we could see."

"Barboursville . . ." Max said, more to help him think. "Wasn't Melissa's car found at the mall in Barboursville?"

"Lenny's dealership is right down the hill."

They both stood.

"I think we need to talk to Lenny."

———

9:10 a.m.

KNOCKING TORE HEATHER from her first uninterrupted night of sleep since leaving those pesky night owl nurses who had nothing better to do than keep the patients from sleeping. Her eyes refused to open. She pulled the covers over her head. "Go away."

The knocking continued.

"Yoo-hoo," a female voice called from outside the front of the cabin.

Heather lowered the covers and peeked one eye open. Light snuck in through the sides of the blinds from the far window. What time was it?

Another knock. "Hello? Kelsey?"

Where was Kelsey? Didn't she hear the knocking?

Cringing, she rolled out of the crater that had formed in the middle of the bed after who knows how many cabin guests had slept there. She needed a pill, but it'd have to wait. She reached for her phone. Ten after nine. She grabbed her wig and opened the bedroom door. Sunlight streamed in from the windows behind the futon, burning her eyes. A large silver Buick sat outside in the parking area, but the Prius was gone.

A pudgy gray-haired woman wearing a denim jacket stood in front of the sliding window to the left of the front door, partially blocked by the wrinkled white linen curtains. Thankfully she'd had the good graces not to be peering in to see Heather's true hair color.

"Be right there." She ducked into the bathroom and tugged on her disguise. Heather raced to the door, trying to stay out of sight. Would it be ugly to close the curtains now?

180

With her back to the door, she asked, "Who is it?"

"It's Margie."

Heather peeked around the curtain at the woman who faced the door. Colorful embroidered flowers decorated the back yoke of the woman's blue-jean jacket. She had a platter, but Heather couldn't tell what was on it. Heather jerked back when the woman began to look her way.

"I'm sorry. Do I know you?"

"We haven't met. I'm Doug's wife—the owner."

"Oh!" Heather cracked the door to Margie's broad smile and cinnamon buns.

"I baked up something homemade." Margie pushed her narrow glasses back up to the bridge of her nose. I figured you might could use some good cooking after all that hospital food."

"That's very sweet, but I'm not even dressed yet." She looked down at her penguins.

"Oh, that's okay, sweetie" Margie pulled open the screen door and pushed her way in. "I don't mind."

Heather did.

Warm cinnamon scents wafted behind Margie as she set the golden treats on the table next to the pumpkin and looked around. "Where's your sister? Isn't she supposed to be taking care of you?"

"I don't know. I was sleeping."

"Oh, My Lord. I'm so sorry. People 'round here usually get up with the sun. There's not much to do after dark." She giggled. "We get lots of sleep this time of year—short days, you know." Margie pulled out a chair. "Why don't you just sit down here, sweetie, and I'll fix you some coffee to go with those buns."

Heather reached for Margie's arm. "No, please—my broken ribs are killing me. I just need to get back to bed."

"What? Doug didn't tell me you broke your ribs. I got kicked once by a horse. Hurt for months."

Months. And she only had four days of pills. "Then you know what I mean." Heather grimaced for emphasis. "I'm gonna go lay back down now."

"Oh, dearie me. Here, let me help you." Margie touched Heather's elbow.

Heather yanked back. "That's sweet of you, but I really don't know you and would feel better if I locked the door behind you.

"Oh, no need." Margie pulled keys out of her jeans pocket and jingled them. "Got the master key to all the cabins. I can let myself out."

"Okay." Signaling halt with her hands, she said, "That freaks me out. Listen, I'm trying to be nice, but I need you to leave."

Margie's mouth dropped slightly.

Great. Now Heather was a jerk.

"I'm sorry. I didn't mean to bite your head off. It's the pain."

Margie's eyes softened behind her narrow brown glasses. "That's okay, sweetie. I understand, but you know—most folks 'round here don't even bother to lock their doors. And we usually don't knock before coming in." She chuckled.

"That's good to know. Right now, I don't know anybody, including myself. Until my memory comes back, I'd feel better locking the door."

"Oh, that's right. Doug told me about your amnesia. I never met anyone who lost their memory—besides some old folks." She giggled. "My memory's all but gone."

Heather pointed to the door, praying she'd leave. "Thanks for the cinnamon buns. They look and smell amazing."

"You're welcome, dearie. Let Kelsey know I dropped by."

Kelsey. She had already forgotten the name thing. "I will." She shut the door behind Margie, then turned and fell back against it. What had Melissa said about being large enough not to have Nosy Nellies?

She retrieved her glass from the bedroom and went to the kitchen. A note was stuck to the refrigerator. How had Nosy Nelly missed that? She pulled it off and read it.

Didn't want to wake you up. Gone to get Abu and
groceries. Be back by 10:30.

Ha. Bet Melissa hadn't anticipated the bun brigade. Heather filled
a glass with water and returned to the bedroom. She counted the
pills again. Twenty-five, minus the one in her hand. Twenty-four. Her
heart raced as she swallowed. She tugged off her wig, went to the
bathroom, and took a much-needed shower. She emerged refreshed
but still exhausted. At least the pill had already started to relax her.
She crawled back into her bed nest, relishing the feel of the sheets
against her skin.

———

9:15 a.m.

MAX LOOKED UP FROM HIS CELL PHONE as Braun eased off the gas
to exit the interstate at the Barboursville exit. After a couple of left
turns, they came to a used car lot featuring several dozen buffed and
polished pickup trucks and cars glinting in the early morning sun.
High-hanging blue and white fringe that looked more like cheer-
leaders' pom-poms than advertising pennants was draped between
flagpoles that marked the business's territory. Oval windshield
stickers announced the vehicles' birthdates.

Braun turned off the four-lane business highway, made his
way between the rows of mostly trucks, and parked in front of the
freshly painted white cement-block building. To the right of the
office, two glass-paned service-bay doors revealed a bygone era
when gas stations performed services rather than selling coffee,
groceries, and sandwiches.

Braun pushed the ignition button off. "Ready for a sales pitch?"

Max pointed to a testosterone-powered Ford F-150. "There's a
blue pickup I wouldn't mind having."

"You're not kidding."

No one rushed them. Not a salesman in sight. The agents looked
at each other.

183

"This is a little spooky," Braun said as if reading Max's mind.

A CLOSED sign hung on the certificate-stickered glass door. Six feet on the other side of the office's plate glass window, a woman sat staring at her desk. Despite their proximity, she didn't look up.

Pulling the door open, Max and Braun stepped into the tiny office, crowded with only three mismatched chairs, a water cooler, a gray metal file cabinet, and a gray-metal desk—every inch covered by a computer monitor, papers, and all manner of office supplies. Between the awards, car posters, cross, and wall-unit air conditioner, there was little space left for the fresh beige paint that still scented the room.

Scattered papers and broken picture frames lay around the desk on the dark wood vinyl flooring. Across the desk from the woman, crime-scene tape blocked the glass door to the service bays, perhaps explaining the mess. A RESTROOM sign marked the short hallway beyond.

Max carefully moved around the debris between the desk and the crime scene as Braun took a position inside the door.

The puffy-eyed brunette, whose gray roots revealed a different kind of midlife crisis, looked up slowly from her papers but didn't stand to greet them. "I'm sorry, we're closed."

Max tipped his hat. "We apologize for intruding, ma'am. We're with the FBI."

While Braun took over the introductions, presented credentials, and identified the woman as Mrs. Feldman, Max peered through the glass door into the sunlit work bays behind him. A hood-up gray minivan awaited repair in the far bay. The empty nearer bay explained the yellow tape. A smeared pool of liquid death cried out from the clean cement floor. Max turned back, eyes meeting the thick grief on the other side of the desk—the same eyes his mother had when she was told his sister had overdosed.

Max looked at Braun, tipped his chin toward the garage, and then exchanged places so Braun could see for himself.

Mrs. Feldman shook her head slowly as if denying the elephant lying on the garage floor would make it go away. Straightening, she said, "I've already talked with the police. I-I don't understand. FBI? Why would you be investigating this?"

Max removed his hat. "Ma'am, we're just here to ask your husband some questions. Is he here?"

Her head tilted, then her eyes narrowed. "You're kidding, right?"

"No, ma'am."

Her face reddened. "My husband's dead." She pounded the desk and then stood. "Someone killed my Lenny!" She pointed out the front door. "First, the police asked me questions like I killed my husband, and now you . . ." she said, pointing at Max, "What? You think my husband's a criminal? We're not criminals! We're the victims here."

Braun pushed his hands down as though that would reduce the tension. "We're very sorry, ma'am. We're not here to blame anyone. We know this is hard. We have no reason to believe you or your husband did anything. We're here to see if he sold a car to someone we're investigating. That's all. Please." Braun motioned to her black executive chair. "Let's talk."

The woman wilted back.

"Do you mind if we sit?" Braun asked.

She nodded.

Max sat in the brown studio chair to her right in front of the window, holding his hat on his lap, as Braun took the tubular white rolling chair across from Mrs. Feldman.

"Can you tell us what happened?"

"The police said it was probably some addicts looking to steal money or a car. But Lenny never kept cash here. I wouldn't know if they took a car. But look around . . ." She waved a hand over the chaos. "Why would kids go through paperwork? What would they be looking for?" She shook her head. "None of it makes any sense."

Braun removed a pad and pen from his inside coat pocket. "Can you tell us when this happened?"

"Last night. Lenny didn't come home for dinner. When he didn't answer his phone, I came down here and found him . . ." She pointed past Braun, then pressed her hand over her mouth and looked away.

Max pointed to the water cooler. "Can I get you some water?"

She shook her head. "I'll be okay." She pulled a tissue from her sleeve and blew her nose.

"So why are you here?"

"Are you familiar with your husband's business dealings?"

"I wish I was." She looked around the room. "After thirty years, you would think . . ." She began crying. "What kind of wife am I? I look at all these papers . . . and I'm lost. What am I going to do?"

"Well, ma'am," Max said, "If you don't want to run it yourself, you could always sell it. When my uncle died, my aunt used a business broker to sell his business."

Her face dropped as if he'd killed Lenny himself. "Sell the business? That would be like selling part of Lenny."

"I guess it would," Max said. "Just something to think about."

Braun stood. "Would you mind if we looked around?"

"What do you think you'll find?"

"Maybe some paperwork for a car sale with our suspect."

Mrs. Feldman's face tensed. "I don't know. I'm not going to have you ruining my husband's reputation—God rest his soul."

"I get that." Braun sat back down. "A little girl might be in danger if we don't find the folks we're tracking. You'd be helping her."

"A little girl?" She pursed her lips. "If you think it'll help."

Braun nodded.

She looked around the room at the papers and shook her head. "Oh my God—do you think the people that did this were looking for the same thing?"

"We don't know, ma'am. That's what we're hoping to find out."

She looked up at the cross on the wall. "Dear Lord. I can't take any more of this today." She stood and gathered her purse. "You men do what you have to. I have to go."

"One of us can give you a ride home if you need," Braun said as he and Max stood.

"No, I'll be fine. Do you need anything else from me before I leave?"

"Can I get your number—in case we have questions?"

Braun recorded her number on his pad. She handed him a key from her purse. "Just put this in the mail slot when you go. I have another set." Max stepped in front of her to open the door. She paused at the threshold. "You'll let me know if you find anything?"

"Yes, ma'am," Max said. "Oh. One more thing." He motioned toward the hallway. "Is there a safe in the back?"

"Yes. It was open when I got here. The police said they must have gotten him to open it before . . ." She covered her face with her hands.

"I'm sorry, ma'am. Can you tell me who's handling the case?"

She looked up. "Barbourville Police—Chief Leggett, of course. He and Lenny go way back."

"One last thing. The computer. Is there a password to get in?"

"Yeah." She half-laughed. "He wrote it on the blotter." She pointed to the desk. "I told him it wasn't safe, just like I told him it wasn't safe to close shop by himself. But he never listened to me. I can't even be mad at him now." She shook her head and left.

Max stepped back in. "Last night—huh? At least we know where Melissa got her new car."

"Yeah. Unfortunately, so do they." Braun pulled out his cell phone. I've got Chief Leggett on speed dial. Why don't you check the computer? I'll start with the safe."

Max nodded and scanned the mess. "Hopefully, they left something behind."

Chapter 21

10:15 a.m.

A BARKING DOG AWAKENED HEATHER to her ever-present companion—pain. When had she taken her last pill? She tried to sit up, but her ribs forced her back. Was it even a week since the explosion? Two more months of this?

The door cracked open. "Heather!" Olivia screeched as the door flew open wide, and she ran to the side of the bed.

"Jasmine!" Melissa called from the other room. "Remember our Virginia names."

The cutest beagle-shepherd mix raced in behind Olivia, jumped onto the bed, and began licking Heather's face. She deflected the mouth-to-mouth kisses but immediately fell in love with the sweetness of the soul.

"And let Aunt Cindy sleep!"

Olivia formed a megaphone with her hands. "Sorry, Mommy!" She turned back to Heather. "Can you come and watch *Aladdin* with me?"

Melissa came to the door with a box of hair color in hand. "No, she can't. Now get Abu down. Aunt Cindy needs her rest. Go on."

Olivia dropped her head. "Come on, Abu." She patted her leg. Abu leaped down, following Olivia out of the room.

"Sorry. I hope she didn't wake you."

"Actually, it was Margie's buns that woke me."

"Now that's a picture."

Heather chuckled but immediately regretted it. Gripping her side, she said, "Don't make me laugh. It hurts. I meant her cinnamon buns."

"I was wondering where those came from. When did she come by?"

"Nine." She eased herself up. "No Nosy Nellies, huh?"

Melissa scrunched her face. "That bad?"

"You have no idea. She barged right in and wanted to take over my caregiving. You—by the way—are awful for leaving me alone."

"Wow. I'd better nip that in the bud."

"Maybe if you tell her she set me back a week by getting me out of bed."

A sly grin stretched across Melissa's face. "Guilt trip. I like it."

"I was kidding. Margie seems nice enough. And her buns looked awesome." Heather grinned, trying not to laugh.

"So, how'd you sleep last night?"

"It was wonderful. No nurses waking me up—but the pain meds had worn off by the time I got up. When I haven't had one, I stress over every move."

Melissa's face tensed.

Heather shouldn't have said anything. "No, seriously. One of the nurses told me I'd heal better with them because they'd relax my body. She said people who try to tough it out heal more slowly."

"That doesn't sound right. I'm going to have to google that."

"Out here in the wilderness? Is there even reception?"

Melissa laughed. "Better than that—there's Wi-Fi. But the cell service stinks. Good luck trying to call anyone."

Who would Heather call? Looking at the pill bottle, she took a deep breath. "Speaking of medicine, I only have pills for a few days. Do you have more?"

"I'm hoping we can switch you to something over the counter by then. I hear that Tylenol-Advil cocktails work as well as narcotics for pain."

Heather's stomach knotted. She needed her pills. She had to figure something out. But they were in the boonies.

"Are you up to coming to the table for some coffee, or can I bring you something?"

She needed to start moving around if she was going to get pills. "I'll get up."

"Good." Melissa waved the hair color box. "Ready for some color?"

"You know, if the wig hadn't been by my phone, I would have forgotten it when Margie busted in this morning."

"I thought about that." Melissa read the box. "Rinsing this stuff out might be painful. Maybe you can hop in the shower to rinse it out."

"That works. Speaking of new identities, we need to get our stories straight."

"Well, actually we don't. That's the beauty of your amnesia." Melissa grinned like a child getting away with something. "If you say something wrong, you can blame the amnesia."

How sad. What if she never got her memory back?

She pushed off the bed. "Do you mind if I come out in my penguins? Changing is a pain—literally."

"Not at all." Melissa pulled a matching robe from the closet and held it up for her.

Heather moaned louder than necessary as she slipped into it and a pair of slippers by the door. Perfect. Maybe now Melissa would be more compassionate about getting her pills.

"Come on out when you're ready. I'll fix your coffee." Melissa left.

Heather tipped the pill bottle and retrieved number twenty-four. Should she take two? She hadn't taken any all night. Palming numbers twenty-four and twenty-three, she put the bottle in her robe pocket and chased it with last night's water.

Twenty-two left. Now she needed to convince Melissa of her genuine need if she was going to get more.

———

190

10:30 a.m.

MAX HUNCHED OVER THE CAR LOT's crumb-infested keyboard, wishing he had taken a few more classes in computer forensics. He knew enough to search by file date, but that only showed that Lenny's sales had been slow—at least the ones on the books.

Braun stacked the collected papers on top of a box of file folders in front of Max. "Nothing here—at least nothing whoever broke in didn't take."

A balding goateed man in a gray tailored suit looked through the glass door and grinned upon seeing Braun.

Braun mirrored his expression and stood to greet the Chief, who matched Braun's stature but not muscle. "Chief Leggett. Long time . . ." The men shook and butted their right shoulders.

"You're not kidding."

"Jim, this is Special Agent Max Enders."

Max stood, returning his right arm to the sling, and did a left-hand pump. "Good to meet you."

Leggett jutted his chin at Max. "Aren't you that agent that took down the sheriff's office in Hearthstone?"

Max nodded. "So much for undercover."

"Well, I doubt the average Joe would know you, but you're a hero around the department. Corruption like that gives us all a bad name."

"The bigger hero is that prosecutor. He almost paid the ultimate price."

"Shocking about that FBI agent. Besides being a knock-out, I heard she was top in her class at the Academy. How could that fat old scumbag sheriff have gotten to her?"

Max shook his head. "I don't know. Bad-boy syndrome?"

"That guy?"

"Maybe he had something on her. We'll never know."

"I worked with her on an assignment five years ago," Braun said. "She was top-shelf. I couldn't believe it when I heard."

Leggett pulled down the crime scene tape and peered into the bay. "You know, I've known Lenny since elementary school. This doesn't smell right. I was glad when you called. I knew there was more to this than junkies looking for money."

Max and Braun filled him in on the Mongrel case, how Heather got involved, and what it boiled down to—a crazy Detroit drug gang coming after their money.

"But even if the Wheeler girl's connected with Detroit, what's the connection with Lenny?"

"Maybe nothing, but Lenny was seen visiting Johnny," Braun said. "And with what we're finding here —or should I say not finding— you have to wonder. We're hoping you can tell us something new."

"Didn't Hawthorne bring you up to date?"

"Hawthorne?"

"Yeah. DEA? We called him yesterday when we made the connection between Lenny and an abandoned car found at the mall. It was registered to Melissa Thomason. Johnny's girlfriend, right?"

"Yeah," Max said, leaning against the desk.

"Lenny sold it to her."

"When did you call Hawthorne?" Braun asked.

"Oh, it must have been about four o'clock or so. Said he'd check into it."

Max looked at Braun, then back to the chief. Maybe Hawthorne wouldn't have called the night before, but surely by now. Something wasn't right.

"I called him again this morning, and he came right over," Leggett said. "Didn't find anything. Didn't he call you?"

"No," Braun said. "I know he's been tied up with some big takedown. You know how those DEA cowboys are."

"Strange. He wasn't too busy to get here this morning."

"I'll follow up when we leave," Braun said. "In the meantime, why don't you bring us up to date?"

192

Max's phone rang. *Alex.* He excused himself before stepping outside to answer the call.

"What's up?"

"Guess what?"

"Seriously?" Did he have to say it?

"Okay, okay. You could suck the hot out of a hot air balloon."

"Alex."

"Anyway, you're not going to believe this. Melissa and Heather are cousins."

"What?"

"Right? You can't make this stuff up. Melissa's mom and Heather's mom are sisters—or *were* sisters."

"Were?"

"Yeah. They both died of cancer. Melissa's mom was a real piece of work. She died in prison while serving a fifteen-year sentence for child neglect. The story will make your stomach turn. I texted a link. Do you think Heather found out about her and went looking for her?"

"That doesn't sound right. Heather wasn't running to something. She was running away from her life."

"That only leaves coincidence. Randomly meeting a cousin?"

"Yeah, it sounds crazy." He needed time to process. "Good work, Alex. I really owe you now."

"You have no idea. Don't ask how I got this."

"Call me if you get anything else."

"You know I will."

Max rejoined Braun and Leggett, who had moved into the service bay and were discussing how Lenny's body had been found.

"You're not going to believe this," Max said. "Melissa and Heather are cousins."

"What? How did our intel miss that?"

"Well, let's just say I'm not sure this came through regular channels."

"And I guess you're not sharing your secret?"

"I'd say over my dead body, but that doesn't seem like the right thing to say here." They simultaneously looked toward the blood pool.

"I've been thinking," Max said. "Maybe Heather's father knows something."

"Oh no you don't." Braun shook his head. "You can't breathe a word of this to Heather's family. We're too close for you to put any information out there."

Braun was right. But how else was he going to find out? "So, where are we, Chief?"

"I think we covered everything. I'm praying Lenny wasn't involved. His wife would be devastated."

"Well, maybe he wasn't." Max noticed a layer of dust covering the minivan windshield—as if it hadn't been moved or worked on for months. He walked around it to a workbench with no tools and parts. Clean, like a desk. Drop cloths covered something bulky.

"Hey, guys."

"What is it?" Braun asked as he rounded the minivan.

Max uncovered a specialty printer. "What do we have here?"

Leggett joined them.

"This sure doesn't look like a mechanic's tool to me."

"What is it?" Leggett asked.

"Sorry, man." Braun patted his shoulder. "I think you're going to have some bad news to deliver after all. This, my friend, is one of the best ID makers not officially on the market."

"You're kidding," Leggett said.

"Nope."

"I don't believe it. Why would Lenny do this?"

"From the sales numbers I saw on his computer," Max said, "I'm guessing money. Do you have any idea what these cost?"

Leggett shook his head. "I'm afraid to ask."

"We need to take this puppy back to the lab, run prints, and have them pull the memory card. I'd be willing to bet we find our missing ladies with this." He lifted his slinged arm. "Can you two get this out to the car?"

He took a quick photo while the able-bodied men gloved up, then held doors for them as they made their way outside and loaded the printer into the back of the SUV.

After ungloving, Braun shook his former colleague's hand. "Sorry, Jim. We'll let you know as soon as we find something."

Leggett thanked them and left.

Max looked at the printer. "So what's up with Hawthorne not calling us? Do you trust him?"

"Have you ever worked with DEA agents?"

"Of course."

"I mean joint-task force—side-by-side years of working together."

"No."

"They go deep into dark places trying to get to the headwaters of the poison. One of three things can happen. We take down dozens if they get it done, or we're looking for body parts if they get found out."

"Or?"

"They get sucked in—like Nicole. It's the old double-agent quandary. You never really know whose side they're on."

"So, whose side is Hawthorne on?"

"Ours, I hope."

Chapter 22

12:00 Noon

STILL SNUGGLED IN HER PENGUIN BATHROBE, Heather sat in the oak dining chair, bathed in the warmth of the hairdryer, Olivia's humming along to *A Whole New World*, and the rich scent of the burning wood from the stove. In the newness of the daylight, the formerly overwhelming oak paneling now provided a glow she could get used to. The mismatched countertops were another thing.

Melissa turned off the hairdryer and handed her a mirror. "What do you think?"

Her hair matched the wig. "You nailed it. I actually like it." She angled the mirror to look at Melissa standing behind her. "You think my tastes are the same?" She handed the mirror back.

"I don't know. You like the same clothes."

"I'm glad one of us knows that."

"Look, Aunt Cindy." Olivia pointed to the TV and ran to Heather's side.

Not wanting to be left out, Abu joined the gathering, tail wagging.

"It's the magic carpet. Remember? You promised to paint this on my wall."

"Did I?" Did she know how? She did that sketch in the hospital. Was painting like riding a bike?

"Oh, sweetie, these aren't the kind of walls you can paint," Melissa said.

"But, Mommy. She promised."

"Well, maybe we can figure something out when she's feeling better." Melissa returned the hairdryer to the bathroom, went to the kitchen area, and pulled a pitcher out of the refrigerator.

Olivia continued staring at Heather—eyes widening as if she were just now seeing Heather. "Wow, you look pretty." She touched Heather's bruised hand and looked where her IV had been. "Does this hurt?"

"No. Just my ribs and my head."

"Why do they hurt?"

"Because of the accident. It feels like someone kicked me really, really hard."

Olivia twirled one of her blond curls as she studied Heather. "Mommy says you don't remember anything."

"I don't. Isn't that weird?"

"Yes, so weird." She continued staring and twirling. After a moment, she grabbed Heather's hand and pulled her. "Can you take me to see the white deer?"

Heather pulled back. "Did you see one?"

"No, but you did. I've never seen one. Can we go look?"

"Honey, leave Aunt Cindy alone." Melissa set a glass of iced tea next to Heather's half-eaten cinnamon bun and removed her cold coffee. "She's got to get better before she goes running around in the woods."

"Okay." Olivia returned to the futon, and Abu to her bed.

Heather smiled at Melissa. "Thanks." She took a sip. Sweet tea made just right.

Abu popped up, facing the parking area, and barked.

"Abu! Quiet." Melissa pointed to the floor. Abu stopped and sat.

"Wow, she's obedient."

"Yes, you said that before." Melissa looked out the windows beyond the futon.

"I did? Must have been BC—before Cindy."

Melissa chuckled until Margie's silver Buick pulled up next to the Prius. "Shoot. It's Margie. The hair-color box." Melissa raced to the bathroom to get it and then tossed it in the back of the linen closet. "We need to get rid of her. Tell her you're tired."

"No problem. I am."

"Knock, knock," Margie sang from the porch.

Melissa opened the door. "Come in, please."

Olivia and Abu raced to her side as she balanced a platter covered in red plastic wrap.

"Careful, sweetie."

"Did you bring me some cookies?" Olivia asked.

"Of course." She delivered the goodies to the table. She pushed her glasses back on her nose and then pulled off the wrap. "I thought you girls could use some lunch." A variety of carefully arranged sandwich halves and a pile of cookies filled the platter.

Abu moved to the table in anticipation.

Olivia beelined for the cookies but knew enough to look to her mother.

"Not 'til you've had lunch."

"I'm not hungry for lunch."

They all giggled.

"Eat a sandwich, then you can have a cookie."

Shaking her head, Olivia pouted her way back to the futon—face focused on the table. Abu maintained her hopeful position.

"Margie, this was so sweet of you," Melissa said. "You didn't have to."

"Oh, I know. But you have your hands full with these two—" she looked at Abu "—three." I just wanted to help. Plus, I needed to make up for waking Cindy this morning."

"No worries. You didn't know," Heather said.

Margie spotted Heather's half-eaten cinnamon bun and frowned. "Were the buns okay?"

"They're amazing. I wasn't even hungry, so you know they're good."

A long moment passed as Margie looked at the empty chairs as if asking to sit and chat. It was hard not offering a seat and some coffee or tea. Melissa tipped her chin to Heather to deliver the 'I'm tired' company line when Olivia hopped up.

"Guess what, Miss Margie? Aunt Cindy saw a white deer."

Margie's face blanched. "Really?" She looked at Heather. "Where?"

Heather pointed toward the porch. "Right in front of the cabin."

"Did anyone else see it?"

"No, just me."

Margie examined Heather for a long moment as if looking back in time.

"You've seen it, haven't you?" Heather asked, hoping for the story.

"Yes, but it's been years." She paused again, looking directly into Heather's eyes as if telling the story would divulge some buried secret. "I'll have to tell you about it sometime."

"Can you take me to look for it, Miss Margie?"

"Not right now, sweetie. We're talking."

"Please, please, please," Olivia said, jumping up and down.

"You know. That might be good for both of us," Margie said.

"No. You don't have to do that." Melissa guided Olivia back toward the futon.

"But I want to go."

"The walk really will be good for me. And I'm sure she's getting fidgety hanging out here."

"Are you sure?" Melissa asked.

"I'd love it. I'll take her to my house to get some walking shoes. We'll eat and then hunt for that white deer. How's that sound, Miss Jasmine?"

Olivia sprung off the futon. "Yay! Yay! Yay!"

"Go get your jacket and shoes on," Melissa said.

Abu followed Olivia to the bedroom.

"Thank you. Bring her back if she gets on your nerves."

"Oh, did I mention? Our church has a half-day daycare. She might enjoy being around some other kids. And I'm sure you could use a little free time."

Melissa's face froze. "Oh, I don't know. I've never let her go to daycare before."

"Well, think about it."

Olivia and Abu returned ready for adventure.

"Can Abu come?" Olivia asked.

"Sure, why not."

Melissa hooked Abu up and handed the leash to Margie.

"Come on, Miss Jasmine. Let's go find that white deer."

They said their goodbyes and left.

Melissa shut the door and then leaned back against it. "Whew." She looked at the linen closet. "While we're alone, I need to show you something."

She went to the closet and pointed to a blanket bag on the top shelf. "There's a couple of thousand dollars stashed in each closet in those bags." She removed the hair color box, took it to the kitchen trash, opened the freezer, and took out a frozen dinner box. "This is money, so it's no use opening any of them if you get hungry. There's money under the mattresses and inside the spare tire."

Johnny also stashed money in different cities. I put the locations in the contacts on your phone. I coded it so no one else can figure it out." Melissa explained the system.

"Why are you telling me all this?"

"Just in case."

Heather's stomach knotted. In case? With their new backwoods venue, she thought they were safe. Was all this necessary? And now that she knew where the money was, if the gang or the FBI caught up with her . . . Heather didn't want to think about it. She needed a pill now more than ever.

"Listen. I'm exhausted."

"You need to eat, you know."

"Maybe when I wake up. I wasn't even going to be released from the hospital until tomorrow."

Heather shuffled to the bathroom, tapped out pill number twenty-two, and downed it with water she cupped in her hand from the sink. She flushed the toilet to complete her deceit, then opened the door. Melissa was sitting at the far end of the table eating a sandwich—examining her the way a dad would a daughter returning home late from a date..

Except for ignoring the four-times-a-day thing, she wasn't doing anything wrong. She was in pain, after all—something Melissa couldn't understand.

Heather took her iced tea, thanked Melissa, and returned to her bed nest, praying she'd never need to know where that money was.

———

4:00 p.m.

THE LOCAL FBI OFFICE COMPUTER FORENSIC LAB was little more than a couple of folding tables at a right angle in the corner of a back room. Metal shelving hung over the bank of monitors and held bins, electronic components, and hard drives. Wires ran everywhere. A fire inspector would have a field day writing up violations. Max had been spoiled by D.C.'s state-of-the-art technology and Alex's lightning-fast research. A scruffy-bearded kid in jeans was hunched over a computer pulling off a panel. How much evidence would this kid miss?

Braun made introductions, then asked, "Whatchu got?"

"You gotta see this." The kid hopped up and waved them over to a desk in the opposite corner of the room. It was as if he had just discovered where Jimmy Hoffa was buried.

They joined him at a computer screen running facial recognition software. Faces flashed on the left side next to the picture of some-one with lines between points on his face. "We hit the jackpot. The printer's drive has dozens of fake IDs on it." The kid hit a button on the keyboard, printed several pages, handed them to Braun, and asked, "Do you know how many gang members we've identified with this?"

Max moved next to Braun to look on as he scanned the pages. The spreadsheet listed names in two columns—"Alias" at the top of one column and "Name" on the second. There were dozens of aliases. Many had matching names.

"You're not kidding." Braun rattled off names that, before today, meant nothing to Max.

The kid held up some photos, naming them as he went through the stack. None of this was helping them find Heather.

"Listen, guys. I hate to spoil the party, but did you find Heather?"

"Sorry, sorry. Yeah." The kid opened a folder and spread out the first few pages. "I'm pretty sure this is her, and these are the other two."

"Bingo." Max pointed to Heather's redheaded Virginia driver's license. "That's Heather, all right." He read the address. "Charlottesville. Interesting choice—assuming that's where they went."

Braun picked up two other pages. "I'm sure this is Melissa. And that must be her daughter's fake birth certificate. It's the right age. Jasmine—cute name. Good job, Ace." Braun patted the kid's shoulder. "Put out a BOLO on these three." He held up the folder. "Is this for us?"

"Yep. All yours."

"All right, send me all the files. Also, pull a list and notify all the daycares in the Charlottesville area. Make it a thirty-mile radius. Be sure to include church daycares. We forgot those once. The abducted child was a block from our office. We found out too late. Not making that mistake again."

"You got it," the kid said.

"Let's go. We'll run by my house first. We should be in Charlottesville by nine. Is your jump bag ready?"

"Always. What about you?" Max jutted his chin toward Braun. "Got more of those suits in yours?"

"Guess you'll have to wait to see."

———

6:00 p.m.

DEXTER NEVER TIRED OF HIS CEDAR-LINED CLOSET—the smell of success. He breathed in the spicy aroma, profoundly marking the end of a busy day resetting the dealership for a new winter marketing campaign after the massive influx of trick-or-treaters the day before. Even with giving the car away, they'd still made six figures.

He breathed in again. Ahhh.

Mary Ellen appeared at the closet doorway, leaning against the door jamb with one arm above her, the other unbuttoning her blouse. Lips red. His heart raced. This woman knew how to do sultry.

Dexter met her in two quick strides across the plush carpeting, drew her into his arms, and kissed her neck as he pulled her to him.

She whispered in his ear, "Dexter?"

"Uh-huh."

"The kids need to get to the church by six thirty. Are you taking them, or should I have the driver take them?"

Mood killer. He took a step back and looked at her.

She winked and ran a finger up her thigh, lifting the hem of her dress not nearly far enough. "I can think of something we can do while they're out."

So maybe there were two things he never tired of—his closet and his wife. He pulled her inside and closed the door, shutting them off from the world.

"Mom? You in here?" Christina called from outside.

Dexter cursed as Mary Ellen pulled away and touched his lips. "Later, big boy." With her face flushed, she buttoned her blouse and opened the door to their teenage daughter.

"Oh gross, Daddy. Get a room."

"We have one. You're in it." Dexter walked out and swatted her. "A little privacy, please."

"Ha, ha. So, you taking us or what?"

"Or what. Your mom and I have plans."

Christina rolled her eyes. "That's just gross. I'll call the driver. Next time put a sock on the door." She headed out.

"Just a minute." Mary Ellen followed her out of the room. "Have you eaten . . ."

Dexter returned to the closet to finish unbinding himself from the day. He emptied his pockets atop the center island of ties and accessories and removed his suit.

He'd like nothing more than to wait in bed for Mary Ellen's return, but he knew better. She wouldn't be relaxed until the kids had been gone for twenty or thirty minutes.

He pulled on a knit shirt and khaki pants and started down the stairs, but his private cell rang from the closet. If only he could ignore it so he could focus on every inch of Mary Ellen's figure. But then again, he'd only worry about it.

He picked up the phone from the accessory center. "Did you call to make my night or destroy the mood?"

"You decide."

"So it's mood-killer. Talk."

Mary Ellen came to the door and frowned when she saw him on the phone. "You coming down to dinner? The kids left for church. You know what that means."

"I'll be right down."

She rolled her eyes. "You have five minutes, or you can spend the evening alone." She left.

Dexter pounded the closet dresser. "I hope you heard that."

"Yes, sir. I'll make this quick. Both ID addresses were bad—an abandoned Virginia house and some North Carolina family's house. But we talked to some people who think they saw them in Virginia. Blue Prius. A redhead and a brunette, just like the ID photos. They were at a gas station just off I-64 in Covington. That's on the way to Charlottesville, so it's likely that's where they're headed."

"What did Hawthorne say?"

204

"He doesn't know anything. He's worried he's being left out of the loop—either that or they really don't have anything. Of course, he can't sound too interested, or they'll get suspicious. He's sure the FBI knows about Virginia. They put out a BOLO there. It doesn't sound like the feds got the North Carolina address."

"You sent a team to North Carolina?"

"Covered."

Rockefeller came into the room and lay down on his dog bed, a sign the kids were gone.

"We'd better find them first." Dexter walked to the window. The driver was pulling out with the kids. *Kids . . . church.* "Didn't you say the girlfriend had a kid?"

"Yeah. Little girl. Three or four."

"Tell them to go to places where kids go. Parks. Daycares. Churches. Kids get antsy. She'll surface soon enough. And tell them to follow the FBI guys. In fact, put two teams on it. We need to end this—now. We have a week until that Hearthstone hearing."

"You got it, boss. And boss, it's the first of the month. Don't forget to burn the phone."

Dexter hung up, pulled out the sim card, filled the bathroom sink with a couple of inches of water, dropped the phone in, then trashed it. He started to retrieve the next one in line but decided against it. He already had some work to do if he was going to get Mary Ellen's engines restarted, and he wasn't going to let these hicks interfere with his evening.

Chapter 23

Thursday, November 2
9:20 a.m.

A DRONING MOTOR AWAKENED HEATHER *from a restless sleep.* What now? A vacuum? A cleaning service? She covered her head, but it was still a splinter needing extraction.

Heather threw the covers back and got up. She grabbed her phone. Nine twenty. Was it too much to ask to have a little quiet so she could sleep? Heather downed pill number fourteen with the water she had concealed from Melissa's purview, then stormed the living area.

Margie looked up from her vacuuming, tapped the button on top of the old Electrolux with her navy-blue-sneakered foot, and rested her crossed wrists on top of the wand.

"Good morning, sweetie. I hope I didn't wake you."

"Of course you did. Didn't you see my door closed? Why can't you leave me alone?"

Margie's mouth dropped open. "I'm so sorry. You're right. I should have known better."

"Yes, you should have. How many times do I have to tell you I need my rest?"

Heather cursed, then retreated to her room, slamming the door behind her. She fell into bed and began to cry.

Margie rapped softly on her bedroom door. "Cindy?"

"Go away!"

Margie came and sat on the edge of the bed. "It's okay, sweetie." She began stroking Heather's head. "I know how much it hurts. I've had broken ribs—remember?"

"Oh, so you've had amnesia?" She turned her back to Margie.

"No, I haven't." Margie spoke softly and continued to stroke her hair. "I think it's time I tell you about the white deer."

"What?" Heather turned back. Margie's eyes were soft.

"The white deer. Did it seem almost magical—did it appear and then disappear?"

Heather wiped her eyes. "Yeah."

"When I was about Jasmine's age, I saw a rabbit in our yard. It scurried off into the woods, and I followed. It got away, and I found myself lost. I wandered around crying and calling out for my parents for the longest time. Out of nowhere, a white deer appeared. I swear it glowed. It looked me in the eyes, then walked away—like it wanted me to follow. The fear left me, and I followed.

"After a while, I heard my parents calling me. The deer turned, looked at me, and disappeared. And I mean disappeared. I had only looked away for a moment, and when I looked back, it was gone. When I told my parents about the deer, my dad said it was the Holy Spirit, Himself."

"Did you ever see it again?"

"Yes." She chuckled. "Most folks who know me now find this hard to believe, but I was like the old song, 'on the highway to hell.' One night, I was driving to the wrong kind of party. A white deer jumped out in front of my car. I veered off the road to avoid it."

Heather's mind flashed a white deer on the road and veering off, but the image evaporated as quickly as it came. A chill ran through her.

Margie examined Heather's face. "What is it?"

"I don't know. It was like . . . like déjà vu, but now it's gone."

Margie patted her arm. "I had to get a tow truck to get my car out of that ditch. But it was the best thing that ever happened to me."

"Why?"

"First, the party kids ended up starting a fire that caused a gas explosion. Several died. If that deer hadn't jumped out in the road, I might not be sitting here."

"Wow." Heather's mind flashed back to the camper . . . the gas leak, but again, it disappeared.

"That's not the best part." She grinned impishly. "The tow truck driver was a Christian. I don't for the life of me remember how it came up, but we talked about my life choices. Then he invited me to church. He was so handsome—I couldn't say no. I fell in love with him *and* Jesus. Forty-eight years later, I'm still madly in love with both of them—all because of that white deer.

"When Jasmine told me you saw it, I don't know why, but I felt led to tell you my story. I don't know what's going on in your life, and I don't need to know." Margie stroked Heather's face. "I'm here for you if you ever need to talk." She stood. "Would you like for me to finish vacuuming later?"

"No, no. It's okay. I'm sorry I barked at you."

"It's okay. I'd be a little stressed too. I'll shut the door. I'll let myself out when I'm done." Margie rose and quietly pulled the door closed behind her.

The deer she saw at the cabin didn't change her life. But Melissa had told her about the one that had caused her to crash. A crash that was course-altering. Instead of going from hell's highway to the stairway to heaven, Heather was trapped in a damned life with no way out.

———

9:30 a.m.

MAX'S HEART SANK AS HE STARED from the street at the sagging porch roof and broken windows of the house listed on the girls' IDs. He'd rescued his sister too many times from these drug-infested flop houses. Why would the girls be in this dump if they had the kind of cash the FBI had recovered . . . unless that was all they had.

"Sure we got the right place?" Max asked as they walked up the steps to a wrap-around porch and carefully chose which rotting boards might hold their weight. Curled paint revealed mold-filled cracks in the siding.

"I guess we'll see."

As Braun knocked on the blistered-paint door and announced their FBI status, Max moved to the bay windows—a single glass pane remaining unbroken. Inside, sofas not fit for animals, broken tables, and fouled blankets littered the living room. Syringes, rubber tubing, plastic bags, and foil were strewn around the floor. Even outside, the smell of putrid human waste accosted his senses. No evidence of life here, but then again, anyone in a drug hole was not really living anyway.

Braun joined him at the window.

Max centered his face in front of a broken-out section of glass. "FBI. Anyone in there?"

No answer.

Max shook his head. "I hope we have better luck with the daycares."

As they turned to leave, a baby cried. They looked at each other.

"Did you hear that?" Max asked.

Braun nodded as the two swiveled back to the door.

Paint flecked off as Braun pounded. "FBI! Open up!" He yanked on the handle, but it was locked.

"The windows." Max held up his sling." I hate to ask."

Braun wrapped his hand in his jacket, cleared the remaining glass from one of the bay windows, and climbed through. A few seconds later, he opened the front door for Max, gun drawn. Max pulled his own and entered the hallway.

The baby cried out again. Braun signaled himself upstairs and Max down the hall. Following his gun and the baby's cries, he entered the kitchen, where he found a blond mid-twenties female crumpled against one of the lower cabinets, a syringe in her hand.

His heart hurt. *Not another one, Lord. Wasn't my sister enough?*

Max holstered his gun. "Clear!"

"Clear!" Braun called out from upstairs.

"Down here!" Max stooped to check the girl's pulse. Only skin covered her cold skeleton. The cardboard box in the corner cried out again—a month-old infant wrapped in a dingy yellow blanket. Max scooped up the baby with his good arm and felt its forehead. Cool but pink with life.

Braun came in. Max jutted his chin toward the girl. "Too late for her, but the baby looks okay."

While Braun called it in, Max placed the screaming infant on the counter to check its condition. He removed the soaked and smelly diaper to discover a girl. She screamed all the more, face turning bright red. No cuts or bruises. He formed a makeshift diaper with his sling, then wrapped her back up and began rocking this precious miracle—another orphan in an already overwhelmed foster system.

"Check upstairs for a diaper bag."

Max took the downstairs, swinging the baby in his arms and singing "You Are My Sunshine" until she settled. His heart ached. He stared into her wide-open blue eyes and wondered if she would end up like her mother. Like his sister. At least his sister hadn't left an orphan.

Braun clumped down the wooden staircase. "No baby stuff." He smirked when he saw the baby sucking Max's knuckle. "Looks like you're a natural. Hey, if you ever need a side gig, I get my rugrats every other weekend."

A siren screamed its way to the front of the house. Paramedics rolled a stretcher in through the open front door. Max placed the miniature human on the adult-size stretcher, swallowing her up like children's feet in their daddy's shoes. The paramedics went to work checking her vitals.

One paramedic chuckled and shook his head. "Nice diaper job."

Max nodded. "Thanks."

"Don't worry." The paramedic tipped his chin to the arm Max didn't realize he was cradling. "We've got slings in the truck."

He didn't really want one back.

"Other than that, she looks like she's in good shape. Lucky you found her when you did. We found one too late just last week."

"You see this a lot?" Max asked.

"Isn't once enough?"

Max nodded as two police officers entered. He gestured down the hall. "The vic is in the kitchen."

One of the officers went back.

"So, what were you guys doing here?" the second officer asked.

Braun explained about the girls and showed him copies of their fake IDs.

"Weren't these the two we got the BOLO on?"

Max nodded.

"They sure are beautiful. Hard to believe they'd be involved in this kind of stuff. Not that it's anything new for us. The University is full of beautiful students with very influential parents who demand special hands-off treatment—if you know what I mean." The officer shook his head. "Privilege. Look what it gets you." He scanned the girls' images again. "Are they suspects?"

"Maybe—maybe not." Braun pointed to Heather's picture. "This one claims to have amnesia due to head trauma from an explosion—"

"Meth lab?"

"No." Braun described the explosion. "We're concerned they're in danger. These IDs were our only lead."

"Well, I hope you find them. Why don't you come back to the station so I can introduce you to the chief."

"That'd be great," Braun said.

The officer watched the paramedics wheel the baby out, then shook his head. "Well, even if you don't find the girls, you sure saved that baby's life. Silver linings."

Max was indeed thankful for that.

211

He forced himself to follow them to the truck to get a replacement sling, then located Braun behind a police SUV across the street. As he checked left to cross, a dark Grand Marquis pulled to the side of the road several houses away.

"Braun!"

The car pulled out and sped by. He dashed after them but couldn't make out the license plate. Braun joined him in the wake.

"It was them," Braun said. "The two guys we spotted at the hospital." He pointed to the officer, then to the officer's SUV. "You know these streets. Let's go!"

The men jumped in without missing a beat, Braun claiming shotgun. Braun rattled off a description of the vehicle and the two men. The officer called in the BOLO as they raced through the neighborhood back to Route 29.

"Go left. They wouldn't head into town."

The officer described the street system as he gave pursuit. After several miles, he pulled to a stop sign and turned to Max. "They could be anywhere. At least we have a description of the car."

"Don't count on it," Braun said. "These guys will have already ditched the car and picked up another—if they didn't already have one waiting. Next time we see these guys, they could be driving a car like that." He pointed to a blue Prius that crossed in front of them. A beagle shepherd hung its head out the window, ears flapping in the crisp breeze.

"Dog and all?" The officer chuckled.

"Well, that would be a first," Braun said, "But I wouldn't put anything past them."

Max cursed. "I bet they're the ones that killed Lenny. If those girls are in this town, they're in trouble."

"Well, the good news is that if those guys came to this house, they got the same wrong address we did," Braun said. "Let's just hope they didn't find something we didn't."

———

10:30 a.m.

ABU BARKED AND SCRATCHED AT HEATHER'S DOOR.

She groaned and turned over under the bedcovers. What *now*?

"Aunt Cindy! Aunt Cindy!" Olivia squealed as she broke into her room. "Guess what we did?"

"Jasmine!" Melissa said, following her in. "How many times do I have to tell you to leave Aunt Cindy alone?"

"It's okay," Heather pushed herself up.

"No, it's not." Melissa swatted Olivia's behind. "Please, go into your room and take off your shoes and jacket, then sit and think about your choice to disobey. I'll be in to talk about it in a minute."

Melissa shut the door behind Olivia as she left. She squeezed up the narrow passage between the bed and the wall. "What's Margie doing here?" she whispered with a pinched face.

"I don't know. She just came in and started vacuuming."

Melissa held a finger to her lips. "*Shh.*"

Heather lowered her voice. "Don't you have housekeeping service as part of the rent?"

"It's not. What if she found the money? How would we explain that much cash?"

"You're asking me . . . *now*? I had nothing to do with any of this. Remember? Innocent bystander." Heather reached past Melissa for her pills and took number thirteen.

"Is that your answer? Pop another pill?" Melissa grabbed the pill bottle and counted. "Oh my gosh, is that it? You only have twelve left? What are you gonna do when you run out? You know I'm not buying you more." She threw the bottle onto the bed.

"Give me a break. It's only been a week since my accident." She searched for the bottle among the comforter's folds.

"Just what I need. An addict."

"I am not addicted." She stopped searching and glared at Melissa. "I'm sorry I'm not healing as quickly as you think I should, *Doctor.*"

"You ungrateful—"

"Mommy?" Olivia said, peeking into the room. "Are you okay?"

Melissa's neck muscles strained. She took a deep breath and glared at Heather. "Yes, baby. Everything's fine." She turned to her daughter. "Go back to your room and stay there until I come in."

Olivia's tiny face looked between the girls, and then she pulled the door closed.

Melissa quickly located and grabbed the pill bottle. "Well, you've made it clear that you consider yourself a hostage, not a guest. But I'm not going to be an enabler." She checked her watch. "Your next pill will be at four-thirty, not a minute before. And if you don't like it, I'll give you money to go wherever you want—no questions asked." Melissa pocketed the pills and left, slamming the door behind her.

Was she serious? Who did Melissa think she was? Had she forgotten that it was her fault she was in this mess? Didn't Melissa understand she would rather be anywhere than here? Melissa's the one who told her not to go back to her family.

How was she ever supposed to find her way back to the life she had before? Instead, she was a prisoner of a crime she didn't commit and a mind she didn't break. She should take the whole bottle of pills and end this. But Melissa had them.

She dropped back onto her pillows and prayed she would never wake up, but sleep evaded her. Even the pill she'd taken wasn't helping to calm her racing heart. After a few restless minutes of trying, she got up and paced.

Muffled voices snuck in under her door. The screen door banged shut. Had Margie left? Had she heard them fighting? Was Margie her friend? Theirs was the only relationship she knew from beginning to end. And now Melissa had probably driven her away.

One thing was for certain—Heather needed those pills. There was no way she was going to make it six hours. She needed to make amends.

Heather donned her robe and opened the bedroom door. She stepped out, fully prepared to humble herself, but the living room was empty. Melissa's voice drifted from her closed bedroom door. A reprieve. A shower was in order.

Once cleaned and refreshed, she put on her robe, inhaled, and opened the bathroom door—time to face the groveling music.

The door to the other bedroom was open, and the cabin was void. No Melissa. No Olivia. No Abu. Where had they gone now? She took a seat at the table, taking in the quiet. Somehow, she was disappointed—despite being saved from groveling. The emptiness penetrated her soul. She put her head down, cried until no tears were left, and then sat up numb.

She didn't know how long she had been sitting when crunching gravel in the drive broke through her fog. Her head turned robotically. Margie's Buick pulled up and parked. The sight of another warm body soothed her heart. But why had she returned?

Footsteps tapped across the porch. A knock.

"Come in."

The screen door squeaked. Keys fumbled. The door opened. Margie's expression shifted immediately to concern.

"Are you okay?" She hurried over and sat next to Heather. "I saw Melissa drive away with Jasmine and Abu. I was worried about your fight." She looked into Heather's eyes. "You've been crying."

"I'll be okay. I'm such a loser."

"Don't say that." Margie reached for her hands, but Heather kept them in her lap. "With all the stress from the amnesia and the pain, it's no wonder you're grouchy."

Why couldn't Melissa understand her like Margie did? Why couldn't she meet her where she was?

"When I hurt my ribs," Margie said, "I wanted to stay in bed all day. But my doctor told me I needed to move around. Didn't your doctor tell you that?"

"Yes, he did." She couldn't tell Margie that she'd busted out of the hospital before getting her rehab instructions. "The swelling in my head had just gone down, so he told me to wait a couple of days before I moved around."

"You've been here that long."

"You're right. I've lost all track of time."

"I've got an idea. Why don't you get dressed? I bet you'll feel better."

"You're probably right." Heather stood.

"In fact, how about we go for a walk at the University to see some Jefferson architecture and have lunch at The Corner? The air is crisp. The sky is blue. It'll give you a fresh perspective. Or we can go for a drive if you don't feel like walking. But I think you'll love the Rotunda and the Serpentine Walls. They're fabulous."

The idea tickled something in her artist's soul. "I'd like that."

She went to the bedroom with an energy she hadn't felt since the accident. She picked out a red and beige mixed-plaid flannel top with a button front to keep her rib movements to a minimum. Putting on the jeans wasn't too bad. She grabbed her purse, then returned to the smell of fresh-brewed coffee and Margie reading a small note stuck to the refrigerator.

"What does this mean?"

Heather ran over and grabbed the note.

> *Cindy,*
>
> *I know I was too harsh with you, but I'm worried about your health. You're the only family I've ever had. I know you're in pain, but don't forget that I just lost the love of my life. Or the risks that I took coming to get you.*
>
> *I've taken Jasmine and Abu to a park.*
>
> *I hope we can talk when I get back.*
>
> *Kelsey*

Heather searched Margie's face.

"Kelsey never said she lost anyone. She said she was running from an abusive ex-husband. She said he'd almost killed her. What's going on here?"

Her amnesia was not going to explain this one. Or would it?

"I'm sorry, Margie. All I know is I woke up in a hospital bed with amnesia. I only know what Kelsey told me. She proved to me that we were related, but other than that, I can only go by what she said, which I am sure is what she told you. I'm as much in the dark as you are."

Margie relaxed, but sadness still covered her face. "You're right."

Heather dropped the note on the table. "Do you still want to go?"

"Oh yes, dear me. Of course. You should get a jacket. You might get chilly."

"I think I'll be fine with my flannel. Besides, dressing hurts." She looked back at the letter on the table. "I'd better leave a note for Melissa so she won't worry."

"Good idea." Margie pulled a pen from her purse and handed it to Heather.

She scribbled a note telling Melissa where she was going. She dare not say more with Margie around. She handed the pen back.

"All right. Let's go."

Margie poured the coffee into two Styrofoam cups, and they headed for a much-needed diversion. If only she had her pills.

————

2:30 a.m.

HEATHER'S HEART BEAT FASTER as Margie pulled up to the cabin and parked beside the blue Prius but didn't turn off the engine. "I'm not coming in. You girls need to work out your differences—especially if you're each other's only kin."

"I hope we can." Heather unbuckled her seat belt. "Thank you. You were right about everything—getting out, amazing architecture, lunch, and perspective. It's the best I've felt since—well since I lost my memory. But my pain's back, and the prison keeper won't give me another pill until four thirty." Just the thought made her heart race.

"She's doing that for your good, you know. Those painkillers are addictive. And based on that note, she's dealing with something big. Maybe you should find out what that is and see things from her shoes."

"When the pain kicks in, it's hard for me to see anything. In the hospital, they gave me more whenever I needed it." She couldn't admit this to Margie, but she needed those pills for more than the pain. She needed them to get a break from the fear of maybe never getting her memory back. And now she feared dealing with Melissa. She wanted to go home with Margie.

Heather opened the car door and groaned through the pain to get out. Margie leaned across the console. "Remember—you are welcome anytime if you need to talk or just get out."

"Can I come now?"

Margie shook her head. "No, sweetie. You need to do this."

"I know you're right." Heather forced a smile and closed the car door. Her good mood and energy evaporated with each step as she prepared to face the woman who held the keys to her relief.

Abu ran to greet her, jumping up for a kiss.

"Abu, down," Melissa said with a taught face. This time, Abu didn't relent.

Despite the pain, Heather squatted and let Abu kiss her. "Good afternoon to you too."

Olivia came out of the bedroom. "Aunt Cindy! You're back." She ran to Heather and hugged her while she was still squatted. Abu was reenergized as it turned into a group hug.

Melissa tipped her head and said, "So much for that nap."

"I'm sorry," Heather said as she stood. "Did I wake you from your nap, sweetie?"

"No—I was in bed, but I wasn't sleeping. Mommy made me go in there because she said she couldn't take any more of me. She said I was her last nerve."

Melissa's face reddened. "I said you were *on* my last nerve." She pulled a chair out, sat at the end of the table with her back to the kitchen, and waved Olivia over. "I'm sorry. Mommy's very sad because Uncle Johnny isn't with us anymore, and because we had to move to get away from the bad men. Remember?"

Olivia tucked her chin. "Yes, ma'am. I'm sad too."

"I know, baby." Melissa touched Olivia's pouting lips. "You know I love you, right?"

"Yes, ma'am."

"Will you forgive me?"

Olivia nodded.

"Now give me a hug." Melissa wrapped her arms around her daughter, pulled her close, then held her back. "Okay, Aunt Cindy and I need to talk. Would you go into your room for a few minutes?"

"Yes, ma'am." Olivia called Abu, and the two disappeared around the corner.

"Come and sit." Melissa motioned to the chair at the opposite end of the table. "We need to clear the air and make a plan. We can't do this again."

"I agree." Heather sat facing Melissa. Her right leg began bouncing. She forced it to stop.

Melissa lifted the note. "So, Margie saw this?"

Heather nodded. "Yeah. She was pretty upset. Said you told her you were running from a violent ex-husband. I played the amnesia card."

"I should never have put that in writing."

"So what are you going to tell her?"

"I never told her how long ago I was divorced. And Olivia is four, so falling in love with another man is believable. I'll tell her he died in a car accident."

"That makes sense. What else did you tell her?" Heather's leg started bouncing again. She put her hand on it to stop it.

"Just that you were in a car accident."

"Isn't that a lot of accidents?"

"I guess." Melissa stared out the window. "I'll have to figure that out—maybe an accident at work?"

"Your call. Just let me know what you decide."

"Maybe I could say you were both in the same accident—even that my ex ran you off the road. Most of that is the truth. The only fib is who ran you off the road."

"Where did this alleged accident happen? Margie might try to look it up."

"I'm not going to say. I already told her that we were using aliases, and that's why I have to pay in cash."

"Good. But how do I explain that I didn't know this?"

"I didn't tell you because you had enough to deal with."

"Makes sense. How did you explain having the money to pay to stay here?"

"I didn't. She never asked, and if she does, I'll remind her of my no-details policy."

"Okay, I think we're good then." She rose to escape to her room to wait out the two-hour countdown to relief.

Melissa's face tensed. "No, we're not. Sit down."

Heather sat.

"Where did you go with Margie today?

"To the Corner for lunch, then to the Lawn and Rotunda."

Melissa examined Heather for a long moment. "I think you know what I mean."

Heather's legs bounced. "Margie came back after she saw you leave. She was worried about me after our fight this morning."

"Yeah. I was good and mad. I shouldn't have taken it out on you—or her."

She dare not agree. She needed to keep Melissa's guard down. Heather quelled her bounding leg.

"Well, I probably deserved it. My pain has been so intense. And I feel like I'm living in a vacuum because of the amnesia. I'm afraid I'll never remember. It's getting to me."

"But that's no excuse for turning to drugs. I'm not going to let it happen."

"I get it." She was getting nowhere fast. She stood, groaning for sympathy. "Well, listen, I've had a big day. I'm going back to bed. At least it doesn't hurt when I sleep."

Melissa stood and pulled the pill bottle from her jeans pocket. She stared at it for a minute, then said, "Here. I'm not your momma." She handed them over, staring Heather in the eyes. "But I was serious—addicts are not welcome here."

"Got it," she said, anticipating the rush she was about to get. "I promise. I'm not addicted." She really wasn't. She could stop anytime—and she would—just as soon as this pain went away and her memory returned.

She headed to her lair, pill bottle in hand.

"Remember, your next pill is four-thirty." Melissa called from the living room.

Heather poked her head back out. "I got this," she said, then immediately took pill number twelve.

She stared at the bottle. Emotionally and physically, this had been a big day—getting out for the first time since they'd come here—seeing new things. Maybe she should take one more to settle down for the excellent sleep she required for healing.

Number eleven.

She slipped off her boots and crawled back under the covers to enjoy the rush. But it never came. She wasn't even sleepy. Maybe it was all the extra anxiety from fighting.

Just one more—just this once. She sat up, took number ten, and lay back down. And then it happened. Finally—the rush of relief.

That was more like it.

Chapter 24

Friday, November 3
9:28 a.m.

ABU'S BARKING AWOKE HEATHER ONCE AGAIN. Light shined in through the crooked miniblinds. Every bone in her body ached—not just her ribs. This pain was deep and all over. The sheets were soaked with her sweat. She pushed off the worn, blue comforter only to be seized with chills. Was she getting sick?

She rolled to her side to avoid the abdominal pull that stabbed her ribs. Even running her fingers through her hair hurt. She checked her phone. Friday morning. Nine twenty-eight. What had happened to Thursday?

Nausea stirred her stomach. Heather opened and tipped the last pill into her palm. She stared at its implications. Should she save it for when she really felt bad—like now?

She opted for the Tylenol-Advil cocktail Melissa had recommended.

Heather donned her robe and opened her door. Five pairs of eyes were trained on her, including Abu, who provided a rambunctious greeting and wet kisses. Melissa and Margie were seated at the pine table. Doug had Olivia tucked under his arm on the futon.

"Down!" She said, harsher than she'd meant.

Abu retreated to her bed and put her head down with a plop of frustration.

"I'm sorry." She put her hand up as if shielding light from her eyes. "I'm just not feeling well today. I think I'm coming down with something."

Doug patted Olivia on the head. "It's okay. We busted in here too early." He turned to Margie. "See the trouble you cause?" He chortled, amused with his own teasing.

"Oh yeah—like it was my idea to get up this early." She looked at Heather. "He's Mr. Early Bird." She winked. "Besides, I did bring a delicious apple coffee cake."

Melissa shifted in her seat but never broke eye contact. "Where would you have gotten sick? None of us are sick."

"You know those hospitals . . ." Keeping her head down, she pulled the robe tightly around her body and moved toward the bathroom. "If you'll excuse me, I'm just going to freshen up."

"You go ahead, little lady," Doug said. "We probably need to get going anyway."

"No, no. Please don't leave on my account. I'll just be a minute. I'd love to chat." Anything was better than Melissa's inquisition.

She slipped into the bathroom and stared at the dark circles under her eyes. Death stared back. She knew enough about addicts to know the symptoms—and she had them. But how could that be? It hadn't even been a week.

She found bottles of Advil and Tylenol on the shelf over the toilet and tapped two of each into her palm. She filled Olivia's Aladdin cup, then downed the pills, chasing them with water. She braced herself on the sink, waiting for relief to take over . . . Nothing. She still felt awful. When would this nightmare end?

Her mouth was like a desert. She grabbed a washcloth and Olivia's bubblegum toothpaste and cleaned her teeth. The minutes passed, and still, nothing changed. She couldn't stay in the bathroom. Even their guests would get suspicious. Time to face her judge and jury.

"Well, that's better," she said as she slinked out of the bathroom and into the vacant seat at her end of the table. Despite her lack of movement, her breathing was fast. Her legs wanted to bounce—both more signs.

"Here." Margie cut a piece of the coffee cake and plated it for Heather.

"That looks delicious." Her stomach tightened. She picked up a fork and cut off a piece.

"Coffee?" Margie busied herself in the kitchen area.

"Yeah—that'd be great." She forced a bite, swallowed, then rested her fork on the plate, hoping no one would notice.

"Well, I've been thinking about your amnesia," Doug said. "Do you realize the great opportunity you have, little lady? You can reinvent yourself."

"Oh, Doug. Leave the girl alone," Margie said. "There's nothing good about amnesia.

As Margie delivered Heather's coffee, she looked at Melissa who was laser-focused on Heather's every move. Heather looked down at her plate. How long had her fingers been tapping? She forced them to stop.

Margie turned to her husband and waved him to come. "Maybe we need to get going."

"No-o-o-o," Olivia said.

"Please don't go," Heather said, sensing the coming storm.

"Doug needs to take some winter clothes down to the church this morning." Margie waved again, then took his hand to help him up. "Come on, old man."

Abu jumped up to take Doug's place.

"Well, I know when I'm not wanted, Miss Abu."

Everyone but Melissa laughed.

With every step the couple got closer to the door, another shovelful of dirt was tossed into Heather's grave.

"Can I come with you?" Olivia pleaded. "I'm bored."

"No, honey," Melissa said, "I'm sure Doug and Margie don't need you underfoot."

"We'd love for you to come," Margie said, "But we do have a few things to take care of today. We have the Harvest Festival at the church tomorrow. You should come. Lots of games and a costume contest. We still have that Jasmine costume." She turned to Melissa. "The kids love acting out their characters. And they can bring their extra candy to ship to our troops overseas."

"What are troops?"

Doug marched in place, arms swinging. "They're the soldiers who are fighting against the bad guys to keep us safe."

"Are they fighting the bad guys who hurt Uncle Johnny?"

Doug's and Margie's expressions blanked. Melissa's stalled for the briefest moment but quickly recovered. "No, sweetie. These bad men live far, far away."

Margie looked at Melissa. "Who's—"

"Ready to leave, honey?" Doug wrapped a hand around his wife before she could say anymore. "She's got to cook her prize-winning pie for the contest." He looked at the girls and beamed. "Her three-berry pie always takes the blue ribbon.."

"There's also a chili contest Doug keeps trying to win." Margie looked up at her man, who was almost two heads taller.

"What can I say? Our pastor's from Texas. He cleans up every year."

"You're just jealous." Margie elbowed him gently, and he kissed her on the cheek.

"Can *we* go to the festival, Mommy?" Olivia crawled into Melissa's lap. "Please, please, please."

"Yes, I think that sounds good. Got any ideas for today? I think we need to get out. Don't you, Cindy?"

"Yes. It was good to get out yesterday." The bed sounded better, but she couldn't tell Melissa that. She put her hands on her lap—where Melissa couldn't see them fidget.

"Oh," Doug said, turning to Margie, "What about Fridays After Five? They'd love that."

"Fridays After Five?" Melissa asked.

"Yes." Margie pushed her glasses back and squinted her nose. "It's at the downtown mall. There's live music in the amphitheater and lots of food. There are all sorts of people—from high society to just plain folks. You'll love it. And you're in luck. They usually shut down in September, but they're doing a special series now.

"I'm assuming it starts at five?" Melissa said.

"Clever, huh?" Doug chortled. "That's what happens when you have a university in town—you get smart folk that come up with this stuff."

"Sounds perfect," Melissa said. "How about it, Cindy?"

Heather forced a smile. "I'm game. That'll be a late night for me compared to my last few days. I'd better rest up." She pushed herself up from the table.

"Well, we'd better go if we're going to be ready for the Harvest Fest tomorrow. I've got a prize-winning pie to bake."

"Cindy, before you go," Doug said, "how 'bout that hug? You think you're ready for it?"

"Well, I can't think of a better person to get my first hug, but be gentle with me."

Heather walked into Doug's wide arms. It was the first time she felt loved—at least, that she could remember. And she liked it. Margie followed. Her embrace was long and too snug, but she was not about to let her know it hurt.

"Jasmine and I will go to the park for a little while so she can play. We'll leave Abu. Can you take her out later?"

"Sure." Heather excused herself to her room. She leaned back against the closed door. What would she say to Melissa if she asked about the meds? The over-the-counter stuff was not doing a thing for her. Since she'd taken them, she only felt worse with each passing moment.

She crawled back into bed, hoping to stay unconscious until they left that afternoon. Then, maybe she could find something more potent when they went out. With all those people at the event, there had to be someone who could help.

Unfortunately, just as she'd feared, sleep evaded her. Chills quickly overtook her. The deep pain returned. Even her skin hurt. She couldn't take it anymore.

She threw the covers back and reached for the last pill.

―――――

12:00 Noon

"HOW MANY BAPTIST CHURCHES CAN ONE TOWN HAVE?" Max said as they pulled up to another white-columned brick church attached to an annexed building sitting on a corner, this one with its parking lot across the street from the sanctuary. "You think the Baptist bylaws require columns and steeples?"

Braun huffed an agreement. "My friends went to churches like this back home. My family only went to church on the holy days. It was more like a cathedral. Then there was catholic school."

"Yeah. My family didn't do church either, but I did hang around a church youth group for a while when I was a teenager."

"You go to church now?" Braun asked.

"No. Guess it didn't stick. Never felt a need for it, if you know what I mean." Unless you counted the times he'd prayed for his sister. A lot of good that had done. It didn't seem like God was really out there. But then things happened, like saving that baby the day before—what were the odds? Maybe there was something to it.

Two dozen cars occupied the closest spots to the street. "There must be something going on. Either that or they have one hopping pre-K," Braun said as he parked.

The two agents got out and crossed the street. A HARVEST FEST: THIS SATURDAY banner hung in front of the large park-like grassy area to the right of the sanctuary, which formed an L with the three-story annex at the back.

Max pointed to the sign. "Maybe that explains all the cars."

The OFFICE sign directed them down a sidewalk to a white door tucked in the corner of the building's L-shape. A small balcony, supported by a white column—of course, covered the entryway. Maybe the pastor delivered summer sermons to a lawn-chair flock from there.

As they reached the door, a tall, seventy-something man juggling three grocery bags approached from across the lawn like a man on a mission.

"Can I help you?" the man asked.

"I think we should be asking you that." Max held the door open for the burdened man.

"Thank you. I'd shake your hand, but . . ." The man lifted his bags topped with flannel clothes and blankets.

"Can my friend grab one of those for you?" Max grinned as he held up his sling.

"I'd appreciate it." He handed all three bags to Braun and laughed. "One of the benefits of gettin' old. Come on. I'll show you where you can set those down."

The man shed his tan jacket as they followed him down a hallway to the left that opened into an area of plush green carpeting encircled by an orderly arrangement of sofas and chairs upholstered in bold floral patterns. A rounded, white-paneled welcome station sat on the room's far side. A perfectly-coiffed silver-haired woman looked up from her post as they entered.

"Morning, Miss Sally," the man said.

The woman's face lit up. "Good morning." She checked her watch. "Or should I say good afternoon, Doug? You here to help set up?"

"Not yet. The warden sent me down with these clothes for the homeless." He gestured to the bags Braun carried.

"Doug Lewis! I'd say Margie doesn't keep a tight enough rein on you." She shook her finger at Doug, feigning reproach, then looked at Max and Braun. "He has the sweetest wife God ever created. Warden indeed."

"Yeah, yeah. All you wardens stick together. But we men know better." Doug winked at the agents. "Speaking of gettin' ready, I need to get back to my chili. This is gonna be the year I knock the pastor off his throne."

"Dream on, sweetie. You don't stand a chance. Pastor said he's got a new secret ingredient. He brought me a sample this morning, and oh my—I dare say it's better than last year's."

"Well, maybe I got a new secret ingredient myself. You just wait."

"Meanwhile"—Sally cleared her throat and pointed to his companions—"are you going to introduce me to your friends?"

"Oh, I'm sorry. Where're my manners? This big fella here is my bodyguard, and this other fella—well, I just don't know. Not much use with that sling." Doug laughed. "Actually, I can't introduce them 'cause I didn't ask their names."

"That's right," Max said. "He dragged us off the street to do his heavy lifting." He tipped his hat. "I'm Max, and the bodyguard is Eric. Nice to meet you, Miss Sally."

Braun lifted the bags at his sides. "Bodyguard doubling as a delivery guy."

"Well, enough small talk," Doug said, starting toward a wide staircase to a basement. "Unlike some women who just sit around looking pretty, we've got work to do. Come on, men."

Sally beamed. "Don't let him lead you astray."

Doug narrated the tour as they made their way downstairs to a vast cafeteria-style room in the basement. "This is where we take care of our friends who live under the stars—'specially in the winter. Some of the ladies come and cook hot dinners for them a few times a week.

"Of course, there's always the church potluck dinner where you find the world's best fried chicken." Doug chuckled. "We Southern Baptists know our fried chicken."

They followed Doug across the room, weaving through the rows of folding tables and chairs to a Dutch door to the right of the serving line. Painted in cursive above the door were inscribed the words, TRULY I TELL YOU, WHATEVER YOU DID FOR ONE OF THE LEAST OF THESE

BROTHERS AND SISTERS OF MINE, YOU DID FOR ME — MATTHEW 25:40. Max didn't remember the verse from his church days. Of course, he wasn't into memorizing scripture—unless a prize was involved.

Doug retrieved a ring of a dozen keys from his pocket. "And here's why you should never get a reputation for being trustworthy." He dangled a dozen keys in the air. "They give you the keys to everything." He unlocked the door, then smiled like he was letting them into a bank vault. "This is where we keep the good stuff."

The room was lined with metal racks of clothing, cabinets filled with blankets, and bins labeled with various types of underclothing. Doug pointed to a table already covered with bags. "You can just set 'em down there."

Braun obliged, then threw his muscle-bound shoulders back. "Anything else?"

Doug laughed and clapped him on the shoulder. "That's a dangerous question around this place. How much time do you have?"

Max chuckled. "I wish we had more. Looks like you're doing some good work for the community here."

"It's never enough, but we try." Doug grinned. He pointed to Braun's suit. "That tie and white shirt tell me you're not here to help in the soup kitchen. Although you—" He looked Max over— "except for the hat, you'd fit right in. Course, you might not be of much use with that arm."

They laughed.

"So what can I do for you gentlemen?"

"Well, I'm Special Agent Braun, and this is Special Agent Enders. We're with the FBI." Max showed his badge. "We understand that you have a pre-K here. Perhaps you could direct us to it?"

"FBI you say? Wow. I know we've got some tough kids. I know firsthand 'cause the warden drags me in there to help sometimes. But FBI? Wait, this isn't about those Blackburn kids, is it? They'll drive anybody crazy." His eyes gave a twinkle as they all chuckled.

230

"No, nothing like that. But we'd love to speak with the pre-K direc-tor if you can point us in the right direction."

"Well now, you were such good sports carrying the bags, how 'bout I take you there? Besides, not even two smart agents like your-selves could find your way there without getting lost—much less make it past Mrs. Anderson. Takes a lot more than FBI clearance to get past her. I tell you, if you're ever in need of a tough cookie, she's your man. Then again"—he tipped his chin to Braun—"from the looks of you, you might could take her on." He winked, then motioned for them to follow. "This way, gentlemen."

Max could not remember a single down-to-earth man like Doug in his church. Holier-than-thou attitudes tainted his church memories.

Doug led them to a narrower staircase in the back corner of the cafeteria, then stopped. "Hold on—my jacket." He hurried back to grab it. "If I got home to the warden without this," he said, holding it in the air as he jogged back across the room, "there'd be heck to pay."

As they trailed behind Doug to the main floor, Braun asked, "You sure have a lot of cars here for a Friday. What's going on?"

"Didn't you see the sign? Harvest Fest is tomorrow. It's a big deal around here. Lots of crafty things—the stuff women swoon over. Good for Christmas presents, though.

"Then there're the cookin' contests. My wife's making her famous three-berry pie. We even let in FBI agents. You should come. I think it starts at ten. I forget. We have to be here at seven to set up."

"Wish we could," Max said. "We'll likely be heading back this afternoon."

They turned down two hallways and arrived at Noah's Ark, the Pre-K's greeting room, as was evidenced by the Eau de baby lotion. Various painted cartoon animals formed a line around the room, headed for the wooden check-in counter modeled after the famous boat. A slender forty-something woman emerged from an office door behind the ark wearing a scarecrow costume with a pointy brown hat over her long black hair.

"Doug." She smiled. "To what do I owe the pleasure?"

"We just came to see your costume. When are you going to be putting it on?"

She shook her head. "You like it?"

"If I were a crow, I wouldn't land here." He laughed. "These men have been wandering our hallways looking for you. I rescued them from eternal damnation."

"And you helped them find their way here?" She chuckled, then addressed the agents. "We find Doug roaming the hallways all the time. You're lucky you made it."

"You know me too well. I'd introduce you, but I'm old and can't remember names too well. These gentlemen are with the FBI. I think they're here about those Blackburn kids." Doug winked conspiratorially.

"FBI?" Her brows furrowed.

"That's right, and before they start asking questions, I'm gonna skedaddle back home to the warden." He turned to the men. "I'll leave you two with Mrs. Anderson."

They shook hands, and Doug started back the way they'd come. "Oh," he said, turning to them, "and when you leave, just head out the door there to the sidewalk"—he pointed to a door on the left—"and turn left back to the parking lot. And steer clear of the animals on the other side of the chain-link fence to the right out there. They might bite."

"Animals? Really?" Max asked, stepping to the glass exit door and seeing only a playground.

"Doug! He's referring to the kids." Mrs. Anderson said.

"Don't say I didn't warn you," Doug said, tickled with himself. "Okay, I'm really leaving this time."

"Thank you." Braun said, "And if I were you, I'd let the pastor win tomorrow. There's probably a bonus in heaven for that."

"You know what?" He pointed at Braun. "Eric, right?"

Braun nodded.

"I like you. Now I can lose with dignity—speaking of which, I'd better get to it. Good to meet you two." He waved and left.

"So, what can I do for you gentlemen?"

Braun made introductions, then showed the woman Olivia's photo. "Have you seen this little girl?"

Mrs. Anderson shook her head as she examined the photo.

"She'd be a little older now. This was taken a few months ago."

"Is this the four-year-old I got the email about?"

"It is," Braun said. "She'd be new here—would have arrived in the last couple of weeks."

Mrs. Anderson laughed. "Oh, heavens no. Most of our kids have been here since they were born—except for the occasional new professor's kids when semesters start over at the university. But most of our kids are just town folk. Definitely nobody in the last few weeks."

"Here's a picture of her mother." Braun showed her Melissa's ID photo. "Do you recognize her? She may have a different hair color or style."

"Only from the email I got. But no, I haven't seen her either."

"Well, if you don't mind, would you keep these photos and let us know if they come in?" Braun handed her a business card.

Mrs. Anderson looked at the card. "Did someone kidnap the little girl? That's what you guys do, isn't it—kidnappings?"

"Yes, but not in this case. The mother is a potential witness. She might be in a lot of danger."

"Is that right? Well, I'll be sure to call if I see either of them."

"We'd appreciate it. And if you see them, please don't say anything. Just call us," Braun said.

"I surely will."

"Thank you, ma'am," Max said, tipping his hat, then following Braun to the door.

"You know," Mrs. Anderson said, stepping around the counter. "We've got the Harvest Fest tomorrow. It's a great event for little ones. We usually get hundreds of kids. Maybe she'll bring her daughter."

"We'll keep that in mind. And thank you for everything."

They exited past the playground, happy with the sound of children's laughter. "You don't think the girls would be stupid enough to go out to a public event, do you?" Max asked.

"If they're even in this town."

They turned left at the sidewalk just as an old Toyota Corolla came around the corner and slowed before the playground.

Max made eye contact with the driver. "It's them!"

The car raced away. Max ran after them to get the plate as Braun called out, "I'll get the car while you call it in."

Max stopped when they turned the corner and made the call. This time he'd gotten the license number—not that it would do any good. The sheriff's office had already found their last car abandoned.

Braun picked him up at the corner. They took off in the direction the Corolla had traveled, but to no avail.

"They must be following the same game plan we are—find the child, find the mom," Max said. "I sure hope we get to them first."

Chapter 25

3:30 p.m.

ABU'S HEAD POPPED UP—EARS ON ALERT—from the spot she had captured on the bed after Heather had dozed off. Heather had started to object but then relaxed into the dog's affection. She hadn't been able to get back to sleep. Abu's snuggle had soothed her. But now, Abu growled.

Heather rolled to get up. "What is it, girl?"

Abu jumped down, raced to the front room, and began barking a dog stranger-danger alarm. Had the gang found her?

Heather's heart raced as she moved to her door to survey the front room and the parking area. No cars, but then again, the gang wouldn't just drive up. They'd park away and sneak up. Abu wasn't going to let that happen. Now in full protection mode on the futon, she stood against the back like a hound dog that had treed its prey. Something or someone outside that window had her full attention.

All the curtains and shades were open, making them easy targets. She closed her bedroom blinds, not that they couldn't just bust in and wipe them out.

Suddenly, something like gunfire banged outside, enraging Abu's barks. Abu was going to get them shot. With her back against the open bedroom door, she called out, "Abu. Come." She obeyed. Heather squatted beside her and held her collar.

Another bang stopped her heart, but it wasn't gunfire. More like a drum. Abu broke loose and ran back to the futon.

Something crashed. No gang members would make this much racket. Focusing on the parking area, Heather hurried across the living room to the door and peeked out the porch window just as a tipped-over metal trash can rolled away from the porch on the gravel. A furry face-masked bandit came around to the top, stood on his hind legs, stared at them, and began working on his mission—getting the bungee-corded lid off.

Abu continued to bark as Heather released the breath she'd been holding. She chuckled at her overreaction, then sat on the arm of the futon to enjoy his antics.

Stopping again, the determined ring-tailed thief glared a dare to stop him, dug his hind feet into the gravel, and used his body as leverage to pull back on the lid. It opened but snapped back shut. The raccoon looked at them and then repeated, this time getting his head in, but when the top squashed his neck, he pulled back. He pushed the can to the picnic table, jumped up on the bench, and started his quest anew from a different angle.

Heather laughed. "Well, Abu. At least I know you're a good watchdog."

Abu licked her face, jumped down, went to the door, and whined.

"Not happening, girl." Olivia would never forgive her if a rabid raccoon bit Abu. Her dad had to put down a dog once—

Her dad. She remembered her dad. "Oh my goodness, Abu! I remembered."

Abu stopped whining and cocked her head.

Like a torrent, memories rushed in. Piece by piece, room by room. Images of her dad's vet clinic, her sister, and his staff rolled in like waves fighting for first position on a beach. Suddenly, pressure crushed her head like a vice. The memories stopped as suddenly as they had come. She fell back to the futon cushions and cried, not from the pain but from the void.

Abu rushed to her side, licking her tears away. She wrapped her arm around her faithful friend.

After several minutes, the pressure relented. At the same time, something metal crashed on the gravel. Heather stood. The trash can lay open, and the raccoon was absconding down the hill toward the A-frame with his loot.

With the raccoon gone, it was safe to walk Abu. The wall clock by the linen closet read three forty. She painfully donned her robe, leashed Abu, then headed out with her tail-wagging friend.

The tree shadows were already lengthening. Abu ran to the limits of the retractable cord, stopping here and there to sniff out the raccoon's parking lot movements. At the end of the line, she paused to take care of an overdue potty call. While Heather waited, she agonized through her rib jabs to re-strap the can—not that it had been effective against its nemesis.

Back inside, Heather jumped into the shower to get ready for their night out. The warm water cascaded over her tense muscles, helping to alleviate the pain . . . until she had to put on her jeans, turtleneck, and sweater top. Man, she needed those drugs. How was she going to pull this off? She'd never done a drug deal before—or had she? Even if she had, it wasn't helping her now. But there was no other option.

Fully clothed and with nothing left to do but wait and observe every ache and pain, Heather paced. She wasn't hungry. Didn't want to watch TV. Her legs bounced as she stared out the window. Was she really an addict? Maybe it was nerves. Either way, Melissa would be home any minute. If Melissa noticed her jonesing legs, she'd keep Heather on a leash the whole time they were out. She needed to move—if for no other reason—than to get her mind off what she had to do.

Heather hooked Abu up. They walked down the hill past the vacant A-frame to the road they had come in by the lake.

Having only passed over the berm as a car passenger, she hadn't experienced the surrounding beauty. The mirror-like lake stretched to her left, reflecting the muted golden colors of late autumn. As she made her way across the berm, the sound of cascading water arose from the gully that dropped down on her right. The rushing waters calmed her soul. Maybe she didn't need those drugs.

She stopped to inhale the cool crispness that defined a wooded fall. She longed for an easel and palette of paints to capture an imagined canoe gliding two lovers toward a far-off mountain destiny.

Unimpressed, Abu tugged her leash, impatient to continue. She pulled Heather up the tree-lined hill to the Y where they had turned to come in. She wondered what lay down the road to her left besides Margie's house, but for now, she needed to stay on the path Melissa would pass by.

The pine office building was bigger than Heather remembered. In fact, bigger than their cabin. The open door welcomed them in. Abu's nose worked overtime as she made her inspections. A desk sat to the left of the entrance, covered with brochures for nearby Jefferson architecture and wine country attractions. Laundry sounds hummed from the doors just beyond. To her right, tables, games, and a sitting area complete with a big-screen television made the space feel more like a home than an office.

"Anyone here?"

No one answered.

Had Margie forgotten to lock up? It wasn't like this was a gated development that would protect them from thieves.

A possible medicine cabinet in the bathroom to her right enticed her to come and look.

Like their cabin, only a shelf holding soap and lotion sat above the sink. The mirror above exposed Heather's miserable state.

Abu tugged.

"Okay, girl. I'm coming."

Abu led her out of the cabin toward the resort entrance—such as it was. Across the road, a large, white home graced the top of a hill encased by a white fence. Smoke escaped its chimney, blowing toward a giant barren oak tree near its side. The land beyond stretched out as far as the hills would allow her to see.

A jacketed horse grazed midway down the pastured hill to her left. It raised its head toward them. Abu barked. Unfazed, the horse returned to its afternoon snack.

An Adirondack chair below the oak tree faced in the direction of the horse. Heather imagined a woman at the chair . . . a painting easel—an image she'd seen before. At least, she thought she had. The woman hummed as she painted the pastoral scene around her. A girl rode up on a horse. Julie? Mom? Was her mind playing tricks on her?

Before she could process it, Melissa's Prius came up the road, stopped next to her, and opened her window. Abu jumped up on the door. Melissa was smiling—something Heather wasn't used to.

"Aunt Cindy!" Olivia shouted from her child seat in the back.

"Hi, sweetie."

"I'm glad to see you're out," Melissa said. "Want a ride back?"

"Please." She let Abu in the back, then went around and groaned as she lowered herself into the passenger seat. Melissa started back.

"You're not going to believe this," Heather said. "I remembered something."

Melissa looked at her, eyes wide. "Really?"

"Yeah. It was just a couple of flashes, but still." She recounted how the raccoon triggered her first memory. Then the woman painting. "Maybe I'm going to be okay."

Melissa pulled up the drive to the cabin. The raccoon was back.

"Look, Jasmine. The raccoon."

"Where?" She struggled against her car seat to see out, but it scurried down the hill.

"I'm sorry, baby. He ran off." Melissa said.

"That's not fair. I never get to see anything."

"I'm sure he'll be back," Heather said. "He's a determined rascal, and he struck it rich last time."

They all climbed out. Melissa returned the trash can to its spot beside the house. The raccoon was pacing down the hill by the A-frame, staring at them.

"Look there, Jasmine. Do you see him?" Heather asked, pointing in his direction.

"Yeah, cool! Can we pet it?"

"No," Heather said too sharply. "They're very dangerous."

"But he's so cute."

"They carry rabies. If you get bit, you could die," Heather said.

"You ready to go to Fridays after Five?" Melissa asked as they made their way into the warmth Heather hadn't noticed she'd missed.

"Yeah, I am. I think it's going to be good for me." Not in the way Melissa thought.

"Good. Have you had your four o'clock pill?"

"No. I should probably go take it." More casually than she felt, Heather went to her room and stuffed the empty pill bottle in her pocket, then went to the bathroom and took the over-the-counter cocktail—hoping for some relief. Then she put a few tablets into the empty bottle so if Melissa asked, she could rattle it.

"Ready?" Melissa asked when Heather emerged from her deceit. Was she ever.

———

5:00 p.m.

OLIVIA FILLED THE TWENTY-MINUTE CAR RIDE to the Downtown Mall with questions about where they were going, how long it would take, and how many kids would be there. Heather filled it with working to keep her legs still and her stomach calm while wondering how she would get away from Melissa long enough to find what she needed.

After parking in the pay lot, they crossed the street they'd come in on and walked up a barricaded road toward the outdoor mall. Margie had told her that the city had converted its Main Street into a bricked park that ran half a dozen blocks, housing stores, restaurants, and al fresco entertainment. She'd also said there would be towns folk from all socio-economic backgrounds. Heather hoped that meant a *medication entrepreneur* because she couldn't believe she'd sunk so low as to be looking for a drug dealer.

About halfway up the side road, a man in a ragged maroon parka sat huddled on the ground against a building, a brown paper bag in his hand and a donation cup and bulldog at his side. He'd probably know where to get what she needed. She'd have to sneak back.

The mall opened up at the top of the road to more activity than she'd imagined. The white-canvas-covered amphitheater they'd come for was on their right at the bottom of the street. They turned toward the large gathering below.

Margie was right about the people. High society strolled in their designer clothes next to Goodwill-clad families bundled for a cold autumn evening. Couples window-shopped. Some waited for restaurants. Others people-watched from their benches. Itinerant guitar players livened the ambiance as the fragrances of Italian cuisine wafted past. But none of them looked like the type she needed.

Folks sat on blankets while others meandered around the grassy areas in front of the sizable canvas-covered stage and three-section seating area. Local ale vendors and wineries hosted various tents around the perimeter.

A man sporting a well-trimmed beard approached them from a tent-covered folding table. He held out a handful of lime-green plastic wristbands. "Will you be tasting any of our local delights?"

"I'm sorry. What?" Melissa asked.

He pointed to the vendor tents. "Wines? Beer? Are you going to be drinking the local fare?"

"Oh, I don't know." She eyed Heather.

Heather didn't dare say yes, but she'd try anything to help her escape her mounting anxiety. Maybe if she drank enough.

Melissa turned back to the man. "Why do you ask?"

"Well, if you're going to drink, we check your ID, then give you a wristband, so we don't have to card you all night. And if you want to do the Taste of Charlottesville, then you can pay once and taste to your heart's content."

Olivia tugged at Melissa's sleeve. "I want a wristband?"

"No, sweetie. They're for grown-ups."

"But I want one."

"I said no." She turned back to the man. "I don't think so. I'm the designated driver, and my sister can't drink."

Heather's face warmed. She elbowed Melissa and whispered. "Tell the world, why don't you."

Melissa kept her eyes on the man. "Sorry. She's recovering from a serious accident—still getting her bearings."

"Oh, I'm sorry to hear that. I hope you feel better."

"Me, too," Heather said, wishing he had a wristband for what she needed.

They crossed the grassy area and scoped out the three sparsely-occupied sections of folding chairs in front of the stage as a couple finished a gospel song while a group waited off-stage. Olivia pointed to another grassy area past the right folding-chair section, where a dozen kids batted a balloon between them. She tugged on Melissa's sleeve. "Mommy, can I go play?"

Melissa looked at Heather as if she was afraid to leave her alone.

Heather prayed she'd go. "You go on." Heather pointed to the folding chairs. "Walking here tired me out. I'll sit and watch from there." She forced a smile. "It's a beautiful night, and with the music and the children, this'll be good for my soul."

"Come on, Mommy!" With one tug, Melissa and Olivia were on their way to much-needed fun.

"Melissa called back, "If you need anything, wave."

Heather nodded and followed until she was halfway down the aisle, then took a seat to watch the adults huddled around the contagious laughter of the kids. A smile tugged at Heather's cheeks. This *was* a welcome change from hostage life.

Olivia joined and began bouncing in cadence with the other kids. Melissa looked back at Heather as if still unsure it was safe to leave her.

Heather smiled and waved as she quieted her own bouncing legs.

Melissa moved next to some chatting parents and gradually melded in, ignorant of anything beyond their joy-filled circle. A moment like this should be captured.

A deep longing arose to find an easel, paint, and brushes. Images flooded her mind—an art studio, students painting the streets of Chicago—the essence of the entire city.

A smile spread across her face as she returned to herself—the artist she was. She knew. And she remembered. Oh, how much she remembered—scenes, family, snapshots, experiences. Her heart quickened with excitement.

Then another image surfaced, this one of two lovers on a bed in the back room of her art studio. Her husband. Her bed. A student. Betrayal knotted her stomach. How could he have done that? She closed her eyes and tilted her head back. These were not the memories she craved. It was too much. She begged them to stop.

Several rows away, a red-faced baby squalled. Heather's mind raced. A baby . . . a pregnancy test . . . a waiting room of young girls not daring to speak . . . a gynecologist table . . . a vacuuming sound . . . blood, so much blood . . . a hospital . . . a doctor's sad eyes and the words no one should ever hear . . . *I'm sorry. You won't be able to have children.*

Tears cascaded down her cheeks. Her baby—the chance for any babies—gone forever. How could she have been so stupid? Is this who she really was? She folded in half, rocking, forcing deep breaths into her lungs to push away the memories of abortion clinic workers lying to her—trying to earn a commission on her grief. Anger competed with shame.

She held her head in her hands as shards of pain shot through. The Downtown Saloon . . . her sister's pregnancy . . . her perfect sister with her perfect life. The bed spinning . . . the dark, winding road . . . the white deer . . . the river . . . the cold . . . Abu . . . the Porsche . . . Tyrone . . . Johnny . . . blood everywhere.

No wonder her memory had shut down—her life had been a total waste. If this was who she was, she didn't want to remember.

————

6:00 p.m.

"YOU SURE THIS IS THE PLACE?" Max asked as Braun slowed and parked in the single open space in front of Yelp's number-one-rated diner. An orange, lighted twenty-foot sign pointed toward the metal patio furniture in front of the Main Street building, confirming they'd found the right place, but number one? Giant menus, hand-written signs, and faded printed ads were taped inside the ground-to-roof sixties-style plate-glass windows, along with the neon open sign Max was beginning to wish wasn't lit. Two garage bay doors midway back on the building told of a former auto-industry-related occupation.

"Just how many reviews were there? West Virginia mining towns have diners more modern than this." Max climbed out of his seat. "I like fried chicken, but soul food?" He grabbed his cowboy hat off the back seat and angled it just right on his head. Immediately, the fried-chicken aroma drew him, but he was not about to confess it.

Braun came around the back end of the SUV. "We got four different recommendations for this place. Two from Southern Baptist pastors, and they know their fried chicken. Besides, they wouldn't lie." Braun grinned and pointed to the packed parking lot. "Looks like they're doing something right. And smell that? What is that? Fried chicken? Umm, umm. You have to admit—you want it."

Max hoped his growling stomach wouldn't expose his anticipation. "We'll see."

Two couples waited in the crisp night air by the glass door entrance. Braun pulled the glass door open, allowing Max to enter first. Two dozen tables were covered with black-and-white checkered tablecloths to match the checkerboard linoleum flooring in front of the old-fashioned ice cream dipping cabinet that displayed children's photos instead of coned treats. A rich history of framed family and friends covered every inch of the wall space above the kitchen pass-through and serving areas.

A smiling woman in a casual Polo shirt looked up from a table where she was chatting and approached them. "Good evenin', boys. Table for two?"

Max tipped his hat. "Yes, ma'am. That'd be fine."

"Well, you's lucky. The folks over at table five is just leavin'." The woman grinned like they'd just struck gold as the couple in the back corner rose to leave. "Ain't many Friday nights you could get a table right away, especially one in a corner where you can both have your backs to the wall." She winked. "I 'spect your kind likes that."

Braun turned to Max, his eyebrows raised. It was true that no one in law enforcement ever wanted their back to a crowd, but how'd she know? Of course, one look at Braun's suit was probably all anyone needed. But Max?

"Follow me." They made their way to the unbussed table. "I'll be right back to clean this up." She winked at Max, then headed toward the kitchen.

"Tell me how it is you're not married?" Braun said. "There's not a woman we met today that didn't act like they wanted you to take them home."

Max grinned. "It's the hat. You should try it."

Braun rubbed his bald head. "And ruin my do?"

The woman returned and handed them the laminated one-page menu listing comfort foods. Some were blacked out. She cleared the remaining items and wiped off the plexiglass table topper. "I'll give you a couple of minutes."

"Thank you, ma'am," Max said as she walked off.

"You know what you want?" Braun asked, still looking over the menu.

"Yeah. I'm here for the fried chicken. And the fried donuts with ice cream."

"Me, too." Braun put the menu down and looked at the fried chicken, greens, and cornbread being served at the next table. He looked back at Max. "That's what I'm talking about."

Max maintained his stoic face. Despite his fake protests, Max was in his element. This place could tempt him to move here.

After checking the status of other tables' families, the woman returned. "You boys ready?"

"Do you know everybody here?" Max asked.

"Pretty much. I've watched their kids grow up, and even some of their kids come along. We pretty much all family here. Soze I know you boys ain't from 'round here." The woman grinned widely.

"No, ma'am," Braun said, trying on some of Max's Southern charm, "we're just here on business."

"Uh uh, don't you go trying to be all sweet with me, looking like a bouncer from one of them fancy New York clubs. Whereas you"— she turned to Max—"you'd fit in at any of the horse farms around here. So what kind of business you two here 'bout?"

"FBI business." Max pulled photos of the girls from the pocket of his jean jacket. "Being as you know everyone in this town"— Max held out the images—"We're trying to locate these two women and this little girl. I bet you'd know if this little lady was in town."

The woman scrutinized them. "They in some kind of trouble?"

"Not likely, but they may be in danger."

"Like witness protection?"

"Not exactly. But they may have witnessed something we're investigating," Braun said. "We're trying to find the girls before our subjects do."

"I ain't seen 'em, but I can keep an eye out for you. You got a card?"

Max handed her his card. "If you see them, don't let on you know anything. Just call. And if they leave, let them go, but watch for what they're driving."

"Ooo, woo! I just love this. I sure hope I can catch 'em for you." The woman shook like lightning struck her.

"Ma'am," Braun said. "Let me remind you—we don't want you to catch them. Just let us know if you see them."

"Got it." She looked at the photos again. "What about the folks that might be following her? What do they look like?"

"Well, aren't you the wise one?" Max nodded to Braun, who gave their descriptions.

Braun's eyes narrowed. "If they come in, be cool. Killing people is their business. Do you understand?"

The woman's eyes looked beyond him as if watching a memory unfold in her mind.

"You okay, ma'am?" Braun asked.

"Yeah, yeah . . . Sorry. I do. I know what you mean. And if I see 'em, I'll call." She paused another moment to look at the pictures. "Well, let me get your meals in so you can get back to finding these guys."

"Well, actually, we're headed back to West Virginia after dinner," Max said. "We've run out of leads."

"Hang on." The woman went to the counter and returned with two flyers. "You might want to head down to Fridays After Five."

"What's that?" Max asked.

The woman described the location and festivities. "If they're in town and have this girl with them, there's a good chance they'll go there. Lots of family stuff. Let me rush these orders so you boys can get over there."

After she left, Braun eyed Max. "I know that look."

"What's another hour or two? Besides, you're driving. I can sleep on the way back."

Chapter 26

6:15 p.m.

A HAND PRESSED HEATHER'S LEFT SHOULDER as she hugged her lap. She froze.

"You okay?" a gruff female voice asked.

Afraid to move, Heather shook her head but opened her eyes. Suede work boots, scuffed around the toes. Rugged jeans. Nobody she knew. But then again, she only knew five people in this town. The shoes shuffled between her and the folding chair ahead. The woman sat next to her and patted her back.

"There, there. Whatever it is, it'll be oo-kay." She emphasized each syllable as if that would calm Heather.

Who was this woman? Was she going to tell her all about Jesus and why He was the answer to all her problems? But then again, Bible thumpers didn't wear work boots.

The woman continued patting Heather's back. "Listen, I know you don't know me, but I'm pretty sure I know you."

Heather shot up and turned to the hefty hillbilly. "How dare you? You couldn't know me. And you have no idea what I've been through. How dare you judge me."

The woman smiled, stretching her drooping jowls. She crossed her arms and leaned back in her seat. "You done attackin' me?" She blew a straw auburn lock back with its straggly cohorts.

"*Attacking*? You came to me, remember? Did I ask you to sit here?"

The woman uncrossed her arms and pulled her olive cardigan tighter across the wrinkled red-checkered shirt she wore underneath. She cocked her head. "Ya done?"

Heather stood. "What do you want from me?"

The woman eyed Heather for a moment. "It's not what I want from you. It's what you want from me."

"What are you talking about?" Heather sat again at the front edge of the chair, almost tipping it over.

"I know what you need—and I have it."

Oh, here it came. Get ready, holy rollers.

"You're in pain. Your body hurts, you feel sick, and nobody understands what you're going through."

Heather stood again, "I don't need this."

The woman grabbed Heather's hand and pulled her down. "Oh? So, where you gonna go then to get what you need?" She pointed toward Melissa and Olivia. "Is your friend over there gonna help you?"

Was Heather's condition that obvious? "What are we talking about here?"

"Oh, you know what I'm talking about. Listen." She rose with a groan. "I gotta go powder my nose." She jutted her chin toward a drab gray building beyond the grassy area to their right. "Wait a couple of minutes, then come if you want the answer." Heather watched her make her way up the aisle, across the lawn, and into the building.

Did she dare go? Olivia was still batting the balloon with the other children, faces beaming. Melissa was leaning back against the wall, engrossed in conversation with another mom. She wouldn't miss her. Without another thought, she took off after the clairvoyant hillbilly.

As she neared the ladies' room door, a woman in a pink sweater came out carrying a pink bundle of joy. Heather paused, letting the door shut in front of her. Was she really about to do a drug deal with children around? *Was* this a drug deal? For all she knew, this woman was undercover. But that hillbilly?

249

Heather leaned back against the exterior wall as her heart thundered in her chest.

An overly-happy brunette, wearing a Virginia Alumni sweatshirt and carrying a beer bottle, approached. "Is this a line?"

Heather's face flushed. "No, sorry." She waved a hand toward the door. "Go ahead."

Heather waited another minute, then took a breath, opened the door, and went down the hallway to the opposite door. As she reached to push into the bathroom, the janitor's door on her left opened. The mysterious hillbilly pulled Heather in and closed the door behind her.

Heather's stomach lurched at the pine-scented disinfectant. The woman leaned back against the concrete block wall next to metal shelving and a yellow mop bucket, arms crossed. She stared, silent. Heather felt like a caged animal being studied for a psych research project.

"What if someone comes in here?"

"Don't you worry your pretty little head 'bout that. I took care of the cleanin' crew."

Took care of them? What did that mean?

"So, how do you think you can help me?"

The woman reached into the pocket of her baggy jeans and pulled out a clear plastic bag containing a dozen oblong yellow pills—just like the ones she'd been taking. Her torturer held it out like a bone for a starving dog and grinned. "This what you need?"

Heather stared. "How did you know?"

The woman laughed and shook her head. "Think I was born yesterdee? I can spot your kind a mile off." She waggled the bag in front of Heather.

"How much?"

A Cheshire grin spread across her face. "How much you got?"

Heather wasn't sure. She opened her wallet and found a fifty, two twenties, and some ones. "Ninety."

"Well, that'll getcha six." The woman opened the bag and removed half the contents. She paused, then put one back in. "I'll give you one extra for good measure." They made the trade—packet for money.

Heather stared at the seven pills. Not a day's worth. Her heart raced. "I'm going to need more."

The woman chuckled. "Yep, I s'pose you will. Lookin' at you, I s'pect you'll need 'em tomorrow. You got more money?"

"I can get some."

"Good. What time? Needs to be in the mornin'."

"It's a ways from here to where we're staying, and I don't have a ride."

"Not my problem. There's an ol' country store out on Route 250 west of town, just past Crozet. It's just before the roadblock. Rockslide closed the old road down, ya know."

"Crozet?" Heather didn't dare tell her that's where their cabin was.

"Yeah." She eyed Heather. "You ain't from 'round here, are ya?"

Heather shook her head.

"My grandpappy used to take me down that way to get rat cheese. They had a big wheel of it settin' on a table. You'd just whack off a piece and go. We'd eat it on the way back up the mountain." She shook her head and huffed. "Nowadays it's all wrapped up. Nice and sanitary." She scrunched her face. "Ain't the same. Anyway, be on the west side of the store at ten o'clock. Don't be late. And come alone, or you won't see me."

Heather nodded.

"Now, be a good girl—go use the facilities, wash your hands, and don't come out for a few minutes." She patted Heather's shoulder. "Go on, now."

Heather left the closet and entered the bathroom. A line of metal stalls ran from one end of the room to the other. Several women went on about the musicians as they freshened their makeup. She went into a stall, took two pills, and choked them down. She retrieved the pill bottle from her pocket, flushed the useless ones down the toilet, and replaced them with her new cache. She looked inside the bottle. Melissa would never know.

She sat on the toilet for a minute, fully clothed, waiting for the feeling. Several minutes passed. Then, finally . . . *ahh.*

When she returned to the seating area, neither Melissa nor Olivia was with the playing kids. She was scanning the crowd on the other side of the seating area when two hands grabbed her shoulder from behind and spun her around. Melissa.

"Ow! I'm still sore, you know."

"Where have you been?" Her face was beet red. She pulled Olivia close against her leg. "We looked all over for you."

"I was in the john. What's the big deal?"

"We looked in there. You weren't there."

"Didn't you just see me come out?"

"No. I've been looking all over."

"I don't know what to tell you. I went to get a drink, then went to the restroom."

Melissa's eyes narrowed. "You should've told me. I thought they'd found you."

"Give me a break. How would they ever find us here?"

"You don't get it, do you?" She lowered her voice. "They can find anybody."

"You're overreacting. Nothing happened." Heather swept her hand over the panorama. "Look around. You see any Detroit gang types here?"

"Mommy." Olivia pulled at her mother's elbow. "Mommy, are the bad men coming to get us?"

Melissa squatted, facing her daughter. "No, sweetie. I'm sorry if I scared you. Mommy just got upset when she couldn't find Cindy."

"But Aunt Cindy asked if you saw the gang men."

Melissa looked up at her. "You didn't mean that, did you, Aunt Cindy?"

"No, no. I was just being silly." She squatted through her rib pain and kneeled next to Melissa. "There are no gangs here, sweetie." She lifted Olivia's chin with her knuckle. "Okay?"

Olivia nodded, mouth still tipped down.

"I think it's time to head back." Melissa hugged Olivia and stood with Heather.

Heather reached out to take Olivia's hand, and the three walked back to the car.

On the drive home, Heather pictured the money bags in the closets and began formulating a plan. "What time are you going to the church tomorrow?"

"Margie said nine."

"Hmmm. I really wanted to go." She slid her hand down to the seat release and pulled. "Boy. I'm exhausted." She stretched her legs out and relaxed heavily against the chair. "I'm starting to think it might be pushing it for me to go after tonight. Especially that early. Maybe I could catch an Uber there later."

"I could come back and get you. I don't like the idea of people knowing where we live."

"That should work. I'll probably sleep until about noon. Then I can have lunch with you guys there."

Heather leaned her head back and pretended to try to sleep. If six pills cost ninety . . . that was fifteen bucks a pill. What was she up to? Six a day? Eight? How was she going to spend so much money without Melissa noticing? She'd have to figure that out later.

———

7:00 p.m.

MAX AND BRAUN MADE THEIR WAY DOWN to the amphitheater where a band played country music.

"Now we're talking," Max said as he joined the line dancers in the area between the stage and the folding chairs. His boots were made for stomping out a good line dance—the true definition of happy feet. He motioned to Braun to join. "Come on!"

Braun crossed his arm. "You're kidding, right?"

When Max made the last turn back, Braun pointed toward a dozen young children kicking a ball around a circle formed by chatting adults. He left the makeshift dance floor, following Braun to the group.

None of the children fit Olivia's description. A man in his early thirties with a well-trimmed beard wearing a University-colored polo shirt squatted as he recorded the children with his phone. When he spotted the agents approaching, he stood and headed toward them. Max smiled. Having worked too many years in child trafficking, he loved seeing a vigilant parent.

"Good evening, sir." Max tipped his hat, then showed his credentials. "We're with the FBI."

The man's eyes frantically surveyed the surroundings. "Something going on here? Are my kids in danger?"

"Oh no—nothing like that."

Braun retrieved photos from his inside suit pocket and held them up. "We're trying to locate these girls. Have you seen them?"

His face lit up with a smile. "You know, I think I did." He leaned in to look more closely. "Yeah. That's them." He opened his phone and showed them a video of the kids playing. "Look. I'm sure that's the girl."

"Do you have any of her mother?" Max asked.

The man stroked his phone. "No, doesn't look like it."

A slender brunette joined them, sporting an orange sweater that showed off about ten thousand dollars of plastic surgery and silicone. "What's going on, sweetie?" she asked the man as she slipped her arm around his waist.

"These men are with the FBI. They're looking for that little blond girl who was playing with Kate."

"Jasmine?" the young mother asked.

"Yeah. Jasmine." He turned to Braun.

"Are they in danger?"

"They could be. We really need to talk to her mom."

"Well, that's easy." The brunette said. "They'll be at Harvest Fest tomorrow."

———

7:45 p.m.

"No, SWEETIE. AUNT CINDY'S HAD A BIG DAY and needs her rest." Heather groaned through the pain to climb out of the Prius into the darkness just outside the reach of the cabin's porch light. She forced herself upright, then held on to the roof and door to allow the dizziness to pass.

"But you promised to watch *Aladdin* with me."

She closed the door on the child's protests. She was in no mood for whining or watching a kid's movie. Uber, money, and a one-hour window to get to that awful hillbilly railroaded all thought.

Melissa bent into the back seat to unbuckle Olivia. "And it's your bedtime anyway, missy." Olivia hopped out. "Oh, Cindy, remember to watch out for the—"

Heather's toe caught the stump. "Oww!" Excruciating pain radiated up her leg. She doubled over, then propped herself on the front fender to catch her breath. "The stump?" she said through clenched teeth. She glared at Melissa. "Do you think you could have reminded me *before* I got out of the car? It's not like anyone can see anything in these God-forsaken woods."

"Wow." Melissa slammed the back door shut, took Olivia's hand, and moved to a position across the front of the car from Heather. "You listen. I've had about all I can take from you. I risked my life to get you out of that hospital, but are you thankful? No. You are nothing but trouble, you ungrateful—" she looked down at her daughter, whose wide eyes watched closely, then bent and scooped her up. "I'm done. Pack your stuff and get out." She spun around to the porch.

"Mommy?"

"Not now, baby." She stomped up the steps, then slammed the cabin door behind them.

Heather plopped herself down on the porch steps. How dare Melissa speak to her that way. None of this was her fault. She didn't ask Melissa to help, and she didn't have to take this. Honestly, she was ready to turn herself in.

Heather reached into her pocket, tapped two pills out of the bottle, and swallowed hard. Three remaining. Maybe if she could get enough, she could end it all. Everyone would be better off without her.

Just then, a moonbeam showed through the trees illuminating the white buck standing ten feet in front of her by the picnic table. His rack was regal, but his eyes pierced her soul. Her heart pounded. She reached down, grabbed a handful of gravel, and launched it at the deer. "Damn you!" With two leaps, the deer disappeared into the woods. Holy Spirit, my butt. That deer was Satan himself . . . if there was a Satan.

And then her head began to spin.

————

8:45 p.m.

"CINDY—WAKE UP." Melissa shook her shoulder.

She opened her eyes. Darkness . . . the faint outline of trees above . . . Melissa was squatting beside her. What had happened? Why was she so cold? She pushed herself up from the dirt-packed gravel. Her ribs. She was so tired of the pain.

"What's going on?"

"You passed out."

Heather wrapped her arms around herself. "How long have I been out here?"

"I don't know." Melissa helped Heather to her feet. "Thirty minutes?"

Her head spun again, and her knees buckled. Melissa grabbed her elbow to steady her. "We'd better get you to bed."

" But I thought you said—"

"Forget what I said. I was out of line. The pressure is weighing on us all."

Melissa guided Heather into the cabin and to her room. She helped her ease onto the bed.

"There you go. Lay down until you get your land legs." Melissa covered her with an afghan she retrieved from the closet.

"I remembered," Heather said, staring at the ceiling.

"Remembered what?"

"Everything—my entire pitiful life." Her eyelids pressed closed. "You'll be better off without me."

"Stop. It's been a long day. We'll talk tomorrow." Melissa turned off the light and shut the door.

She didn't have the energy to argue. As she lay in bed, surrounded by darkness, memories continued to move in and out of her self-induced fog, turning one by one into nightmares.

Chapter 27

Saturday, November 4
8:30 a.m.

"CINDY, WAKE UP." Melissa nudged her shoulder.

"What?" She squinted against the sunshine pouring in the opened blinds. Her head pounded. Was Melissa trying to kill her with shards of light? "What time is it?" Her dry throat rebelled against the words.

"Eight-thirty."

"Eight-thirty?" Ten o'clock. Country store. She had to get ready. She sat up. "Aren't you going to Harvest Fest?"

"I wanted to make sure you're okay . . . after the things you said last night."

"What did I say?"

"Don't you remember?"

She shook her head. "I don't know what you're talking about." All she knew was her aching to get "comfortably numb," as the great philosophers of Pink Floyd had sung.

Melissa's eyes were soft. "You said you wanted to die. And now I'm worried. How about we wait around a while and see if you're up to coming? Maybe getting out again will be good for you."

"It didn't work last night." What didn't work was that she didn't get enough pills to be done.

"Mommy!" Olivia flew in wearing her Jasmine costume. Abu followed. "Come on, Mommy, let's go." She grabbed her mother's hand and pulled her toward the door. "It's time for the costume contest."

"Wait, sweetie. We need to be sure that Aunt Cindy's okay."

"But you said she was leaving. You said she's nothing but trouble."

Melissa's face reddened. She squatted and pulled Olivia to her. "That's not what I said, sweetie."

"Uh hu-uh," Olivia eyed Heather with pouty lips, her head tipped down.

Melissa pulled Olivia's chin toward her. "Look at me. Mommy was wrong. I should never have said those things. They were ugly and not true. Do you understand?"

"No. Aunt Cindy is a liar. She promised to paint my room and watch *Aladdin* with me, but all she does is lay in bed and be mean. I want her to go."

Olivia's brutal honesty sliced Heather's heart in two. How had this happened? She'd always loved kids, and they'd always loved her back.

"Jasmine, you take that back. Aunt Cindy's sick." Melissa turned Olivia toward the door. "I think you need to go into your room and think about your attitude, young lady."

"But, Mommy. The contest."

"There'll be no contest if you don't change your attitude. Now go."

Olivia stomped from the room, Abu following. "I hate Aunt Cindy," she said as she rounded the corner and slammed the door on Heather's hope of getting to the country store on time.

Melissa stood. "Jasmine!" She turned to Heather. "I'm sorry. I've got to deal with this now." She pursued her daughter with the determination of that raccoon.

This was all Heather needed. She prayed Olivia would get right—right now. Heather was still dressed from the night before, her pocket still loaded with relief. She snuck to the bathroom and took two pills, leaving just one. She had to make that meeting.

She freshened herself, went to the kitchen, poured a cup of coffee, and grabbed a cookie. Not that she was hungry. But she needed Melissa to believe she was okay. She sat in what had become her chair facing the front door.

Moments later, Melissa emerged from her bedroom with Olivia tucked in tightly behind her legs. Abu wove around them from behind and hopped on the futon. "Abu. Get down." Melissa pointed at the dog bed. Abu hung her head and obeyed.

Melissa sat next to Heather at the table. Olivia tried her best to stay hidden behind her mother, but Melissa pulled her around to face Heather. "What do you say to Aunt Cindy?"

"Sorry," she whispered.

"It's okay," Heather said.

"That's not going to do it, young lady. Hug her and tell her again—like you mean it this time."

Pout firmly maintained, Olivia gave the mandatory hug. "I'm sorry," she said, returning immediately to her mother's side.

"It's okay. Aunt Cindy is just in a lot of pain. Do you understand?"

"Yes," she said, keeping her head tucked.

Heather ducked her head to make eye contact with Olivia. "Do you know how it feels to be really sick?"

"Yes."

"Aunt Cindy is really sick, but I promise I'm getting better."

"Okay." Her face remained blank.

"And maybe we can get some paint when I feel better so I can get started on your Aladdin painting. How would that be?"

Olivia's face instantly lit up. "Can we go now?"

"I thought you wanted to win that contest"—she gently tugged the sleeve of her costume—"Princess Jasmine."

Olivia's eyes shifted back and forth to Heather's eyes while she processed this life-altering decision. "Can we do both?"

"Absolutely. You go win that contest. Later we'll see what kind of art supplies we can find."

Olivia bounced in place. "Really?"

"Well, only if you forgive me for being so grouchy."

"Yes—yes!"

Melissa laid a hand on Heather's. "Are you sure you're up for that?"

"Well, if you guys let me rest up, I think I'll be good this afternoon. Maybe this is what I need instead of going to Harvest Fest." She pointed to a pad of paper on the table. "I'll sketch out some ideas she can pick from later." Heather's heart lightened as a mural materialized in her mind, tickling her soul. It felt good.

"I guess that's okay." Melissa hesitated, her focus on her beaming progeny. She glanced toward the wall clock and stood. "We'd better get going."

Abu headed her off at the door. "No, no. Abu. We just took you out."

Olivia put a hand on her hip and shook her finger at the dog. "Yeah, Abu. We just took you." Abu hung her head and again retreated to her bed.

Melissa laughed. "Ready, baby?"

Princess Jasmine rushed to her mother's side. "Yes, yes, yes."

Melissa grabbed her purse from the coat rack by the front window. Her face puzzled as she scanned the room, then looked at Heather. "What are you going to paint with these wood-paneled walls everywhere?"

"Well, I've got some ideas for that, too," Heather said, bluffing as Melissa opened the door for Olivia.

Melissa slipped out on the porch behind her daughter. "I'm looking forward to seeing what you come up with." She smiled, then closed the door.

How *was* she going to manage the mural? A large canvas, maybe? She picked up a pencil and began sketching, imagining the breeze through her hair as she flew on a magic carpet with her prince. Wholly absorbed in getting Aladdin's world just right, she lost track of time—until a wave of nausea overcame her. She'd never be able to paint feeling like this. She turned to the clock behind her. "Nine o'clock?" Panic set in.

Abu perked her ears. Her head cocked to one side.

"What?"

Her head tipped the other way.

Abu wasn't the only one questioning her actions. She couldn't believe she was contemplating a drug deal. But she'd still be getting them on demand if she were in the hospital. It wasn't her fault she couldn't get a prescription. She had to do what she had to do. And right now, that was to focus her fuzzy brain.

Money. She rushed to her bedroom closet with Abu on her heels. Melissa had said the money was for her. She looked down at the dog, who watched her every move. "You're the lookout. Bark if they come back—got it?"

Abu cocked her head.

Heather stood on the bed and reached for a shoebox on the top shelf. She lifted the lid. A pair of sneakers. Duh. Melissa had said the blanket bags. She quickly pulled the bag down to the bed and unzipped it. Hidden within the fold of the blanket were stacks of twenties wrapped in quantities of five hundred dollars each. Jackpot.

So how much would she need? She hated math, but she remembered enough to know tens and hundreds were her math friends. Fifteen dollars per pill times a hundred pills equaled fifteen hundred dollars. She pulled out three bundles. How many days would that be? A hundred pills divided by ten per day is ten days. What if she decided to leave? She would lose her Crozet connection—although finding the hillbilly hadn't been hard. But to be safe, better make it a month's worth. Forty-five hundred was nine bundles. She'd worry about getting another round later. After that, she should be pain-free.

She took seven more bundles, one for good measure.

Melissa zipped the bag closed. Too flat. Melissa would notice. She put nine back, then hurried through the house, quickly finding nine other bags and removing a bundle from each. She stuffed them in her purse.

With her phone, she downloaded and attempted to sign in to Uber, but she needed an email address. She dared not use hers and didn't have time to make a new one. The time on the phone's face mocked her. Nine fifteen. She cursed again. How was she going to get there in time?

A taxi!

She googled "Charlottesville taxi" and dialed the first number that popped up. *No service.* Great. Holding her phone up, she moved around the cabin for a signal. Nothing. She stepped outside. None there either. Wait. The office was on higher ground.

Apologizing to Abu, she headed to the office, holding up the phone like a divining rod for a satellite signal.

Bars lit up at the fork in the road just before the office. Margie's Buick was parked in its drive. What if Margie saw her? How would she explain? But Margie couldn't be there. She had a pie contest to win. Doug must have taken her.

She tapped "Call" on her phone again and held the phone to her ear.

"Welcome to Charlottesville Cab," the digital female voice said. "Please press one to order a cab now."

Heather complied.

"Please state your location, followed by the pound sign."

What was her location? Something Resort. She hung up. Nine thirty. She was never going to make it now. She walked to the sign at the entrance—MOUNTAIN HAVEN RESORT. She dialed again and gave her location. She didn't know the country store's name, but how many could there be? She tapped zero several times until she was finally transferred to a real person.

"Charlottesville Cab," a woman said in a thick Appalachian accent. "How may I help you?"

"I need a cab." Heather turned and walked back toward the office.

"I see you're at Mountain Haven Resort. Oh, that place out by the winery in Crozet?" She drew out every second syllable. "That's a great place."

"Yes, yes. Listen. I'm running late. How long will it take for you to get someone here?"

"Well, let me see . . ." Her voice became distant as she spoke to someone in the background. "Well, alls my drivers are tied up right now, but I should be able to have somebody—what did you say?" She spoke again to someone whose voice Heather couldn't make out.

"Hello?" Heather reached Margie's Buick and leaned against the trunk.

"Just hold on to your britches. I'm trying to find out where Jackson is."

Heather waited impatiently as the discussion continued.

"Okay, okay. We can have somebody there in twenty minutes."

"And how long will it take to get to the country store?"

"You mean the Rockfish Gap Country Store? I love that place. My daddy used to take me out there to get maple syrup candy back when I was knee-high to a grasshopper—oh, and rat cheese. We'd cut off a big ol' slab and eat it on the way home. Momma never knew we didn't bring her the whole thang."

Rat cheese again? "Listen. I'm late." Heather paced by the car. "I'm supposed to meet someone there by ten. Can you make that happen?"

"Oh, it'll probably be fine. That place is only about ten minutes from where you is—if you don't get stuck behind a tractor—if you know what I mean."

"Okay, I'll be at the office. The first building when you enter. Please ask them to hurry. Tell them there's an extra hundred in it if I get there on time."

"Well now, I'll come and gets you myself for that much."

"Whatever. Just get here."

Heather hung up and went inside the empty office. Everything in its place—including Margie's car keys hanging on a hook by the laundry door.

Margie had said she could borrow her car.

She snatched the keys and ran to the Buick. She started the engine just as the white buck appeared at the edge of the woods in front of her—staring her right in the eyes.

Margie's words echoed. Was Heather on the highway to hell?

No, she was just a broken girl in pain. What did that deer know? She laid on the horn.

The deer leaped into the woods and out of sight.

She plugged "Rockfish Gap Country Store" into her phone's GPS. Twenty-four minutes. That stupid dispatcher hadn't even been close. She checked the time. Nine forty-five. She'd be at least ten minutes late. Should she even try? Well, she had nothing to lose. Or did she?

———

9:45 a.m.

MAX AND BRAUN FINISHED THEIR HEARTY COUNTRY diner breakfast. Max left a tip for the waitress and paid the bill at a register that must have once served Thomas Jefferson himself. He tipped his hat to the matronly clerk. "Thank you, ma'am. You've been an absolute delight."

She blushed. "Y'all come back now."

Braun shook his head and walked out ahead of him. "See?"

"I'm telling you, it's the hat."

The church could not have ordered a more perfect day for Harvest Fest. Nothing but blue skies and crisp air. They'd arrive about fifteen minutes early, giving them plenty of time to show the photos around before the girls showed up--if they showed up at all.

Max had expected some of the event volunteers to be there already, but for blocks leading up to the church, cars were parked in "not-so-legal" spots along curbs and on any patch of grass they could find. Max's stomach knotted. "Look at this crowd."

Braun cursed. "Didn't that woman say it started at ten?"

"I think we were misinformed. Unless this is like those garage sales where people show up early to get the best items."

Braun passed the church and found a parallel spot along the road several blocks away. They trekked back toward the festivities, deciding they would separate when they got there to cover more ground. Hopefully, if the girls were coming, they weren't early.

A couple of police cruisers flanked the church—a presence that might dissuade any gang members from showing up, although Max doubted it. They had a history of in-your-face retribution.

Two clowns greeted newcomers at the edge of the park-like lawn—turned fairgrounds. One wore a painted smile, the other a frown.

"Welcome to Harvest Fest," the smiling clown said. "You two don't look dressed for fun." The happy clown used his fingers to pull up at the corners of his mouth as if inviting them to do the same.

"Sorry. We're in a hurry." Max pulled out the photos. "We're with the FBI. We're looking for these ladies. Do you recognize them?"

"No, can't say as I do. Pretty girls, though. They—"

"FBI!" someone called in a friendly voice from a distance.

Max looked around to find Doug making his way between the craft and game booths toward them. He shook their hands. "You guys come to win my bride's pie? Eric and Max, isn't it?"

Max tipped his hat. "Yes, sir, that's us."

"So what are you guys doing back here? I thought you'd be gone by now."

"They're here looking for two girls who are in some kinda trouble," Frowny said.

"Is that so? Who are you looking for? I'm pretty good at sizing folks up."

Max showed Doug the photos. His face tensed.

"Why are you looking for these gals?"

"You've seen them?" Max said.

"They're renting one of my cabins."

266

Max exchanged glances with Braun.

"Yeah." He pointed at one of the photos. "This is Kelsey and her daughter Jasmine. And that's Cindy," he said, indicating the other.

"You say they're at your cabin?"

"Well, right now, Jasmine's at the costume contest with her mom." Doug pointed to the building they'd visited the day before. "Did they do something wrong? They sure don't seem like the type."

"They're witnesses to a crime and may be in danger," Max said.

"Well, come on." Doug motioned them to follow. "I know the shortcut."

———

How long had it been since Heather had driven? Never a Buick. She carefully backed out and drove down the hill along the horse pasture to a stop sign at the two-lane paved road. A dog was barking from somewhere. She checked her rearview mirror. Abu was running down the hill toward her full speed, ears flopping. How had she gotten out?

She didn't have time for this. She'd have to deal with her later. She gunned the engine and made the turn, but Abu didn't give up. Her dog-loving DNA wouldn't allow her to do this. She stopped the car just as a pickup truck flew up from behind, almost hitting Abu as he crossed the double-yellow line and raced past. Heather hopped out and gave him a one-finger salute.

Abu slowed her pace as she neared.

"Bad dog, Abu. How did you get out?"

Her tongue bounced up and down as she caught her breath, but she still managed to lick Heather's face.

"Get in the back. You're making me late."

She followed the GPS's guidance, sailing along pastures lined with vineyard signs. If she couldn't get the drugs, a couple of cases of wine might do the trick. She could use a glass right about now.

As she passed through the small downtown area of Crozet, the town's only traffic light changed just in time to make her wait.

Naturally. A uniformed deputy that could have doubled for a marine sergeant exited a corner coffee shop and stared directly at her. What if he recognized Margie's car? She sank down.

Mercifully, the light changed. Heather passed through the intersection, half expecting a high-speed pursuit, but instead, the deputy stopped to talk to someone who had just pulled up next to his SUV in a brown pickup. Her imagination was getting the best of her.

She continued to Route 250 and turned west toward the store. Detour signs directed traffic away from her destination, so only store traffic continued past the signs making their rendezvous point less conspicuous.

"Your destination is on the right."

Besides the barricade that blocked the road ahead, even without the GPS, Heather couldn't have missed the store. The almost billboard-size sign on the end of the store boasted its name, unique gifts, kids' toys, antiques, local art, April Cornell, and Virginia Wine. She had imagined a house-like structure with a small porch, but this place ran a city block. Red roofs were mounted atop off-white walls, complete with a red rooster weather vane mounted on the red-roofed cupulo at the center.

Red columns supported the red porch roof that ran along the front of the building. She had to agree with the WINE A BIT — YOU'LL FEEL BETTER banner hanging off the porch. Where were the rat cheese ads? Garden furniture and decorations stretched the length of the patio. Heather would have been shocked if there was a garden gnome, wind spinner, or house banner they didn't have. Lady bugs, hearts, sunflowers, stars, flamingos. They had it all. And that was outside. She was sure she'd spend days exploring the "unique gifts" inside under different circumstances.

While there was head-in parking for a dozen cars along the front, Heather was glad there were only three cars today. Fewer witnesses.

As instructed, she pulled past the store to the cracked pavement that formed a circular drive on the west end. Woods ran up a hill behind it and the building and bordered the highway beyond. The drive dumped cars back on Rte 250 just before the barricade. She wondered how far it was to the rockslide. She parked near a two-foot tall hand water pump sticking out of the ground. How long had this place been around?

She scanned the area—no drug-dealing hillbilly. Ten-fifteen came and went. Sweat formed, and her legs started to bounce. She hoped money talked louder than threats. She partially opened the windows for Abu and got out.

From where she stood, the store blocked her view of the road to her left, including where the detour directed traffic away. A truck pulled up to the blockade and drove through a ditch and over craggy rocks around it, like in one of those tough truck commercials.

Abu stuck her head out of the window and begged for attention. Leaning against the car, Heather petted Abu's head. Other than the one truck, only minutes passed.

Her phone rang. Melissa. Had she gone back to the cabin and found her missing? Heather let it go to voicemail. Almost immediately, the phone rang again. Didn't she know when to stop? She couldn't answer in case the hillbilly showed up. How would she explain where she was?

A voicemail notification dinged.

Contemplating her single pill left, she began to pace. The sweats returned. Her stomach hurt but wasn't queasy. It was lower abdomen—more like constipation pain. When was the last time she had gone? When was the last time she had eaten?

A sheriff's SUV came around the building and slowly pulled up next to her. The deputy looked like the same one she saw in town. He rolled down the passenger window and leaned across the console. "Ma'am? Can I help you? You don't look so good."

Was it that obvious? She crossed her arms. "No, sir. Just waiting for my friend."

"Yeah? Anybody I know?"

"I doubt it. We're from out-of-town. Just stopping here to get some rat cheese."

He chuckled. "My momma used to bring me here for the rat cheese."
Of course she did.

"That's an interesting vehicle for someone your age." The deputy
jutted his chin toward Margie's car. "You don't look like a Buick
kind of girl."

Heather looked back at the car. "Well, I'm not. It belongs to my
landlady, or whatever you call her. We're renting a cabin from her."

"Margie?"

"Uh . . . yeah. You know her?" Had the shock registered on her face?

"Everybody knows Margie." His eyebrows furrowed. "So, she
just let you take her car?"

"Yeah, she's great, isn't she?" Heather forced a grin. "She didn't
need it today 'cause she's at the Harvest Fest. Said I could use it."

The deputy looked long at her. "Well, I saw you in Crozet. It's
been a while since you passed by."

So it was him, and he had noticed her. She was so busted.

"Is your friend lost or something?"

"No, just running late, I guess. I'm thinking she may have gotten confused with the detour signs." She pointed to the blockade. "I
should call her. Thanks." She waved to the deputy and got back in the
car, hoping he'd leave. Abu was glad she returned. If the hillbilly was
watching, she'd never come now.

The deputy rolled up his window, then tilted his head toward his
shoulder mic. Was he calling her in? He glanced at her one more
time, waved, then pulled out.

Finally.

She put her head back. Now, what was she going to do?

A sharp thud hit the window, causing her to jump so hard that she
nearly smashed her head against the headliner.

Abu barked furiously at the bending forward outside the passenger door to reveal her surly face. Heather unlocked the doors. The
woman jumped in, carrying a brown paper bag.

"Go 'round back." The hillbilly pointed toward the front of the store?

Trees blocked the access to the back of the store. "What?"

"Are ye deaf? Drive 'round the store."

Abu continued her protest as Heather pulled out, heart racing.

"Shut that dog up, or I will." The hillbilly's jowls shook with her bobbing head.

"Quiet, Abu."

Abu lay down with a groan.

With the hillbilly pointing the way, Heather circled back to the east side, and up the drive she hadn't noticed before. She turned behind the store and parked the Buick next to a blue portable toilet situated at the end of the store's single, decades-old loading dock. Trees blocked the view to the store's west side and covered the hill above them. No one from either direction could see them back here.

"What kind of crap is this? What part of ten o'clock didn't you understand? You said you didn't have a car, and next thing, you're driving this thing and gabbin' it up with Bobby."

"The deputy? You know him?"

"You're really stupid, ain't ya? I knowed every deputy since they was sucking at their momma's teets."

Heather's mouth dropped open. What could she say to that?

"How much money d'ya bring?" She pointed to Heather's purse.

"What if Bobby comes back?"

"For what? He'd never come up here. He'd pee in the trees 'fore he'd use that blue can. Look around. Nobody ever comes back here. So how much money you got?"

"Three." Her stomach knotted as she said it.

"Thousand?"

"Yeah, three thousand."

The woman's sunken eyes were cold as steel. "Where'd a girl like you get that kinda money? You steal it?"

"You wouldn't believe it if I told you."

"Try me."

Heather stared at the woman's weathered face. "Yeah, I stole it."

"You ain't smart enough to steal that kinda money."

"What difference does it make? I got you the money. Now I believe you owe me two hundred pills.

"You think I carry around that many pills?"

"I told you that's what I wanted."

"Well, that's too damn bad, ain't it? I pegged you for a loser. Brought you something cheaper." She pulled out a syringe filled with a brown liquid and a rubber tube. "This'll make you feel better than oxy. Here, try it." She pulled off the needle's cover.

"You crazy?" Heather leaned away. "I'm no junkie."

"Aren't you?" Her eyes narrowed, then she recapped the syringe and dropped her arms to her lap. "Your choice."

"Forget it. It's Percocets or nothing."

"Have it your way." The woman opened the door.

Heather breathed harder at the thought of the last pill. "Wait."

The hillbilly pulled the door closed. She looked Heather over. "Give me your arm."

Heather checked for witnesses, then held out her arm. The woman pushed Heather's sleeve up, checked her veins, and tied the tube above her elbow. Abu whined. The hillbilly uncapped the syringe and plunged it into Heather's tattooed arm.

Immediately, a warmth enveloped her, traveling to every part of her body. The jitters dissolved. She put her head back, closed her eyes, and . . . all was well. Heather had never felt this good. She wanted it to last forever.

"Three thousand?"

Heather opened her eyes. The hillbilly had her purse and was taking out her money.

"Looks like you got five here."

"Give me that." Heather struggled against the euphoria to retrieve her things.

"Now, I know you're trouble." The woman grabbed six bundles of cash back as Heather pulled the purse onto her lap. She climbed out of the car, then tossed the brown bag on the seat behind her. "That should hold you for a while." She slammed the door, smacked the window with her palm, then headed up through the woods.

Heather wanted to be mad, but she felt so good. She couldn't care. She put her head back and closed her eyes, never wanting the feeling to end.

Chapter 28

10:15 a.m.

MAX AND BRAUN FOLLOWED DOUG, weaving between the various food and game booths to the same door they had entered the day before. Turning right, they navigated two hallways while Doug answered Max's question about what the girls were wearing. They arrived at a foyer full of costumed cuties filing out of an open auditorium. Max scanned the pirates and princesses for Jasmine.

"Pastor Stuart," Doug said as they approached a group of three chatting inside. "Did we miss the costume contest?"

"Sure did. They were all winners . . . unlike you." The pastor grinned at Doug, then turned back to the couple, patted the man's shoulder, and said, "Hope to see you tomorrow." The couple smiled, nodded, and left. Turning back to Doug, he said, "You ready to lose the chili contest again this year?"

"You know that's not happening." Doug turned to the agents. "These are Agents Max and Eric with the FBI. They're looking for these ladies."

Max held up the photos.

The pastor's face lit up. "Princess Jasmine. She's a precious one. That's her real name, you know." The pastor craned his neck toward the remnant of people milling outside the auditorium. He turned back to them. "Sorry, I didn't see which way they went."

"Thanks, anyway," Braun said. "If you see them, don't approach. Just let us know." Braun handed him a card.

The three men fanned out and made the rounds, asking a dozen families who still lingered inside the auditorium and foyer if they had seen the girls. Some had seen them, but none knew where they'd gone.

Max rejoined Braun and Doug in the foyer. "Any luck?"

They shook their heads.

"Let's get back outside," Max said just as Frowny ran in, breathing heavily. He made a beeline for the agents.

"I saw them," he said between breaths. "Something spooked them. The mom grabbed the little girl and ran back inside. They must not have come this way, or you would have seen them."

Max looked at Doug. "Any idea where they might have gone?"

"Likely toward the daycare."

"What kind of car do they drive?" Max asked.

"A blue Prius."

"Any idea where they parked?"

"Yeah. Near the playground by the daycare where you came out yesterday."

"What's the fastest way there?"

"Follow me."

Doug led them through the labyrinth and out the daycare door. The blue Prius was backing out of a spot near the corner. The agents sprinted down the sidewalk to the curb just as two men in black leather jackets holding guns rounded the corner and shot at the Prius as it sped past.

"Everybody down!" Max screamed. He and Braun pulled their guns as they took cover behind two vehicles.

"Stop! FBI!" Braun popped up and aimed his gun at them.

The Prius banked the corner and disappeared. Max jumped up and aimed at the men. Shots rang out as one of the thugs jumped in front of a passing Jeep and yanked the driver out at gunpoint. Both men scrambled into the vehicle, then raced past them. Max held his aim but couldn't shoot—too many pedestrians. The Jeep turned in the direction the girls had gone.

Max cursed as several police officers rounded the building, holding their guns toward the ground as they surveyed the scene.

"Agent Enders, FBI." He holstered his weapon and held out his badge. "That's my partner, Braun," he said as Braun joined them. "We need a BOLO on a late-model blue Prius and a red Jeep Cherokee. The suspects just stole the Jeep and took off." He pointed to the displaced driver. "That's the man they hijacked. Get the Jeep's tag numbers from him. The Prius is being driven by a woman with another female passenger and a young girl."

"One passenger." Doug appeared at his side. "Jasmine. Cindy's back at the cabin."

Max nodded, then described the two men. "They belong to a gang. They are armed and dangerous. Got it?"

The older officer grabbed the mic on his shoulder and began reporting the BOLO. Max turned to Doug. "Where can we find Heather?"

Doug gave them the address. "It's just north of Crozet. They're in the Apple Blossom Cabin."

"Do you know where that is?" Max asked the officers.

"Out by the winery. It's the Albemarle sheriff's department," one said. "It might take them as long to get out there as it takes you. It's a big county. They don't always have a deputy out that way."

"Okay, we don't want to spook her, but we don't want to put her in danger. Tell me about the property."

Doug described the office and the drive to the cabin. "It's about a half mile back. But she's going to see and hear you coming."

"Is there a back entrance?"

"Yeah, but you'd have to know that road to find their cabin. It winds around some other cabins. But you can come in unnoticed from the hill above."

"How many roads are there to your place?"

"Just one. The front and back roads split off near the office."

"Is there a spot where we can post a deputy?"

"Yeah, there's a house just across from the entrance. They can see anyone coming for a mile from there."

Max turned to the officer. "Let the deputies know not to approach the cabins. Just monitor the activity from that house—unless the suspects show up, in which case, all bets are off. The woman's a key witness."

The older one stepped away as the younger approached the Jeep's driver. An EMS truck pulled into the church property and stopped behind several parked cars. Four police SUVs followed and parked at angles blocking the streets around the church.

"Thanks, Doug," Max said.

"If it's okay, I'll ride with you. The cabins are in the boonies. I can show you a shortcut and the back way to their cabin."

"Agreed," Braun said. "Whatever it takes, we've got to beat those guys there."

————

10:30 a.m.

THE RING OF HEATHER'S PHONE SHATTERED the bubble of euphoria that had floated her away from her pain and trouble. Crashing back to reality, she yanked her head forward. Abu jumped into the front seat and began licking her face. "Stop," she said, pushing Abu away. The phone stopped.

Finally. She leaned back into her peace.

It rang again. Heather retrieved the maniacal device while Abu kissed her. Melissa. She silenced the ring, but Abu couldn't be ignored. As much as she loved dogs, she loved the bliss more. She pushed Abu's backside down into the seat, then rubbed her back. "It's okay, girl. Just relax." Abu curled up on the passenger seat, alternately raising each eyebrow to inspect her surroundings. She finally closed both eyes. Heather leaned her head back and followed suit.

A voicemail dinged.

Quiet returned.

The phone rang again. Abu's head popped up.

Heather cursed as she grabbed the phone from her lap. She switched it to mute and threw it to the passenger floorboard. She was sick of Melissa's judgments and done with her mothering. Her new-found cousin wasn't going to control her. Melissa could never understand all the things Heather was dealing with. This was all Melissa's fault—her and her drug-dealing boyfriend. If it hadn't been for them . . . then what? She couldn't think about that. Even now, Melissa was managing to ruin the best moment of her life.

————

10:40 a.m.

DEXTER DIDN'T KNOW WHICH VIEW he loved better—his lingerie-draped wife sleeping soundly in the bed of their vacation home or the fresh snow on the Vermont mountains beyond her, framed by floor-to-ceiling windows. He ran his fingers tenderly down her arm. Mary Ellen opened her eyes, smiled, and closed them again. Total contentment.

He missed Rockefeller's morning kisses. His faithful companion always waited at his bedside for Dexter's first movements to start their day together. But this time, Mary Ellen said if the kids weren't coming, she wanted Dexter all to herself.

Skiing away their mornings with the twins was their original dream, but the teenagers now preferred time with their peers. At first, Mary Ellen had pouted, but now she was enjoying sleeping in—or at least staying in bed to enjoy each other. Since the twins weren't likely to ever set foot here again, perhaps he should sell the place.

He touched his wife's neck. She moaned, opened her eyes, and pulled him to her for more. On second thought, maybe he should keep it.

His secure phone rang. Mary Ellen pushed away. "Really? You couldn't turn that thing off for one night?" She got up and wrapped herself in a thick robe.

"No, wait."

She turned and narrowed her eyes. "Are you going to answer it?"

He couldn't respond.

"That's what I thought." She left the room.

Dexter's heart raced as he grabbed the pants his wife had hurriedly ripped off him the night before. He tapped the phone, then unloaded his entire cursing vocabulary before asking Charlie what was so important.

"Sorry, boss. It's ten. I didn't think—"

"Well, that's obvious. You never do."

"I'm sorry, but I thought you'd want to know. Bones' guys found the girlfriend and the kid, but the FBI—"

"Hold on." Stepping into the hallway, Dexter peeked over the balcony toward the kitchen. Mary Ellen was at the counter sipping coffee with the housekeeper—no doubt commiserating with her about how men never understand them. He'd never be able to reprime Mary Ellen's pump now.

Dexter padded into the bathroom and turned on the shower. "Did they take care of them?"

"No. The FBI was there. They got away."

"Where's the sister?"

"You gotta love this. One of our retailers was selling her some product when it all went down."

A grin slid across his face as he considered her slide from grace. "Since when did she become a customer?"

"Probably became a fan at the hospital—our best referral source. She was looking for pills. They upgraded her."

What delicious irony. The only thing more painful than the death of a child was them becoming an addict. This was getting better.

"Where'd they go?"

"We don't know yet. We alerted the North Carolina team.

"One other thing. One of our guys found the Wheelers. They're at their family summer house in Chincoteague. A couple of marshals are protecting them."

"Chincoteague?"

"You know. That island on the Virginia Eastern Shore where they have that wild pony auction? It's pretty deserted in the winter. Maybe a thousand residents. Everyone-knows-everyone kind of place. House is in a small community—ten or twelve homes on the water. Neighbors' houses are empty for the season. Easy access by boat. Wood home with lots of tinder around, if you know what I mean."

"You think the sister might go there?"

"Who knows? If she's in Virginia with her cousin—"

"What cousin?"

"Didn't I tell you? Hawthorne found out the girls are cousins."

Was it time to get rid of Charlie? "Anything else you forgot?"

"Sorry, boss. I've been trying not to call. Bottom line—she could go to her dad's home in D.C., head to North Carolina, or Chincoteague—if she doesn't still have amnesia. What do you want us to do?"

"Send a team to Chincoteague. Somebody that would blend in, not any of your thugs. You said waterfront?" Dexter considered how vulnerable his lake house was. "Is it duck hunting season there or something? Maybe camouflage outfits and a boat. Just make sure they blend. Got it?"

"Yes, sir."

"And tell them not to approach the house until the girls get there. We don't want to interrupt the happy reunion, at least not until they're all settled in."

"I like the way you think, boss."

"One of us has to. The Wheelers have to show up for the hearing Wednesday if you haven't gotten rid of the rat problem. The FBI would want to prepare them for the hearing. Let's assume they're headed back Sunday. Do you think you can handle this before I get back home after Sunday dinner?"

"Yes, boss."

Dexter tapped to disconnect the call. Why didn't he believe Charlie? He pounded the sink. Now he'd be the one who couldn't get in the mood.

———

10:45 a.m.

A LANKY DEPUTY LEANED against the sheriff's SUV posted at the house across from the entrance to Doug's place. The kid must have just graduated from the police academy. Max rolled down his window and tipped his chin toward the kid.

"Good morning, Deputy. We're with the FBI. Has anyone been by here?"

"Not a soul." The deputy leaned in to see all the passengers and smiled when he saw who was in the back seat. "Hey, Mr. Lewis."

"Chip. How's your momma?"

"Still got some pain. She's gone back to work, though."

"Good to hear. We've been prayin' for her."

"Yessir, I know you have."

"You didn't go to the cabin, right?" Max asked.

"No, sir. My instructions were to wait right here and call if anyone came or went."

"Good man."

"Yep," Doug said. "His momma done raised him right."

Chip's face reddened.

"Keep up the good work," Max said as Braun put the car in gear. Max half-saluted and raised the window as Braun turned the SUV around. "Doug, you said you have a map of the property?"

"Yes, sir. Just head back to the resort entrance."

They returned down the hill, turned left at the resort sign to the office, pulled into the drive, and parked. Doug retrieved a map from inside, put it on the hood, and explained the layout. A serpentine route weaved by a lake and a dozen cabins. Doug showed them the back way up the hill they'd just turned off of and where they should park to come in behind the girls' place.

"Any other guests on the property?" Braun asked.

"Not this time of year. Now, if you boys are done with this old man, I'm gonna get out of your way and head back to my house." Doug stood back and pointed down the gravel road ahead of them. "My place is straight down there. The girls' is to the left at the Y."

Braun shook Doug's hand. "You've been a tremendous help."

"Before I go, let me just say a quick prayer for you boys." He put a hand on each of their shoulders.

They didn't have time for a holier-than-thou sermon-of-a-prayer, but something kept him from protesting.

"Dear God, You know what's going on here. You know the mess these girls are in. We know You can handle it. Please keep them all safe. Your will be done. Amen."

"Amen," Max said mechanically as he tried to reconcile this prayer with the kind he'd grown up with—filled with dozens of thee's and thou's. It was as if Doug knew God . . . like he was talking to a friend.

"Max, you okay?" Doug asked.

"Yeah, sorry." Was his confusion that obvious? "You'd better get going."

Doug looked him in the eyes like he knew something Max didn't, then patted his shoulder and started down the road.

"Let's go," Braun said. They drove up the hill just past the crest, parked so the car blocked the road, then crept down to the back of the cabin.

The blinds on the back of the house were all closed. Max leaned near the first window he came to. No sounds, which made sense if Heather was sleeping. Max motioned for Braun to go around the opposite side of the cabin, then went to the porch and climbed the wooden steps, careful not to make them creak. The door was ajar. Had the suspects been here and gotten to Heather?

Max removed his arm from his sling, drew his gun, and took a position beside the door with his back to the wall. Braun came around to the closed end of the porch. Max held two fingers to his eyes and then turned the fingers to the open door. Braun quietly came around the porch and joined him on the other side of the door. Max pulled the screen door slowly to avoid a screeching spring, then pushed the door open. "FBI! We're coming in!"

Guns leading, they cleared the living room, then checked the bedrooms. "Clear," they both called simultaneously, then returned to the living room. Everything was in place. No signs of struggle. Dishes on a drying rack. Dog bowls on the floor with water and food.

"Looks like they have a dog." Max returned his arm to the sling. "Maybe Heather's walking it."

"Keep an eye out." Braun pulled on rubber gloves and opened a linen closet. He searched its contents as Max inspected papers on a dining table. A beautiful sketch of Aladdin's famous magic carpet ride lay unfinished at the far end. In place of the monkey, a dog was wearing the same red vest and fez. How funny. He grabbed the drawing and held it up for Braun. "Check this out."

"*Aladdin.* That's my daughter's favorite movie." Braun emptied a blanket bag from the closet onto the futon. "Look what I found." He picked up several bundles of cash, then fanned them out on the cushion. "I'd say the gang hasn't been here. I wonder how much the girls have. We need the sheriff to get a team in here."

"I'll call them. Do you think Melissa will come back for it?"

"After being shot at, my guess is she's in the wind. Although it might depend on what else is here."

Braun snapped photos as Max dialed the sheriff. *No service.* Max cursed. "See if you have service."

Braun pressed a few buttons. "Me neither. I'll go up to higher ground while you go through the rest of the place."

Max raised his sling. "Maybe I should go. Two hands and all."

Braun nodded. "I'll check the bedrooms."

Max scanned the parking area through the window behind the futon, then opened the door just as a loud bang rang out from close by.

Max jumped back, drew his gun, then moved to the front corner between the futon and the front door—back to the wall. Braun poked his head around the bedroom wall, gun drawn. "Where'd it come from?"

Max shook his head. The sound had been loud and close.

Another loud bang.

Max's heart raced. He peeked out into the parking lot, then through the porch window down the hill toward an A-frame cabin. No vehicles. Nothing moving. He moved to the other side of the porch window next to the door. Pulling back the curtain, he scanned the road below. A metal trashcan rolled from beside the porch toward the picnic table, a raccoon pushing. The animal looked back at Max from behind his bandit mask.

He let out his breath, lowered and holstered his gun, and tipped his chin toward the perp. "Rocky."

Braun lowered his gun. "Racoon?"

Braun came to the window and watched as the culprit tried removing the bungee cord holding the garbage can lid. He shook his head. "He doesn't know how lucky he is to be alive." He returned to the bedroom as Max headed out.

Rocky glared at Max as if daring him to stop him. He might have been tempted to shoot the trashcan just to watch him scamper away if it were not for the forms he'd have to fill out for discharging his weapon. He circled away from the feisty animal and backed around the cabin.

No sign of Heather anywhere. Must have been some walk.

Max located a sheltered perch behind some evergreens up the hill. Except for birds singing and Rocky's antics, nothing rustled. His phone rang. An unknown number from a local area code. He tapped the screen.

"Enders."

"Max. It's Doug. I completely forgot that Margie and I went to the church in one car. We left hers at the office, but it's gone. Sorry I didn't notice before. Cindy must have taken it."

"Any idea where she would have gone?"

"I thought she might have gone to the church, so I called Margie. She never saw her." Doug gave him a description of the car.

Max called in a BOLO on Cindy and the Buick, then requested a team to inventory the cabin's contents. He returned to the cabin where Rocky was still trying to get lucky. Braun was emptying another bag on the futon.

"There must be two to three hundred thousand here," Braun said. "I still have to go through the other bedroom. Did you get ahold of the sheriff's office?"

"Yeah. And get this. Doug called. Cindy took Margie's car. She's gone."

"You've got to be kidding. Do you think Melissa called her after the shooting?"

Max shrugged. "No idea, but can you imagine them leaving all this money behind? Between the half million we got from the camper and this, they have to be running out."

"You'd think so."

Max's phone rang again. Now it worked? He checked the screen— another unknown local caller.

"Enders."

"This is Deputy Smith from the Albemarle Sheriff's Office. One of our men spotted the Buick and the suspect at the Rockfish Gap Country Store out on Route 250, just south of you."

"When?"

"'Bout an hour ago. She was in the circular drive on the west side of the store. Claimed she was waiting for someone. He's sure it was her and that she was alone."

"Text me the address." Max hung up. "They saw Heather. We have to go."

"We can't leave this money." Braun snapped pictures of the loot on the futon, then went to the sink and located trash bags. "Sheriff's office will have to take care of the rest." Braun stuffed a sack with the money. He looked like Santa as they raced up the hill and back to the SUV. But there was nothing Christmassy about this day—unless you counted Rocky—who had finally gotten the lid off the trash can.

———

10:55 a.m.

EUPHORIA AGAIN—FINALLY. What could be better than this? Heather floated as her mind painted a magic carpet ride until Abu jumped in her lap and barked, ripping her mind's canvas in two.

Abu pawed at the driver's window and whined at a thin plaid-clad man standing outside the car. He wore a John Deere cap. A long brunette wig and a denim jacket hung from his fingertips.

"Open up!"

It was a woman's voice. Heather examined the stranger. *Melissa?* Heather unlocked the door.

Abu launched herself at Melissa as she yanked the door open and pulled Heather out. "What are you doing back here? And why do you have Margie's car?"

"I . . . uh . . . just needed to get out for a while."

Melissa stared into Heather's eyes. She cursed. "I know that look. What have you done?" Melissa glanced toward the drug paraphernalia inside the car. "Really? You're doing heroin now?"

"Who do you think you are? My mother? You don't know the pain I'm in." Heather pushed Melissa back. "Leave me alone! I didn't ask for your help."

"Fine. You want me to leave you alone?" Melissa threw the wig and jacket at Heather. "Great. Take care of yourself, you brat. I don't have time for this. And P.S., don't call me when the bullets start flying."

"Oh sure. Like that's going to happen."

"Are you that stupid? Bones' guys found us at the church. They shot at us. They could have killed us. Heather, they could have killed Olivia. Or are you so self-centered you don't give a damn about anybody but yourself?"

"*What?*" Killed Olivia? Heather fought her brain's fogginess. The photo of Johnny's brothers and mother lying dead on the street popped into her mind, but with Olivia's tiny body in a pool of blood next to them.

"Come or stay. I don't care, but I'm leaving. I don't even know why I bothered to come back for you." Melissa stormed toward the corner of the building, Abu following.

"Wait!"

Melissa stopped and looked back.

"Please don't leave. I'm sorry. I'm so very, very sorry. I'll do whatever you say. I'll throw the drugs away. Please."

Melissa came back and stared into Heather's soul. "I want you to understand—this is the last time."

"I promise. I'll do anything. Please."

Melissa shook her head. "I know I'm going to be sorry." She scooped up the Cher-like wig and jacket, and shoved them at Heather. "Put those on."

Heather tugged them on while Melissa and Abu went to the passenger side. Fingering the pill bottle in her pocket, Heather eyed the brown bag knowing she couldn't say anything. She followed Melissa to try to intercept the bag. "I need my purse."

Instead, Melissa collected the bag and the elastic band and threw them in the bushes. She removed the sim card from the phone and tossed the phone too.

Every sinew in Heather's body screamed for her to go after the bag. But Olivia . . .

Melissa held out her purse. "No more drugs, right?"

Heather touched her pocket where the bottle was. "Right. I promise." She took the purse.

"Come on. I've left Olivia alone long enough." Melissa touched Heather's elbow, prompting her to head around the store.

"What about Margie's car?"

"We can't worry about that now."

They made their way down the steep incline that ran alongside the building. Tail wagging, Abu ran ahead as if she knew where they were going, sniffing every rock and tuft of grass as she went.

"Where's Olivia?"

"She's in the horse trailer I got. No one will be looking for a single man pulling a horse in rural Virginia. It's decked out inside to live in. You'll see." She held out her elbow like an escort. "We have to be cool. We're going to walk to the truck like a happy couple." Rounding the building to the front of the store, Melissa pointed to the roadblock. "I'd planned to head west . . . I guess we'll head south for now. I'll stop in about forty-five minutes to map our route."

"How'd you find me?"

"I pinged your phone."

She should have known. But if she had turned it off, Melissa would have left without her. And then what would Heather have done?

They hurried across in front of the store to the drive where she'd met the deputy earlier. A faded two-tone truck with a horse trailer awaited them. Melissa unlocked, opened the trailer's side door, and stood back for Heather to climb in.

"Aunt Cindy!" Olivia rushed to the door and jumped into Heather's arms, knocking her weakened frame to the ground. Her rib took the brunt of it. She prayed it hadn't broken in two.

"Jasmine, stop!" Melissa pulled Jasmine up and helped Heather back to her feet.

Olivia's face reddened, and tears began to pool in her eyes.

Melissa quickly bent and wrapped her arms around her. "I'm sorry, baby. It's just that the bad men might be around. We have to hurry."

"I'm scared, Mommy."

"I know, baby. We're gonna be safe. We just need to get going, okay?"

Tucking her chin tightly to her chest, Olivia nodded.

Melissa lifted Olivia's arm to help her up the steps into the trailer, followed by Abu and Heather.

Melissa wasn't kidding about the interior. A full-size bed filled the back with a locker at the foot of the bed, while the front contained a storage cabinet, ice chest, folding table, and folding chairs. In the center stood a play table covered with some of Olivia's puzzles, books, and dolls.

"Wow. You thought of everything."

Melissa pointed to a car seat someone had mounted on a low rack by the play table. "Can you buckle her in? We're going to be on a highway." Melissa shut the door, then reopened it and tossed Heather a phone. "Sorry. Here's a new phone. Call me if you need me to stop. My number's programmed in." She closed the door again.

Heather buckled Olivia into her seat and kissed her forehead. Just as she slid the play table toward Olivia to keep her busy, the trailer lurched, then crunched over gravel before bumping onto a smooth surface. Her head spun. She needed to lie down if she was going to survive her promise not to take the painkillers.

"Can you sit with me?" Olivia's eyes pleaded.

"Aunt Cindy's not feeling well. I need to lie down, okay?"

Olivia pouted her lip. "Okay."

Heather crawled under the covers. Abu jumped on the foot of the bed and settled in. Heather should have shooed her off, but after this day . . .

"Aunt Cindy?"

"Yes, sweetie."

"Can I come and lay down with you?"

"No, sweetie."

"But Abu's on the bed."

"It's not safe for you if we suddenly hit a bump or stop."

Olivia looked at Heather for a long moment. "Have the bad men gone?"

"Not yet. But your mom isn't going to let anything bad happen to us, okay?"

"Okay."

If only Heather believed it.

——

11:10 a.m.

MAX POINTED RIGHT AS THEY APPROACHED the light at Route 250. "Go past the detour signs, and the store will be ahead on the right just before the roadblock."

The orange and white barricade confirmed what the deputy had told them. They turned into the store's parking lot as a man pulling a horse trailer came out of the circular drive on the far side of the store. A handful of cars were parked along the front of the harvest-decorated porch, but no Buick and no Heather. After parking, the two went inside.

Behind the front counter, a fit middle-aged woman wearing a solid orange sweater and jeans stopped pouring coffee grinds into a filter to look at Heather's picture. Neither she nor the hoodie-clad teenage stockboy, whose head bobbed to whatever was playing in his earbuds, had seen her. *But y'all are welcome to look around,* the woman had said with a wave and a smile. Braun went to the second floor as Max searched the surprisingly large ground floor.

The store's many nooks and crannies were packed with some of the most unexpected items—the perfect mix of a corner store, souvenir shop, and antique store. Max picked up an antique egg beater that his ex-wife would have loved. In fact, she would have loved everything there. If he'd spent more time taking her to these places rather than being away for months undercover, maybe they'd still be together. Instead, a new man was enjoying buying egg beaters with her.

The smell of the freshly-brewed coffee filled the store as he returned to the front counter, reminding him that the coffee he'd had earlier was doing its work.

"You got a restroom?"

The woman grinned. "Well, in case you hadn't noticed, this ain't the Hyatt, but if you go 'round back, there's a portable john back there." She pointed out and to the left. "Up the drive. Cain't miss it."

Max checked Braun to see if he, too, was struggling to believe this. One corner of his lips curved up. "I think I'll just wait here."

Max went out the front door and up the drive. And there it was, as if waiting to be found—Margie's car. He called Braun.

"You're never going to believe this . . ."

"I'll be right there."

Max removed his sling, gloved up, and inspected all sides of the car before opening the driver's door. He leaned in and found nothing unusual. Braun joined him as Max walked to the passenger side.

"You're right. I don't believe it. I'll check around and call the sheriff's office for backup."

Max contorted his body to look under the seats. The passenger's side was clean, but the driver's side revealed a used syringe. His mind flashed back to his blue-lipped sister lying on her bedroom floor, a needle beside her—just sixteen.

Please. Not another one.

Max snapped a picture, then held the syringe up for Braun to see. But even as he did, something didn't sit right. He'd lived through his sister's addiction. But Heather had shown no signs. Besides drowning herself in beer and tequila, Heather was as straight as they came. How could she fall this far this fast?

"Was she a drug addict?" Braun asked.

"She wasn't a couple of weeks ago."

Max walked around the back of the car and handed the syringe to Braun as several deputies made their way around the corner of the building. "I'll let you handle this. I'm gonna hit the head."

Max walked the few yards to the plastic john. The odor inside was as nasty as he'd expected. Should have opted for one of those trees.

Max didn't want to believe any of this. Heather's dad had charged him with finding his daughter—alive. Surely "and not addicted to heroin" went without saying. Max's sister started heroin after the doctors got her hooked on pain meds. Was that what happened to Heather?

Max emerged from the portable potty. Several deputies were making their way through the car while Braun and another stood back. One emerged from the wooded area holding up a brown bag. "Found the drugs—heroin."

Braun motioned Max over and away from the others. He turned his back to the activity and spoke in a low voice. "There's nothing new on the gang or the girls. So what do we know?"

"We know Heather was here when everyone thought she was at the cabin. We know Heather was alone when the deputy saw her and that she said she was waiting for someone who clearly was not Melissa because Melissa was supposed to be at the church. Has to be a drug deal."

Braun nodded. "Agreed."

"We know she had access to a lot of money. We also know that the gang is after them for that money."

"But we don't know if they caught up with her."

Max checked his watch. Just after eleven. "No way the suspects could have been at the church at ten and still had time to dump the car, get another, and find Heather. Heck, we wouldn't have found the car if it hadn't been for my nature call."

"Unless the gang was able to catch up to Melissa and then used Melissa to find Heather."

"I don't know. Wouldn't they have gone to the cabin? That's where the money was." Max shook his head. "It doesn't make sense."

"Well, the only explanation is that Melissa came and picked her up."

"I guess." Max's mind worked through possible scenarios.

"I can't believe Melissa would want Olivia around drugs. Even living with Johnny, she never had it in the house." Braun said. "Our intel indicates she's a good mom. And clean."

Max shook his head. "You never know about people." He pictured the lifeless woman they'd found with the baby. "So where does that leave us?"

Braun shook his head. "Back at square one? We need to go back over everything. I'll call the lab to see if they've found any other identities."

"I'll call Heather's dad to let him know she's alive."

Braun glared at Max.

"I'm not going to give any details—just that she's alive."

For how much longer, he didn't know. And even if they had managed to elude the gang, weren't drugs the greater danger now?

Chapter 29

11:15 a.m.

"AUNT CINDY." OLIVIA SHOOK HEATHER AWAKE as the trailer droned along.

She pushed herself up. When would she stop hurting? Every jiggle and bump ratcheted up the pain. She needed that pill. She needed more drugs. But her promise . . .

"Aunt Cindy." Olivia stood beside the bed, legs crossed with Abu at her side. "Me and Abu have to pee."

"Okay, sweetie. I'll ask your mom to stop." She glanced at Olivia's car seat. "How'd you get out?"

"I'm a big girl now." She smiled proudly. "I know how to unbuckle."

"Okay, Miss Big Girl. Now, do you know how to buckle yourself back in?"

Olivia giggled and nodded.

"Good, get back in your seat. It isn't safe for you to be walking about."

Olivia obeyed as Heather got up and retrieved her phone. She tapped Melissa's number and explained Olivia's emergency.

"That's fine," Melissa said. "We're coming up to a town now. I'll stop at a gas station. But don't come out until I check around. I don't think anyone's following us, but I need to be sure."

Heather tapped the phone off. "Mommy's stopping in a minute. Okay?"

Olivia nodded. "Will the bad men be there?"

"No, sweetie. We got away from them. Everything's going to be fine." Heather forced a smile.

Olivia did not.

Heather snatched a twenty from her purse and stuffed it in her pocket to buy a drink so she could take a pill—the last one. Her stomach cinched.

The trailer turned, throwing Heather to the side, but she was able to stabilize herself before it came to a stop. Olivia popped out of her seat.

"Wait. Don't open the door."

Olivia and Abu danced in anticipation of their relief. After a long moment, Melissa opened the door and stepped in holding two matching John Deere ball caps.

She still couldn't get over how different Melissa looked in her manly getup. "What am I calling you, anyway? Bob?"

"Sure, why not?" Melissa put one of the hats on Heather, then helped adjust her wig.

"No new aliases?"

"We have to talk—"

"Mommy, I need to go!" Olivia put her hand over her crotch.

Heather chuckled. "I don't think 'Mommy' will be a good name for you . . . And you can't exactly take her to the women's room in that getup."

"Okay, you take her. I'll walk Abu. Then I'll go."

A grin took over Heather's face as she pictured Melissa facing a urinal. "How are you going to manage a men's room?"

"Ha, ha." Melissa chuckled mechanically. "We're parked on the side of a convenience store. The restrooms should be inside. Keep your head down when you walk in to stay off camera." She pulled a pair of sunglasses from her shirt pocket and handed them to Heather. "Don't talk to anyone."

Melissa pulled the other cap over Olivia's head. "There you go."

Olivia peeked up from under the oversized cap. "Look, Aunt Cindy, we match."

"I know. Isn't this fun?" Heather began to open the door, then stopped. "By the way, those guys that caught up with you back at the church—what were they driving?"

Melissa shook her head. "I'm sure they've ditched their car by now, with all the police and FBI agents there."

"Agents?"

"Yeah, the guys from the hospital. The bouncer dude and the cowboy."

Heather had forgotten all about Jake, or whatever his name was, being FBI since her memory had returned. She'd seen his picture in the news. It didn't make sense he'd be following her. Wasn't he involved with the Hearthstone mess?

"How'd they catch up to us?"

She made a face toward Olivia. "Not here. We'll drive up the road and figure out our next moves."

Heather took Olivia's hand as they stepped down and went inside. After using the restroom, Heather grabbed a couple of power drinks and a boxed fruit drink from the cooler and carried them to the register.

"Aunt Cindy," Olivia tugged at her jacket. "Can I have some candy?"

She looked down at Olivia. "Not right now, sweetie."

The clerk stopped ringing up the transaction and looked between them. Had he heard her name? "Y'all want me to hold this?"

"No, we're good."

Olivia pouted her lip.

Melissa and Abu met them at the trailer as they returned from a wooded patch at the back of the store. Melissa pointed to the bag and stepped inside. "What's that? Didn't I tell you not to talk to anyone?"

"We didn't. We just got some drinks."

"Yes, she did," Olivia said. "She talked to the man."

Melissa's face squeezed. "Really? Are you that stupid? I have drinks."

"How was I supposed to know? It's not a big deal. Not like they're gonna recognize us with these outfits and this horse trailer."

Melissa's eyes darkened underneath the bill of her cap. "Can't you do anything without screwing it up?" She clasped her face, then shook her head. "I can't deal with you now. We have to get away from here." She turned to Olivia. "Get back in your seat, baby."

"Are you mad at Aunt Cindy, Mommy?"

"Yes, baby. She broke the rules."

"Are you going to make her leave?"

"I don't know. Maybe."

"But *I* talked first, Mommy." She teared up. "Are you going to make me leave too?"

Melissa squatted and grabbed Olivia's hands. "No, baby. I would never leave you."

"But I broke the rules."

"But you're family. You're my daughter."

"Isn't Aunt Cindy family too?"

"Yes, she is. I'm sorry. Mommy was just mad. We won't make her leave, okay?"

"You promise?"

"I promise." Melissa pulled her daughter close.

Olivia pulled back and crossed her arms. "Now you and Aunt Cindy have to hug and say you're sorry."

"It's okay," Heather said. "Your mom is right. I broke the rules."

"But that's what Mommy makes me do when I get mad."

"You're right." Melissa stood and gave her a stiff hug. "I'm sorry."

Despite Melissa's empty words, Heather said, "I'm sorry, too." It was only a matter of time before Melissa broke her promise. Everyone pushed her out of their lives eventually.

———

12:00 noon

Fifteen minutes after leaving the store, the trailer rumbled to a halt. Why'd Melissa want to talk about their next steps anyway? It wasn't like she'd ever taken Heather's advice.

The last pill had not relieved her pain. But that wasn't the worst part. Now she felt sick—really sick—nausea, aches, jitters. She needed . . . what? A fix? Like a junkie? Not her. This was temporary. She could kick it later when they got settled.

The trailer door opened, and Melissa stepped in. She pointed to two folding chairs and asked, "Can you set those up?" Melissa unfolded the table. Olivia ran over and sat in the first chair Heather set up, then giggled as if she was getting away with something.

Melissa grabbed two packages of peanut butter crackers from the cabinet, opened them, and put them on the play table. Abu beelined for the table and looked among them for a treat. "Come and sit at your table, sweetie. There's one package for you and one for Abu. Can you share?"

"Can't I sit with you here?"

"No. Aunt Cindy and I need to talk. Besides, Abu's waiting for you."

Olivia slid out of her seat and joined Abu for their snack. She began humming, "A Whole New World."

"What about you?" Melissa asked, holding out a package as Heather took a seat.

Her already nauseous stomach rebelled. No way could she eat. She held up a hand. "I'm not hungry."

Melissa squinted but said nothing. She opened the pack, popped a cracker in her mouth, and then sat and stared at Heather.

Was she going to talk? Silent treatments had been one of her stepmother's favorite tortures. "So, what do you want to talk about?"

Melissa tapped a finger on the table. "We have to figure out what we're going to do."

"Really? I thought you had all the answers."

Melissa's lips pursed. She glanced at Olivia, then kept her voice low and controlled. "Listen. I've had all I can take of your attitude. I don't have to put up with this—or, let me rephrase—*you* don't have to put up with me. You clearly don't like the way I handle things. You're welcome to leave. Anytime."

"Fine. I will." Heather jerked up and went for her purse. She was sick of being disrespected—and she needed drugs. But as soon as she'd pulled the purse strap over her shoulder, Olivia jumped up and wrapped herself around Heather's leg.

"No. You can't go." She looked back at her mother. "Mommy, you promised."

"It's okay, sweetie," Heather said. "I've got to go back to my family." She made a weak attempt to walk toward the trailer door.

"But *we're* your family. Mommy, *please.*"

With her heart breaking, Heather stopped. Olivia may well be the only person who truly wanted her around.

"She's right." Melissa stood and motioned for Heather to sit. "How about I tell you my plan? Then you can decide."

Beads of sweat were forming on Heather's forehead. "I don't know." If she stayed, how would she get her drugs?

As if reading her, Melissa turned to the cabinet and pulled out a bottle of pills. She stared at it for a long moment. Had those been there the whole time?

"Okay, just so we're clear . . ." Melissa looked down at her. "I know you think I'm a bitch, but my best friend died from an overdose last year. I didn't try to stop her. I'm not going to stand by and watch you do the same thing."

With wide eyes, Olivia hopped up and ran to Heather. "Are you going to die?"

Heather ran her fingers over Olivia's cheek, then lifted her chin. She looked into her tear-filled eyes. "I'm not going to die, sweetie. Those pills are my medicine. They make me feel better. That's all. Your mommy's friend took too many. I'm not going to do that."

Melissa tucked the bottle in her pocket, then retrieved a pudding cup and a box of plastic spoons from the cabinet. "Here, sweetie. Why don't you have some pudding, but don't give this to Abu. Chocolate is bad for dogs."

Heather hugged her, and Olivia returned to her table with her treats.

Melissa opened the pill bottle and shook one into Heather's palm. "I'm only going to give you these as prescribed—every six hours. Do you understand?"

"I'm not a baby." She popped it in her mouth and chased it with the warm power drink that had caused all this trouble.

She eyed Heather again. "Baby or not, are we clear?"

"I'm crystal clear." Heather sat back, closed her eyes, and inhaled deeply, praying for the pill to take effect. Whether imagined or real, peace filled her. Not like the amazing rush of comfort the heroin had delivered, but enough to take the edge off. She yoga-inhaled deeply once more, then exhaled as her body relaxed.

"You feeling better?" Melissa's face had softened.

"Yes, thank you."

Melissa returned the bottle to her pocket.

Could she make it six hours? And one pill at a time? Her shoulders pulled higher as her body tensed.

Melissa sat back down. "All right. First, let's talk about how they could have found us."

"Are they coming back, Mommy?"

"No, baby. That's why we left." She got up and pulled an electronic tablet from the locker. A few moments later, the opening sounds of *Aladdin* filled the trailer. She set the tablet on Olivia's table, then returned to Heather.

"There was only one person who knew our plans—Lenny. He made our IDs and got our vehicles. Remember stopping at his place?"

"Yeah, where we dropped you off."

"I'm guessing some of Bones' men followed Johnny that day . . ." Melissa looked away briefly as tears built in her eyes.

The camper flashed in Heather's mind with a new remembrance. "At the camper, one of them had a tattoo . . . 'MCM?'"

"That's them. Motor City Mongrels."

"That's a stupid name. That guy picked up Johnny's duffle bag, but I had switched the money for my clothes. Wish I could have seen their faces when they opened that bag." Heather half-laughed.

"What did you do with the money?"

"I put it in the suitcase we bought. That's what the FBI got."

"Anyway, after they . . ." she inhaled deeply, "after the accident, they must have gone to Lenny's and found the info on our IDs. It's the only explanation. No one else knew anything." She eyed Heather for a moment. "You didn't call anyone, did you?"

"Like I could have done that. I had amnesia, remember?"

"Yeah, but you got your memory back." She waited for an answer.

"No. I didn't tell anyone. Who would I even call?"

"How about whoever you met up with at the store?"

"I didn't call her. I don't even have her number. We set that up at the Friday thing. The only phone call I've made since this whole thing happened was to the taxi service this morning after you left. But that wouldn't have told them you were at the church."

"Wait—what? When?"

"Before I found the keys to Margie's car."

Melissa's face tensed as if about to explode, but then she glanced at Olivia and caught herself. Good thing she couldn't send Olivia to her room while the grown-ups talked.

"Any *other* phone calls?"

"No, that was it."

"And what about this woman? Did you tell her anything?"

"No. Of course not. She picked the time and location. I didn't tell her anything. There was nothing to tell. She gave me some pills in the restroom at the Friday thing. Then we met at the store. That was it."

Melissa took a deep breath, then let it out slowly. "You know I grew up with a liar, right? My brother would say or do anything to get out of trouble. He had no conscience." Her eyes narrowed. "Do you?"

"What kind of question is that?"

"You didn't answer my question."

"It's a stupid question."

"It might have been a stupid question when I first met you—when you were still kind and sincere. Now . . ." Melissa shook her head. "Now I'm not sure who you are or what you're going to do next. You're just like any other junkie who would say or do anything for your next fix."

"Mommy, what's a junkie?"

Melissa glared at Heather before turning to Olivia. "Baby, I said this is an adult conversation. How about you go sit on the bed with your movie?"

Olivia climbed on the bed and lay on her stomach, propped up on her elbows. Abu joined her. Neither woman objected.

"So, are you?" Melissa asked, turning her full attention back to the table. "Would you say or do anything to get a fix?"

"No. It's not like that." *Or was it?* The truth was, ever since those pills had come out of the cabinet, they had been her singular focus—how to get them or how to get out so she could get more? Her knees bounced.

Melissa did another torturous pause. "So? Is there anyone else you contacted?"

"No, I'm sure. That's it."

Melissa stood and retrieved an envelope from the cabinet. She pulled out a pair of North Carolina driver's licenses and dropped them on the table.

Heather stared at the black-haired image. Melissa's was a blonde. She couldn't help but laugh. "Didn't like the man thing?"

Melissa cracked a smile. "Yeah, those urinals are nasty."

Her grin faded as she ran her fingers across the envelope. "This is the last set, but if they got our Charlottesville details, they're sure to have these as well. I'm thinking we can still use them as long as we don't go to North Carolina. And we can't use them for anything big like checking into a hotel or renting an apartment." She sat back in the chair. "The cash will have to speak for us."

"Chincoteague."

"What?"

"My dad has a place on Chincoteague. He hardly ever goes . . . at least since he married Cruella. And they never go in the winter. There're only a few thousand people who actually live on the island. All the tourists would be gone this time of year—well, except for hunters—and I'm pretty sure it's not duck season yet. We'd be safe there."

"Where's Chincoteague?"

"On the eastern shore of Virginia."

Melissa tapped the table several times with her index finger, then looked up a map on her phone. "No, I don't like it. Bones does his homework and might have found out about your family connections."

"Even if we don't stay at Dad's, the Eastern Shore is perfect. There are only chickens and farms out there. No way they can find us."

"Are you kidding? Bones and whoever he works for have a huge network. I don't know if they do business in Chincoteague, but I've heard rumblings about Baltimore, and that's not far. The boys he sent after us might not be the brightest, but trust me, the organization is well-run. They'll know."

Heather looked at the IDs. "If the gang has these pictures, they'll look for these two women." She held up the ID next to her black wig. "We can't use these." She tossed the license on the table, then stripped off her cap and wig. "Face it. We're screwed."

"Okay, Miss Brains. What do you think we should do?"

"What's there to do? I'm done running and doing disguises. I'm Heather Blanchard. You're Melissa Thomason, and that sweet girl is Olivia. I want to go home. Maybe not to my sister's or Dad's, but Chincoteague is safe. And I'll figure out something when I get there. I'll lay low and get back to my painting." Heather's heart warmed as she remembered the loft studio her dad had designed for her, perched atop the house like a giant cupola with a peaceful view of the bay. "I need to paint. I need to hear seagulls. I need to smell the ocean. I need to see nature. I need to be somewhere I can think. When I figure it out, I'll call Dad."

"You're dreaming."

"Well, at least I have a dream that doesn't involve running with stupid IDs that the gang already has."

"Your dream is a nightmare if those guys find you. You'll be dead before morning."

Olivia jumped out of bed and ran to her mother. "You said Aunt Cindy's not going to die."

Melissa picked her up and rubbed her back. "Baby, I was just trying to warn Aunt Cindy about something. You know how Mommy tells you to watch for cars when you cross the street? I'm just suggesting that Aunt Cindy make a good decision to stay away from the bad guys. I didn't mean that she'd actually die."

"Yes, you did." Heather stood as her pulse quickened. "My name is Heather. Heather Blanchard. And I'm done with the cloak-and-dagger routine. I'm going to Chincoteague!" She grabbed her purse, flung the door wide, climbed down to the pine-forested roadside, and slammed the door against Olivia's shrieking protests.

Her stomach knotted as she walked away. Was Melissa right? Would she be dead by morning? She couldn't think about it. She had to get away—to Chincoteague.

Behind her, twigs broke from within the canopy of pines. Her heart fluttered as she whipped her head toward the sound. A white buck stood erect, glaring at her. Time stalled as its eyes pierced her soul.

"Leave me alone!" She kicked the gravel toward the deer. It leaped back into the vegetation and out of sight. She watched to be sure it was gone. What did he want from her?

Heather turned back to the road ahead. Which way should she go? She had no idea which direction they'd come from. Fifteen minutes of driving since they'd left might mean ten miles. But at least she knew there was a store back there somewhere. She crossed the road and headed back, taking one final look at the trailer. It still hadn't moved. Poor Olivia. Melissa must still be consoling her.

As she walked, she checked over her shoulder. Each time, the trailer appeared smaller as it got farther away until it disappeared beyond the crest of a hill. Except for the passing cars, she was finally alone. The scenery didn't change as she journeyed. Rolling hills. Barren trees interspersed with spots of green—pines and other evergreens—the promise of life in a dead forest.

An old pickup with a gun rack mounted along the back window pulled off the road ahead of her. She slowed her pace and waved for them to go on. The truck didn't move. She took a wide path around it. The passenger window lowered as she came alongside. A man whose long, stringy hair hung below his ball cap draped a camouflaged arm out the window. She couldn't see the driver's face.

"Hey, baby, need a ride? We'll make it worth your time." Both men laughed.

Heather ignored him and kept walking by. The truck door slammed behind her. She didn't dare turn.

Roadside gravel crunched from a man's footsteps. "Didn't you hear me, darlin'?"

She still didn't look back. "I heard you. No, thank you."

"What—you think you're too good for us, bitch?"

She'd dealt with guys like this before. Like wild animals, the smell of fear fueled their fires. With bears, you stand tall and pretend to be bigger than them. She took a deep breath, turned, and faced the evil that stalked her.

"Bitch? You got that right." She stared him down. "I've had one of the worst days of my life, and I'm not in the mood for your crap. So back off, or you'll give me an excuse to do something we'll both regret." She opened her purse and put her hand inside as if reaching for a gun. "Go ahead. Give me an excuse. Looking at you, any cop will buy self-defense."

The man put his hands in the air and backed away. "Hey, we was just trying to have a little fun. Didn't mean nothing by it."

"Go on." She jerked the purse forward. "Get out of here."

The man turned and ran for the truck. Gravel erupted from the back tires as they sped away.

Heather let out the breath she didn't know she'd been holding. How many more of these guys would there be?

Not even five minutes passed before another vehicle pulled off the road behind her. No way. She spun around, ready for a fight. Relief flooded her at the sight of Melissa's truck.

Melissa hopped out of the cab carrying a large backpack and brought it to Heather. "I know you hate me right now, but I have to think about Olivia first. And I really believe they could find us at your dad's."

Heather looked into Melissa's soft eyes. Maybe she was right, but Heather couldn't live like this. There had to be a way out.

"I do understand. Nothing's more important than Olivia. Maybe if I can get to safety, I can help you."

"Don't be naive. They'll send me to prison. Then what would happen to Olivia?"

Prison? Was Heather an accomplice? She should have turned herself in at the hospital. No, she should have walked away at the mall. None of this had to happen. But Olivia?

"I'm sorry, Melissa. It's an impossible situation."

Melissa handed over the backpack. "There's enough money in there to get you by for a while. Clothes. And yes, I remembered bras."

They both chuckled.

"There're some snack bars, and . . ." she bit her lip, "and the rest of the painkillers. I'd throw them away if I were you." She pointed to Heather's purse. "You haven't used that cell phone to call anyone but me, right?"

"Yeah, just from the trailer."

"It should be safe. You have my number, and I have yours. If you need me, call. I hope I can call you too."

"Of course. We're cousins, after all." A weak smile fought against the sadness of the moment.

"This stinks. I finally have family, and I may never see you again." She opened her arms and embraced Heather.

"We'll figure this out," Heather said when they'd pulled apart. "I promise."

"From your lips."

Heather looked at the trailer. "Can I give Olivia a hug before you leave?"

"I think that would be perfect. I don't want her to remember you . . . well, you know."

They walked back to the trailer. Olivia squealed when she saw Heather.

"You're back. Can she stay, Mommy?"

"I'm sorry, sweetie, I can't. I've got to get back to my daddy and sister. Maybe someday you can come and visit us, okay? My sister has a horse you can ride."

"Really, Mommy? Can I?"

"Someday."

Melissa took her John Deere cap off and put it on Heather's head. "There, keep your head down. Give me a couple of hours before you contact anyone so I can get far enough away."

They said their goodbyes, and Olivia convinced her mother to let her ride in the truck. After long, final hugs, Melissa and Olivia drove off, leaving Heather alone. The farther her new family moved away, the more profound the void in her heart grew.

The only question now was whether she should call her dad for a rescue mission or head to Chincoteague and lay low. Decision time. Well, at least when she got to the town. She opened the bag, took another pill, and then took her first step toward the decision she'd have to make.

———

1:00 p.m.

After taking the last bite of his half-pound cheeseburger, Max balled up the paper wrapper, stuffed it in the empty French fry container, and tossed it on the plastic tray between him and Braun. They'd spent the last thirty minutes reviewing their options. With no leads, there was only one—heading back.

Max rose from the fast-food restaurant booth. "Ready?"

Braun's phone rang. He tapped the screen.

"Braun." He listened. "North Carolina?" Braun nodded. "You sure?" He nodded again. "Text it to both of us. We're on our way." He tapped his phone off and looked up at Max. "The lab recovered another set of IDs that had been partially deleted." He scooted out of the booth and stood. "Let's hope we're the only ones who found them."

Max grabbed the tray, emptied it in the trash, and joined Braun at the door. "You don't think the girls would be stupid enough to go there after we found them here? They have to know that we got the info from Lenny."

"It's our only lead."

They jumped in the car. Max scrolled back and forth between the pictures of the two driver's licenses. "I don't know which hairstyles and colors I like better. Heather, the blonde, seemed so innocent when I knew her in Hearthstone. Well, maybe not innocent, but certainly not caught up in this kind of trouble." Why was she running?

Braun nodded. "Disguises certainly haven't taken away their beauty."

Max pulled up the address on the GPS. "It's due south by rural roads—if that's where they went. Probably another abandoned house."

"Even though the girls weren't there, saving that baby was something." Braun put the SUV in reverse and pulled out.

"Yep. Something I'll never forget. Makes it all worthwhile. Doesn't it?"

Braun nodded. "Call the office and get them to send a team to scope out the address."

"Might spook the girls."

"Tell them to move only if any gang members show up. Meanwhile, the girls are bound to get hungry. Let's stop at restaurants on the way south to check if anyone's seen them." Braun smiled. "And gas stations. Ever traveled with a four-year-old?"

After a dozen stops, they came to a gas station with a convenience store. The clerk's face lit up when they showed the North Carolina IDs.

"Yeah, yeah." He pointed to Heather. "That one. She was with a little girl. Called her 'Aunt Cindy.' I don't remember seeing the other one."

Max and Braun exchanged looks.

"How long ago were they here?"

"They came right after I got here—'round noon."

Max checked his watch. "Did you see which way they went or what they were driving?"

"No. They didn't get gas. I didn't see where they was parked."

"Did they buy food?"

"Nope, just some drinks." The clerk chuckled. "The little girl was beggin' for candy."

"Anything else you can tell us?"

"That's it. Is there a reward or something?"

"Only the reward of knowing you helped with an ongoing investigation. Thank you."

The two returned to their SUV.

"Well, only a couple hours' head start." Braun backed out and headed south.

"And if they didn't get food here, maybe we'll get lucky at a restaurant."

Chapter 30

1:30 p.m.

A Black-rimmed white historical marker came into view—something Heather would never have cared about as she whizzed past in a car. Did anyone really stop to read these signs? It was bad enough having to study history in high school. Now, it was her only distraction from her walk and her decision about whether to call her dad.

The sign declared the number of square miles the county contained and that it was formed in 1761. Was America that old? And what was up with the French and Indian War? Was it fought here? Benjamin West had painted one of her favorite pieces of American art—*the Death of General Wolfe.* The portrait revealed a time of gray skies and misery but was masterfully crafted. It was impossible to imagine this beautiful countryside overrun with red and blue-coated men trying to kill one another. And Indians? Had the modern, politically-correct society changed the war's name since she graduated high school only a decade before?

A few miles later, a town came into view. Heather walked past the first few businesses to a crossroads. At the sight of a drug store, her backpack suddenly became heavy with the weight of the pills. Thus far, she'd managed to take only one, but now, her mind turned against her. If she believed in the devil, she'd have sworn he was whispering in her ear—tempting her like in that story about Eve. How many pills were there? One more pill wouldn't hurt. She should stop and take one.

She tapped her head with the palm of her right hand as if the action would push the evil thoughts from her brain. "Stop." If she were going to call her dad, she'd need to get straightened out first. Getting to Chincoteague would buy her some time to quit. But right now, she needed one—maybe two little helpers to get by.

Just past the drugstore, a gas station boasted its world-renowned fried chicken—like this place was actually known beyond this county. But the smell made her wonder if it was true. Not that she was hungry. Maybe a bite or two would help chase away her growing anxiety.

She entered the aging market and approached the glass-front counter at the back of the convenience store. After scanning too many options above the clerk's head, she ordered a two-piece, white-meat box, then grabbed a table in the separate dining area to the right and managed to eat half the juicy breast she would have devoured any other day.

She folded the flaps of the greasy box back over the biscuit and styrofoam mashed potatoes container and stared at it. Now was the moment of truth. She checked the time. She had given Melissa enough time to get away, but could she call her dad? Her leg bounced. Sweat formed on her brow as she considered the painkillers.

A few tables away, a gray-haired version of Andy Griffith eyed her, his bushy eyebrows emphasizing his glare. He shook his head as if he could read her thoughts. She didn't care—she needed those pills. Now. She spied the restrooms and grabbed her backpack as she rose and headed toward the restroom sign at the back.

"Hey."

Heather turned back, expecting a look of condemnation and ready to defend herself.

"The table is not a trash can." He pointed a crooked finger at the chicken box she'd left behind. "We don't take too kindly to folks treating us like we're their servants."

Blood drained from her face. She wasn't raised like that. Turning back, she collected the box. "Sorry. I'm not feeling well. I guess I lost my mind."

His features softened. "You do look a little flushed. Can I help you? I'm a doctor."

She cursed under her breath. "No, no. I'm sure I'll be fine. I need to take my medicine."

"Mmm hmm, I think I understand. I hope you're not gonna do something you'll regret. You look like a sweet young lady."

"Oh. No, sir. Nothing like that. Just recovering from a bad accident—broken ribs, you know."

"Yeah, I'm sure I do." He tipped his head. "They got you hooked on those pain pills, didn't they? What is it, oxycodone? Percocets? Or have you moved on to heroin?" He watched her quietly, like a worm squirming under a magnifying glass burned by the intensified sunlight. "Just last week, we lost another girl 'bout your age. Not even thirty. I delivered that girl . . . and her momma too, for that matter. She had a good job. Bright future. Good family." He shook his head. "We've lost so many."

"Well, that's not me." She shoved the box through a hinged flap on the orange trash can lid and left the building.

That man didn't know what he was talking about. She wasn't going to die. She'd be able to control this when she got to Chincoteague and didn't have all this stress.

———

2:10 p.m.

"Now I'm sorry we stopped for a burger," Max said, pointing to the "world-renowned" chicken restaurant attached to a convenience store/gas station. "My aunt makes the best fried chicken, so that sign is like throwin' down a gauntlet."

They pulled in and hopped out of the SUV. Max's mouth watered as they entered the restaurant. Braun jutted his chin toward the counter. "I'll check with the clerk."

Max nodded and headed for the dining area to the right. The only patron—a gentle-looking gray-haired man was packing chicken remains in a logoed box in the dining area to the right. He tipped his hat. "Sir."

The man stood. "Well, I don't know if I'd call myself a sir, but can I hep you?"

"Before I get to business, is that chicken as good as they claim?"

"Ain't none finer. And I know 'cause I'm a Southern Baptist." He pinched the only inch of fat on his otherwise-lean torso. "Fifty years of fried chicken." A grin spread across his face. "Now how can I hep you?"

"I'm Special Agent Max Enders with the FBI. We're looking for two young women and a child." Max showed him the pictures.

The man nodded and pointed to Heather's ID. "Yep, yep. That one—and I can tell you, she's in some kinda trouble."

"What do you mean?"

"Addicted. I know it when I see it. Said she was taking pain pills from an accident. That's how it always starts. And then you're hooked." He snapped his fingers. "Just that easy. I'm a doctor, by the way—Doc Hallaway." He shook Max's hand. "Yep, lost a young girl just last week. Same story."

Max knew all too well, and now—Heather. His heart dropped. Her family was going to be devastated. "Do you know where she went?"

"Sorry. When I tried to help her, she ran out the door. She went right—south, but that's all I know."

"Did you see anyone with her?"

"Nope. She came in, ate a few bites of chicken, then trashed the rest of her lunch and left. Is she in some kinda trouble with the law?"

"Not with the law. Thank you." He handed the doctor a card and asked him to call if he remembered anything else, then joined Braun in the SUV and relayed the sighting.

Braun's phone rang. "It's the chief." He answered and gave an update on where they were, then grew silent. He frowned. "But, sir—" He shook his head. "Yes, sir." He tapped off his phone.

"That didn't sound good."

"The chief says a team checked out the North Carolina house. A family lives there. They don't know anything about the girls. Said if we don't have a lead on Melissa, then we need to come back. Heather's not our focus."

The words punched Max in the gut, but there was no arguing. He knew how the agency operated. If he weren't a passenger, he might ignore the orders. After all, he was supposed to be on medical leave.

Braun must have been reading his mind because before Max could devise a plan of escape, Braun pounded the steering wheel. "How about we try the other restaurants and gas stations in town first?"

———

2:35 p.m.

THE FAST-FOOD RESTAURANT'S ACCESSIBLE STALL provided the perfect hideaway for Heather to dig through her backpack without inquiring minds finding her out. Hoping the diaper-changing table was clean was likely in vain, but she emptied the contents there anyway. Various tops, jeans, and underwear came out first. A rolled-up beach towel hid packets of cash. She didn't dare take the time to count now in case that old doctor had alerted the police to look for her. She took five hundred and rolled the towel back up. She removed a pouch from the bottom. Her pills. She shook the bottle, then opened it and counted. Nineteen. She had to make them last. But right now, she needed to take the edge off. She downed two, shoved the bottle and the cash into her pocket, then repacked the bag.

The bathroom door opened to the cry of a baby. Someone pounded on the stall door. "Hey, you gonna be long? I gotta change my baby."

"Sure, sure. I'm done. Give me a minute." Heather zipped the bag and opened the door to a towering, thin woman worn beyond her years. The screeching four-month-old on her hip was red-faced and plump.

The woman eyed her backpack. "You'd better be careful. They don't put up with no druggies 'round here."

314

"I'm not a druggie, thank you. I have broken ribs. Just taking my meds."

The woman stared at her. "Well, your face screams druggie. What're you on anyway? Oxy? Heroin?"

Heather brushed past the woman, then exited into the dining area, where she caught a glimpse of a black SUV pulling into a parking space on the side of the building. The passenger got out, seated his cowboy hat on his head, and then turned toward her. *Jake.* Heather rushed back into the restroom.

Trying to catch her breath, she pressed her back against the cold tiled wall.

The woman came out of the stall with her now-contented infant sucking happily on her thumb.

Heather grabbed her forearm. "You got a car?"

The woman pulled away. "Sure, don't you?"

Heather pictured her red Prius at the bottom of a river. "Yeah, but not here. I need to get out of here. There are a couple of guys out there. Can you help?"

"What's it worth to you?" the woman asked as she rubbed her fingertips together in classic show-me-the-money style.

The woman's wardrobe spoke of Salvation Army. Heather didn't want to be her meal ticket to Niemann Marcus, but what choice did she have? "How much do you want?"

"Depends on where you're trying to go."

"I need to get to the next town east of here. Can you do that?"

The woman stared at Heather's brand-new backpack as if she knew its contents. "Five."

"Five hundred? I should call an Uber."

"Good luck with that." The woman turned to leave.

"Wait."

The woman stopped.

Despite her bankroll, Heather squeezed her face as if desperate. "That'll wipe me out."

"Not my problem. My guess is, whoever's out there is more trouble than broken ribs."

"Okay, five hundred."

The woman held out her hand.

"You think I'm stupid? I hand you the money, and you run off."

"Well then, show me the money."

Heather pulled the five one-hundred-dollar bills from her pocket and waved them in the woman's face as her baby watched wide-eyed.

"Okay, who am I looking for?"

"Two guys. A tall, dark-haired guy in jeans, boots, and a cowboy hat. The other looks like a bouncer—dark suit, white shirt, and tie. They got out of a dark SUV."

"Okay, I gotta get a sandwich before we go anyway. I'll scope it out. Be back in a couple of minutes. Here." The woman handed the baby to Heather. "I bet they won't expect you to have a baby." She laughed, then pulled the door open and disappeared.

Heather was in no shape to be holding a baby, but her anxiety lessened. Strangely, the baby hadn't fussed when her mother handed her over. She cooed as Heather patted her back. How could this woman let a stranger take her baby—especially one she thinks is a junkie? Then again, why was Heather trusting a woman who could rob and leave her in the middle of nowhere?

The woman returned to the restroom with a food sack. "They're showing pictures and asking about you, another woman, and a little girl. Didn't sound like anyone saw you. Must be that stylish hat."

The baby reached for her mother and grunted. The mother smiled as she accepted her child. "They left already. You know they're offering ten thousand dollars for information leading to you?"

Heather's breath caught. "And you didn't turn me in?"

The woman shrugged. "I've had my fair share of trouble. But I don't think I've ever been worth anything to the authorities. Ten grand sure would go a long way with my family, though. So what's the deal with the other two?"

"It's my cousin and her daughter. We decided to split up and go in different directions. Did the men identify themselves?"

"Yeah, FBI special agents—the suit called himself Braun, and the cowboy was Enders." She pulled a card from her pocket. "Here's his card."

Heather examined the card. Max Enders. Special Agent. She would never have guessed that the sweet farm hand could have been undercover. Heather rubbed the card. Maybe she should turn herself in. Jake had always been kind. "Can I keep this?"

The woman nodded as she swayed with the baby.

Good. Maybe she wasn't planning to turn her in. Of course, she could always call the FBI without the card.

"Sure makes me wonder what you did. Doesn't seem like the FBI'd be lookin' for a junkie with no money or car."

"I honestly don't know why they're looking for me. Whatever it is, it's nothing I chose to be a part of. That's for sure. Wrong-place, wrong-time . . . on steroids."

"I've heard that before."

"Are you going to help me or not?"

"Yeah, but I don't know why. But I bet you're not good at this stuff, so listen. I'll go out the side door, then come back if they're still around. Wait a couple of minutes. If I don't come back, come out to my car. It's a green Corolla. Get in the passenger seat. Keep your head down, and don't look around."

She nodded, and the woman went out. Heather followed a minute later, found her way to the car, and got inside. Without a word, the woman backed out and pulled out of the parking lot. Jake's SUV was in front of the chicken place down the street she'd left less than an hour before.

"Keep your head down. They're talking to Doc Hallaway out front."

"There was a doctor there questioning me." Heather peeked a glance. "That's him." She cursed.

"Doc Hallaway's a good man. Delivered me, my daughter, and all my siblings. He even delivered my mom. But he loves to talk. If you told him anything, he'll spill it."

Heather cursed again.

"Listen, I got a friend who can take you anywhere. You interested?"

It would be great to have someone drive her to Chincoteague, but with a reward on her head, that was too risky. "No, I don't have money for that. Besides, I'm not sure where I'm going yet. Just need some distance for now."

"Fine with me. Just thought you might need some help. You still want to go east?"

"Yep. I'm pretty sure they think I'm going south."

"Why's that?"

She shook her head. "I think I've said enough."

"Okay, then."

They traveled for about twenty minutes without sharing a word or their names. The baby had fallen asleep. The pills had calmed her, but she felt sick. She spent the time mentally rerunning her life in Hearthstone—trying to figure out the connections between Jake and the gang. She still refused to believe that Tom was a criminal. He was the only bright spot in that town. She could use his shoulder right now.

They arrived in a town hosting a dozen businesses on its main street. Heather pointed to a fast-food restaurant. "That'll be fine. You can drop me off there."

The woman pulled around back. "Thanks for not turning me in." Heather handed over the money and got out.

The woman lowered the passenger window. "Well, Heather, I'm sure I'm going to regret it. Or are you still going by Cindy?"

How did she know Heather's name? The agents at the restaurant. "Heather. Can I look you up after I get all this cleared up? You've gone beyond kind."

"Yeah. Pretty sure I'll never escape my small-town life. I work at the hotel cleaning rooms. Name's Angel."

Heather smiled. It fit. "Well, Angel, here's hoping I can get my life back so I can find you one day and properly reward you."

"I know this sounds hokey, but I've already received my reward. And this five hundred will go a long way." She fanned the bills. "Good luck."

Heather stood back as Angel pulled away, then crossed the mostly-vacant parking lot to find the restroom and down two pills. They weren't doing for her what the heroin had. She looked in the mirror. She'd aged ten years. Angel was right—she had the face of a junkie. And that red hair. Who had she become? She wanted to find some ruby slippers, click her heels, and go home.

She shook it off, pulled her hat low over her eyes, shouldered her backpack, and pushed the restroom door open. The quicker she could get away from that reflection, the better.

Heather tucked her head as she passed a slender sixty-something woman dressed in a tailored brown-wool sweater suit that belonged in a metropolis, not a hick town.

"Excuse me." The woman called out, loud enough to draw attention.

Heather paused but didn't turn.

"Young lady?" the woman said.

Peeking from under her hat, Heather turned back. The woman's perfectly-coiffed hair matched her out-of-place wardrobe.

"Do I know you?"

Heather couldn't place the familiar voice. Forcing a baritone, she said, "No, I'm sure you don't."

"Wait. I know. You're one of Doc Blanchard's girls. Heather. Right? I'm Mrs. Forsythe, your first-grade Sunday-school teacher. Don't you remember me?" She opened her arms and started toward Heather.

Heather didn't remember much of anything from those dark days after her mom died. Nor did she want to. Leaving Mrs. Forsythe calling her name, she rushed out the door, rounded the building, and stole a final glance through the plate-glass window. The woman pulled a phone from her suit-matching purse, tapped the screen, and put it to her head. Was her dad on speed dial? This couldn't be happening.

She ran until the restaurant was out of sight, then raised her thumb, praying no tormentors would come along. A faded black pickup truck pulled in front of her, sporting Pennsylvania license plates and a solo male driver. Answered prayer or someone looking for a good time? She ran to the opened passenger window while her father's admonitions to never hitchhike screamed their warnings.

An adorable curly-haired man with a five-o'clock shadow tapped the steering wheel with his thumbs to the beat of *Good Directions* playing in the background. His smile would have invited her to join him anywhere. "Need a ride?"

She did, but was it safe? *Be logical.* What did she know about this man? Southern accent. Eyes sincere, not malicious. Clean. Good music taste. But then again, she'd never been a good judge of character—especially where men were concerned. She glanced over her shoulder. No Mrs. Forsythe. What choice did she have?

"I'm heading east."

"Me, too. I'm headed up to Richmond. Gonna meet up with some friends there. You'd be saving me from a boring trip."

The crooked line of his smile charmed her. Maybe he was a Godsend. Not that God had ever sent anyone—or anything. She looked around for the white deer—no sign of him.

"Thanks." She opened the door and hopped in. "I appreciate this." She tossed her backpack on the bench seat between them and settled in as he pulled onto the road. If only she could just shut her eyes and ride in silence. But this guy might get suspicious if she clammed up.

"My name is Crystal. What's yours?"

"John."

Really? As in Doe? At least she had come up with an original name. She didn't dare press it. "You from around here?"

"Not really from anywhere." His tone was folksy, a trustworthy voice. "My dad was military, so we moved around a lot. What about you?"

Not an answer. And that accent—Texas, maybe? Sounded more like someone who'd grown up in one place, not a military brat. Her stomach knotted, but she was unsure if it was related to her diminishing trust level or the meds. She needed to keep the conversation going.

"Illinois." Not technically a lie. "So, where do you live now?"

"Well, funny enough, I'm between gigs. Been staying with a buddy over in the Shenandoah Valley near Luray. I'm hoping to get a job in Richmond."

"What do you do?"

"Jack—or in my case, *John*—of all trades." His smile was so endearing. He glanced at Heather as if to invite her to join in his amusement. That was always how it started with her and guys, wasn't it—at least, that's what Julie said. She had to prove she could keep her heart out of this. Fact-finding. Who was John?

"What have you been doing lately?"

"I was working a horse farm, but it was time to move on. I'm hoping to work at a factory just south of Richmond. I like working with my hands." He lifted his right arm and flexed his bicep. Even through his blue denim shirt, it was impressive. "What about you?"

"I've moved around. Waitressed mostly."

"I was sure you were going to say modeling. You're prettier than a spotted horse in a daisy pasture."

Now she knew he was lying. "Thank you, but we both know I'm no model."

John checked his side mirror, then floored it to overtake the tractor poking along ahead of them. He didn't speak for a few more miles as the road ribboned through the pine forest. Her knee began to bounce. A flush heated her face. She wiped her sweaty palms on her jeans and then used them to still her legs.

John glanced at her with furrowed brows. "You doing okay over there?"

"Yeah, I've just been a little under the weather. No big deal."

He glanced at her again. "Where're ya headed?"

She stopped her bobbing knee again. "No place in particular. Just checking my options. I can waitress just about anywhere."

"That's true." He was quiet for another moment. "You got a place to stay tonight?"

There it was—checking if anyone would notice her missing. "I'll be good. I just need a ride."

"Happy to oblige. Just let me know where to drop you off."

"I will."

She looked him over again out of the corner of her eye. He was just the charmer type she always fell for. Too good to be true. But in another life . . . *whew*. She leaned her head back, intending to keep an eye on their travels, but before she knew it, the pills kicked in, and she was out.

———

5:30 p.m.

"WHAT DO YOU SAY WE STOP FOR DINNER in Beckley?" Max said after checking the time to Huntington. He was still licking his wounds after the chief had chastised them for not heading straight back. *You boys can't go in four directions—time to pack it in.* The worst part was knowing how close they had come to finding Heather.

The doctor from the chicken spot had called them back—not with more information—but with gratitude for the work they were doing.

Fried chicken. That smell.

"You know, I'm dying for some good fried chicken."

A smile pulled at Braun's lips. "I know just the place. They cook everything from scratch. And the cheddar fries . . . Oh, man, now my mouth is watering."

"I'm in."

The brick-arched restaurant interior reminded Max of old forts. They were quickly seated, and seconds later, the waitress brought their menus.

"Either of you boys interested in a Painkiller cocktail?"

Max winced and shook his head. "I think we'll pass. Someone we know just got hooked on those killers."

Her face dropped. "It's a stupid name, especially for this state—the reigning champion of drug overdoses. My cousin OD'd last month. Half my school is hooked on something."

"Not you, I hope," Braun said.

She shook her head. "I'm not that stupid."

"Good. Keep it that way."

Max glanced at the menu. "You know, I came here for one thing. Fried chicken. What do you have?"

"Most folks get the country-fried chicken, but the chicken tenders are just as good—real chicken breasts, just not as messy."

"How 'bout the chicken tenders with your cheddar fries."

"The cheddar fries are an appetizer—enough for a family to split."

Braun nodded. "She's not kidding. We'll split the fries, and I'll have the country-fried steak. Cola for me and sweet tea for my friend."

The waitress took it all down, then returned a couple of minutes later with their drinks.

Max's phone rang. Heather's dad. He turned the screen to Braun, who shook his head. Max steadied himself before answering.

"Doc Blanchard, what can I do for you?"

"It's Heather. An old family friend, Elizabeth Forsythe, saw her in a fast-food restaurant on Route 60 in Cumberland, Virginia."

"Cumberland? Hold on." Max held his phone away and switched to the map. He looked at Braun. "Heather. She's headed east on Route 60 from Amherst." He put the phone back to his ear as Braun opened the map on his own phone. "Did Mrs. Forsythe talk to her?"

"She tried, but Heather ran out. Her hair was red, so she didn't recognize her at first."

"Did she say if she got in a car?"

"No. She had a backpack. Thinks she was hitchhiking but might have gotten in a black pickup she saw pulling away when she went after her. She didn't get the license tag."

Half the vehicles in rural Virginia were black trucks.

"Max, what's going on? Who are you talking to?"

All Doc Blanchard was supposed to know was that Max was poking around. "I'm talking out loud. I'm just looking for your daughter, sir. Just like you asked."

"Should I be worried?"

"My momma used to say worrying is for fools. You ain't no fool, sir. Just know I'm looking."

"You said she's moving east. If that's true, she might be heading for our summer home in Chincoteague—where Julie and Richard went. She won't know they're there."

Max wanted to say more, but he couldn't. "Great. Thanks for the information. I'll check into it. Text me Mrs. Forsythe's contact information. And Doc, I know you might be tempted to tell Julie and Richard about this, but please don't. You understand? Let's not get anyone's hopes up."

Doc Blanchard hesitated. "I don't like it, but yes. Only because I know you have her back."

"Thank you."

"Max, please find my girl."

"I will, sir." Max hung up, not worried if they would find her, but in what condition that would be.

Max filled Braun in, then Braun called the chief and gave him the update. "Can we go after her?" As he listened, Braun shook his head. "But sir, these are the people—" He continued his negative shake. "Yes, sir." He hung up.

"Sorry, man. He said you had to be back in the office Monday to prepare for your testimony, and they don't want you getting caught up in this mess. The Hearthstone hearing is too important."

Max cursed and pounded the table just as the waitress approached with the fries. Her eyes widened. Braun moved their drinks to the side to make space, then motioned for her to set down the platter. "It's okay. He just got some bad news."

"Okay, then. Your orders will be up in five minutes."

"Sorry," Max said as she left. He looked at Braun. "I guess I'm on my own time until Monday, wouldn't you say?"

"Max, you can't—"

"Who says? It's my time. I'm supposed to be on R and R, remember? Come on, man. Take me to get a rental. I can't just let her walk into something I know is bad. I need to be there. We wouldn't have Hearthstone if it weren't for this family."

Braun shook his head. "Well, I don't have any plans for my weekend."

"No, I can't let you get involved in this—"

Braun held his hands up. "Too late. I'm in. My ex has the kids this weekend anyway."

The waitress returned with their meals.

"Should we get them to go?"

The server waited as Max considered it. "No, we'll eat here." It was already late afternoon. Heather would probably have to stop in Richmond unless she was going to try to make it all the way, no matter which place she went to. But if she was hitchhiking, she might not get a ride right away. And hitchhiking at night, especially for a girl, was downright crazy. If they went to Richmond, they'd be pretty central to whichever way she might go—a couple of hours from D.C. and three hours from Chincoteague. Richmond was a three or four-hour drive from them. They needed to eat.

"Anything else?"

Max held up his glass. "More tea?"

She took the glass and left.

"Thanks for doing this. Let's get to Richmond tonight. I have a lot of local contacts around there. I'll make calls while we're on the road. Maybe we can get a lead."

Chapter 31

_6:30 p.m._

"Crystal. We're here."

Crystal?

Someone nudged Heather's shoulder. She struggled to lift her lids from her dry eyes and her brain from its fog. "What?" The truck was parked in front of an old two-story farmhouse tucked into a small fortress of trees and bushes. Chickens scurried toward their coop near an old red barn. Fenced barnyards were empty. John's was the only vehicle.

Heather turned to him. "Sorry. Guess I dozed off. Where are we?"

"At my buddy's house. I need to drop off my stuff. Then I can take you wherever you wanna go. You can stay in the truck if you want. I'll only be a minute. Or, if you'd like, you can come in for a while and have a beer with my friends. They should be back soon."

Beer with friends sounded good—normal. She needed normal. But his friends weren't there? Alone with a stranger in the middle of nowhere? Her stomach tensed.

"Come on. I promise we'll be out of here within the hour. You don't have anywhere to be right now, do you?"

This was bad. He knew no one was expecting her. What if there were no friends? No one to hear her scream. "Well, let me call my dad first. He'll be worried if I don't check-in. Can you tell me where we are?"

He gave her an address for a town right outside Richmond. Of course, they could have been in Kalamazoo for all she knew. She was so stupid! Why had she fallen asleep?

Heather slid out of the truck and stepped away to fake a call since she couldn't call her dad yet. But if this guy was an ax murderer, she should tell someone where she was. Maybe then they could at least find her body. She texted Melissa the address, a description of the truck, and a tag number, then held the phone to her head and spoke loudly enough that John could hear. When she'd completed her ruse, she returned to the truck for her backpack.

Duffle bag in hand, John retrieved a key from under a gnome at the edge of an unplanted garden plot and met her at the front door. A silly grin crossed his face as he held up the key. "I guess you can tell we're good friends." He winked. "Come on."

The screen door creaked as he propped it open with his back and unlocked the red front door. He pushed it open, then stepped back like a gentleman to hold the door for her. What did the spider say to the fly in the creepy poem her dad used to recite at bedtime?

"Here, let me get some lights on." He flicked a switch on the wall.

This was no tangled web. White contemporary furniture splashed with wonderful lavender and blue throws. Everything in place. A woman's touch.

"Set your backpack there." He pointed to an armchair in the corner of the room. I'm just going to put my stuff in *my* room." His mouth formed an impish grin. "Boy, are they going to be sorry they invited me. Missy's a great cook. I may never leave." He laughed as his boots clomped up the wooden staircase.

His casual attitude had finally abated her fears. She needed to text Melissa not to worry. She set her backpack in the chair and called upstairs. "Do you mind if I use the bathroom?"

"No, go right ahead. Under the stairs."

Heather's first text hadn't been read. She quickly texted Melissa that all was okay and that she'd be heading to Chincoteague in the morning. She felt foolish—John had been nothing but polite. Now she could relax.

She sat on the closed toilet and took a deep breath. Her broken rib sharply reminded her that was not a good idea. She downed two more pills. That should take the edge off.

John stomped down the stairs above her. "Crystal?"

"Still in here."

"Sorry, sorry. Didn't mean to invade your privy time. Don't rush."

Heather came out of the bathroom to an empty living room.

"Can you believe this?" John called from the back.

She followed his voice down a short hallway to a dream kitchen. Oversized appliances gleamed in the perfectly-angled track lighting. John stared into a double-door refrigerator as large as two normal-size units put together

"It's a crime to have this magnificent piece of equipment without a single beer inside."

The front screen door creaked. "John?" A female's voice called out.

"Back here, Missy."

An Irish setter bounded into the kitchen and jumped on John.

"Finney. How're you doing, old boy?" John hugged and patted the dog until Finney relented and made his way to Heather. She stooped for a defensive hug before he could hurt her with the full force of his weight.

Missy and the man Heather supposed was her husband came into the kitchen, each burdened with several grocery bags. Heather stood. Missy's smile could warm a homeless man on a cold, damp night. The couple dropped their bags on the island counter.

John motioned to Heather. "Meet my new friend Crystal."

Blood rushed to Heather's face as her heart screamed for her to confess her deception.

"So, you're the cute hitchhiker John called to say he was bringing home. Welcome to our humble abode." Missy opened her arms and hugged Heather, then backed and pointed to her husband. "Crystal, this is Bobby, my better half."

Bobby reached out to shake Heather's hand. "Crystal? Nice to meet you."

"I'm sure the pleasure's mine." She eyed everyone as they stared back as if awaiting her true name. She scrunched her nose. "I have a confession. My name isn't Crystal. It's Heather."

John's mouth opened.

"Sorry, you never know who to trust, especially when John Doe is picking you up."

Missy chuckled and hugged her again. "I love it. You were right to be cautious with this one. With that messy hair and five-o'clock shadow, I'd think he was a serial killer too."

"Thanks a lot." John leaned down to pet the dog's head, provoking a vigorous tail wag. "At least Finney knows a good man when he sees one."

"Aww, John." Missy pinched his cheek. "Did we hurt your feelings? You know we love you."

"I'll feel the love if one of those bags has a six-pack." He moved toward the counter as Bobby pulled out two.

"Feel the love, buddy." Bobby tossed John a bottle.

John's face lit up. "You guys are the best." He uncapped the bottle and tipped it toward Heather. "Crystal?"

"Stop it. I feel bad enough as it is." This guy was getting cuter by the minute.

He laughed. "Just kidding. Heather, will you join me?"

"We also have wine for the more refined," Missy said.

"Beer's good by me." Heather accepted the gift.

"Oh, looky there. A gentleman behind that fuzzy face." Missy retrieved a bottle of wine, poured herself a glass, and then raised it. "To new friendships."

They clinked their glass vessels together, then took their swigs. Heather's stomach settled until she took a second swig, reeling her head. Mixing alcohol and pills. She should've known better. She sat on one of four barstools at the island counter and struggled to maintain a smile.

Missy pulled some packaged chicken out of a bag and began putting the groceries away. "John said you were going to a hotel. We have another room if you'd like to stay over. It has a lock so you can keep the mass murderer out." She winked at Heather. "And I'm cooking John's favorite—fried chicken, mashed potatoes, and southern-style green beans with some good ol' Smithfield ham, followed by my famous apple cobbler a-la-mode." She held up a container of ice cream."

A grin stretched John's face. He licked his lips.

Missy handed Bobby a can of dog food and pointed to the dog bowl. "Won't you stay? At least for dinner?"

Heather couldn't remember the last time she had been so warmly greeted. Her heart was full, but she was feeling sicker by the minute. "I think I'd like that. Would it be possible for me to lie down for a while before dinner? I'm recovering from broken ribs, and my pain meds are starting to make me a bit dizzy."

"Pain meds?" Missy's face blanched. "What are you taking, sweetie?"

"Percocet," Heather almost whispered.

The boys' faces tensed.

"You shouldn't be drinking." Missy held out her hand for Heather's beer. Heather stared at her before handing it over. She didn't want to be rude, but she had just escaped one control freak. She didn't need another one.

"You don't need to treat her like a child," John said.

The air chilled as Missy stared at John, mouth open. She shook her head, then bolted from the room.

Bobby pushed off the counter, cutting his eyes toward John. "You, of all people, should know better." He looked at Heather. "Sorry. She just lost her sister. Started with pain meds and ended with a heroin overdose." He left.

"She's right, you know," John said. "Alcohol and pills are a dangerous combination. You shouldn't mix them."

Heather hated being scolded or compared to some loser who didn't know when to stop.

"I'm guessing her sister was troubled?"

"Not hardly. She was happy. Full of life. Valedictorian. Pre-Med in college. On top of the world until a horse threw her. Even then, she was a trooper. Dedicated to her physical therapy regime. Nobody realized she had gotten hooked on the painkillers. When her prescription ran out, she found a dealer who gave her heroin. Dead two days later. The heroin had been laced with fentanyl."

"Wow" was the only word she could manage.

Heather wanted to assure Missy that wasn't going to happen to her, but it already had—at least the finding a dealer part. What if hers was laced with something? Somewhere between mad and scared, Heather knew she needed to be alone.

"John, I hate to ask you, but can you take me to a hotel?"

"You don't have to go. She'll be all right."

The cold sweats returned. "I don't know. I think I'll get an Uber."

"No, no. I'll take you. Let me leave a note." He started for the hallway just as Bobby returned.

John put a hand on Bobby's slumped shoulder. "I'm just gonna run Heather to a hotel."

"I'm sorry," Heather said. "I didn't know."

Bobby shook his head. "It's not your fault. You couldn't have known. It's been a hard time. We'll have to do a rain check."

John man-hugged Bobby. "I'll stay out a while so you guys can have some alone time."

"That's all right. I suspect she's down for the night, but you might want to grab yourself some dinner before you come back. ."

John nodded and turned to Heather. "Ready?"

"Yeah." She gave Bobby a long hug, thanked him, then pulled back and looked into his sagging eyes. "Please let her know . . ."

Bobby nodded.

Heather retrieved her backpack and headed out the door into the darkening night.

———

8:00 p.m.

HEATHER LEANED HER HEAD BACK against the headrest, then lifted it again. Not only was she sick from the guilt of having inflicted deep emotional pain, but her physical malaise was increasing by the moment. "I feel so awful."

"You didn't do anything wrong unless—"

"Not you, too, Brute."

"I'm sorry. But you seem like a sweet girl. *Are* you okay? I mean, you're hitchhiking, recovering from a bad accident, and taking pain-killers. To be honest, you don't look all that well—not that I have anything to compare that to, but just in the few hours I've known you, you . . ." He shifted in his seat. "I'm just saying, shouldn't you be recuperating in a nice home somewhere with someone who cares? What about your dad?"

There was no place she'd rather be.

"Like I said, you seem like a sweet girl, and I'd like to help you if I can. It's how my momma raised me." He turned to her with a sympathetic smile. "Anything I can do?"

He really was a knight and just the cutest kind of cute, but she couldn't trust anyone right now. "I'll be fine."

He handed her a card. She looked down at it.

John Bremmer—John of All Trades.

"Just call my name, and I'll be there." He hummed the song.

A smile tugged at her cheeks. If only.

"Got any idea what hotel you want to go to?"

As a young partier, she'd been to downtown Richmond with friends. Barhopping was the last thing on her mind now. "Where's a safe hotel on the way to Virginia Beach?"

"Virginia Beach? Really? This time of year?"

"I have a friend there." She hated that she had to lie again.

"Well, it's early, and Virginia Beach is just two hours away. I can drive you there. Tomorrow's Sunday, so I can sleep in."

Was this guy for real? She wanted to tell him the truth, ask him to save her, take her to Chincoteague, and make all her troubles disappear. But, the reality was there were no champions in her life.

"I appreciate it, but I need some rest. I may even stay in the hotel for a few days to recuperate before heading to my friend's."

"Well, I'm not familiar with hotels in this area. How about I hop on I-64 toward Virginia Beach, and you tell me when to stop?"

"Perfect. I'm sure we'll run into a good hotel somewhere."

"What's your budget?"

"Nothing economy, but not expensive either. Safe, clean, and sooner than later."

John nodded and took the interstate ramp—the same road that had brought her out of West Virginia just days ago. Several exits later, signs boasted three upper-end chain hotels. She raised a heavy arm and pointed. "Any one of those will do."

"Your wish is my command." John took the exit ramp and pulled into the first hotel. "How's this?"

"Perfect." At that point, a sleeping bag in an alleyway would have worked.

Heather slid out onto her weakened legs, not sure she could stand. She willed herself to appear okay. John opened his door to get out.

"No, please don't come in. I'll be fine."

John climbed back in the driver's seat. "I'll wait here to be sure they have a room."

"You don't need to."

"Oh, yes, I do." He winked, then examined her face. His own face tensed. "You don't look good. I'm gonna help you get checked in."

"No, please." She held up a hand. "I need to be left alone."

Heather lifted her backpack and closed the truck door. She turned as the automatic doors drew her into the minimalist, almost sterile lobby.

A suit-clad man with a single black-leather roller bag was finishing up with the desk clerk. Heather set her backpack on a chair and retrieved another five hundred dollars. The businessman turned and looked her over as if she needed to be swept out with the trash. She was too sick to care.

The uniformed front-desk clerk, a slender blonde, pointed the man to the elevators, then Heather made her way to the desk. The woman smiled at Heather as she approached. "May I help you?"

"One night. King-size bed." Heather fidgeted with the money as the clerk looked her over.

"Are you okay, ma'am?"

How bad did she look? "I've felt better. Do you have a room?"

"Yes, ma'am. That'll be two hundred twenty-nine dollars."

Heather handed over three bills.

The woman stared at the cash, then tapped the end of her pen on the desk. "And may I have a credit card for the incidentals?"

"There won't be any."

"I'm sorry, ma'am." She shook her head. "It's a company policy."

Heather looked back to John, who was still sitting in the drive. She turned back to the clerk.

"I'm feeling awful right now. I just got out of the hospital. My dad was supposed to pick me up, but he had to deliver a . . . a baby. That nice man out there gave me a ride here. Please, the doctors told me to get rest, and I'm starting to feel woozy. I have some extra cash." Heather gave her two hundred more. "How about you keep the change, and we call it a night?"

"Well . . ." The woman glanced back toward an office door. "How about I put this on your account, and you can pick up the balance if you haven't damaged anything or ordered anything from the bar."

"Bar?" Heather looked around. Jazz music she hadn't noticed before wafted out from behind faux wall panels. Under normal circumstances, a bar would have been a requisite for her stay. But tonight, her stomach lurched at the idea. "I don't need a bar. I need a bed."

The clerk put the plastic room key in a machine, placed the card in an envelope, and held it up. "Your room number is there." She pointed it out. "The password for the internet is here." She passed it to Heather. She pointed past Heather and said, "The elevator is just over there."

"Thank you. You're a lifesaver." Heather turned back toward the automatic doors. John was still there. She waved him away.

Sweat formed on her brow as she entered the elevator. Once on her floor, she went down the designer carpeting to her room at the far end of the hall. Her room's furniture matched the modernity of the lobby. A bold painting blazoned with broad turquoise, pink, and black brushstrokes hovered just above the ultra-contemporary headboard and plush, white bedding. In the corner, two turquoise, retro-style Naugahyde chairs formed a seating area with a light gray coffee table between them.

She plunked her backpack down on the bed, then looked out the window to ensure John had left the property. *No way.* His truck was now parked in one of the spaces out front.

She was so stupid. She should never have let him bring her or shared her real name. But there was nothing she could do now. She popped two more pills, downed them with one of the complimentary bottles of mineral water, and crawled into her made-to-order bed.

9:00 p.m.

PAIN RACED THROUGH EVERY SINEW of Heather's body. Two paramedics flanked her where she lay on the hotel floor's plush carpeting. She convulsed upright and then back down, where the thick padding did little to diminish the floor's ungiving nature. She cursed, pulled herself up, then pushed the men away. "Stop!"

"Ma'am, please relax. You overdosed. We're just here to help—"

"What do you mean? I'm not an addict." Heather tried to get up, but her body rebelled. Everything hurt.

The red-headed paramedic reached to help her, but she smacked his hand. "Get away from me. I'm fine." She forced herself onto the bed.

"Ma'am, we need to get you to the hospital."

"I said I'm fine."

"You're not fine. We've just revived you with Narcan. That only works on opioid overdoses."

An opioid overdose? How many stories had Richard told at her sister's dinner table about junkies getting revived by paramedics and refusing to go to the hospital? She hadn't understood it then, and yet here she was.

"But I'm not an addict. I only took my prescription painkiller."

"Really?" The strapping marine-cut paramedic tipped his head knowingly. "One tablet every six hours?" His deep voice emphasized his disbelief.

She didn't respond. He was right, but the hospital would ask questions—questions she couldn't answer. Besides, what could a hospital do for an overdose anyway? Give her fluids and take her pills away?

Heather inventoried her body. She'd never felt worse but sensed no specific pain other than the constant torment of her broken rib. She shook her head. "I'm not going."

Red looked at her with pleading eyes. "Ma'am, you might stop breathing again. The meds only work for a few hours."

She hadn't taken that many drugs. It was probably just something they said to get people to go to the hospital. "No."

The paramedics shook their heads. GI Joe turned toward the turquoise chairs in the corner of the room. "Maybe you can convince her."

She looked in the direction he'd spoken. *John.*

"What are *you* doing here," Heather asked. "Didn't I tell you to go?"

"Yeah, but you left your cell phone in my truck." He stood and took a step toward her. "You didn't answer when the clerk called up here. I told her you hadn't been well, and she agreed that you had said the same thing when you checked in. We found you lying on the bed—white as those sheets." He choked up for a moment. "The clerk called 9-1-1. You had a pulse but weren't breathing. The 9-1-1 operator told me to do rescue breaths, but . . ." his face twisted, "Nothing. There was nothing. You were dead, Heather. You were dead."

Dead? "No." She shook her head as if denial could make the truth go away. "No, that's not possible."

John sat at the foot of the bed and reached for her hand, but she pulled away.

GI Joe moved in front of her. "It's your call."

"Listen. I'm no junkie. I swear. I've been through hell lately, that's all. I was in an explosion. I got knocked unconscious. I had amnesia, broken ribs . . . It was just a few painkillers."

Red patted the stretcher she hadn't noticed until now. "All the more reason to take you to the hospital to get checked out."

"I'm fine." She rose from the bed and wobbled but willed herself to keep upright. "See?" She retrieved the pill bottle from her pocket and poured the contents into her palm. "Only eleven left. How much trouble could I get into with that?" She slid them back in. "I must have just taken too many. I won't do it again."

John looked as if he wanted to say more. He didn't. Perhaps he realized she wasn't going to change her mind.

The paramedics began gathering their equipment. Red snapped a picture of Heather, then asked her to sign a release. She stared at the paper. "And no police report?"

Red looked to GI Joe, who said, "There's no evidence of illicit activity here. We don't need to report it."

"Good, then please leave." Heather handed the unsigned paperwork back and pointed to the door. "All of you. Out. I need to get some rest."

GI Joe reached into a bag and handed John a package. "It's a Narcan kit. You need to watch her for three hours, in case her breathing slows too much. Here's how it works." He opened the nasal spray pack, showed John how it worked, and then gathered the last of their things. "Watch her."

John nodded as he returned the contents to the package. "Thank you."

"Even if you don't need it tonight, you might find a need for it later. If she detoxes, she's going to be sick—nausea, diarrhea, anxiety, nervousness, headache." GI Joe turned to Heather. "You have a rough time ahead, but it will only worsen the longer you put it off." He tipped his chin toward the door for Red to open it. GI Joe pushed the stretcher out, followed by Red.

Heather waved her hand as if to sweep John out with the paramedics. "You, too. Out."

"You heard the men. Someone needs to watch you." He took a seat. "I won't make a sound. I'll just sit in this chair."

Heather let out the breath she didn't know she was holding. "Whatever. I'm too sick to argue."

"Do you need anything?"

"Can you wave a magic wand and make this nightmare stop?"

John shook his head. "I wish."

She slipped into the king-size, comfort-top bed with down pillows, keeping one eye on her guardian.

Chapter 32

Sunday, November 5
8:00 a.m.

MAX FINISHED HIS THIRD HELPING OF BISCUITS and gravy in the hotel's complimentary breakfast area as Braun grabbed a coffee to take. They had decided D.C. was a more likely direction for Heather even if she still had amnesia. She'd be able to research her family and find out that much, but it was unlikely she'd have found out about the summer house. Max retrieved the hotel bill while Braun brought the SUV around.

Max's phone rang as he reached for the passenger door. He tossed his bag in the back seat and answered. "Enders."

"It's Sheriff Watson. I sent out that BOLO on the Blanchard girl. The overnight 9-1-1 operators were crazy busy—Saturday night, you know—so they didn't notice immediately. But the morning crew caught it. There was a 9-1-1 call for an overdose at a hotel here in Richmond. It's your girl. I'll text you the picture."

Max's stomach dropped. He didn't want to ask, but he had to. "Is she alive?"

"Yep. I called the EMTs. They said she was pretty feisty. She wasn't breathing when they got there. Revived her with Narcan. She refused to go to the hospital. Wouldn't sign the paperwork or give her name. Desk clerk said she paid cash. There was a man with her—John Bremmer. He told the paramedics her name was Heather. It's her, all right."

"Where is she now?"

"They left her at the hotel. Bremmer said he was going to stay and keep an eye on her. That's all we know. I'll text you the report and the name and address of the hotel."

"Did they ask about Bremmer?"

"The desk clerk said he was just a nice guy who had given her a ride. Hero type."

"Thanks, Sheriff. I owe you a big one."

"After all you've done for us? Anytime, my friend."

Max hung up and joined Braun in the truck as he opened the Sheriff's texts. "Let's go. I think we got her."

———

8:30 a.m.

SUNLIGHT BROKE THROUGH THE SLIT between the curtains, stabbing Heather's eyes. She struggled to pull her lids open. A hotel room. Still in her jeans. Her body ached beyond her injuries. Flashes of the previous night. *John.* He wasn't in the room.

She groaned as she rolled out of bed and checked the parking lot. His truck was still there. She had to get out before he returned.

Heather checked her phone on the bedside table—dead—like he said she had been. With the way she felt, death would have felt better. She was just so sick of being sick. She needed relief.

She retrieved her pill bottle and dumped two in the palm of her hand. She examined them, tilting her hand from side to side. Could these really kill her? But what was she supposed to do? It's not like she was trying to get high. She couldn't be expected to suffer like this. She downed them quickly.

Her charger was in the outside pocket of her backpack. She plugged her phone into the bathroom outlet. How had it gotten to her bedside table anyway? John said she'd left it in the truck, but hadn't it been in her pocket? She hadn't used it since she texted Melissa from the bathroom at Bobby and Missy's house.

Her abdomen suddenly seized, forcing her to the throne. Diarrhea emptied what little she had consumed the day before. Her mouth tasted like someone had rinsed it with scummy pond water.

When the cramps finally yielded what she hoped was the last of the purge, she stood on her shaky legs. Using a washcloth, she removed the moss from her teeth. How long since she had brushed?

Her breath caught at the image of the dead woman she had become. Where was the happy girl she used to be? Had she ever really been happy? Short moments of happiness were constantly ripped away. Her mother. Her marriage. Her motherhood. Now all she had was her love of painting and animals.

If her stepmother hadn't been so awful, she could have gone home when her fiancé dumped her. Or after her husband had cheated on her. Her dad would have supported her when she found out she was pregnant. She could have had her baby. But Cruella had made that impossible. She would have ruined the child's life like she'd ruined hers.

Heather pressed the power button on her phone and waited. Almost a quarter till nine. John might return any moment. She unplugged her phone, grabbed her backpack, and headed down the emergency stairwell at the end of the hall, then out the side door and into the blinding sunlight.

Only a handful of cars were parked on this side of the hotel. She was scoping out a plan when a dressed-for-success woman exited the door behind her, pulling a small suitcase.

Heather turned toward the woman. "Ma'am?"

The woman passed by her and continued to her car.

"Please." Heather followed her, keeping enough distance so the woman would feel safe. Heather stopped at the front of the car. "Excuse me."

The woman loaded the suitcase into the trunk without acknowledging her, then slammed the lid shut. She acted as if Heather wasn't even there.

"A man is stalking me. If you could give me a ride for a mile or two in any direction—just so he doesn't see me leave. I can pay you. Anything you like. I have money."

The woman moved to the driver's side and scanned Heather from head to toe. She scowled. "I'm sorry. I have a meeting." She opened the driver's door and slid inside.

Heather rounded the car to her door. "Please, I'm scared."

"Call the police." She slammed the car door, started the motor, and pulled away.

Heather closed her hanging mouth. Did she look that bad, or was this woman just a cold-hearted witch?

There was no one else in the lot to help her. A few restaurants were within walking distance, but John might be in one. Hitchhiking was the only answer.

Just as she started for the road, John's truck raced toward her and stopped. He rolled down the passenger window. "Get in. Now!"

"What?"

"No time to explain. Just get in." He leaned over and opened the door. Her body climbed in while her brain still worked to decide if that was wise. John took off before she could buckle.

"What on earth have you gotten yourself into?" John asked, heading back to the highway.

"What do you mean?"

John pulled onto the interstate heading east. "Two guys were asking about you at the front desk."

"How do you know that?"

"I went down to get coffee and a newspaper, and I overheard them."

A shiver ran through her. "Were they dark-skinned? With tattoos?"

"No, these were white guys. Official looking—like some alphabet agency. Said they were following up on a 9-1-1 call. Which brings me back to my question: What have you gotten yourself into? It must be big to bring guys like that in. And they'd have to be well-connected to have tracked you here from a 9-1-1 call."

Enders and Braun. Would she ever be rid of them? She didn't dare tell John the truth. He was too bright. Almost as if he was part of them. "Roll up your sleeves."

"What?"

"Just do it."

John complied. "Satisfied?"

Heather shook her head. "I'm satisfied you don't have tattoos, but why should I trust you?"

"You shouldn't—but I suspect you trusted the wrong people some-where along the way, and that's what got you in trouble."

Heather refused to speak.

"Am I right?"

"Yes, but . . ." Heather shook her head again. "No, it's not like that. All I did was catch a ride after a car accident." Heather pictured the white deer. Was he still in the woods waiting for a chance to mock her again?

"And the drug addiction?"

"I'm *not* addicted."

He gave her a look for longer than any driver should take their eyes off the road. "Take any of your *pain meds* this morning?"

Heather looked away without answering. Not that he wouldn't know—he certainly did—but because she didn't like the answer. She needed those drugs. But wasn't that the definition of an addict? "I'm sick, and I'm serious about the pain."

"Have you ever heard of dope sick?"

She hoped he wouldn't enlighten her.

"It's the sickness you get when you go through withdrawal. It comes from 'chasing the dragon.'"

"Would you speak English?"

"It's when drugs make you feel sick, so you take more drugs to feel better, but they make you sicker. Forget about getting high. You take more drugs just to not feel sick."

The arrow of truth struck Heather's heart. "But I was never trying to get high. I was telling you the truth—I truly was in a bad accident. I really was blown up. I had amnesia. They gave me painkillers at the hospital. I can't help that they made me sick. It's not my fault."

"Well, maybe it's not your fault that you were blown up or that doctors gave you pain meds, but you're taking more than what they prescribed. Right?"

She didn't answer.

"And none of that explains people asking about you or . . . why were you blown up in the first place? Really? That's not normal, Heather."

Heather crossed her arms. "It's not that simple. The less you know, the better."

"Better for who?"

"For you." She unfolded her arms.

He reached across the cabin and put his hand on her arm. "Let me be the judge of that."

His touch felt too good. She jerked her arm away. "They call it 'aiding and abetting.'"

John stared straight ahead for a long moment. "Seems to me I'm already doing that."

"Not if you don't know what I'm involved in. You're just giving a girl a ride."

"I doubt any law enforcement agency will believe I'm driving someone I just met on the road to a place where I have no business."

"You wouldn't be the first man to take a girl for a ride. And who says you haven't kidnapped me." Heather grabbed the straps of her backpack and pointed to the side of the road. "Here. Drop me off."

"No, I'm taking you to your friend's."

"There is no friend. Not in Virginia Beach, or anywhere else for that matter. Drop me off!"

"Well, I guess that means there's something else taking you there."

"Nope. Just getting away from it all."

"All what?"

She couldn't keep up with her stories. "Remember what you said about me trusting the wrong people? Why wouldn't that apply to you?"

"You got in the truck, didn't you?" He looked into her eyes. "I saved your life, didn't I?"

"That doesn't mean you're the right person to trust—I'm such a poor judge of character, right?"

"You're right. You shouldn't trust me." He paused for a long moment as he checked his mirrors.

"What are you looking for?"

"Just checking to see if anyone followed us."

Heather's stomach knotted. "And?"

"I don't think so, but I'll exit here and get back on just to check." John slowed and took the exit ramp down to a suburban road lined with shopping centers. He couldn't cross over directly, so he turned right, made a U-turn, then headed back for the highway.

"Anyone following us?"

"Nope."

They got on the ramp and fell in with the other traffic. Was this an act to make her afraid to leave?

"How would you know if someone was following us? Do you know all the cars in the hotel parking lot?"

"There weren't that many. Maybe a dozen. There were five family-type SUVs, one black, late-model SUV—that was probably your alphabet friends—two white Lexuses, one red Corvette—"

"Okay, okay, you do know. But why?"

"Why what?"

"Why would you have paid attention to the cars?"

"I used to work in security."

"And now you rescue damsels in distress?"

A mischievous smile reclaimed John's face. "Like I said, my momma raised me right."

"But, security—you must have been working on the right side of the law, not with criminals like me."

"So, you admit it?" John smirked. "You're a criminal."

"No, I'm not. At least not willingly."

"You're willingly running from something. And it's not just those agents. What is it? Who are these tattooed men? Maybe I can help." He reached for her again, but she pulled away before his touch could sway her. It always started with a touch.

"The only crime I willingly committed was turning my back on my family when all they were trying to do was help me."

"Nice try. I don't think that would get you followed by tattooed men."

"Okay, let's just say wrong place, wrong time."

"So why does the law want you?"

It was a good question—one she still couldn't answer. "I can't believe I'm telling you this, but here goes. I was driving one night not long ago, and this stupid white deer jumped in front of my car. I swerved and crashed my car in a river. I lost everything. I was in the middle of nowhere, freezing to death, so I hitchhiked. The guy drove me to his brother's house for the night, and they ended up being drug dealers—part of some gang. But I didn't know it. I know this'll sound strange, but I figured out the guy's girlfriend was my long-lost cousin the next morning." She paused to gauge his reaction.

"Go on."

"At this point, I still didn't know about her boyfriend—his name was Johnny—I still didn't know what Johnny was involved with. I admit that I had suspicions when he handed Melissa a wad of cash. But I don't believe Melissa was involved in his business. But she knew what he was into. Back to aiding and abetting, right?"

She turned to John for acknowledgment. He made circles in the air with his finger.

Heather continued the story, filling him in on all the details that had brought her to this point and all the questions still plaguing her. When she'd finished, she leaned over and buried her head in her hands.

"Wow."

Heather sat up. "That's it? Just 'wow'?"

"A white deer, huh?"

"All that, and what you heard was 'white deer'?"

"Well, the rest of it makes sense, but the crashing in a river because of a white deer? Are you sure you weren't doing drugs before the accident? Sounds like a hallucination to me."

"No, I wasn't taking drugs."

John raised his eyebrows.

"Well, I had been drinking a little."

He gave her a squint-eyed look.

"Okay, a lot."

"So, you swerved to miss the deer, crashed into a river, didn't drown or suffer from hypothermia, despite being drunk, and I suppose your car is still in the river?"

"Somewhere on a back road in West Virginia. I can't even tell you where. Gone—along with everything I owned."

"Do you know how lucky you are to be alive?"

"Lucky? Are you kidding? Did you hear the rest of it? Blown up? Amnesia? Murderous gangs? Forgive me, but I'm not feeling very lucky right now. And now I'm being held hostage in a truck with a guy I have no reason to trust, and I've just said way too much."

"Well, lucky may not be the best word . . ." He quieted for a moment. "But you do have me. Don't I count for something?"

Was he coming on to her? He was adorable. But as warm and comforting as his smile was, it didn't make her safe. And it didn't ward off her growing sickness.

He rechecked his mirror. "How much money are we talking about?"

There it was. "Why? Do you want to know where it is too?"

"Still don't trust me, huh?"

The location of the money had been on her previous phone. Was it on her new one? She didn't even want to know. That money was nothing but a curse. She examined John's face. No tension anywhere. Her guard dropped as his eyes softened. Not that she'd had one to begin with.

"Well?"

"I'm not sure. I'm sure it was a lot at some point. The FBI got a bagful from the camper—maybe half of what there was. Then Melissa stashed the rest in the cabin where we were staying. I'm sure the FBI or the gang found that by now. I don't think there's that much left." Maybe if John thought it was all gone, he and everyone else would leave them alone.

"And how much do you have in that backpack?"

Her body froze.

"So, you do have their money."

"I don't know whose money I have. Melissa gave me some to get to a new place and set up house. That's it."

"Relax, Heather. I'm not after your money. In fact, if I were in my right mind, I'd drop you off so they won't come after me. But we both know they probably already know about me by now. If these guys are as connected as I believe they are, they'll find you again. Once I get you safely tucked away, I can call some very trusted friends. Lots of connections."

"And the FBI, Mr. Security? Why shouldn't I turn myself in?"

"I would love to say that you'd be safe with them, but if my job taught me anything, it's that there's always someone on the take. If this organization is as big as I suspect, that may not be the best idea. But if I can get you to the right agents, they could protect you."

"I don't know." Her brain clouded as her bowels rolled and her sweats returned. The pill bottle called to her. "I need to use the restroom—quick." She pointed to the green exit sign listing upcoming restaurants. "There. Any of those fast-food restaurants will do. Hurry."

10:00 a.m.

HEATHER BARELY MADE IT to the bleach-scented accessible stall. Squares of toilet paper littered the floor. She raced to unzip her jeans and sat, but nothing came forth. When had she last eaten?

Pulling herself together, she tossed back two pills, cupped some water from the sink, and awaited her relief. Just knowing the pain would abate soon made her feel better.

She leaned back against the cold tile, not wanting to stay, but not wanting to go. What a place to find refuge.

Maybe she should let John take her to a safe house. He seemed like he knew something about bad guys. Or maybe Julie was right about her lack of man-sense. The mere hint of shining armor and *boom*—her heart's doors swung open.

Heather's phone chirped. Melissa was the only person with the number, unless . . . John said he'd brought her phone to the hotel room. Had he gotten her number out of it somehow? But that was impossible with phone locks.

She pressed the message icon. *Melissa.*

> *Got your text. I was wrong to leave u. Headed to Chincoteague. Text me the address. Almost to Norfolk. B there in 2.*

Norfolk? Her heart lightened. They could meet up there. Ditch John. She hadn't been to the area since her dad took her crabbing when she was a kid. There was a restaurant next to a mall. They could rendezvous there. She texted back.

> *Not there yet. Can u meet me in Lynnhaven?*

> *Where are you?*

349

Between Richmond and Norfolk. Newport News, maybe?

With?

A guy. Think he's ok but need to ditch him. Can u meet me?

Yes. Where?

Mall next to restaurant. Let me ck if still there.

Heather turned and leaned sideways against the wall as she checked the restaurant and the mall websites. The location was even better than she had remembered. The satellite view showed a nice set of woods between the mall and the restaurant that would conceal her flight. She took a screenshot and sent Melissa the satellite scouting report with instructions for their meeting.

This would work. It had to.

She pushed off the wall to grab her backpack from the hook. *Oh no.* She'd left it in the truck with John.

She rushed to the parking lot. The truck was gone. No John. No money. She smacked her forehead with both palms. He'd been after the money all along. Or maybe he was with the gang. But wouldn't they want to use her to get to Melissa? And he had introduced her to his friends and even given her his card. Then again, it wasn't like she could call the cops. He'd really played her.

What was she going to do now? Couldn't anything go her way?

She retrieved her phone. Dead again. She had only charged it for a few minutes at the hotel. She checked her pocket. Twenty dollars. That should cover a charger—what, maybe ten bucks? But what was in the area? Which way should she even go?

No one was dining inside the restaurant, but there were a couple of people in line who, when asked, said they didn't know the area either.

"Next." A uniformed teenager motioned her over from the "Wait Here" sign.

Heather approached the slight but muscular young man—Jayden, his name tag said. A sweet radiance emanated from his eyes despite teenage attempts to be cool. His cheeks were high and toned—extreme smiling workouts? His attempts at a mustache highlighted the mischief of his cocked smile. She'd love to capture that face on canvas.

Jayden bobbed his head. "Today?"

She shook hers to refocus. "I'd like a medium cola, please."

He keyed it in. "Zat all?"

"Yes."

"Two sixty-five."

A manager-type woman delivered her drink. She pulled out her only twenty and stared at it before handing it over. She studied Jayden as he made change. She held up her phone.

"Jayden, I lost my phone charger. Do you know where I can get one?"

"Sure. At a store." He gave the sarcastic smirk of a tormenting sibling.

She grinned back. "Okay, smart guy. Is there a store nearby you can point me to?

He tipped his head to the right and pointed. "Drugstore. 'Bout a block."

She gestured in the same direction. "A block down that way?"

He eyed her for a moment. "Listen. I got an extra one in my ride. Lemme see." Jayden held out a hand for her phone. Heather held it up. "Yep. It'll work. Hang on." He punched a coworker in the arm. "Cover for me."

Jayden gestured toward a hallway door. Heather followed him outside to an old, faded-top convertible with buffed-out metallic panels. He was probably saving to restore this old muscle car to its former glory.

He popped the trunk, dug around in a box, then held out a cord but pulled it back when Heather reached for it. "Ah, ah, ah. Twenty bucks."

"What? For a used charger? I can get a new one for ten." Heather didn't know if that was true, but she didn't have twenty anyway. "Forget it." She turned to walk away.

"Wait. Fifteen, but not a dime less."

She returned and retrieved fifteen from her pocket but didn't hand it over. She pointed to the car. "Does this thing run?"

"Whatchu mean—does it run?" He got in and revved the motor. It roared like a male lion declaring his domain.

Heather scanned the parking lot for John. No trucks in sight. "You want to make some serious cash?"

"Who don't?" He swung his legs out of the car. "What we talking about? Nothing illegal."

"No, nothing like that."

He watched her closely. "You looking for a fix? I can't help you with that. I'm cool, not stupid. You in some kinda trouble?"

"No." Guilt jabbed her. Should she get him tangled in this? All she needed was a ride, and it was less than an hour away. How much trouble could they get into in that short time? Besides, she could really help this kid out. The car sure needed a paint job.

"My ride bailed on me, and I need to get to Lynnhaven. Know where that is?"

He eyed her for a moment. "Yeah, I know where Lynnhaven is. My granddad used to take me crabbing there. It's, like, an hour away. That'll be some serious Benjamins, though. I'll have to leave work early. My boss ain't gonna like it."

"So, what's it worth for your trouble?"

He tilted his head back. "Ten big."

"A thousand?"

He crossed his arms and waited.

What alternative did she have? "You got a lighter plug for my phone?"

"I got all the tools, lady. You got the money?"

"My cousin does. That's who we're going to meet. You know that ride that ditched me? He stole my backpack with all my stuff."

"You is in trouble, ain't you? Why should I trust you?"

Hadn't this been her question with John all along?

"You shouldn't. All I can say is I need a ride. My cousin has enough money to make this car shine. I'm thinking candy-apple red."

"Red? You crazy? Teal. And with all this trouble, the price went up to twenty."

An entrepreneur. She really liked this kid. Besides, it wasn't her money. Why not spend it on a good cause? "Deal." She held out the fifteen dollars. "Here's my deposit."

Jayden shook his head, took the money, and handed over the cord. "You better be good for this. Now I gotta go beg the boss lady so I got a job to come back to."

"Can you start the car and give me the plug for the charger first?"

"So you can steal my ride? Not happening." He leaned in and yanked the keys from the ignition, then headed for the restaurant.

Smart kid. Smarter than she'd been. Time she took a lesson from him. She scoped out the parking lot for John once more, then went to the front of the car and sat out of sight on the ground, a few feet from a small cluster of trees. She kept checking behind her for the stupid deer.

How was she going to work this out without endangering Melissa? What if the kid held them up for all their money? Jayden seemed like a good kid, but then again, she'd thought John was a good guy.

Jayden returned with a bag of food. "Here. You look like you need something to eat."

"Thanks." Heather stood but wobbled.

Jayden reached out to steady her. "You sure you're okay? You don't look so good."

She pictured the house in Chincoteague. "I'm good. Or at least I will be when I get to where I'm headed."

She'd be safe there. Right?

Straightening herself, she made her way to the passenger door and lifted the handle. Locked. She tapped the window. Jayden leaned over and opened it.

"Sorry. Gonna fix that soon with all my money."

A Bible stared up at her from the seat. When she was a teenager, neither she nor the cool kids she hung out with would have been caught dead carrying a Bible.

Jayden grabbed the book and put it on the back seat. "Sorry."

"No worries." Heather lowered herself into the holy bucket seat. "Hey, isn't today Sunday?"

Jayden shifted the car into reverse. "Yeah, what of it?"

"Bible? Church?"

"I go Saturday nights."

"Does your family drag you there like mine did?"

Jayden's face pinched as he turned onto the I-64 ramp east toward Virginia Beach. "You know, I used to feel that way—I mean after my momma died . . . Cancer."

"I'm sorry. Cancer got my mom too."

They were quiet for a few miles before Heather spoke again.

"I don't go to church anymore. Haven't been in a long time. Does your dad go?"

"Ha. No. Only place my dad goes is in and out of prison."

"Sorry."

"What's your excuse?"

Excuse? She shrugged. "Why should I go to a church that worships a God that lets moms die."

"So you're mad at God?"

"What?"

"When my mom died, I was pissed. I started getting into trouble. Ended up in juvie. Then Big Al from the church came down. Told me my grandpa wasn't coming to bail me out. Said it was time for me to make a choice. Then he told me stories about some of the dudes in the Bible—like David. He got a man's wife pregnant, then killed the man to cover it up. That is some kinda messed up." Jayden shook his head. "Anyway, then his baby died when it was born. Big Al said that was David's man-up moment. He coulda been mad at God. I know I woulda been. But David chose God and repented. Big Al said all men are messed up, but God is good. He fixes our messed-up selves. He said I could be mad at God and end up in destruction like my dad or repent and get on the God path.

"Next time he came, he told me about Joseph. His brothers sold him into slavery. Then he was thrown in jail because he wouldn't sleep with the Pharaoh's wife. He never got mad at God. And God rewarded him. Put him in charge of all of Egypt. Then Joseph ended up saving the brothers who'd done him in. Talk about mad? I probably woulda kilt 'em.

"So, after he told me about these dudes and the different paths they'd chosen, he asked me which path I was gonna choose?"

Had this teenager really figured out something that she still didn't understand as an adult?

Jayden shook his head. "It's just crazy 'cause I'd heard all these stories before. But sitting in that jail cell, something changed. *I* changed. Jesus became real to me. He *is* real. And I knew the truth. Since then, Big Al's been by my side. He even helped me apply for college. Me—going to college. It's crazy."

Jayden reached into the back seat. He handed her a ragged bookmark.

For I know the plans I have for you," declares the Lord, "plans to prosper you and not to harm you, plans to give you hope and a future. (Jeremiah 29:11, NIV).

Heather stared at the bookmark. She had despised her life, and here was this kid with hope and a future. What did *she* have? Danger and trouble. Some path she'd chosen.

Suddenly, an overwhelming feeling poured over her. She looked out her window. And right then, a white buck emerged from the trees.

"Stop the car!"

Jayden hit the brakes and pulled over. "What? What is it?"

"Did you see that—the white deer? It was right back there."

He looked over his shoulder toward the trees. "A white deer? You sure you're not trippin'?"

She shook her head as she looked back. He was gone. There was no way Jayden was going to believe her. If Margie hadn't shared her white deer story, she'd be checking herself into the looney bin. "I'm sorry. I must have imagined it."

"You think?" Jayden pulled back on the road. "Don't be scarin' me like that."

Heather retrieved her phone and the power cord. "Got that plug for the cigarette lighter?"

He pulled one out of the center console. She connected the phone, then set it down to wait for enough juice to start it up. She grabbed the food bag from between her feet and opened it. A breakfast biscuit. She wasn't hungry, but she needed to eat. It'd be a while for another opportunity.

That stupid deer. Why had she known to look? Was this her "man-up" moment? She took a bite of the sandwich.

"Don't you be getting crumbs in my ride."

He was right. The car's interior was worn but immaculate. She held it over the bag as she managed a few more bites before returning the biscuit to the bag, then adjusted the seat back and settled in.

"Where're we going in Lynnhaven?"

"It's a restaurant my dad used to take us to when we'd go crabbing there."

He smiled as she talked about it. "Guess we have something in common. We didn't have no money for restaurants back then, but we sure knew how to crab."

Heather pictured herself with a net, standing knee-deep in water and pulling in a crab clinging to a chicken neck on her line. "What did you use for bait?"

"Chicken necks. They love them chicken necks. Our whole church goes crabbing together in late summer. We bring back bushels of 'em, then cook 'em all up. Mmm mmm. Corn. Greens . . . Don't you think that's what the big banquet in heaven is gonna be like?"

Heather tried to picture Da Vinci's *Last Supper* with crabs. "Newspapers on picnic tables?"

"Yep, with nutcrackers, hammers, and melted butter."

Heather giggled. When was the last time anything had tickled her spirit? It felt good. But her smile evaporated when she remembered where she was going. If she hadn't had her temper tantrum, she might have been heading for family time instead of running for her life.

She lifted the phone from the console and powered it on. She entered their destination into her maps app. Thirty minutes.

Heather texted Melissa about John taking off with her backpack. She suggested that Melissa meet her in the restaurant's ladies' room with the money and leave Olivia hiding in the trailer at the mall. They wouldn't need to worry about her overheating with these fall temperatures. She gave Melissa their ETA so she could head over ahead of their arrival. That would keep Melissa out of Jayden's sight.

Melissa texted back her misgivings but agreed.

Heather's stomach knotted again. What if something went wrong? What would happen to Olivia? She pushed the thought away. The phone directed them to take the ramp one mile ahead.

Jayden moved to the right lane. "Everything dope?"

"What?"

"You know—cool?" Jayden's cheeks formed perfect balls above his smile. "You really that old?"

"I didn't think so." It hadn't been that long since she'd spoken in the secret teenage language.

They made their way to the surface street. Heather confirmed Melissa was ready.

Jayden weaved between the Sunday drivers. "Looks like church is letting out. The restaurant's gonna be packed. You sure you want to meet up with your cuz there?"

It was a good point, but then again, they weren't there to eat. And a crowd would make them less noticeable. Heather grinned. "Yeah, we're dope."

As they pulled into the parking lot, Heather's stomach snarled. Seven pills called to her. She'd have to take a couple before her rendezvous with Melissa, who was sure to want to count them. What was she going to tell her?

"You wait here, and I'll go get the money."

Jayden's eyes squinted. "I'm crazy for trusting you, but go ahead."

Heather pushed the door open.

"On second thought, let me hold your phone till you get back." He held his hand out.

It was her only link to Melissa, but she'd already confirmed she was in place. And Jayden was right not to trust her. She locked the screen and handed the phone over.

Heather entered the restaurant and pointed to the back as she passed the hostess counter. She made her way to an area just outside the restroom. She downed two pills without liquid, then pushed the door open. The door to the accessible stall was closed.

"Melissa?"

Melissa opened the stall door. They hugged for a long moment, spewing sorrys and a few tears. Melissa's embrace made her feel like she had come home. How could that be after only knowing her for a couple of weeks?

Melissa pulled back. "Here." She handed Heather a pink children's purse. "We need to get going. You weren't followed, were you?"

How had she forgotten to look? She hadn't checked once to see if John or anyone else was behind them the whole way there. But Jayden had stopped for the deer, and no one had stopped with them. "No. I'm sure of it."

"You think this kid is okay?"

"Better than okay. He's a great kid. He's going to be someone someday."

Melissa smiled. "I've got to get back to Olivia. I'll go out with a group so I'm not obvious." She described where the truck was parked. "After you give him the money, come back inside and wait twenty minutes. Tell the hostess you're waiting for someone. Then head over. There's a clear path through the woods at the back of the lot."

They hugged again, and Heather left Melissa to do her part.

Jayden was standing outside the car, holding her phone. She held out the girly purse.

"Really?" He held his hands open.

"Well, if you don't want it—"

He grabbed it out of her hand, opened it, and grinned. "I gotta say, I wasn't sure you'd be good for it." He popped the trunk, dropped the bag inside, opened his car door, and retrieved the worn bookmark. "Here, you need this more than me."

She stared at him, then the bookmark, almost afraid to accept the weight of the message she didn't quite believe. Somehow though, this kid was living proof of the hope it offered. She took it and held it to her heart. "Thank you." Before she thought better of it, she embraced him. "You don't know what meeting you has meant to me." They released. "I don't know if I ever will, but can you give me your contact information in case I ever want to reach out to you? I feel like I might need to talk to you again."

He stared at her, then held out his hand. "Phone." He tapped in his information and returned it. "I hope you do. Can I pray for you?"

Heather held her breath. What was it about this kid? She nodded, though she wasn't sure why.

Jayden put his hand on her shoulder, bowed his head, and prayed for her life, her health, and her safety as if he were talking to his best friend. Warmth enveloped her. He released her shoulder.

"Don't forget. God's got the plan."

Heather hugged him again. He got in his car and returned the way they'd come. Heather started for the restaurant just as a pickup truck caught the corner of her eye. She swung her head to look, but it was gone.

She raced back to the restaurant. Melissa had already left. She waited the twenty minutes, walked out, checked for the truck, then headed through the woods.

Knocking on a horse-trailer door conjured images of that show from her father's childhood. Was Mr. Ed going to answer? Instead, Abu barked. Olivia squealed as Melissa swung the door open.

"Aunt Heather!" Olivia bounced in place, ready to launch herself at Heather as soon as she stepped in.

The walk through the woods had been harder than she'd anticipated. She was sick—sicker than she'd ever felt. Maybe it was the turmoil of the day. Or perhaps it was the anticipation of Melissa's interrogation.

Melissa scanned Heather's face and shook her head. "Really?" she mouthed.

"Come, Aunt Heather. Play with me."

Melissa held Olivia back as Heather stepped in. "No, baby, Aunt Heather's not feeling well." She glared at her.

"But I've been waiting for her."

"I'm sorry, sweetie. I didn't sleep last night. I need to lay down." Heather barely made it into the bed. Abu jumped up and nestled next to her.

She was sicker than she'd been the night before at the hotel. What if she stopped breathing again? No—that was because of the heroin. Surely that was out of her system. It wouldn't happen again. Besides, once they got to Dad's, it'd be much easier to kick this— whatever it was. She just needed peace and quiet and a chance to stop running.

"Come on, baby," Melissa said. "You can ride in the truck with me."

Good. If she did stop breathing, at least Olivia wouldn't be the one to find her. Abu jumped off the bed, leaving her alone. The door closed, as did Heather's eyes.

Chapter 33

1:30 p.m.

COULD ANYTHING ELSE GO WRONG? Max cursed, kicked a flattened soda can, and paced around the shattered beer bottles along the roadside next to the broken-down SUV. Braun waited for the tow truck in the driver's seat. The engine had died after being stuck for more than an hour waiting for an accident to clear just before the bay bridge to the Maryland Eastern Shore. Since they weren't on official business, they couldn't request official help.

Time was running out. Max had to be back Monday morning to prepare for the hearing. They had wasted time on their hunch that Heather would have gone to her dad's. Still, they would have made it to Chincoteague in time until this. He kicked the can again.

Traffic was finally moving—albeit at five miles per hour—but the tow truck was still delayed. Even if it came then and hauled them somewhere, would a car rental be open on a Sunday afternoon? That alone would take hours. Add to that two and a half hours to Chincoteague, whatever time they spent there, plus eight hours to West Virginia, meant time was up.

Besides, if Heather had made it there, the marshals would have taken her into custody by now, so their mission would be in vain. And if she didn't go there—it's what the chief had said—she could be anywhere. He hated being wrong.

Max lowered his head and returned to the SUV, where Braun was checking his phone. "I'm sorry I got you into this."

"Are you kidding? Best weekend adventure I've had in a long time."

Max shook his head. "Right."

"What? Can't I go to the Eastern Shore on my own time? Besides, I'm not ready to pack it in. I've got a bad feeling. A two-person marshal's detail and a small police force are no match for Bones' guys. And they never give up."

"It's a long shot she's even going there. Won't Bones' guys be chasing Melissa?"

"Bones has an army of people spread over more than a dozen states we know about. It's nothing for him to use his network to get every last dollar the girls have taken and then get rid of them."

"But, I've done the math." Max tapped his watch. "We're out of time."

"I've done the math too. How about this? Wherever we are at midnight, we head back to West Virginia."

Max nodded, knowing getting a rental car was a long shot. He hoped Braun was wrong about Bones.

———

3:30 p.m.

"Aunt Heather." Olivia nudged her shoulder.

She cracked open one eye. Melissa stood over her.

"Hey, we're by the NASA Wallops Center a few miles from Chincoteague. I thought it'd be easier if you came up front to show me how to get to the house."

She pushed herself up, the full fury of her addiction bearing down on every inch of her body. Olivia reached for her hand, but Melissa pulled her back, like keeping a child away from a dead animal. Even Abu stayed away.

"We're at a convenience store. We've already gone in. Do you need to go?

"Yes, I'm not feeling so well." She wavered as she rose and grabbed the wall to steady herself.

"You okay, Aunt Heather?" Olivia asked, eyes wide.

Melissa crossed her arms.

Heather reached for Olivia's head to comfort her, but she pulled back behind her mother. Did she look that bad?

"I'm fine, baby. I need to go to the bathroom and freshen up. It's been a rough couple of days."

Melissa and Olivia stepped back for her to pass. The sun blinded her as she stepped out, facing the NASA facility. Yep. As a child, it was the sign they had arrived.

Customers eyed her as she passed through the store to her tiled haven. She heaved the three bites of breakfast, then nothing. Thankful the stall had a separate sink, she rinsed her mouth and face. How had it come to this? Even Olivia's smile couldn't lift the darkness compressing her soul. She wanted to die, but she had to hold it together . . . for Olivia.

She leaned back against the wall. Two more pills would sure be nice, but were they helping? She wasn't getting any better. She pictured the fear on Olivia's face and began to cry. Who had she become? The mirror said it all. Dark circles. Drawn face. Death was winning the battle for her body. Did she have the strength to find her way back?

She retrieved the bookmark from her back pocket and stared at it. God clearly had plans for Jayden, but what about her? She slumped to the cold floor and sobbed.

"Aunt Heather?" Olivia bent down and peeked under the stall door. "Are you crying?"

"Yes, baby. I'm just not feeling well. I'll be right out."

She stood and retrieved the poison from her pocket. She looked inside the bottle. This—her addiction—was stealing Olivia's innocence. She couldn't let that happen. She took a shaky breath, emptied the last five pills into the toilet, watched as they swirled and disappeared, then opened the door.

Melissa stood facing her.

"I dumped them." She handed her the empty pill bottle. "I'm so sorry."

Melissa's face softened as she shook the bottle. She tossed it into the trash can and turned back with a sympathetic smile. "Well? Are we going?"

She opened the bathroom door and held it for Heather to pass. Olivia reached for her hand. What was it about children that sent light into the dark spaces and brought clarity—no hope—to the worst situations? Whatever it was, she was thankful that her tiny hand had the power to rescue her from the sinking sand. Heather could do this.

"I picked up some groceries to get us by for the rest of the day. Is there anything you need?"

The thought of food twisted Heather's stomach. "No, I'm good with whatever you got."

After retrieving Abu from the trailer, they piled into the quad cab and wound past the NASA base and across the bridge onto Chincoteague. They had finally arrived. Straight ahead was the Island Creamery. Heather pictured herself around Olivia's age, begging her dad to go there first.

As they waited for the light to make their left turn, Heather pulled down her visor to watch Olivia's face when she enticed her with her memory. "Olivia, guess what?"

"What?"

"They have the world's best ice cream here. Do you want to go get some tonight?"

Olivia bounced in her car seat. "Yay, yay, yay! Can we Mommy? Can we?"

"If Aunt Heather's up to it, sure."

"Can we go without her if she's not?"

The words pierced Heather's heart. But truth often does.

"I think we should wait for Aunt Heather to feel better, don't you?"

Heather smiled at Melissa and mouthed a thank you.

Olivia pouted her lips. "I guess."

When the light changed, they made the left and drove to Pirate's Cove. They turned left again and passed through a white gate, past a couple of ponds, across a wooden bridge, and into a cluster of homes nestled in a grove of pine trees. There were no signs of life around. No cars in any of the drives. The perfect hideaway.

"Over there." Heather pointed to the grayish brown, two-story, cedar-shake house. It was just like she remembered, with whisps of green moss and pine needles clinging to the roof and shake. A single red maple sapling revolted against the drab gray day. They rolled to a stop in front of the two-car detached garage. Heather and Melissa slid out onto the pine needle carpet.

"Wow." Melissa stood, looked over the stilted waterfront refuge, and helped Olivia out of the back. Abu jumped down and ran back and forth as she picked up critter scents.

"Better get a leash on her," Heather said as she punched Julie's and her birth years into the garage door's keypad. "There're lots of animals for her to chase out here." The garage door lifted, exposing a cavernous void that used to house her boating memories. Selling that boat was one of Cruella's first orders of business when she came in to ruin their lives.

She rummaged through the shelves for the rusty Maxwell House coffee can holding the house key. "Bingo." Heather turned back to the trailer. "You know, if we want to stay off the radar, we should probably back these in the garage out of sight."

Heather directed Melissa between the randomly-spaced pine trees to make the awkward maneuvers required to back in the trailer. Heather had only tried to back a horse trailer once. Her dad said never again.

While they waited for Melissa to back the truck in, Olivia pointed to the upstairs studio perched in the middle of the house next to the master bedroom. It could have doubled for an enclosed widow's walk with its views of the bay and the property. "Is that a castle tower?"

Heather laughed. "Of course it is." As little girls, she and her friends would pretend they were damsels in distress. They would call out to the bay for princes to rescue them by ship.

After concealing their presence, they made their way to the house and climbed the eight wood-plank stairs to the porch. Heather unlocked the door, and they entered a hallway that led to the kitchen at the back and the living room to the right. Dad's study door was closed, as always. Several lights were on in the living room. Jackets hung on the coat rack by the front door. A faint smell of food drifted in the air. Something wasn't right. No one should have been there. Was Dad doing VRBO?

Melissa, Olivia, and Abu turned into the living room, Abu sniffing every inch of the way. "Wow. This is fantastic." They continued back to the dining room with floor-to-ceiling views overlooking the deck and Chincoteague Bay.

Heather followed her nose to the kitchen. Dishes were in the dishrack. Towels tossed on the counter. Dog food in bowls on the floor. What was going on?

Abu ran to the dog food from the dining area and began crunching away. Melissa and Olivia came around the corner from the living room, appreciating every beach and pony treasure Heather's real mother had incorporated into the decor. "This is great."

"Somebody's here."

Melissa's face blanched. "Now?"

"No—at least I don't think so. No cars. But somebody's living here." She pointed as Abu finished off the food. "Somebody with a dog."

Heather ran up the stairs as quickly as her weakened legs allowed. A partially packed red suitcase lay open on the bed—*Julie's* clothes.

It couldn't be.

Melissa came to the door. "Do you know whose it is?"

367

Heather stared at her, trying to piece it all together. "Julie."

"Your sister, Julie?"

"Yeah." Heather paced. Was Julie coming or going? What had the news said about the arrests and Richard? She held her hands to her head. How long had it been since she'd been in Hearthstone? Had it only been two weeks? "Julie's pregnant. Maybe they came to celebrate."

"What should we do?"

She eyed the suitcase again. It was Sunday. Half full. "I think they're packing to leave."

Abu began barking a warning downstairs. Heather went to the window. A yellow Mustang convertible drove up with Julie, Richard, and Dog. "It's my sister!"

As Richard and Julie got out, Dog jumped out of the car and barked at the house as a dark SUV pulled in behind them. Two men wearing black windbreakers and jeans got out and drew guns. They motioned for Richard and Julie to get back.

Heather ran down the stairs and slowly opened the door but stayed back from the opening. "It's me—Heather!"

Dog ran inside and began licking Heather. Abu joined them as the dogs checked each other's rears, their tails wagging. "It's okay, Dog."

"U.S. Marshals! Come out with your hands up!"

Heather lifted her arms and walked out. She had never had a gun pointed at her, much less two. Her knees buckled, and she dropped to the porch.

"Heather!" Julie jumped out of the car and raced up the steps to help her up. "It's okay, men. It's my sister." Julie enveloped her. "Look at your red hair. How did you get here? We've been worried sick." Richard joined them on the porch and hugged her.

"Heather Blanchard?" the buff marshal asked in a James-Earl-Jones baritone that shook the earth's foundations. "We're going to have to take you in." They holstered their guns and moved toward them.

Julie stood in front of her at the top of the steps. "No. You're not taking her anywhere."

Richard tipped his chin to the men. "Can we talk?" He started down the steps as Melissa came to the door with Olivia. The dogs rushed out to Heather and Julie as the marshals pulled their guns again.

"Ma'am, step out of the house. Hands up."

"Stop it!" Heather positioned herself between Olivia and the men. "These are our cousins. You're scaring her."

"Cousins?" Richard asked, looking between Heather and Melissa, then to Julie, who shrugged.

"Yes," Heather said. "Long story."

"Gentlemen, please." Richard motioned with two hands for calm. "Put your guns away. These ladies aren't a threat. Let's just go inside and sort this all out."

The marshals looked between themselves, then holstered their guns. Mr. Baritone pulled out a pair of handcuffs as he walked up the stairs and pushed past Heather and Julie, turning Melissa around. "Melissa Thomason. You are under arrest for aiding and abetting in the commission of various crimes."

"Jackson, stop! Put those cuffs away." Richard glared at him. "You know her name? Did you know they were cousins?"

Both dogs began their barking again. The marshals spun toward the road. "Everybody inside!"

Richard pushed everyone through the door and shut it behind them. "Stay away from the windows!"

"The house is full of windows." Heather looked around, then pointed to the hallway floor. "Here." She looked at Julie. "Hold Dog." Heather grabbed Abu's collar as they all huddled together.

Olivia cried in her mother's arms. "The bad men are back. Mommy, I'm scared."

Melissa rubbed her back. "It's okay, baby." She glared at Heather. "I told you this was a bad idea."

She was right.

From outside, Jackson yelled, "U.S. Marshals! Put your hands on the dash."

Richard crawled to the living room window and peeked out. "No way. It's Max!" He bolted to the door and called out. "It's FBI Special Agent Max Enders." He disappeared out the door, followed by Julie and the dogs.

The girls untangled and stood in front of the overstuffed sofa to watch through the front window. After Dog almost knocked Max down, Julie got a hug. Then the group talked. Heather didn't know FBI-agent-Max. Was he on her side? The last time she saw him, he carried her drunken self up the stairs at Julie's.

A wave of nausea and pain overcame her. She dropped onto the sofa and, shaking, curled into a ball. Melissa stood crying, holding onto Olivia for life. "You know they're going to take me in. Heather, promise me that you'll take care of Olivia."

"No, Mommy! You can't leave me!" Olivia squeezed her mom with everything she had, crying hysterically.

Tears poured out of Heather's eyes. "Nothing would make me happier, but look at me. Even if they don't convict me, she's better off with my sister until I can do what I need to do to get straightened out—whatever it takes."

"Please make sure she doesn't grow up in foster care like me."

This couldn't be happening. She had come here looking for an escape, and now they were facing the worst possible outcome—prison and a child growing up without her mother. Were these the plans God had for them?

"I'm so sorry. This is all my fault. I'm such a loser." She pounded the sofa cushion.

Melissa and Olivia dropped next to Heather on the sofa, and the three huddled together. "I'd like to blame you, but I can't. As much as I loved Johnny, I should never have let him into our lives. There had to be a day of reckoning."

"But if it hadn't been for me—"

"If it hadn't been for you, we'd still be running. And Bones' guys could have gotten to us first. I hate to admit it, but I'm glad it's over, and Olivia is safe. Maybe this will break my family's tragic cycles."

"No, Mommy, no!"

Melissa consoled Olivia, who held on like a monkey clings to its vine-swinging mother. Heather's heart was in shambles. The three held each other and cried as Heather tried to wish away the reality waiting outside.

———

4:00 p.m.

"You *will* come for Thanksgiving Dinner, though, won't you?" Dexter's mother spoke into the phone as she turned away from the dining room and headed into the kitchen.

Matty shook his head. "Uh, oh. Michael's not coming for Sunday dinner again."

From his position at the head of the table, their father simply shrugged and took another sip of wine.

Dexter glared at him, tossed his linen napkin on his plate, and followed his mother into the kitchen. He couldn't stomach his father's defense of Michael's crucial lifesaving work one more time. Especially since it was more likely that Michael was bedding some hot nurse while lying to his wife and kids—something their father taught by example. How often had the boys caught their father mounting some nurse on his hospital office sofa? Without apology? Instead, his father had yelled, *Get out, and keep your mouth shut!*

And he had. Even now, he couldn't bring himself to acknowledge his father's infidelity. If his mother knew, she never let on.

All Michael had to do was come to one stinking meal at a house only twenty minutes from his own. When had he become so insensitive? Their mother had given up so much to help him get to where he was. She'd been his biggest cheerleader and continued the role at her heart's peril, forced to relive whatever pain she'd faced with Dad.

He found her staring out the back windows from her stool perch—her haven for contemplating life. She dabbed her eyes. Dexter gently put his arm around her shoulder and kissed her cheek. "I'm sorry, Momma."

"I'm glad you and Mary Ellen came all the way from Vermont. And for sending Matty for the weekend. We've just had such a lovely time. I should be thankful for that instead of sitting here crying."

"It's okay, Momma." He held her as she wept.

"I can't take being rejected every week—just like your father did. And now he makes excuses for Michael. I should have divorced him years ago—like modern women do."

"Don't say that. You know you don't mean it."

"You think I don't know what your brother's really doing or what your father did? And then to have to hear your father defend him? It makes me sick."

She knew.

Matty came into the kitchen. "You okay, Momma?"

His mother hopped up, wiped her eyes with her apron, took a deep breath, and turned to face Matty. "Yes, I'm fine." She hugged the innocent one, locking her eyes with Dexter's over his shoulder.

Dexter's private phone rang. He didn't want to leave Mom like this but knew he had to answer. He pulled it from his pocket.

Matty let go of his mother and pointed. "That's Dexter's trouble phone. The one that makes him sad."

"At least he still manages to come for dinner, even while running a successful business. You two are my good boys." Momma reached out and pinched both boys' cheeks, then kissed them. "Go on. Take your call."

Dexter checked his watch as he walked out back. Charlie shouldn't have been calling yet. He tapped the green icon. "What's going on, Charlie?"

"Boss, you okay?"

"What does that mean?"

"Well, you're usually . . . nevermind. Just wanted to let you know that both girls showed up at the vacation house. And you're not going to believe this—that undercover FBI agent's there—the one who's supposed to testify this week. Everyone's there. Party time."

Dexter looked back toward the kitchen, too sad to enjoy the moment. "Call me when it's done."

"You sure you're okay?"

Dexter tapped the red icon. His mother stared out the kitchen window as if staring into the past. How could he be okay?

———

4:30 p.m.

DESPITE THE SUNLIGHT STREAMING in the wall of windows overlooking Chincoteague Bay, the living room might as well have been a prison. At least Max and Richard had started a fire in the closer of two oversized stone fireplaces that ran the room's length to their left, providing the room's only warmth. Family photos on the mantle reminded Heather of the family's love she had taken for granted—that stinking attitude that had started this awful chain of events.

Heather pulled Melissa and Olivia closer as they cuddled on the rose-colored sofa facing vacant floral upholstered armchairs. When they were children, her parents held court and ruled on their infractions from those chairs. She wondered what they would say today.

The dogs stayed close by as if wanting to comfort them.

Behind them, Jackson stood guard on the front porch while the blond thinner marshal played sentinel in her artist loft. From there, he'd be able to protect them from anyone approaching in any direction, including the water. Or maybe his perch was a guard tower to ensure they didn't escape.

Muffled voices drifted from the study on the other side of the entry hallway as their defenders pleaded their cases to the various agencies. It was taking way too long. What could society possibly gain from sending Olivia's mother—or her—to prison? And yet, what else could the authorities do? They both knew what they were doing was illegal.

Pitches and volumes ebbed and flowed behind the closed door. Even muted, Julie's pleas for them, especially Olivia, couldn't be mistaken. How had Heather ever doubted her sister's love?

Richard and Julie emerged from the study, leaving Max and Braun inside, reclosing the door after them. The dogs jumped, tails wagging, to check that the couple was okay. Tears flowing, Julie rushed past the dogs to Heather, then sat on the floor next to the girls. The dogs joined Julie as she took Heather's hand.

Richard sat in one of the judgment seats across from them. "Where do I begin?" He looked between her and Melissa. Heather had never seen him stuck for words. "I'm sorry, I still can't get over your resemblance. Julie and I are stunned." A sad smile crossed his face. "And overjoyed to learn you're all cousins. We can't wait to get to know you."

Julie turned onto her knees and hugged Melissa and Olivia. "We're family now, and we're going to get through this together."

Heather swiveled to put her feet down and shifted forward on the sofa. "But?"

Richard held up a hand. "The FBI agents called in and pleaded your cases, trying to get you released to us, but they said that won't work on several levels, the most important being the witness status of us all."

Heather looked at Melissa, then back at Richard. "Are you saying Melissa might not go to jail?"

"Let's not get ahead of ourselves. The immediate priority is securing everyone for the preliminary hearing Wednesday on the Hearthstone matter, which involves you, Heather. You may have witnessed something important and not known it."

Heather's heart broke. "You mean Tom? Was he really involved?"

"Unfortunately, yes. But what you don't know is that if it weren't for him, Julie wouldn't be alive. He turned on them, and now he's in witness protection. He's a key witness."

"So he was a good man after all?" Heather looked at Julie.

Julie nodded. "From what I can gather, crime was a family business, but somewhere along the line, he got a conscience. Hopefully, with a fresh start, he can live a good life. But other than at trial, you'll never see him again."

Heather braced herself for a wash of sadness for not being able to see him again, but it didn't come. Cruz had been a good friend, but what they shared was a victim mentality. She was done with that attitude. She needed a fresh start too.

"What about me?" Melissa asked.

Richard's eyes saddened. "You and Olivia will be taken to a safe house where you'll stay until you've testified against the gang."

"You mean Olivia can stay with me?"

"For now, but I can't guarantee anything. They know you won't testify if they threaten her, so they have to keep you both safe until these guys are convicted."

Melissa continued to caress Olivia. "But I don't know anything about how they operate."

"I'll bet you know more than you think. Just identifying some of the men will go a long way. I've spoken to the U.S. Attorney's office, and they will recommend no jail time. But that's not set in stone."

Melissa held Olivia tighter. "Thank you. Thank you." She began to sob. "No one has ever stood up for me—ever."

Heather smiled at Richard. "He's the best."

"What happens after they're convicted," Melissa asked. "Won't they still come after me?"

"You won't be a threat to them any longer. However, we can't account for revenge. You'll have to decide what you think is best. You can be relocated and given new identities, or you're welcome to join us in Hearthstone—for as long as you'd like. We'll help you get your new start there."

Melissa wiped her tears. "I don't know what to say. I've never had family."

"You need to turn over all the money in your possession."

"Happily. Besides what I have here, the rest is in the Charlottesville cabin and West Virginia storage units. I'll give you all the locations."

"I can't represent you, but we'll get you the best attorney and ensure you're taken care of financially, okay?"

Melissa nodded as tears spilled down her cheeks. "It was never about the money. It was only ever about providing for Olivia. She's the only thing that means anything to me."

Richard nodded. "No one ever believed you were a gang member. We're going to work hard to get you into the safest and best place you can be."

Richard turned to Heather. "First, let me say that I love you as a redhead, but I must admit I miss the blue stripe."

Heather smiled weakly. "I miss it too."

"Please answer me honestly. Are you addicted to opioids? Don't lie because I suspect you're in the middle of a dope-sick episode right now."

Everyone's eyes turned to her. Would they arrest or lock her up in some drug rehab if she admitted it? Who was she kidding? They all knew it.

She nodded.

"You need to say it."

"Yes," she said, speaking past the knot forming in her throat, "I'm addicted."

"Thank you. Believe it or not, that makes everything easier for you. The agents will take you into custody, get your statements related to the Hearthstone case, and then get you into a drug rehab facility. They don't think you're a high-value target, so providing protection there should be sufficient until the trial is over. Do you believe you know anything the gang will worry about?"

"Not if all the money is turned over. I can't think of any reason for them to come after me . . . except I did see one of those MCM guys. He had a tattoo. They might be afraid I can identify him."

Richard frowned. "Well, we'll have to see. If he's convicted, then it shouldn't be a problem. I'm fairly confident you won't be charged with any crimes. But don't confess to anything until they've given you a written guarantee that you won't. Otherwise, don't say a word. You got it?"

Heather nodded.

Max and Braun came out of the office as Blondie descended the stairs. "Everyone ready?" Max asked as the dogs jumped up, anticipating an adventure. Max pulled his arm from his sling and petted the animals. "Wow, looks like Dog healed faster than me."

Max seemed like the same guy she had known as Jake, but she was still wary. "Ready for what?"

"To go," Braun said as Blondie went out the front door. "We have reason to believe Bones' guys are in town. We need to get on the road. All of us in one place is trouble, especially with the water access. Wood structures don't provide much protection against any kind of assault."

Clutching Olivia, Melissa jumped up to scan the windows and then went to the hallway entrance as everyone else rose and checked for themselves.

"Are the bad men here, Mommy?"

"Not yet, baby." Melissa eyed Braun. "But these men will take us somewhere safe, right?"

Braun nodded. "You betcha." He smiled and pinched Olivia's tucked chin. "Did you know I have a little girl about your age?"

Olivia shook her head as Melissa rocked nervously, still scanning the windows. "Did they find us because of you?"

Braun's eyes squinted. "What do you mean?"

"I mean, how'd you find us? Did they follow you here?"

Braun shook his head. "You're kidding, right?" He narrowed his eyes at Melissa. "You've been around Bones' guys long enough to know how deeply connected they are. He has people everywhere. We know we weren't followed. In fact, we almost didn't make it here.

Our car broke down in Maryland. We were stuck for a couple of hours waiting for a tow truck. We were about to give up when a guardian angel, dressed as a biker, pulled over and rigged a timing belt for us."

"So how do you think they found us?"

"Actually, we're not sure it's so much that they found you or that they were here for the Wheelers. Our source said a couple of guys trying to pass themselves off as duck hunters came into town late this morning with all the right camouflage clothes and a boat. Problem is duck season doesn't start for a couple of weeks. It's snow goose season now. Real hunters would know the difference. If the situation weren't so serious, their stupidity would be funny.

"They made themselves more obvious when they met with a couple of guys who've been hanging around one of the pubs tossing back beers and playing pool for about a week. In this town, strangers stand out, and people talk. That pair was probably sent to sit on this place. Either way, both pairs of men were here before you got here. Don't know if they were anticipating Heather would come here after the shoot-out yesterday or if they had already planned to come after the Wheelers. But now that you're all here, your target value has gone through the roof. That's why we need to get you out of here."

Heather shook her head. "Wait, wait, wait. Why would Johnny's gang care about Julie and Richard? Are you saying they're connected?"

Braun nodded. "I can't say more, but yes."

Heather looked at Melissa, then at Richard, trying to connect the dots in her drug-fogged mind. It made no sense that a corruption case in Hearthstone could be related to a drug ring in Huntington. Or crazier than that—that there was an unknown family connection that was revealed. What if Heather hadn't crashed that car?

Jackson opened the front door. "We need to get going."

The dogs' tails showed their readiness as they weaved around the group.

"What about the dogs?" Julie asked.

"Dog is FBI trained," Max said as he patted him. "I'm sure it's fine to bring the other one. They're good early detectors."

Braun turned to Melissa. "Does she need to go potty? I know my daughter would."

Melissa nodded as she put Olivia down.

"Anything we need to get from your truck?"

"There's nothing in the truck, but the money's in the trailer. You should probably grab some toys to keep her busy on the ride. Oh, and some snacks." Melissa shook her head. "How about I go with you after I take her?"

"I've got this." Smiling, Julie touched her belly as she held out her hand. "I'm going to need the practice." Olivia took it.

Heather's stomach sank. "Oh my gosh, we haven't even talked about your baby. I'm so sorry."

Julie hugged her. "We'll have plenty of time for that, *Aunt* Heather." She looked down at Olivia. "Come on, sweetie. Let's go potty so you can get away from the bad guys." They headed to the half bath off the kitchen and deck.

Jackson opened the front door for Melissa. "After you."

"Wait, you need the garage door code." Heather gave it to them, and they went out.

Max reached to catch the door. "I should get the money." He closed the door behind him.

Richard looked at Heather. "Do *you* need to get anything?"

Heather laughed. "No, between what drowned with my car and my stolen backpack, what you see is what I have."

"And your drugs?"

"Literally down the toilet. I got nothing."

Richard put his arm around Heather. "That's the best place to start. We'll get you through this."

Julie returned with Olivia. Braun held out his hand. "Well, little lady. Time to say goodbye to your aunts."

Olivia scrunched her face. "Aunts?"

Heather squatted and looked up at Julie. "This is your Aunt Julie."

Olivia looked up. "You're my aunt, too?"

Julie smiled and also squatted. "Yes, sweetie." She pointed to Richard. "And that's Uncle Richard."

Olivia's eyes were wide. "Really?"

Heather nodded.

"And now," Richard said, "we need to say goodbye. We can't get all these people in one car, so you're going to go with your mommy and those two nice men outside. They're going to take you to a safe place where there aren't bad guys. Okay?

Olivia nodded. The new family hugged and said goodbye as the dogs gave Olivia their goodbye kisses. She drew in her shoulders and giggled until Dog's head jerked toward the door with ears perked. He let out a low growl. Abu began barking, but Heather reined her in.

"Quiet, girl."

Braun moved toward the edge of the front window. "Get down in the hallway."

The girls crouched together. Sniffling tears, Olivia clung to Heather. Richard stayed behind the hallway wall by the front door. "What is it?"

"Everyone's gone."

Dog's ears flattened as he growled again.

"Richard, stay with the girls. I'm going out the back." He signaled Dog to come, which he did. They slipped out the kitchen door to the back deck and disappeared around the corner.

Richard moved into the living room, popped his head around the curtain, then returned to the hallway. He looked toward the glass back door. "I don't like this. We're too visible. Let's get to the loft."

Richard led her, Julie, and Olivia up the stairs, past the master bedroom to the loft door, and climbed the short staircase to Heather's art studio. An unfinished painting of wild ponies running along the shoreline awaited her finishing strokes. All she had wanted to do was come here and escape with her subjects in the wild. Heather had forgotten how much she adored the peace of this sanctuary. But now, it was anything but peaceful.

Looking down, they craned to find someone—anyone. Maybe they had all gone into the garage with Melissa. Perhaps it was nothing. But it was just too quiet.

"A boat," Richard said, pointing to a small craft at the dock. "Everybody down!"

Olivia began to sob. "I'm scared. I want my mommy?"

Heather held her tight, stroking her precious head. "Shh, shh. She's right over there in the garage."

Abu growled.

"Hush, Abu."

Abu sniffed the air. The faint scent of something burning wafted in. Richard stood. "Oh, my God! The garage is on fire! Call 9-1-1 and stay put. And don't open that door for any reason." He left.

"Mommy!" Olivia shrieked and tried to go after Richard, but Julie held her back.

Abu started barking.

"Quiet!" Heather pushed her down. "Julie, Call 9-1-1!"

"I don't have my phone."

"Neither do I. What are we going to—"

A gunshot pierced the air as glass shattered from somewhere in the house.

"Oh my gosh! Richard . . ." Julie's eyes were wide. She started to get up.

"Sit down!" Heather grabbed her sleeve and pulled her down. He said to stay here.

"How can I stay here? He might be lying downstairs bleeding. I have to get to him." She started to rise.

Heather yanked her back down. "You can't. You have to take care of your baby. I'll go."

Peeking above the window sill, Heather surveyed the scattered pines in the front. Another shot rang out, but this time outside.

Heather couldn't see anyone. Suddenly, one of the skylights in the garage exploded, and smoke billowed out. The side door flew open, allowing Max, Melissa, and Jackson to escape, but shots quickly followed them as they crossed to the space under the house where they would only be concealed from the front. The shooter must be there."

"You have to get to Richard." Julie's eyes pleaded.

"I need to get my bearings. I don't want to walk into an ambush. Just wait a minute."

A man poked his head out from the far side of the garage doors, then pulled back. Was he the shooter? He stuck his head out again. *John.* She knew she shouldn't have trusted him. How did he find her? She had to warn the others.

She cracked the door open and slid into the hallway, back to the wall, inching past the bedroom. It was quiet. No movement. She poked her head around to look down the stairs. She quietly placed her foot on each stair, checking in front and back every step. When the last step creaked, Richard whipped around the hallway wall next to the front window, gun drawn. Seeing Heather, he lowered his weapon and yanked her to his corner by the window. A camouflaged man lay motionless on the other side of the entryway next to the wall, blood pooling around him.

Heather shielded her eyes. "Did you kill him?"

"Shh! I told you not to come out."

She whispered. "Where did you get a gun?"

"Don't you think the FBI trained me for my work in Hearthstone? Now quiet."

"I had to warn you. That guy who gave me a ride and took my backpack is on the other side of the garage. It's in flames. Max, Melissa, and Jackson ran under the house, but they're exposed from the back. I don't know where Braun or that blond marshal is."

"Shh!"

Just then, an explosion shook the house. Heather looked out the front as John ran from the garage blaze and took cover behind a pine tree. "He's out front."

Richard looked toward the back of the house. "I don't suppose there's any point telling you to stay put." He put a gun in her hands and positioned her fingers around the handle and the trigger. "Don't let anyone up those stairs. If anyone comes through the front door, aim and pull the trigger. I'm going to warn the others." He moved down the hallway, leaving her with Mr. Camouflage.

Heather's hand shook as she looked at the gun in her hand. It was cold and hard—a merchant of death. She'd never even seen one up close, much less held one. But Olivia and Julie were upstairs. She prayed she could shoot if she needed to.

Two shots rang out from the back. Heather slid down the wall hoping to disappear. Another shot in front of the house. She crawled to the window in time to see John ducking behind a pine to the right of the house as another shot rang out. Then he looked right at her, took aim, and fired, shattering a pot on the front porch. She ducked out of sight.

She couldn't believe it. *He actually shot at her.* If she had doubts about his intentions before, now she knew she had been in the company of Satan himself.

She looked around for the best position when he breached the front door. The wall by Mr. Camouflage. Her stomach knotted. She took a deep breath, closed the living room curtains, and took her position, pressing her back into the wall so she couldn't be seen from the door. When he came in, she'd roll around the corner and shoot. *Please, God, don't let him come in.*

A shot pierced the silence. Someone yelled from the back, "Clear!" Had they gotten him?

The screen door creaked. She leaned forward and peeked around the doorframe as the door handle turned and the door cracked open.

Drawing back, she took a deep breath, ready to swivel, aim and shoot. If only her hands would quit shaking.

A shot cracked the air, followed by the thud of a body dropping outside the door. They got him. It was quiet for a moment. Was it over?

Heather released her breath, came around the door, and reached for the handle just as footsteps pounded up the porch steps. She stepped back to the base of the staircase, drawing the gun to eye level. *Aim and pull the trigger.* Her hands trembled as the door flew open. *John.*

Time slowed as simultaneously she aimed and pulled the trigger, John yelled "DEA," someone else yelled "No!" and Dog lunged at her from the left, knocking her to the ground. John fell back over the camouflaged body that lay at the door. Her ears rang. Braun rushed in from somewhere. She looked up at him as Dog checked her, then ran to John and whined.

Braun helped Heather up, took the gun from her hands, and sat her on the stairs. "Heather, what did you do?"

Shaking her head, she said, "I pulled the trigger. Richard said to aim and pull the trigger. It's him. The one who stole my backpack and left me stranded. He shot at me. Richard said to aim and pull the trigger."

Braun stepped over the camouflaged body in front of the door and knelt beside John as Dog licked John's face. "Hawthorne, you okay?"

Hawthorne?

John slowly made his way to his feet, blood becoming visible on his left sleeve. Eyes wide, he looked at it, then Braun. "She shot me. She really shot me." He looked toward the body in the living room, then at Heather, and pointed. "Did you shoot him too?"

Heather shook her head slowly, ears still ringing. *DEA? Hawthorne?* Turning to Braun, she said, "You know him?"

"This is Special Agent Brad Hawthorne. He's been working deep cover for the DEA."

Heather's body wouldn't stop quivering. "But he shot at me."

"I didn't shoot at *you*. I shot at him!" Hawthorne kicked the body at the door.

Braun checked Hawthorne's arm. "Looks like you'll live."

"By the grace of God." Hawthorne looked at Heather and smiled. "And Dog." He patted Dog. "If he hadn't knocked you down . . ."

By the grace of God?

Richard and Melissa ran in and surveyed the scene. "Where're Julie and Olivia?"

Heather pointed up. "They're fine."

Richard and Melissa stepped around Heather and vaulted up the stairs. The others poured in from the back, questioning what had happened and if everyone was okay.

Olivia squealed from upstairs. "Mommy!"

Stepping around Heather, Richard and Julie joined the others at the bottom of the staircase, holding each other with a new tenderness. Melissa and Olivia joined Heather on her stair, putting their arms around her as Olivia stared at the camouflaged man in the doorway.

"Is that man dead, Mommy?"

"Yes, baby. He's dead."

"Is he one of the bad guys?"

"Yes, he is."

Olivia buried her head in her mother's chest.

Heather inventoried each person—all fine.

Braun looked at Heather. "Hawthorne risked blowing his cover to come here. Thanks to you, he found out Bones had sent guys here after you and Melissa but didn't know about Richard and Julie and their protective detail."

"And, of course, I didn't know about you two." Hawthorne tipped his chin toward Braun and Max. "I was told you were ordered back."

"Well, we weren't exactly on the clock," Max said, grinning.

"I left you and took your money, hoping you wouldn't make it here," Hawthorne said. "Then I lost you when you did that disappearing stunt at the restaurant."

Heather's face heated up.

"And that horse trailer. Brilliant. Bad for me, but brilliant."

"That was all Melissa," Heather said.

Braun patted Hawthorne on the shoulder. "All I can say is Melissa, Max, and Jackson would be dead if he hadn't gotten here when he did." He shoved the dead guy with his foot. "One of these goons had locked them in the trailer, then set fire to the garage. Heck, Julie and Richard would likely be dead, too. These guys were military special ops."

Hawthorne shook his head. "Let's not forget, as well-trained as any of us are, it took all five of us to take them out. So I'm no hero. Not one of us was prepared individually for this. This was God at work . . . His grace at work. There's no other explanation."

The wail of sirens blared in the distance.

Hawthorne turned his head toward the sound. "That's my cue to leave."

"Leave?" Heather asked. "You're wounded."

"It's just a flesh wound," he said in his best British accent and grinned.

Only Max chuckled. "Monty Python? I love that scene."

Hawthorne bobbed his head toward Max to acknowledge their mutual love of the movie. "But seriously, I need to get out before anyone else sees me and blows my cover. It's taken years to gain the organization's trust—and it goes much higher than Bones."

Heather's brain was still processing. She could have killed him. She managed a weak "I'm sorry."

"You did the right thing." Hawthorne pulled her to her feet, hugged her gently, and whispered in her ear. "I forgive you. Don't let the dragon get you—for Missy's sake. I'll be praying for you. And always remember, God has plans for your life." He turned and walked down the front porch steps.

Everyone followed him down and watched as he disappeared into the bushes to the side of the house just as fire trucks, paramedics, and police arrived.

Heather couldn't take her eyes off the bushes where he'd gone. Olivia wrapped her arms around Heather's legs just as a white buck jumped into the clearing. Everyone stood silent as the magnificent animal surveyed the group, almost glowing.

Olivia pulled Heather's sleeve. "Aunt Heather, it's the white deer."

"Yes, it is."

Heather looked into the deer's eyes. Instead of piercing her heart, cascading warmth and peace enveloped her soul. The buck lowered his head and then leaped into the foliage.

Heather pulled the worn bookmark from her pocket.

> *"For I know the plans I have for you," declares the Lord, "plans to prosper you and not to harm you, plans to give you hope and a future."*
> —*Jeremiah 29:11 (NIV)*

It was true. All true.

Thursday, November 23
Thanksgiving Day—2:00 p.m.

MAX OPENED THE WHEELER'S BACK DOOR for Dog and Abu to come in after their romp in the fields. They wasted no time sniffing their way around the kitchen island piled high with Thanksgiving goodies, their noses on overdrive. He kept his eye on Abu. It's well known that you can't turn your back on a beagle when there's meat around. At least Dog was well-trained.

Julie busied herself with serving utensils for green bean casserole, stuffing, mashed potatoes, gravy, and sweet potato casserole, while Catherine plated the cranberry sauce. Max's mom collected the wine glasses from the shelves and took them into the dining room. Sarah pulled a crispy brown turkey from the oven and set it on a carving board.

How he missed her cooking. He almost declined this dinner until they invited his mom to join them. Since his father and sister died, he could never leave her alone on a holiday. Julie had even asked them to stay for the weekend, but Jake suggested that staying in the house with Catherine might test even his mom's sainthood. So they settled on staying overnight in the barn loft since the farmhand position hadn't been filled yet. His mom could always change her mind if Catherine was behaving—which would be great for him. Save him from sleeping on the floor.

Max kissed his mother's cheek, then slipped into the living room, where Richard, Doc Blanchard, and Sarah's husband Joe watched the Detroit Lions game. He still couldn't stomach anything related to Detroit but sat down anyway. He enjoyed every score against them. Any city that provided that volume of drugs should have consequences—even if it was just losing a game.

"So, Joe, just so you know, when I lived here, I was ready to run off with your wife if she would have had me."

"Join the club." He tipped his head toward Doc Blanchard. "This one's been first in line for years."

"Does Catherine know?"

Doc Blanchard gave an impish grin. "Thankfully, her hearing ain't what it used to be."

They all laughed.

"So, Max, have you given any thought to taking the Sheriff's position?" Richard asked.

The other two men's heads spun toward him. "Really?" Joe said. "How cool would that be? But I'm not sharing my wife or her cooking with anyone else."

Richard shook his head. "And give up the glamour of undercover work?" The men laughed, but there was something very attractive about settling down in this wonderful community he'd grown to love.

Max stood and tipped his chin toward the dining room. "Well, the girls say dinner's about ready."

Richard reached for the remote and clicked off the TV. "Guess we'd better go round up the ladies and help them get the vittles on the table. Otherwise, they might rebel next year."

Before long, they were as busy as ants carrying the picnic food home until every inch of the table was covered. Max was most intrigued that there were three types of dressing, which had always been one of his favorites of the annual culinary tradition. When all the fixings were in place, Doc Blanchard took his seat at one end of the table, Richard at the other.

"Would you do the honors?" Richard asked.

Doc Blanchard said grace, thanking God for their safety, the upcoming baby, their guests, Heather's recovery, Cruz's new leaf, Melissa and Olivia's safety, and, of course, the food. Then, he removed the carving knife from its sheath and sliced away.

Catherine held her plate out to her husband for some turkey. "I understand the hearing went well. When will the trial be?"

"They have seventy days to try the case—sometime after the beginning of the year. There are a lot of moving parts to this case and a lot of defendants, although one of them almost died in prison last week. This organization has no qualms about taking out the trash. It will be interesting to see who's left at the trial."

"What does that mean for Melissa and Olivia," Doc Blanchard asked. I can't wait to meet them."

Max scrunched his face. "They have a ways to go. They still haven't issued indictments, so it'll be at least six or seven months. And even then, they may stay under their new names in their new place. If I had that sweet little girl, I'd think twice about giving up their new identities."

Julie nodded. "My heart breaks knowing that we can't be with them and get to know them. I still can't believe we didn't even know they existed."

Doc Blanchard started to say something but then didn't.

"I hear Heather is doing well," Max said. "It's incredible they opened that drug rehab here when they did."

Doc Blanchard nodded. "They're telling us she should be out by Christmas. Isn't that wonderful?"

Max's mother's body tensed. "I hope you won't take this the wrong way, but my daughter went right back to drugs every time she was in those short-term places."

Everyone grew quiet for a minute, then Doc Blanchard said, "I don't know. She wasn't *really* addicted, was she? Well, I mean, not for long. She shouldn't have any trouble."

Max caught Richard's glance. But what could they say? Doc Blanchard only knew animals. And he wasn't one to confront or challenge others. For better or worse, he always tried to smooth things over. He had a lot of training. Catherine was constantly ruffling people's feathers. He made a career of covering for her.

"That's right," Catherine said. "She'll be out soon, and then we can get her back to D.C."

Max raised a brow for Richard to see.

"Well, Catherine, I'm sure she'll want to be here with the new baby," Julie said. "She promised to paint the nursery walls with Aladdin and Princess Jasmine on their magic carpet in honor of Olivia."

"I saw some of her sketches of that at the cabin. She's talented."

"Well then," Catherine said, "perhaps we'll come and help with the transition when she gets here. It will be hard on you with your pregnancy and all."

A broad smile beamed across Doc Blanchard's face. "Oh, that would be wonderful, wouldn't it, Julie?"

Julie dropped her fork, stood, shoved her knuckles onto the table, and glared at Catherine. "Do you ever stop imposing yourself on people? Nobody asked you to help with Heather. She's where she is because of you. She's going to need a stress-free environment, which is impossible with you around."

"What are you saying?" Catherine asked.

"I'm saying that you stress her out. In fact, you stress me and everyone whose life you invade." Julie threw her napkin down and stormed out of the dining room.

Catherine's mouth opened. She tried to say something, but what came out was mumbled and unintelligible. Then, she fell to the ground.

"Catherine?" Doc Blanchard shoved his chair back and stooped beside her. "Call 9-1-1! I think she's having a stroke."

———

3:00 p.m.

DEXTER EYED THE "BRILLIANT CARDIOLOGIST" sitting across from him. Momma sat at the table's far end, wearing the smile of a mother whose child had won the Nobel Peace Prize. Had Momma blackmailed Michael with his secrets to get him here? He'd already checked his watch a dozen times since the turkey was carved—something Dad was oblivious to or ignored. He should know. Somewhere out there, some buxom girl was spending the day growing increasingly frustrated with how long an Italian Thanksgiving dinner could last—one course at a time. Momma had slowed the pace even more this year, likely just to torture him.

Mary Ellen had been chatting it up with Kelley and the girls, even engaging the twins, who weren't shy about making it known they'd rather be anywhere but there. But Mary Ellen was a pro at setting people at ease and drawing them into conversation. She had such a knack for making each person feel like every aspect of their lives was vital to her. And she'd remember every detail. People believed she truly cared. And she probably did, although Dexter didn't understand why. But it was her gift and served her—and him—very well.

He was particularly thankful this year. His new Hearthstone rehab center was up and running. And his genius plans for the next Super Bowl were well underway. He smiled at his vision. Even the Sheriff's screw-up had worked itself out. Hawthorne had convinced him that the Wheeler sister knew nothing of their operations and didn't have their money—the DEA and FBI saw to that. Charlie had just texted that the one gang member she could identify was no longer a problem.

Knocking her off was a brief consideration, but, as Hawthorne had pointed out, Dexter was already exposed with the large volume of hits they'd put out lately. And he didn't need to make an example of her. She didn't steal the money. It was those Johnson boys, and they were gone.

But that's not to say he was done with her—and especially not that brother-in-law of hers. Death is too quick. Slow roasting—the drawn-out death of an addict—was much more delectable.

Once an addict, always an addict. He'd ensure she never broke the cycle. And the Wheelers would pay. Boy, would they pay.

The great Dr. Michael rechecked his watch, then looked over at Mom. She smiled across the table. His mother, too, enjoyed the slow roast.

"Oh, I forgot the white asparagus. I made my special homemade mayonnaise that you love so much, Michael. Let me get it." She snuck a wink to Dexter and looked back to Michael, and smiled. "It's your favorite, isn't it?"

Michael forced a smile, then peeked at his watch under the table.

Anything to keep Michael at the table. Was there anything better than this?

COMING IN 2024

POISONED SERIES—BOOK 3

VANISHED

What's going to happen when Julie finds herself
helping to take care of Cruella while dealing with her
recovering sister and her pregnancy?

Will Heather relapse?

What kind of business has Dexter cooked up for the
Super Bowl?

And what happened to Frank Rizzo?

Many thanks to . . .

JAN RADER, former Fire Chief in Huntington, WV, who continues the good fight against the drug epidemic in her role as Director of the Mayor's Council of Public health & Drug Control Policy.

As one of the featured heroines in the Netflix documentary *Heroin(e)*, she has been instrumental in changing the treatment of heroin addicts, helping to offer hope and an opportunity for a way out. Thank you for the blessing of your insights into the opioid epidemic. You have been a treasure to me.

JESSICA EVERSON, my editor extraordinaire. You taught me much with each chapter. Who knew those bullets could go through cars?

MY BETA READERS: Valerie Covalt, Sharon K. Crosby (Author of *Praying for Your Addicted Loved One*), Marjorie Maxey, Anne Alper, Denise Parrotta, Jim & Mary Geiger, and Jan Rader. Your suggestions and guidance have helped mold this piece into a better story.

MY FELLOW WORD WEAVERS: Anne Alper, Elizabeth Brickman, Kristen Brown, Deanna Coffin, Mimi Finesilver, Jennifer Garcia, Jim Geiger, Patrick Hartman, David Haun, Sonia Kaiser, Jeffrey Keene, Melanie Prada, H. Irving Wilson, Yvonne Anzolone, Ana Bright, Kyla Carpenter, Dawn Day, Roberta Fish, Patricia Nicholas-Boyte, and Ava Pennington. You have listened, read, suggested, encouraged, and guided me along this long path. Your friendships and love are beyond measure.

PATRICK HARTMAN: my lover, my friend, my Kingdom co-laborer, my traveling bud, and best of all, my honey bunny. Thanks for putting up with me. I love you so much!

OUR AWESOME GOD, who covered me with this mantle and provides the way as I struggle with each jot and tittle in my humble effort to honor Him with my words and enjoy Him forever. To God be the glory!

OTHER BOOKS BY PATRICIA HARTMAN

"A FUNNY THING HAPPENED ON MY JOURNEY TO HEAVEN"

Want to know Patricia Hartman better?

Join Patricia Hartman in a *funny* look at life and how the *funny* (amusing, odd, or coincidental) events of life have shaped her. These stories have taken her from a rebellious atheist to the woman of faith that God is still working on today and will work on as she journeys toward heaven's gate. Each funny story reflects upon God's scriptures for the truth, wisdom, and the meaning of God's lessons.

Grab a cup of coffee and a tissue box and join her journey.

"THE CHRISTIAN PRENUPTIAL AGREEMENT: THE POWER OF MARRIAGE UNLEASHED"

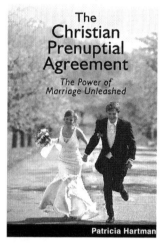

Patricia's divorce attorney friends insisted when she got married that she should have a prenup. At first, she explained that Christians don't do prenups. But as she went through her vows, she discovered that we do (or should) have a prenup that expressed the vows we take—they are just oral, instead of written. She went back to her friends and told them, "Yes, and mine will say if I cheat on your or divorce you, I will give you everything."

"Nobody would sign that!" they said.

But isn't that exactly what we sign up for as Christians?

This marriage manual covers examines both God's law and man's law, "love drugs" (chemicals of the brain released when "in love), history of marriage, vows, and the implications of "for worse," agreements (boundaries) with in-laws, and what it means to become like-minded. This is a must-read for all engaged couples and already married couples as well.

Both books are available on Amazon in Paperback or Kindle editions

Made in the USA
Columbia, SC
21 April 2023

15427803R00238